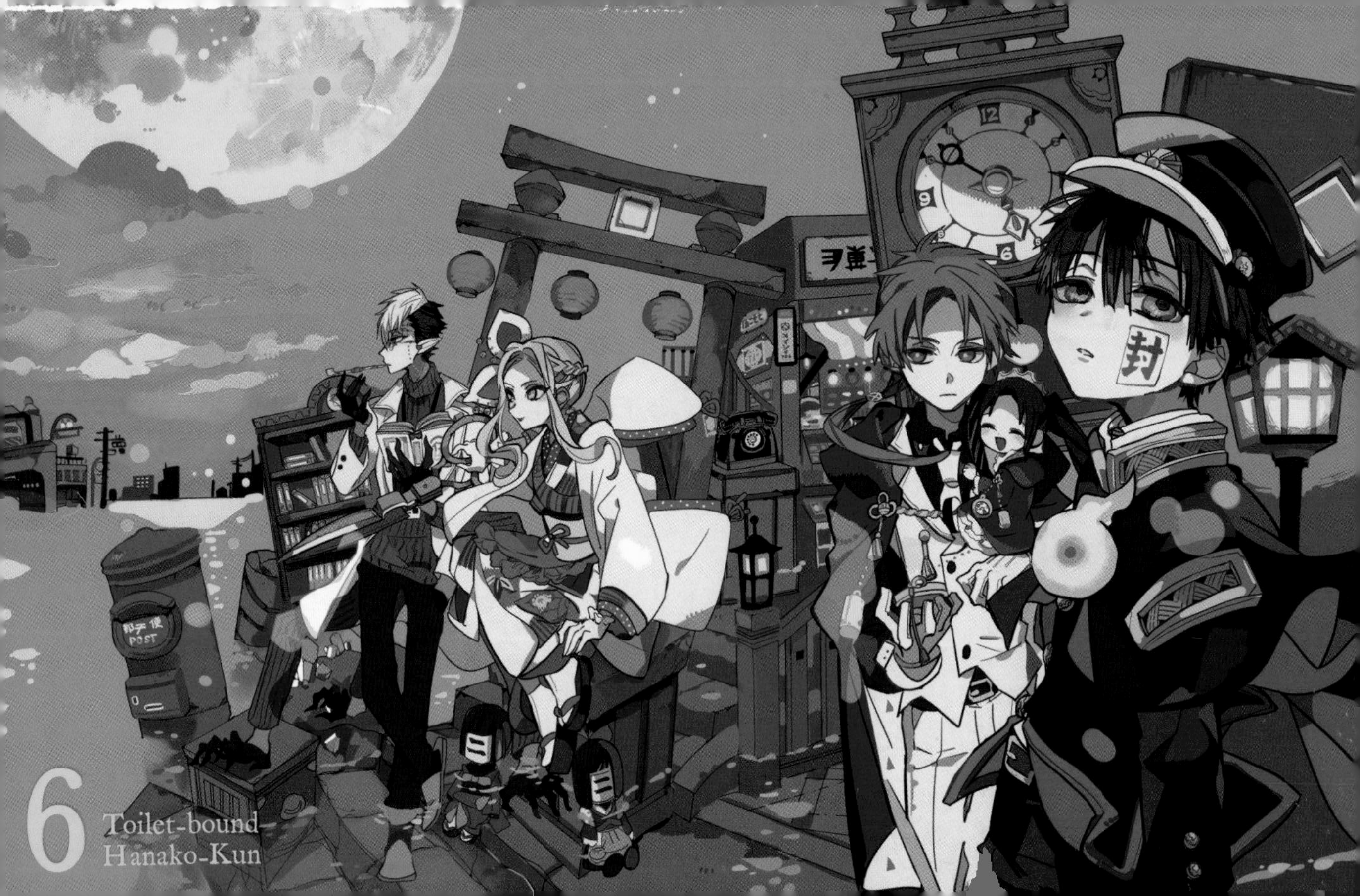
6
Toilet-bound
Hanako-Kun
POST
封

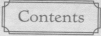

Contents

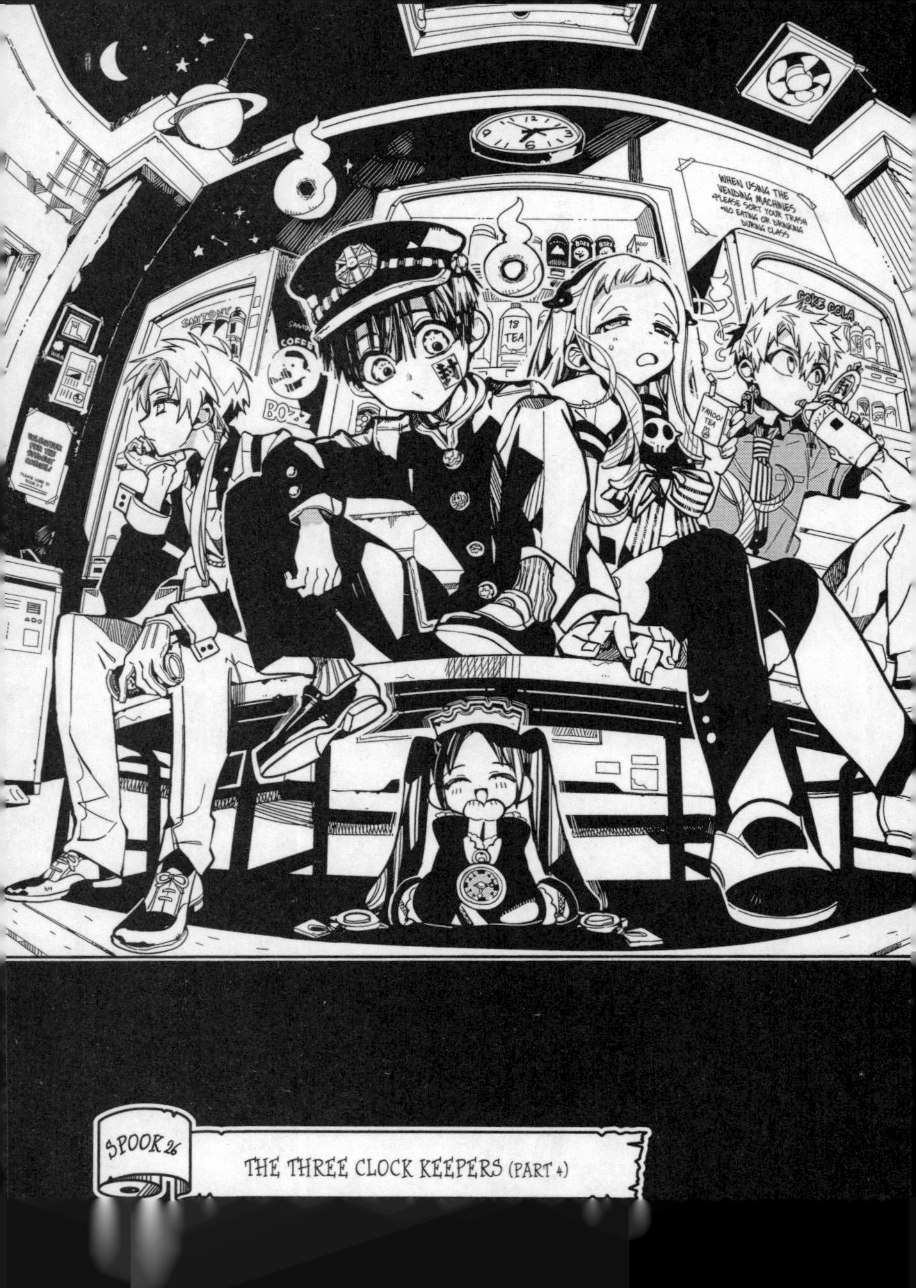
WHEN USING THE VENDING MACHINES
•PLEASE SORT YOUR TRASH
•NO EATING OR DRINKING DURING CLASS
COKE COLA
YAHOO! TEA
18 TEA
COFFEE

SPOOK 26

THE THREE CLOCK KEEPERS (PART 4)

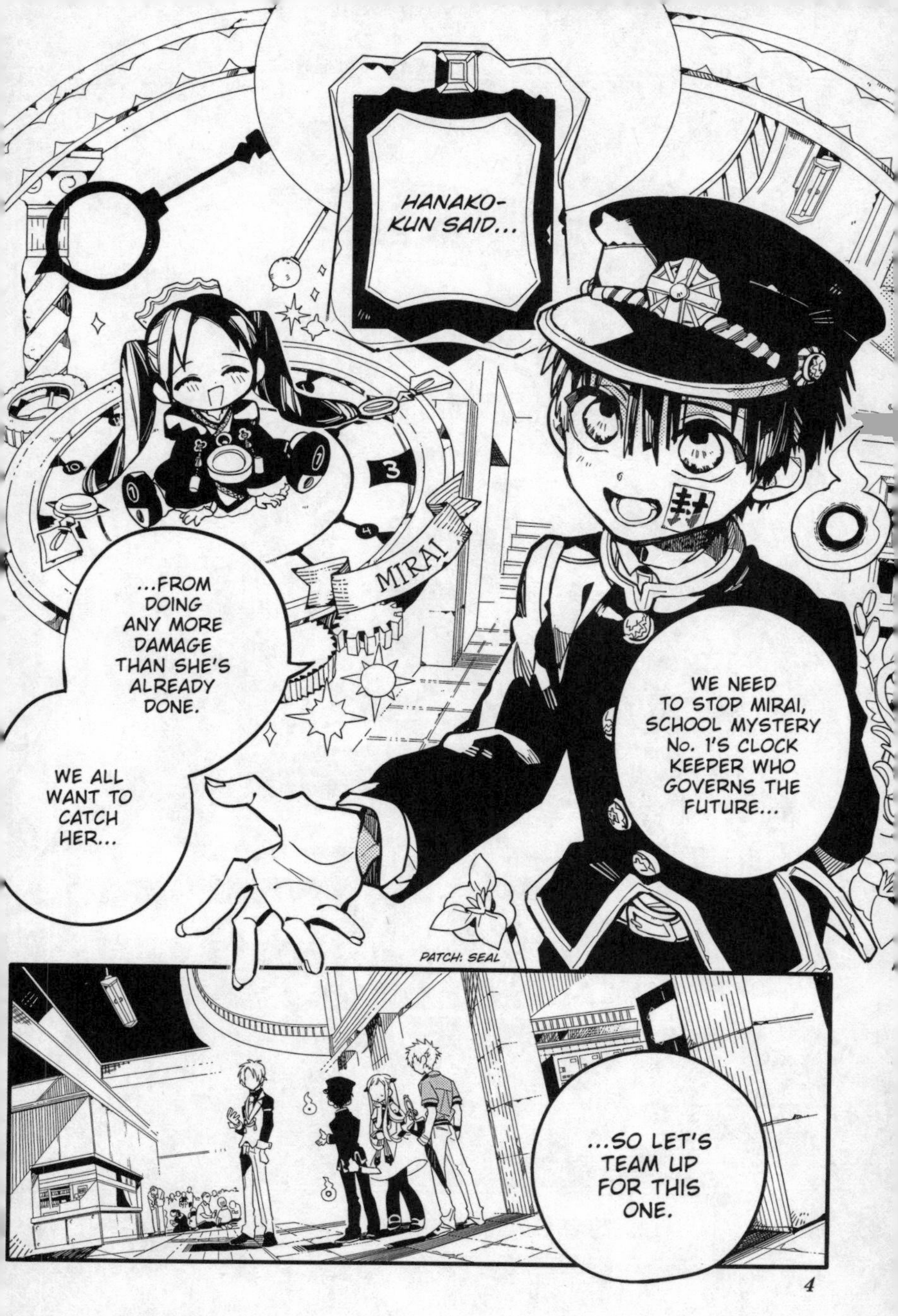
HANAKO-KUN SAID...
WE NEED TO STOP MIRAI, SCHOOL MYSTERY No. 1'S CLOCK KEEPER WHO GOVERNS THE FUTURE...
MIRAI
...FROM DOING ANY MORE DAMAGE THAN SHE'S ALREADY DONE.
WE ALL WANT TO CATCH HER...
PATCH: SEAL
...SO LET'S TEAM UP FOR THIS ONE.

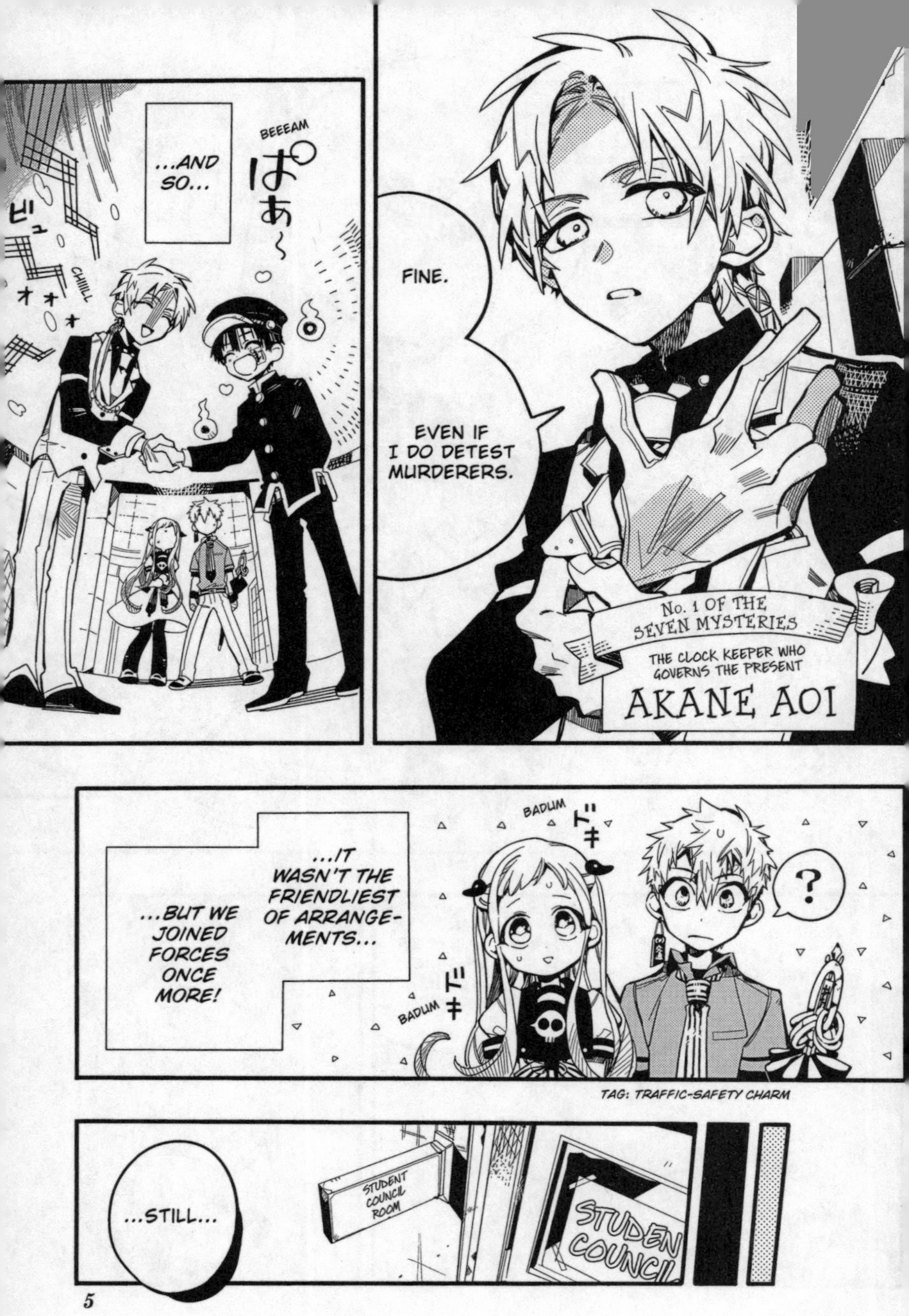
FINE.
EVEN IF I DO DETEST MURDERERS.
No. 1 OF THE SEVEN MYSTERIES
THE CLOCK KEEPER WHO GOVERNS THE PRESENT
AKANE AOI
BEEEAM
ぱあ～
...AND SO...
CHILL
ビュオオオ
...IT WASN'T THE FRIENDLIEST OF ARRANGE-MENTS...
...BUT WE JOINED FORCES ONCE MORE!
BADUM
ドキ
?
BADUM
ドキ
TAG: TRAFFIC-SAFETY CHARM
STUDEN COUNCIL
STUDENT COUNCIL ROOM
...STILL...

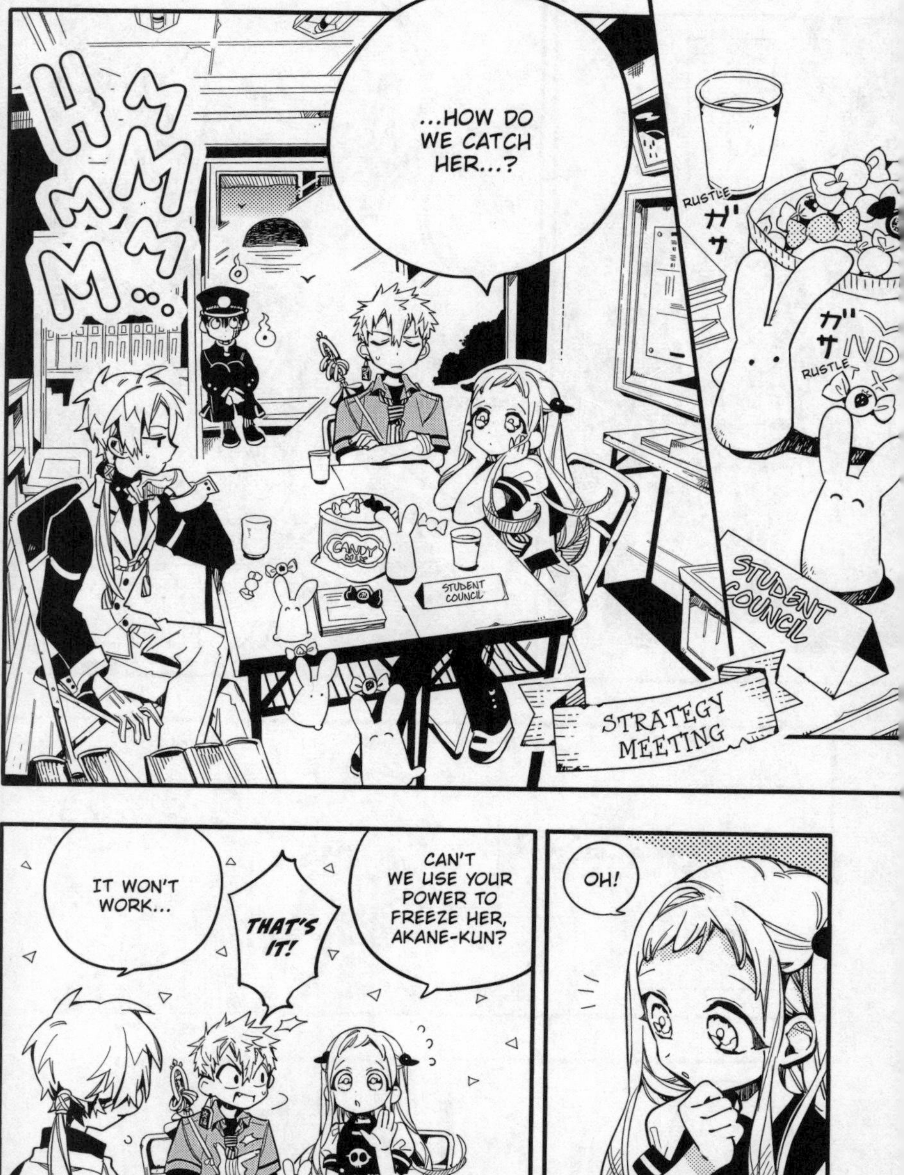
RUSTLE
ガサ
ガサ
RUSTLE
STUDENT COUNCIL
HMMMMM...
...HOW DO WE CATCH HER...?
STUDENT COUNCIL
STRATEGY MEETING
OH!
CAN'T WE USE YOUR POWER TO FREEZE HER, AKANE-KUN?
THAT'S IT!
IT WON'T WORK...

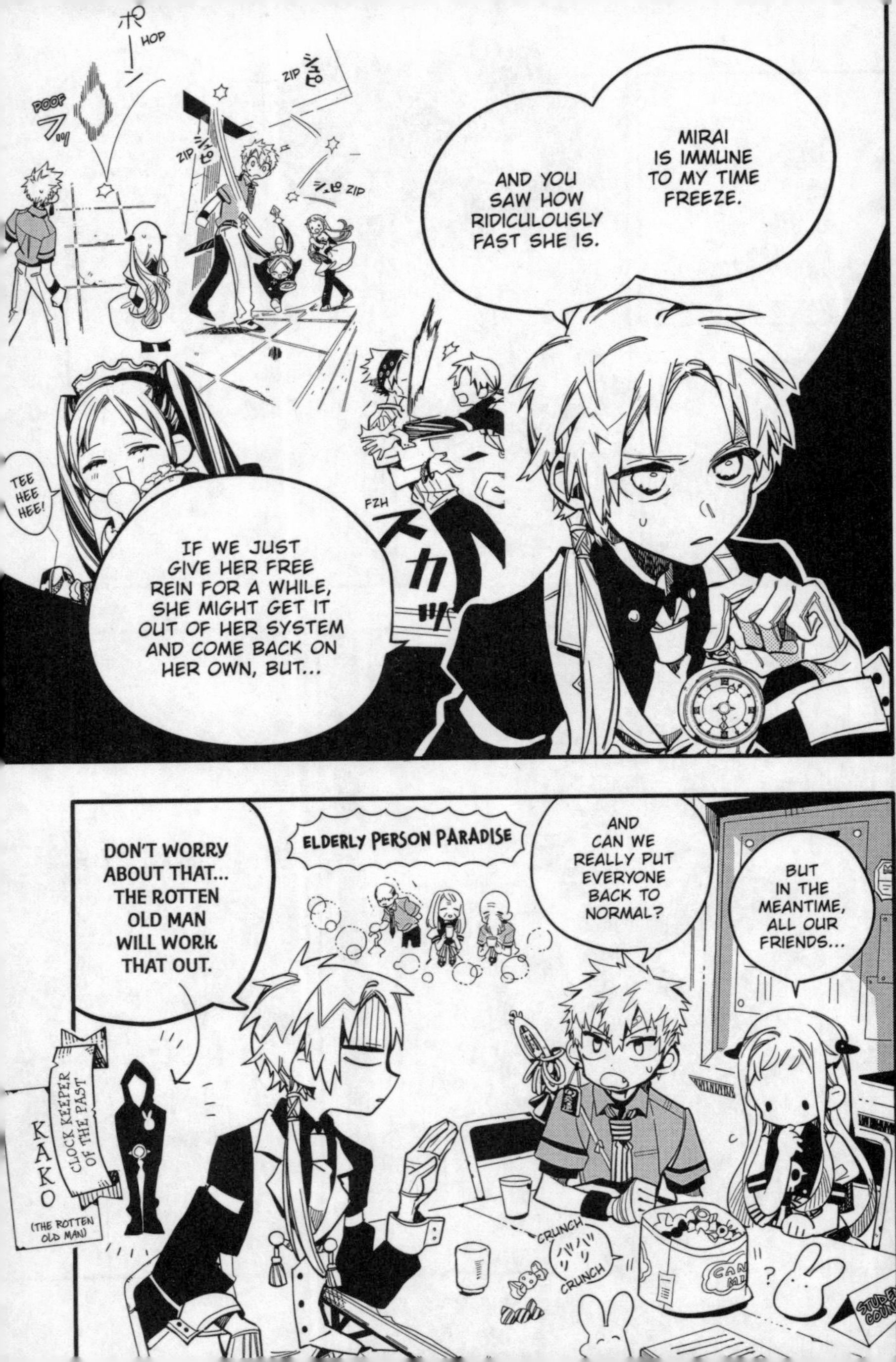
MIRAI IS IMMUNE TO MY TIME FREEZE.
AND YOU SAW HOW RIDICULOUSLY FAST SHE IS.
HOP
ZIP
ZIP
ZIP
POOF
FZH
IF WE JUST GIVE HER FREE REIN FOR A WHILE, SHE MIGHT GET IT OUT OF HER SYSTEM AND COME BACK ON HER OWN, BUT...
TEE HEE HEE!
BUT IN THE MEANTIME, ALL OUR FRIENDS...
AND CAN WE REALLY PUT EVERYONE BACK TO NORMAL?
ELDERLY PERSON PARADISE
DON'T WORRY ABOUT THAT... THE ROTTEN OLD MAN WILL WORK THAT OUT.
KAKO
CLOCK KEEPER OF THE PAST
(THE ROTTEN OLD MAN)
CRUNCH
CRUNCH

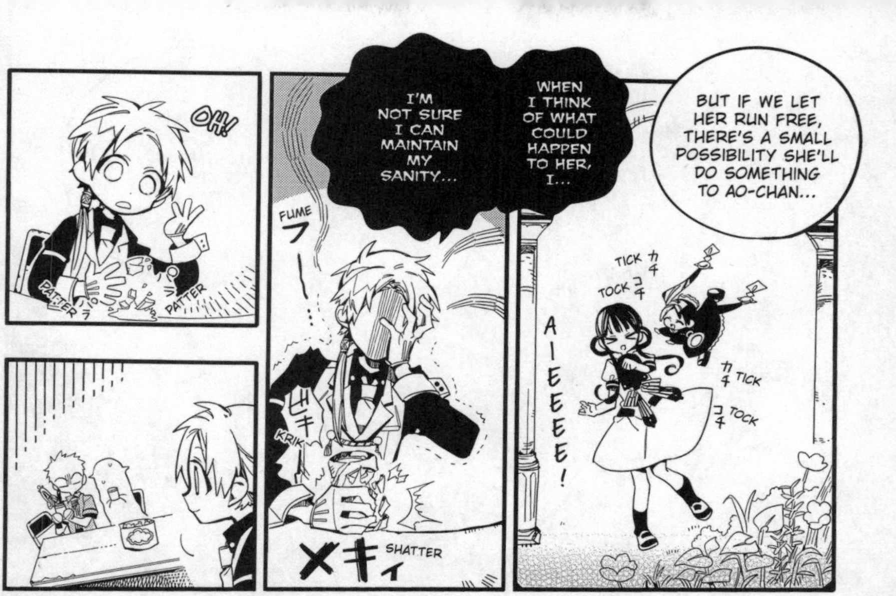
BUT IF WE LET HER RUN FREE, THERE'S A SMALL POSSIBILITY SHE'LL DO SOMETHING TO AO-CHAN...
TICK
TOCK
AIEEEEE!
TICK
TOCK
WHEN I THINK OF WHAT COULD HAPPEN TO HER, I...
I'M NOT SURE I CAN MAINTAIN MY SANITY...
FUME
KRIK
SHATTER
OH!
PATTER
PATTER

SIGN: PLEASE DON'T LEAVE YOUR PERSONAL BELONGINGS.

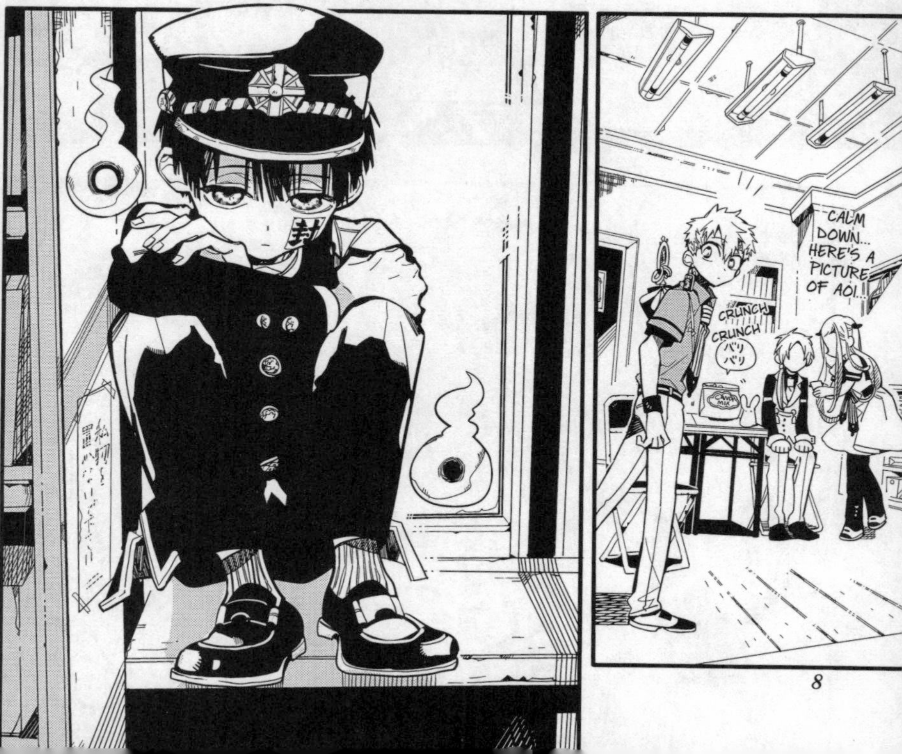
CALM DOWN... HERE'S A PICTURE OF AOI...
CRUNCH
CRUNCH

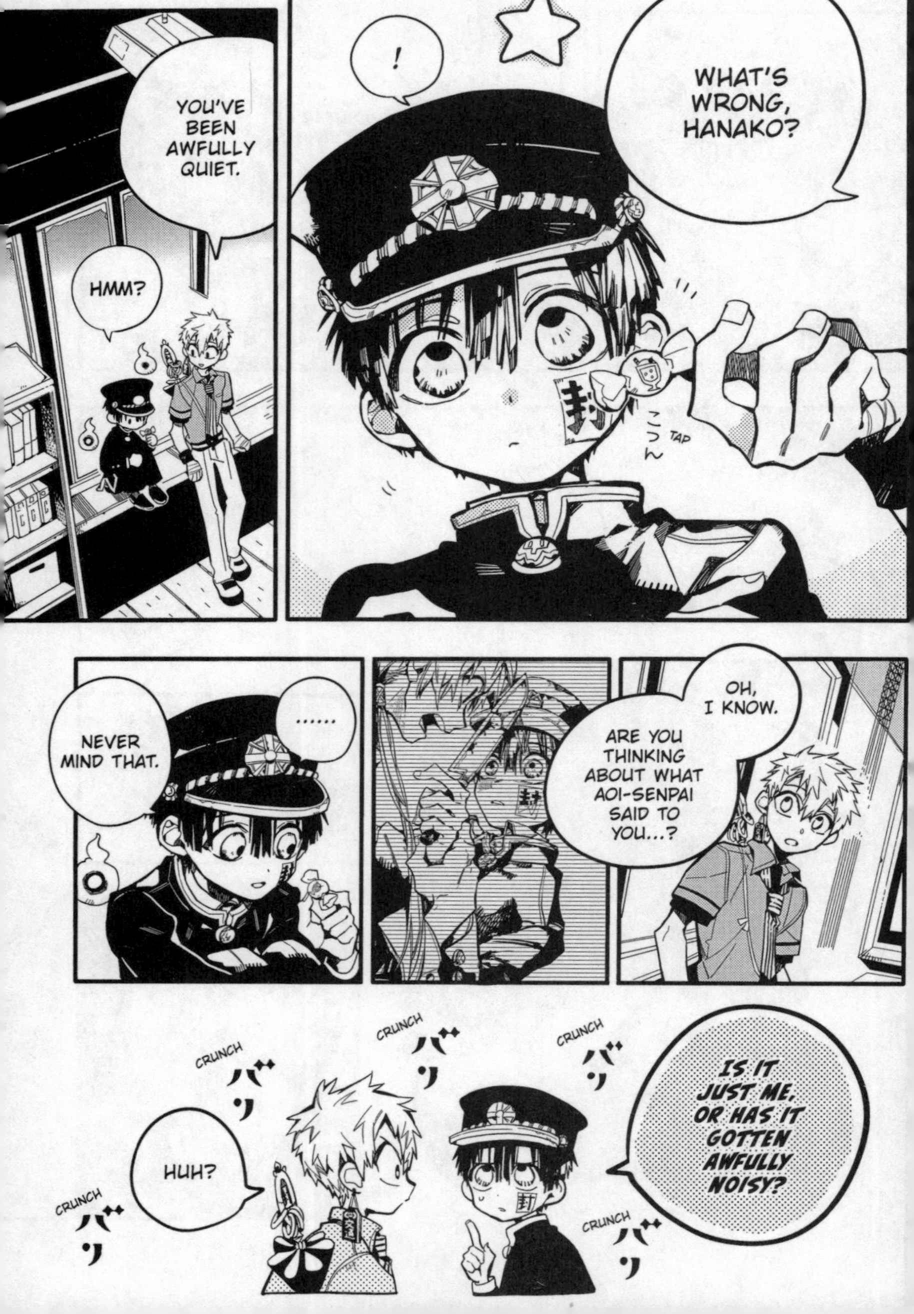

WHAT'S WRONG, HANAKO?
!
こつん
TAP
YOU'VE BEEN AWFULLY QUIET.
HMM?
OH, I KNOW.
ARE YOU THINKING ABOUT WHAT AOI-SENPAI SAID TO YOU...?
......
NEVER MIND THAT.
CRUNCH
バリ
CRUNCH
バリ
IS IT JUST ME, OR HAS IT GOTTEN AWFULLY NOISY?
CRUNCH
バリ
CRUNCH
バリ
HUH?
CRUNCH
バリ

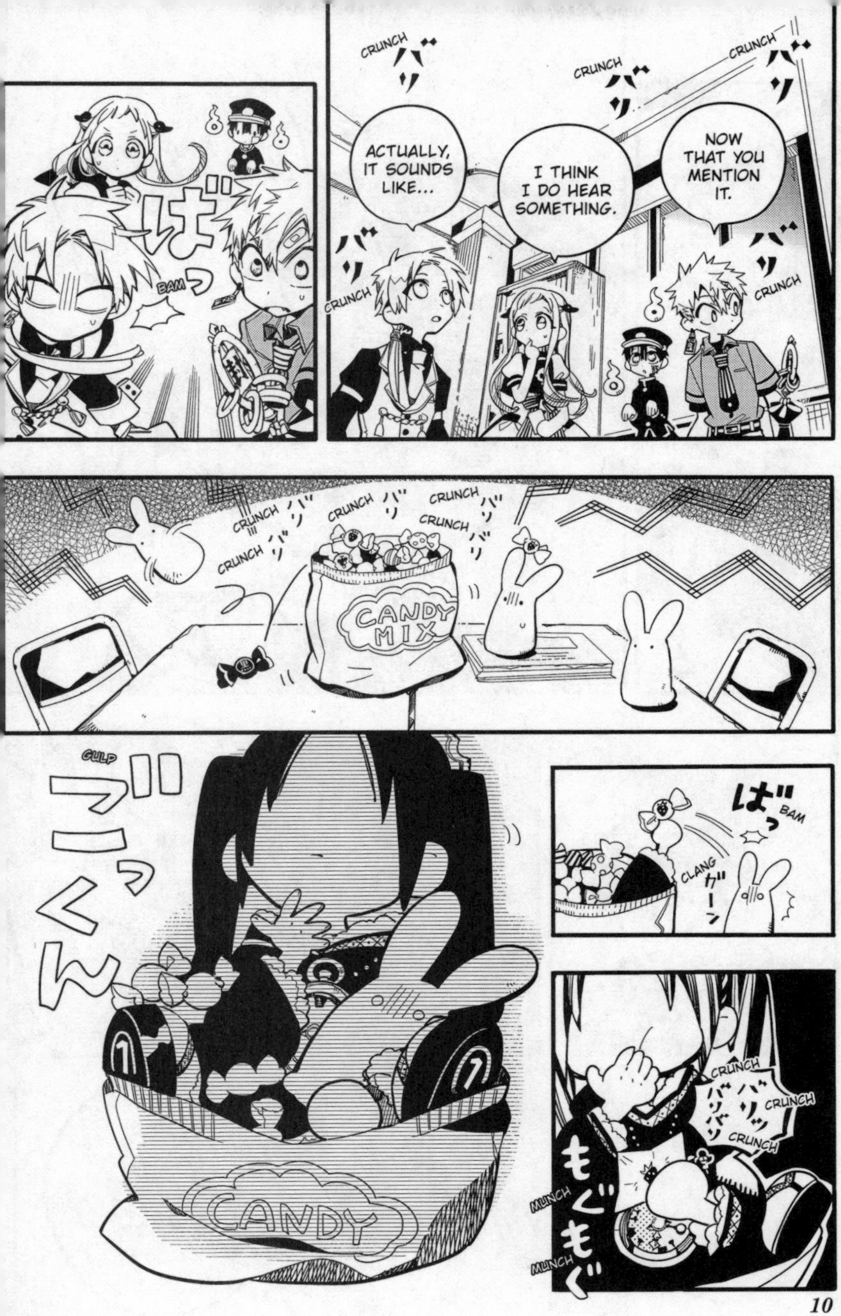
CRUNCH
バッ
CRUNCH
バッ
NOW THAT YOU MENTION IT.
I THINK I DO HEAR SOMETHING.
CRUNCH
バリ
ACTUALLY, IT SOUNDS LIKE...
バリ
CRUNCH
バリ
CRUNCH
ばっ
BAM
CRUNCH
バリ
CRUNCH
バリ
CRUNCH
バリ
CRUNCH
バリ
CRUNCH
バリ
ばっ
BAM
CLANG
ガーン
CRUNCH
CRUNCH
バリッ
バリバリ
CRUNCH
MUNCH
もぐもぐ
MUNCH
GULP
ごっくん
CANDY MIX
CANDY

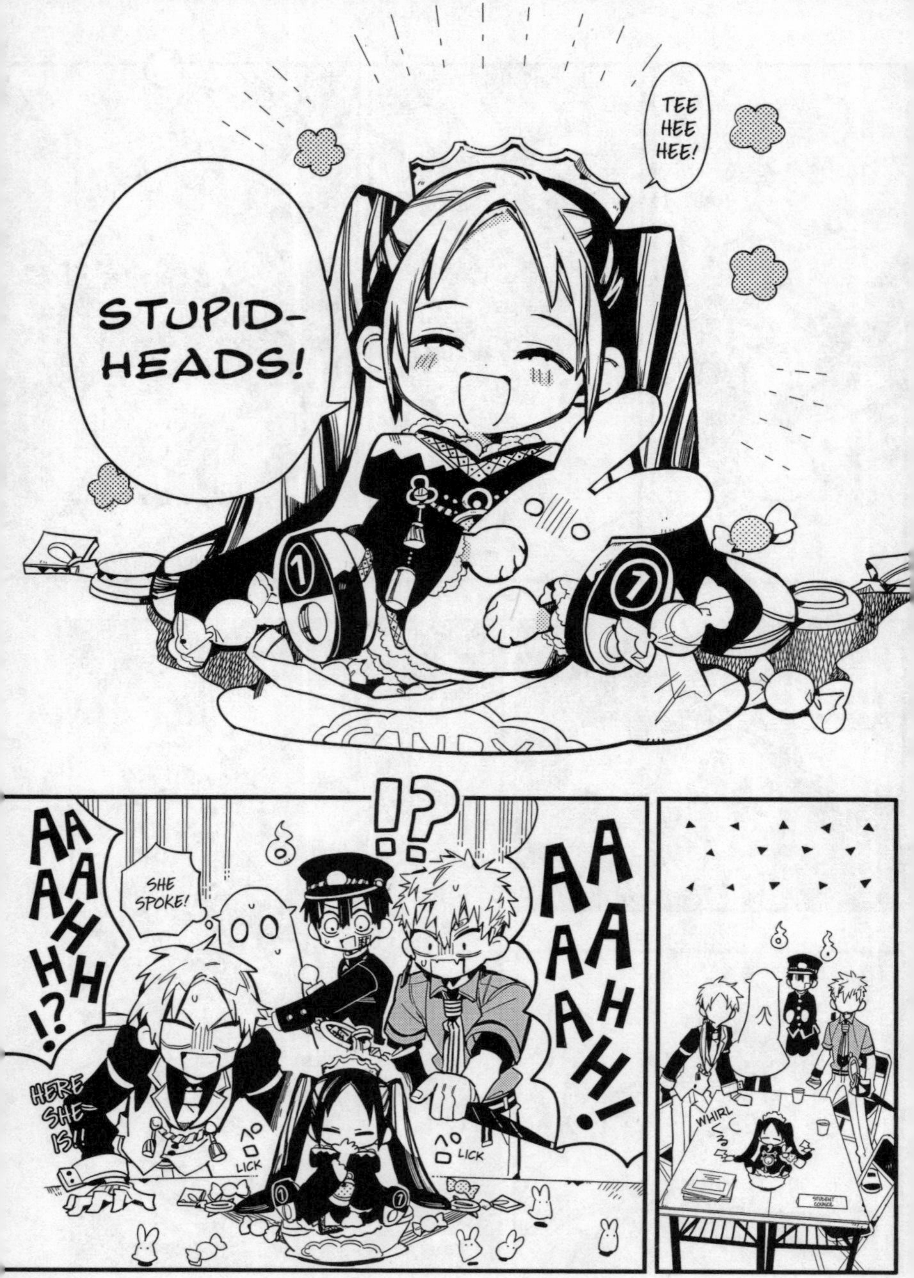
TEE HEE HEE!
STUPID-HEADS!
CANDY
WHIRL
くる
STUDENT COUNCIL
!?
AAAAAAH!
SHE SPOKE!
AAAAHH!?
HERE SHE-IS!!
LICK
LICK

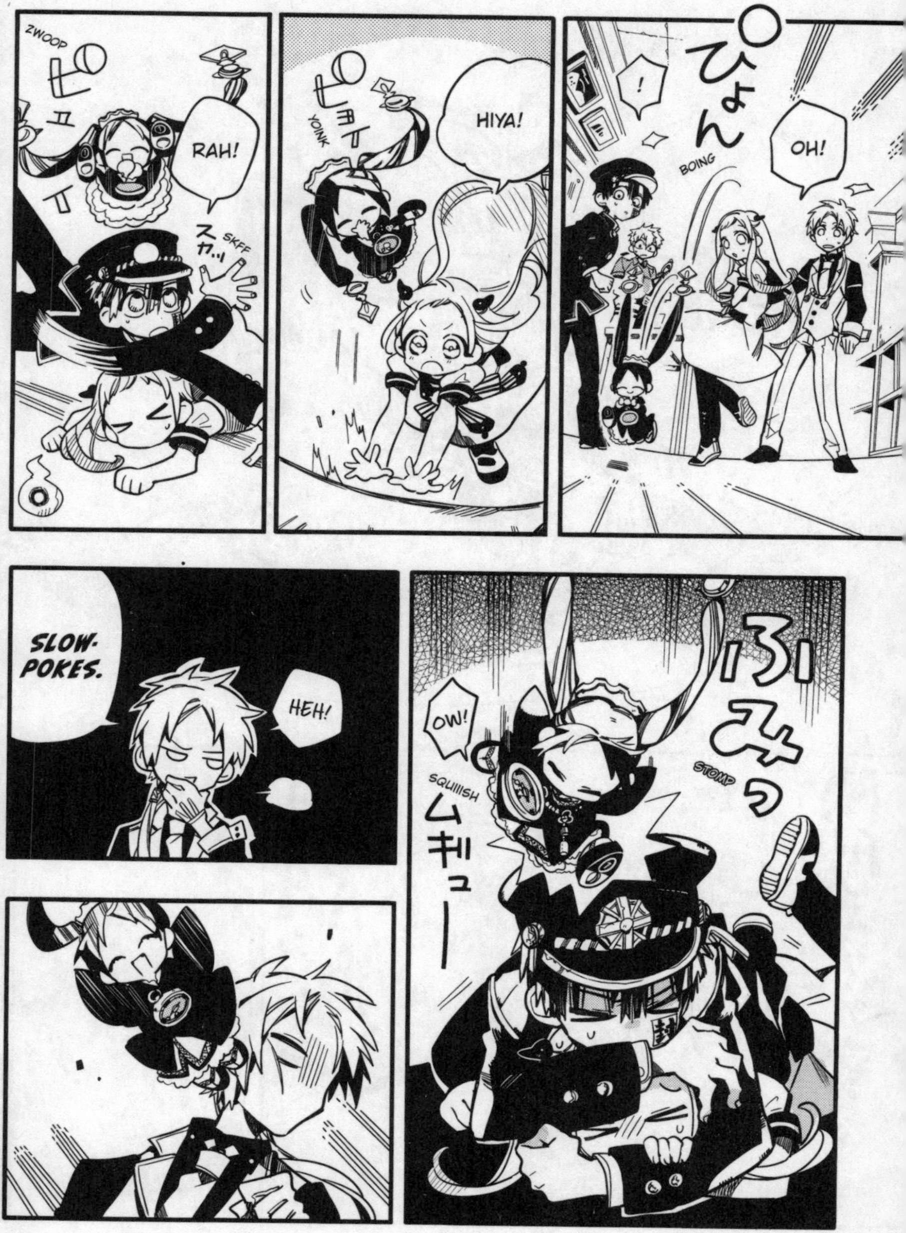

ぴょん
BOING
OH!
!
HIYA!
ピョイ
YOINK
ピュイ
ZWOOP
RAH!
スカッ
SKFF
ふみっ
STOMP
OW!
ムギュー
SQUIIISH
SLOW-POKES.
HEH!

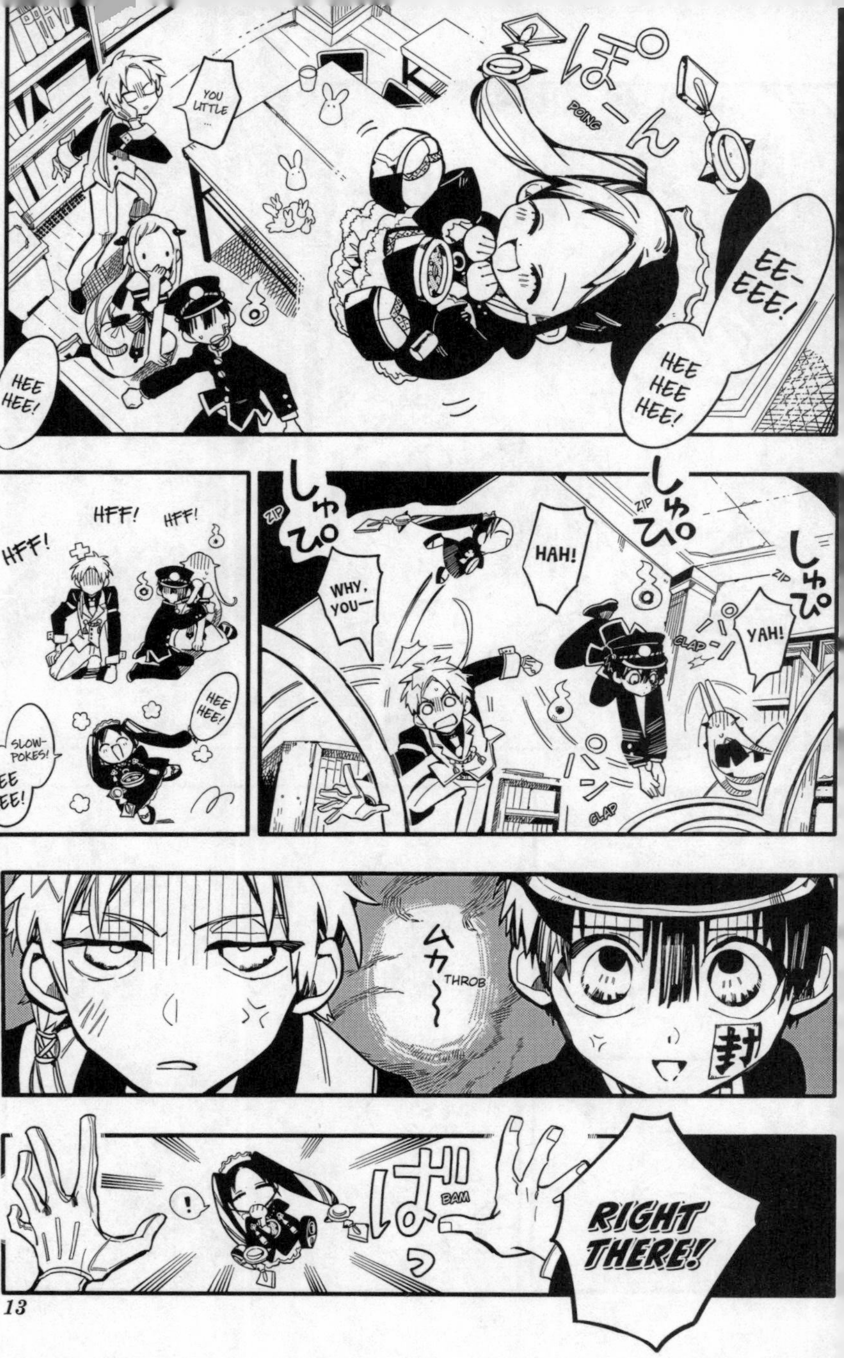
ぽ〜ん
POING
EE-EEE!
HEE HEE HEE!
YOU LITTLE...
HEE HEE!
しゅぴ
ZIP
YAH!
しゅぴ
ZIP
HAH!
パンパン
CLAP
CLAP
WHY, YOU—
しゅぴ
ZIP
HFF!
HFF!
HFF!
HEE HEE!
SLOW-POKES!
HEE HEE!
ムカ〜
THROB
RIGHT THERE!
ばっ
BAM
!

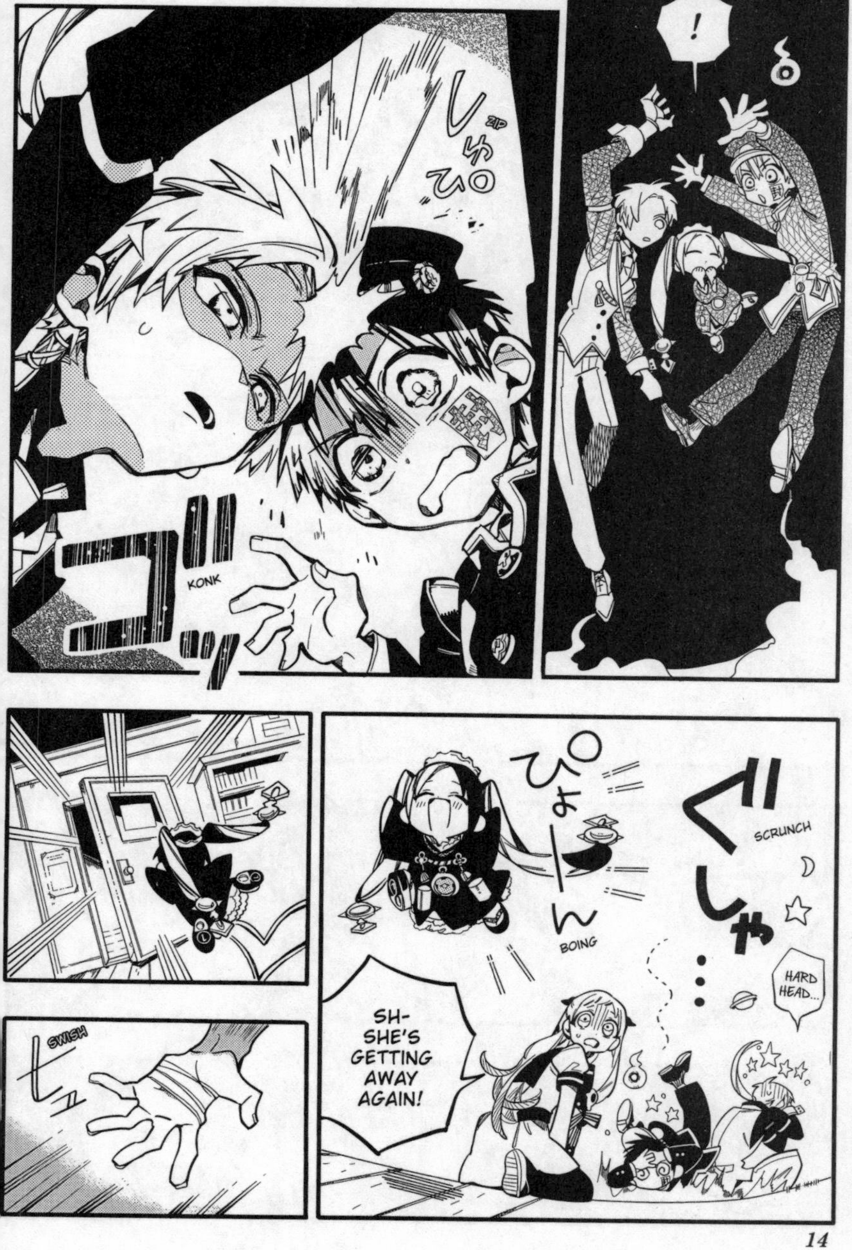

!
ZIP
ゴッ
KONK
ぐしゃ…
SCRUNCH
ぴょーん
BOING
HARD HEAD...
SH-SHE'S GETTING AWAY AGAIN!
SWISH

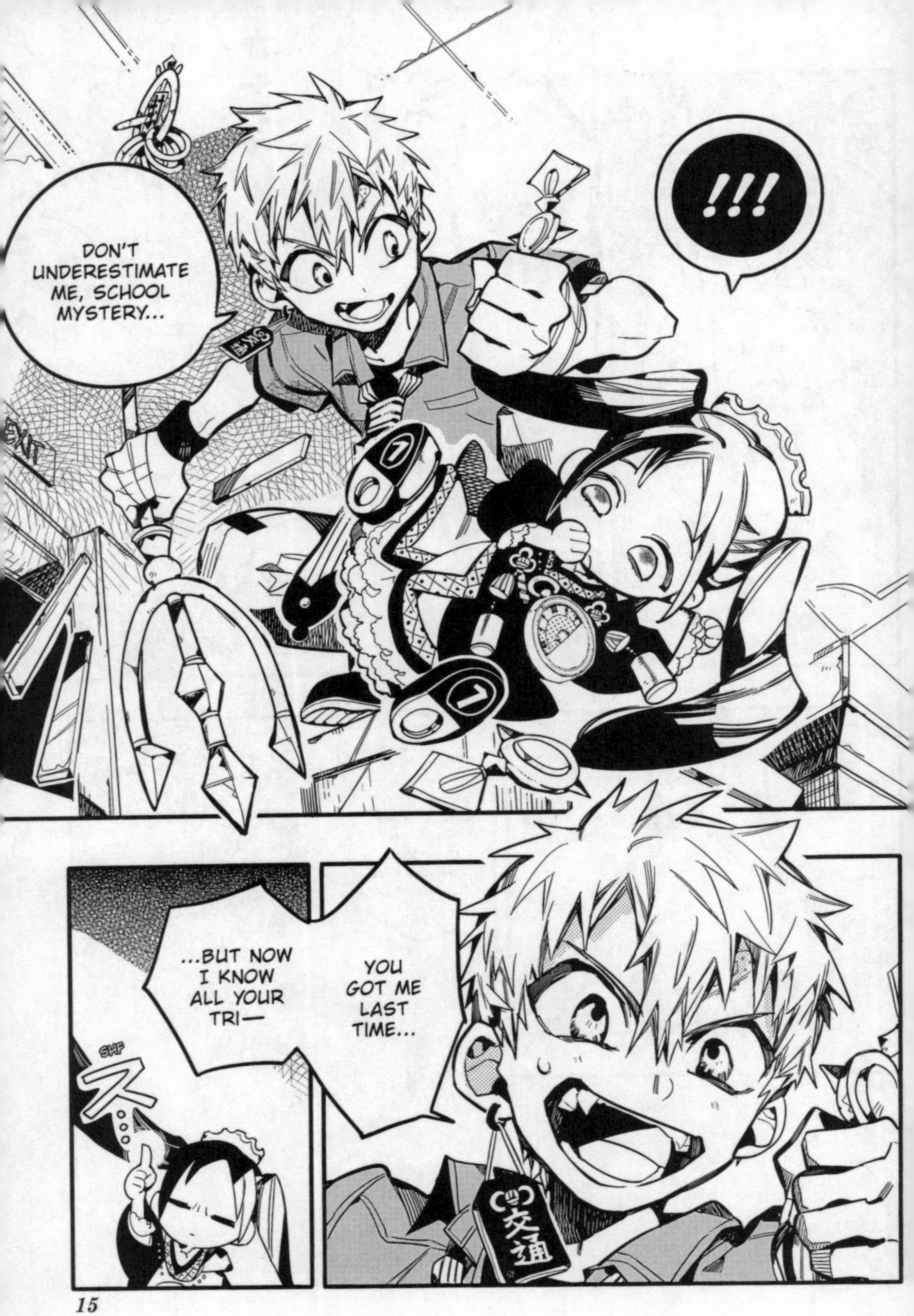
!!!
DON'T UNDERESTIMATE ME, SCHOOL MYSTERY...
EXIT
YOU GOT ME LAST TIME...
...BUT NOW I KNOW ALL YOUR TRI—
交通
SHF
ス

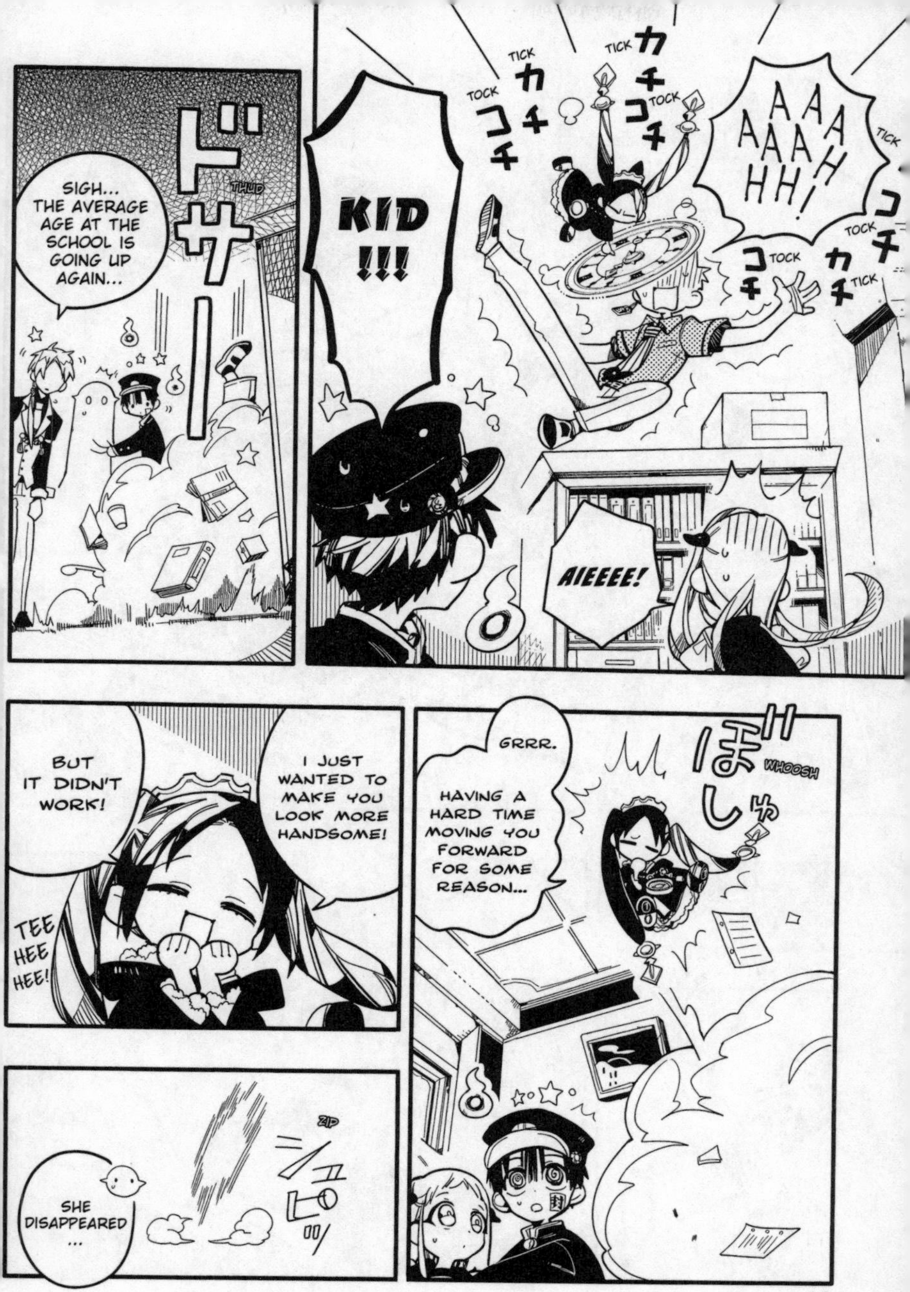

AAA
AAAAH
HH!
TICK
コチ
TOCK
カチ
TICK
TOCK
コチ
TOCK
TICK
カチ
TICK
カチ
TOCK
コチ
TOCK
コチ
KID!!!
AIEEEE!
ドサー
THUD
SIGH... THE AVERAGE AGE AT THE SCHOOL IS GOING UP AGAIN...
ぼしゅ
WHOOSH
GRRR.
HAVING A HARD TIME MOVING YOU FORWARD FOR SOME REASON...
I JUST WANTED TO MAKE YOU LOOK MORE HANDSOME!
BUT IT DIDN'T WORK!
TEE HEE HEE!
ZIP
シュピッ
SHE DISAPPEARED...

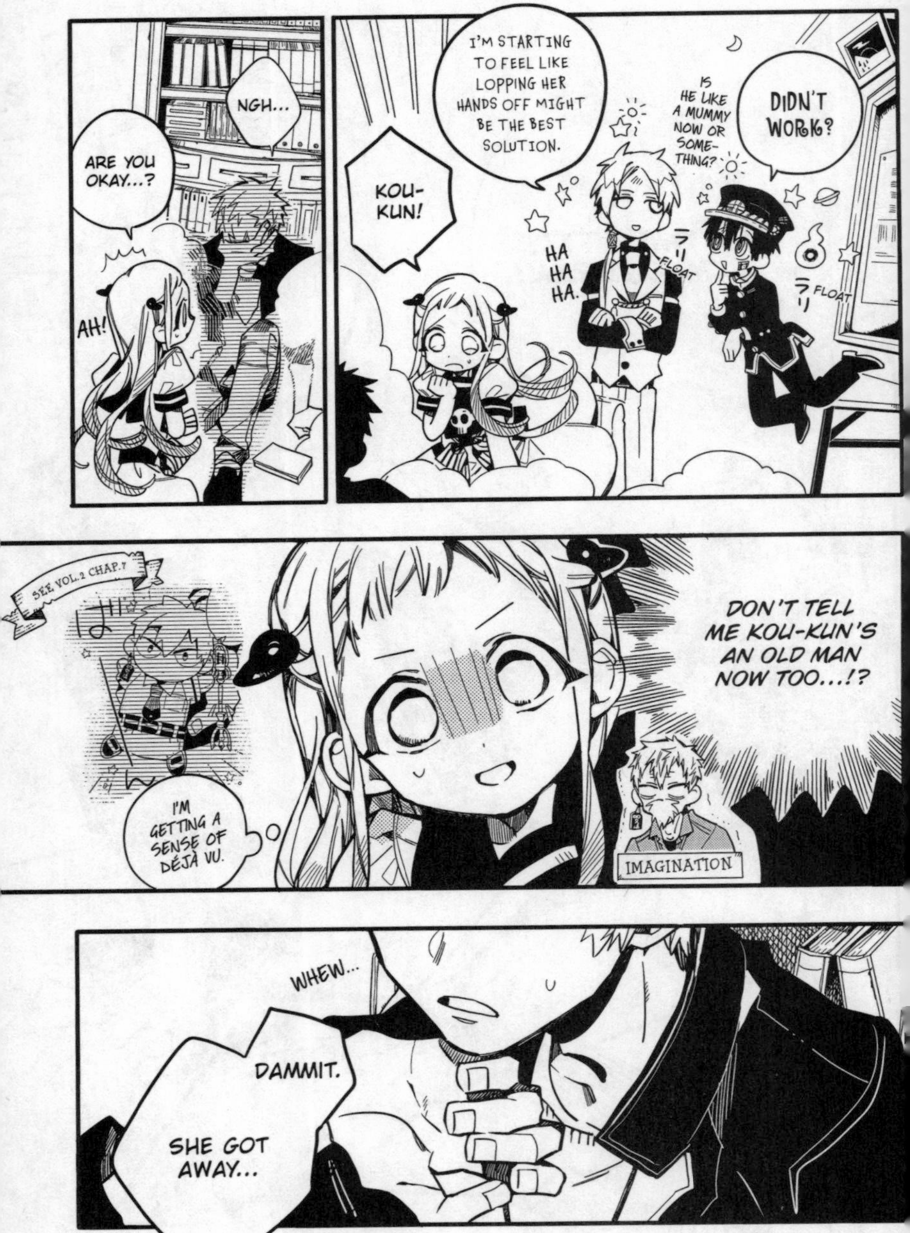

DIDN'T WORK?
IS HE LIKE A MUMMY NOW OR SOME-THING?
FLOAT
I'M STARTING TO FEEL LIKE LOPPING HER HANDS OFF MIGHT BE THE BEST SOLUTION.
HA HA HA.
FLOAT
KOU-KUN!
NGH...
ARE YOU OKAY...?
AH!
DON'T TELL ME KOU-KUN'S AN OLD MAN NOW TOO...!?
IMAGINATION
I'M GETTING A SENSE OF DÉJÀ VU.
SEE VOL.2 CHAP.7
WHEW...
DAMMIT.
SHE GOT AWAY...

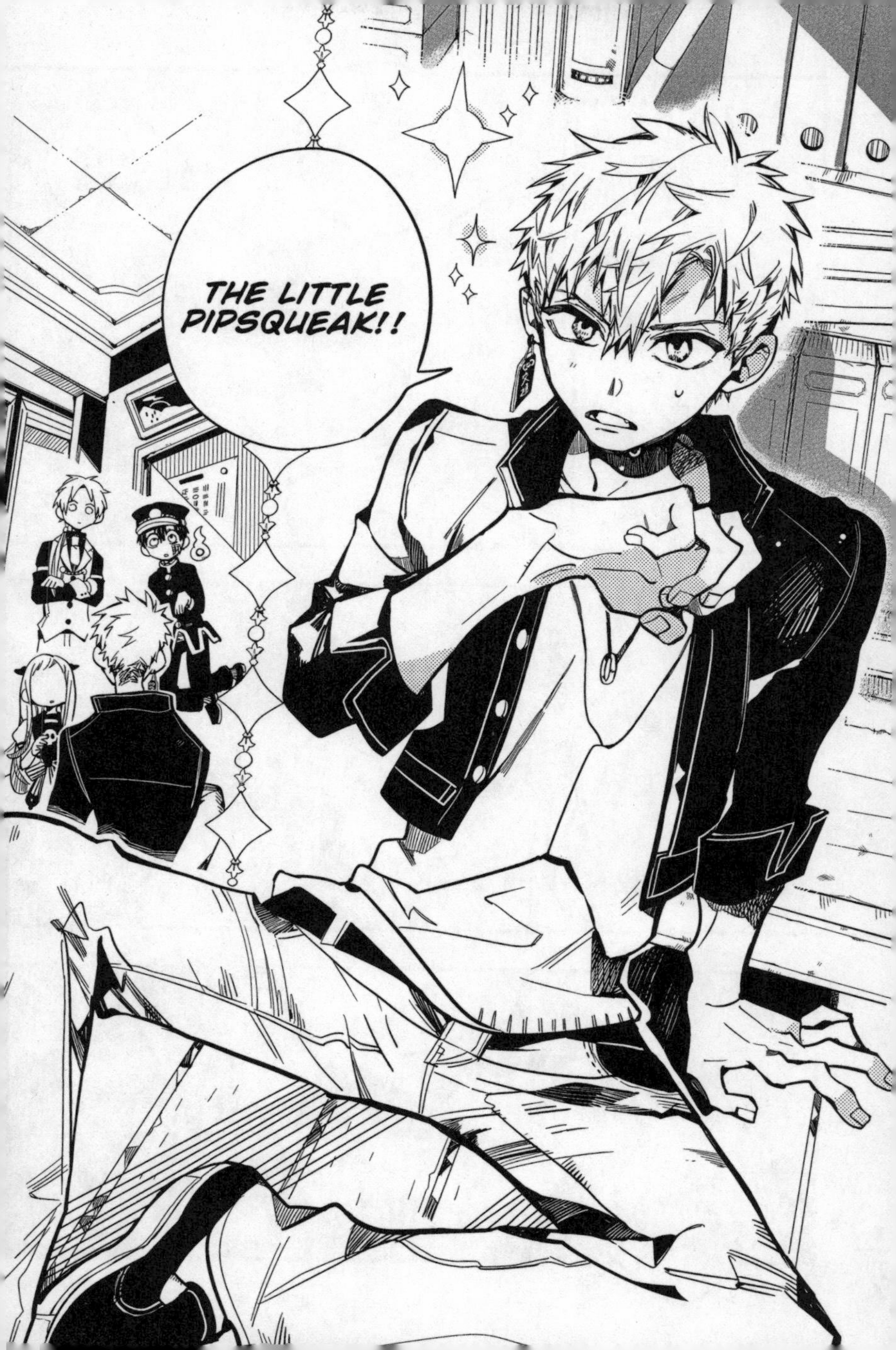
THE LITTLE PIPSQUEAK!!

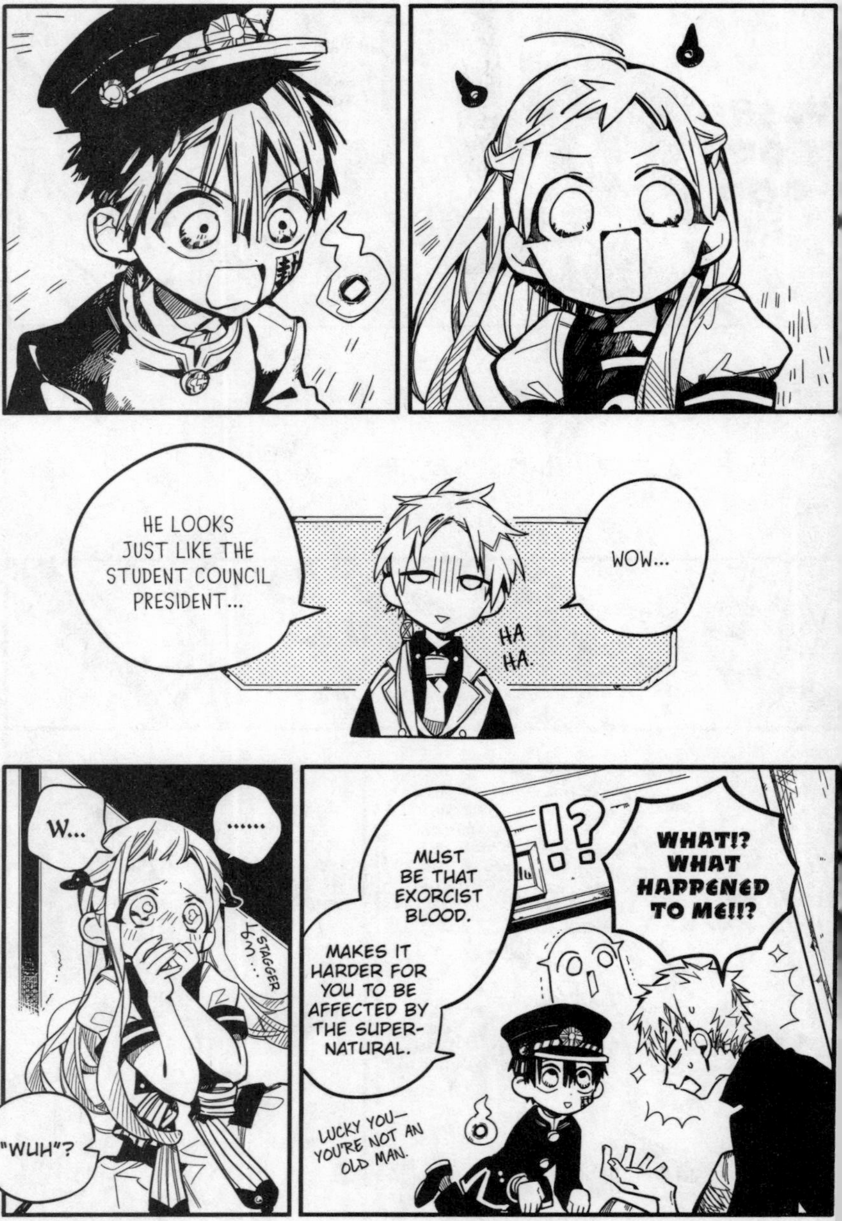
WOW...
HA HA.
HE LOOKS JUST LIKE THE STUDENT COUNCIL PRESIDENT...
WHAT!? WHAT HAPPENED TO ME!!?
!?
MUST BE THAT EXORCIST BLOOD.
MAKES IT HARDER FOR YOU TO BE AFFECTED BY THE SUPER-NATURAL.
LUCKY YOU— YOU'RE NOT AN OLD MAN.
......
W...
STAGGER
"WUH"?

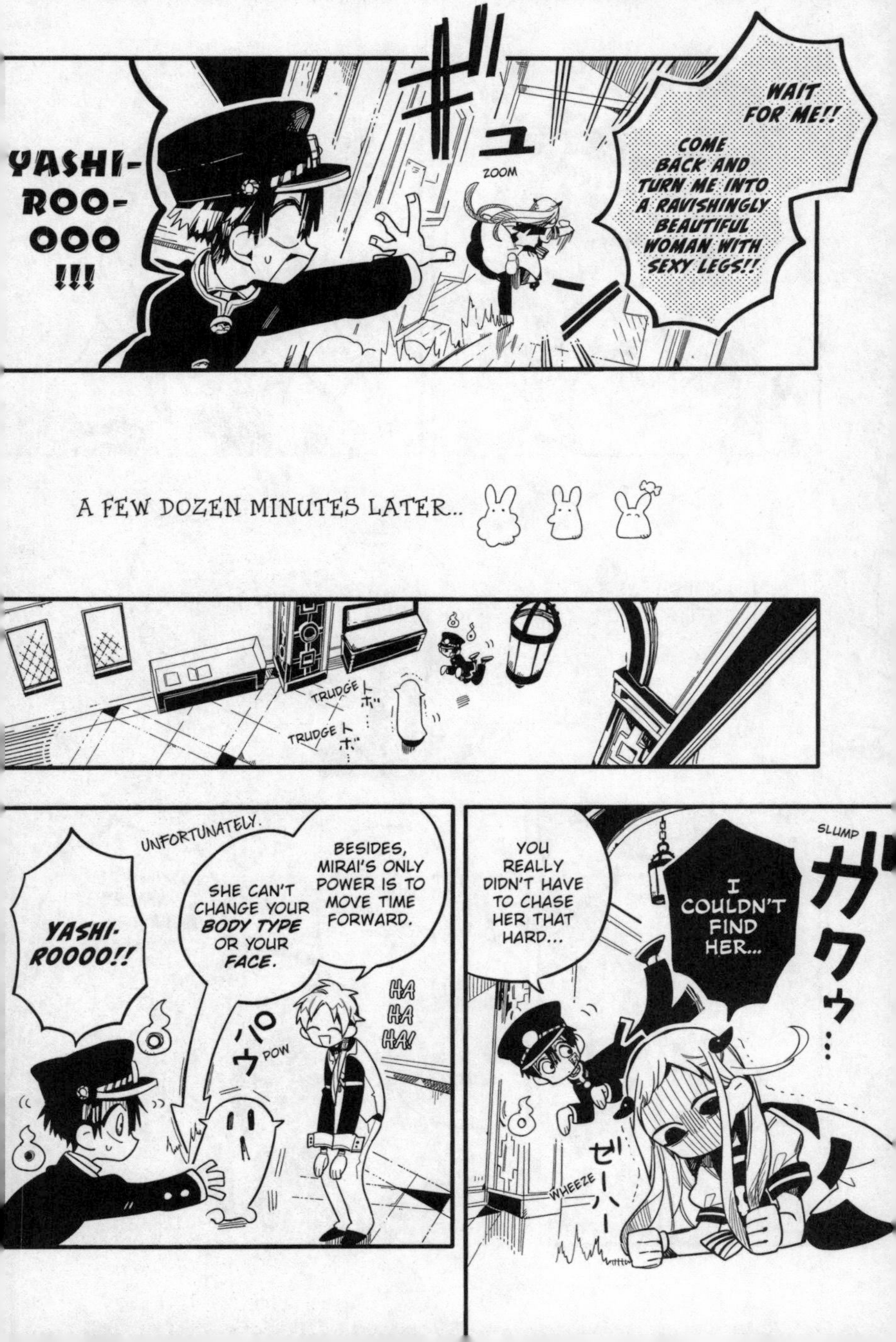
WAIT FOR ME!!
COME BACK AND TURN ME INTO A RAVISHINGLY BEAUTIFUL WOMAN WITH SEXY LEGS!!
ZOOM
YASHI-ROO-OOO!!!
A FEW DOZEN MINUTES LATER...
TRUDGE
TRUDGE
SLUMP
I COULDN'T FIND HER...
YOU REALLY DIDN'T HAVE TO CHASE HER THAT HARD...
WHEEZE
BESIDES, MIRAI'S ONLY POWER IS TO MOVE TIME FORWARD.
SHE CAN'T CHANGE YOUR BODY TYPE OR YOUR FACE.
UNFORTUNATELY.
HA HA HA!
POW
YASHI-ROOOO!!

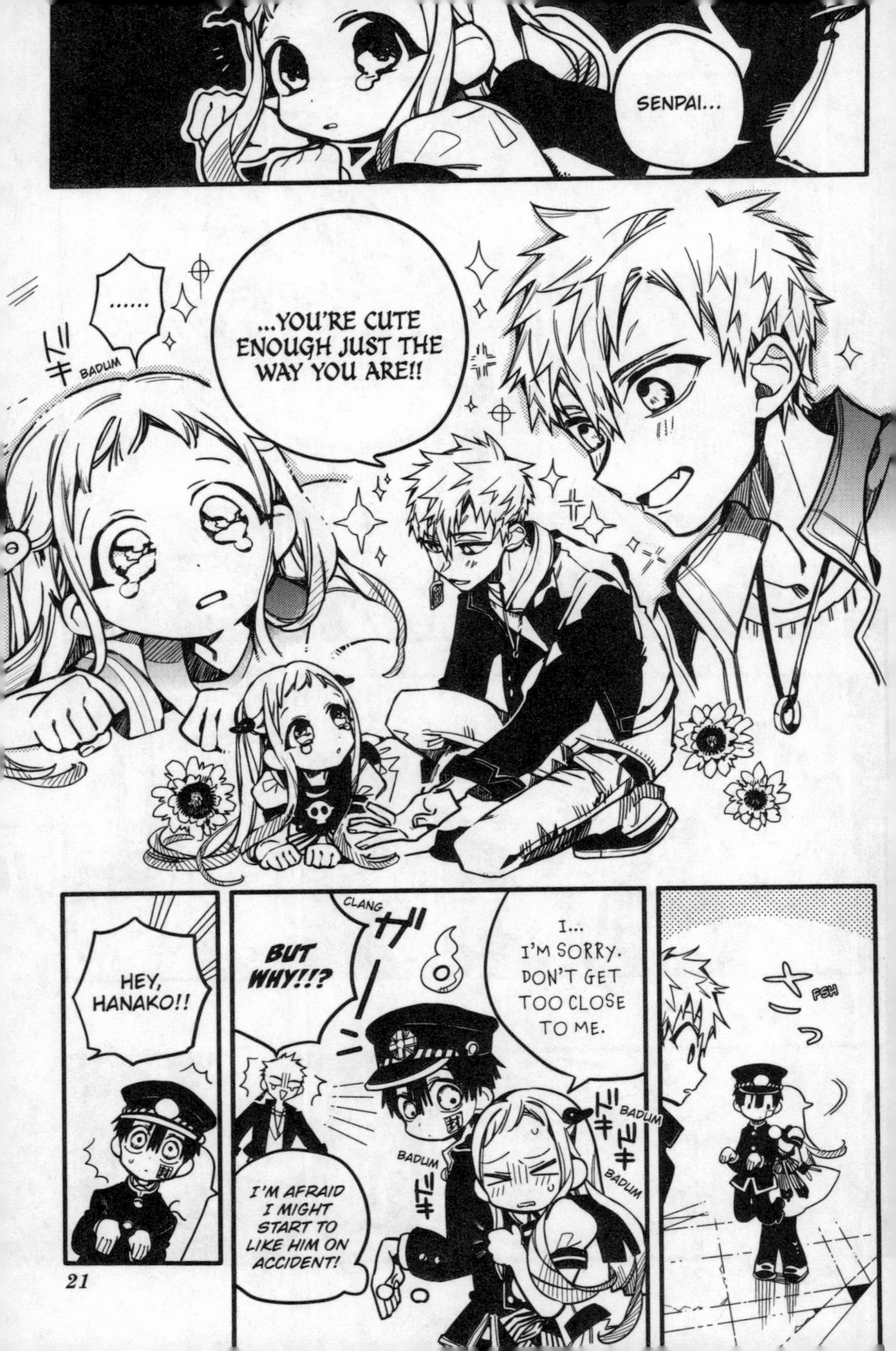
SENPAI...
...YOU'RE CUTE ENOUGH JUST THE WAY YOU ARE!!
......
BADUM
FSH
I... I'M SORRY. DON'T GET TOO CLOSE TO ME.
CLANG
BUT WHY!!?
BADUM
BADUM
BADUM
I'M AFRAID I MIGHT START TO LIKE HIM ON ACCIDENT!
HEY, HANAKO!!

ARMBAND: STUDENT COUNCIL

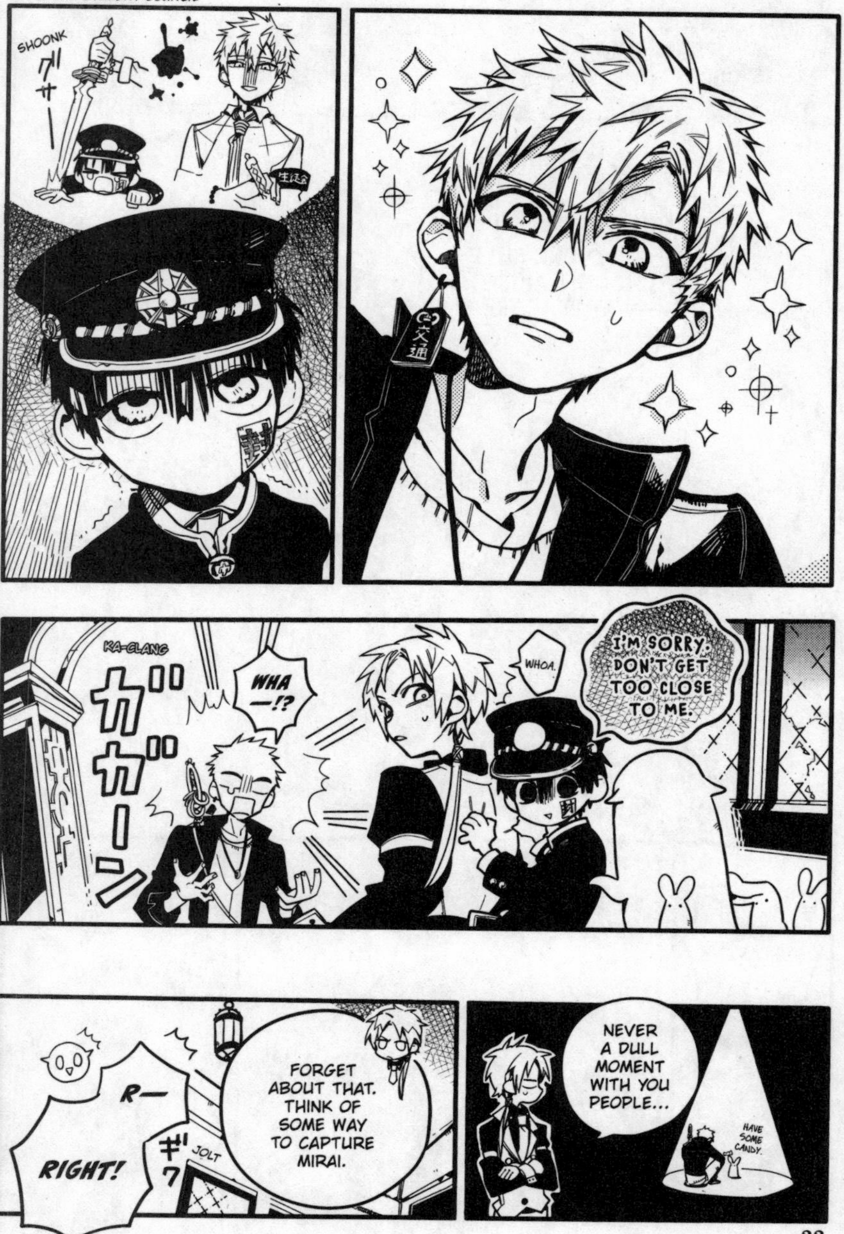
SHOONK
グサー
生徒会
I'M SORRY. DON'T GET TOO CLOSE TO ME.
WHOA.
WHA—!?
KA-CLANG
カガーン
NEVER A DULL MOMENT WITH YOU PEOPLE...
HAVE SOME CANDY.
FORGET ABOUT THAT. THINK OF SOME WAY TO CAPTURE MIRAI.
JOLT
ギク
R—
RIGHT!

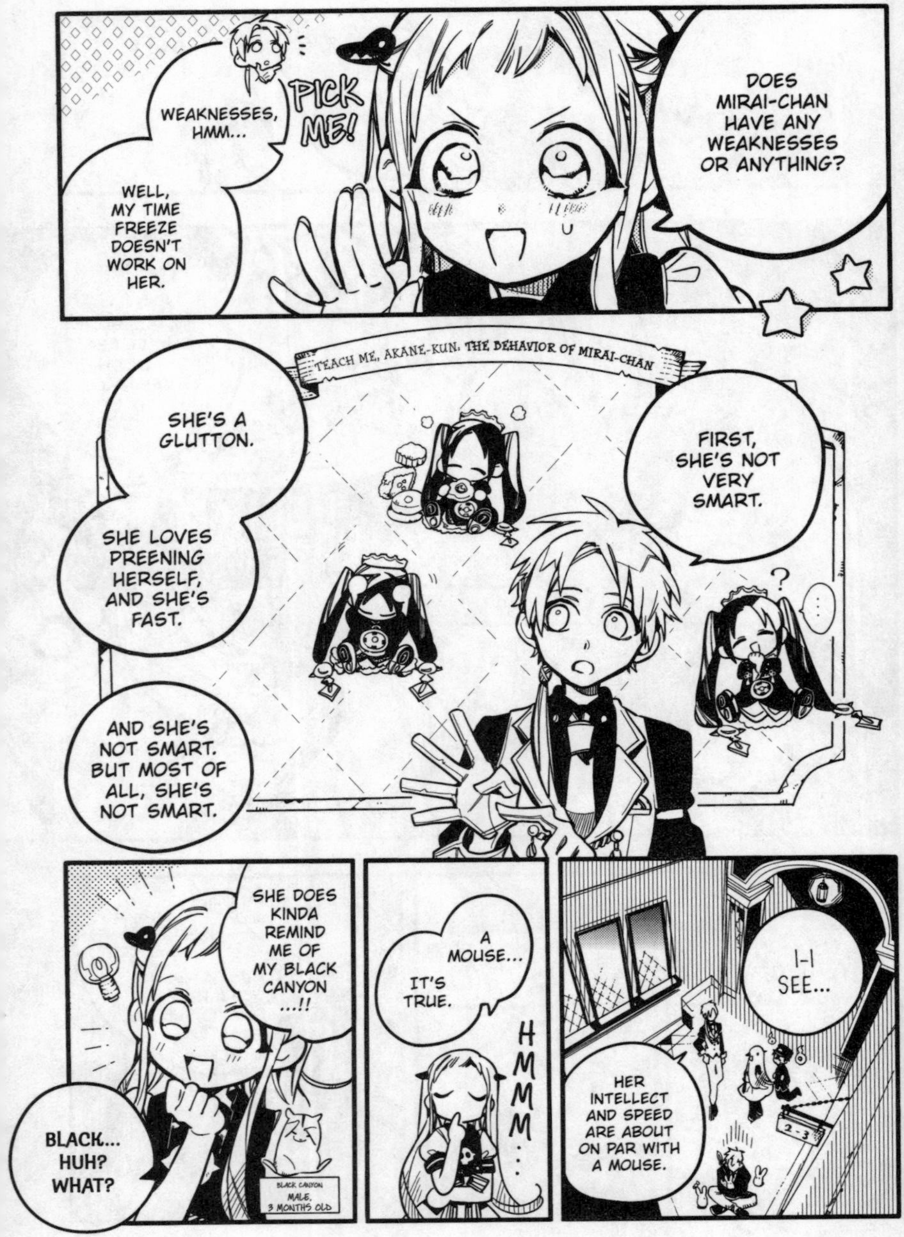
DOES MIRAI-CHAN HAVE ANY WEAKNESSES OR ANYTHING?
PICK ME!
WEAKNESSES, HMM...
WELL, MY TIME FREEZE DOESN'T WORK ON HER.
TEACH ME, AKANE-KUN. THE BEHAVIOR OF MIRAI-CHAN
FIRST, SHE'S NOT VERY SMART.
?
...
SHE'S A GLUTTON.
SHE LOVES PREENING HERSELF, AND SHE'S FAST.
AND SHE'S NOT SMART. BUT MOST OF ALL, SHE'S NOT SMART.
I-I SEE...
HER INTELLECT AND SPEED ARE ABOUT ON PAR WITH A MOUSE.
2-3
A MOUSE...
IT'S TRUE.
HMMM...
SHE DOES KINDA REMIND ME OF MY BLACK CANYON ...!!
BLACK... HUH? WHAT?
BLACK CANYON
MALE, 3 MONTHS OLD

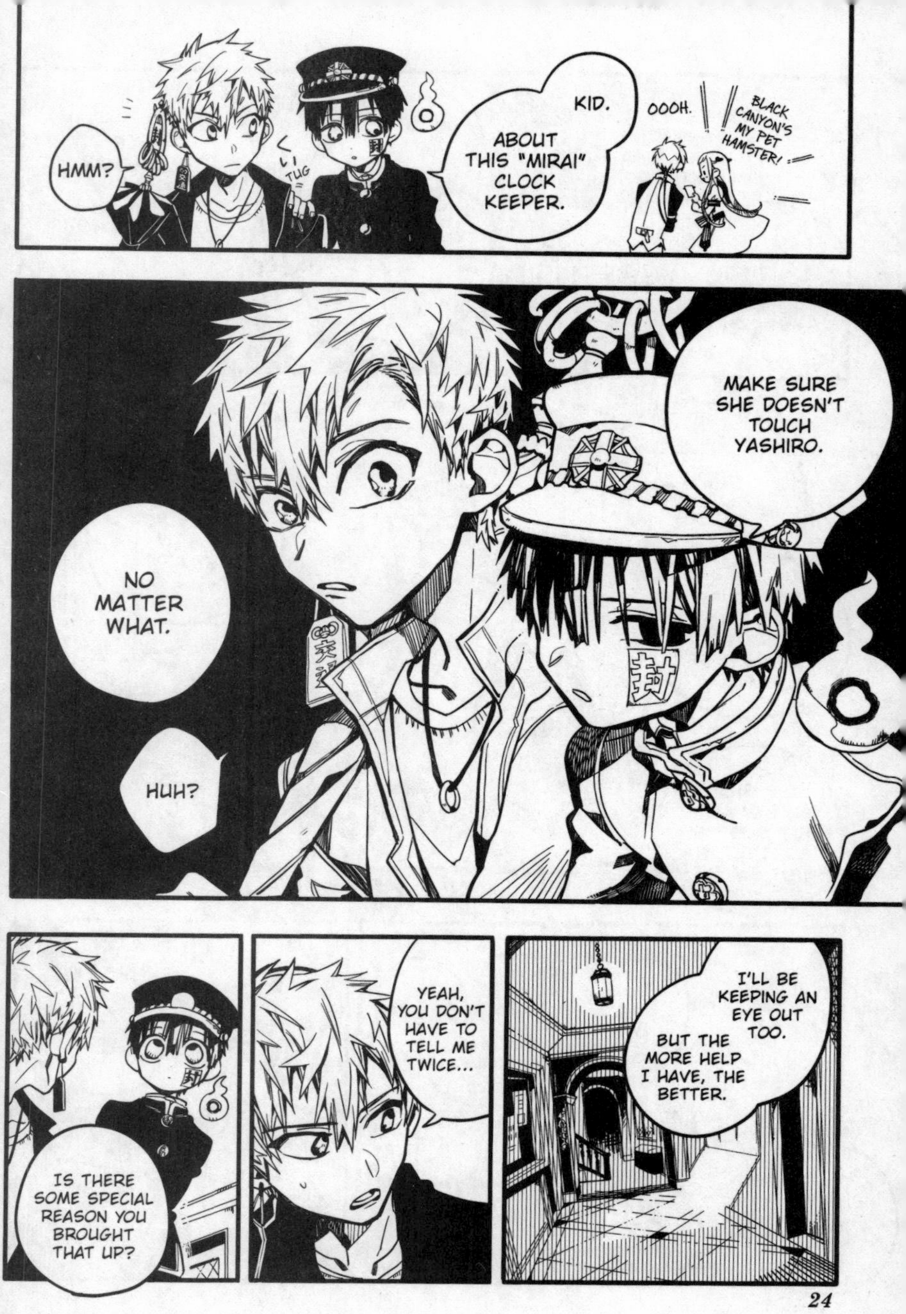
BLACK CANYON'S MY PET HAMSTER!
OOOH.
KID.
ABOUT THIS "MIRAI" CLOCK KEEPER.
TUG
HMM?
MAKE SURE SHE DOESN'T TOUCH YASHIRO.
NO MATTER WHAT.
HUH?
I'LL BE KEEPING AN EYE OUT TOO.
BUT THE MORE HELP I HAVE, THE BETTER.
YEAH, YOU DON'T HAVE TO TELL ME TWICE...
IS THERE SOME SPECIAL REASON YOU BROUGHT THAT UP?

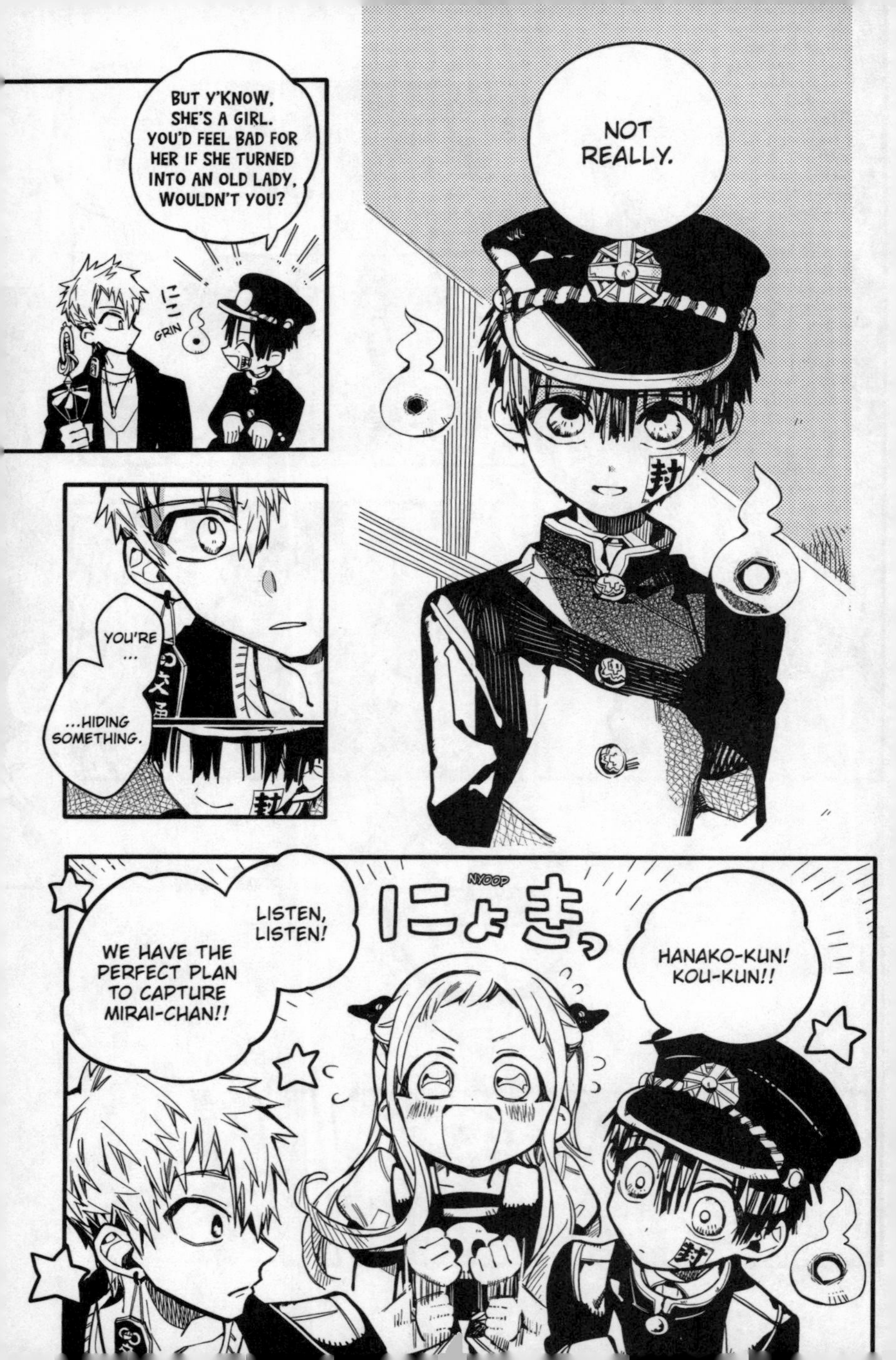

NOT REALLY.
BUT Y'KNOW, SHE'S A GIRL. YOU'D FEEL BAD FOR HER IF SHE TURNED INTO AN OLD LADY, WOULDN'T YOU?
にこ
GRIN
YOU'RE ...
...HIDING SOMETHING.
HANAKO-KUN! KOU-KUN!!
NYOOP
にょきっ
LISTEN, LISTEN!
WE HAVE THE PERFECT PLAN TO CAPTURE MIRAI-CHAN!!

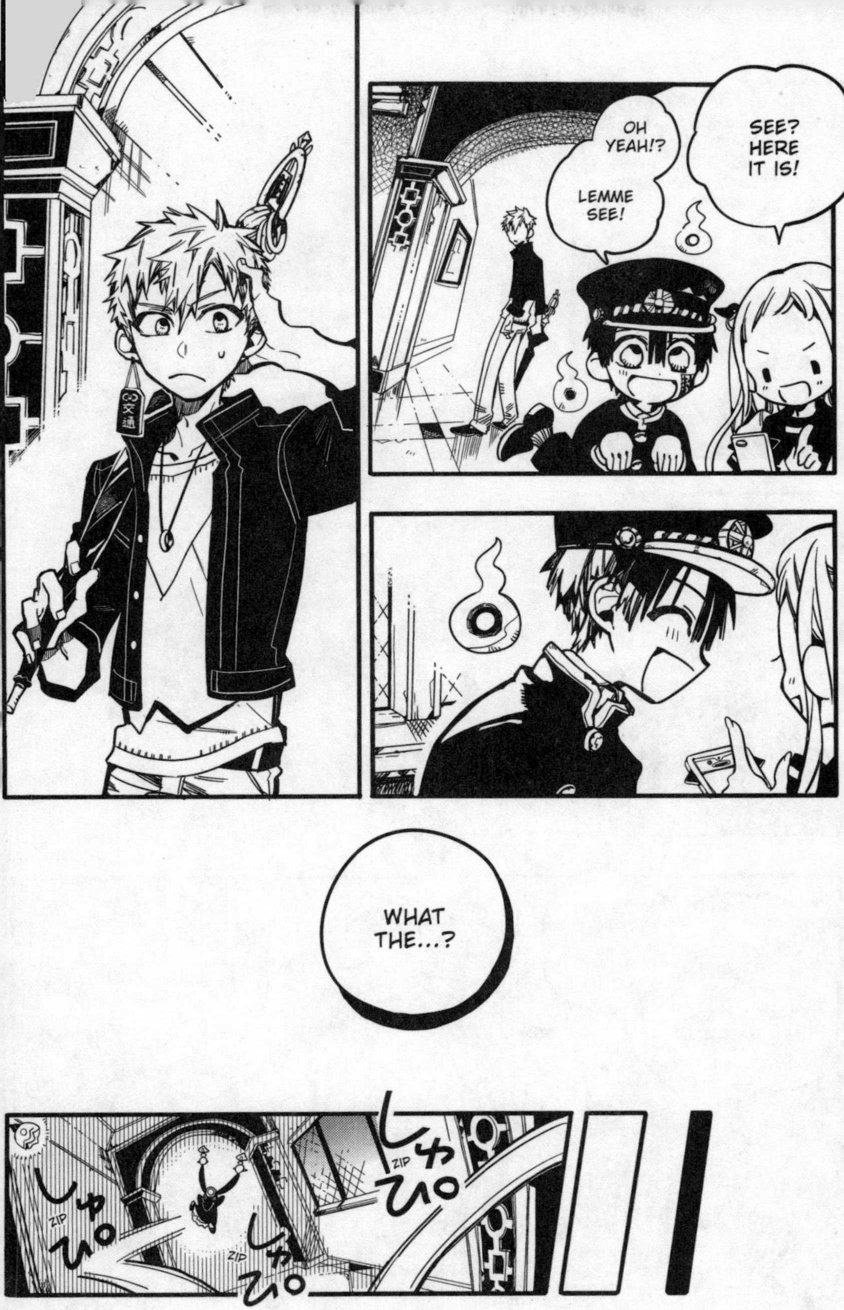
SEE? HERE IT IS!
OH YEAH!?
LEMME SEE!
WHAT THE...?
ZIP
ZIP
ZIP

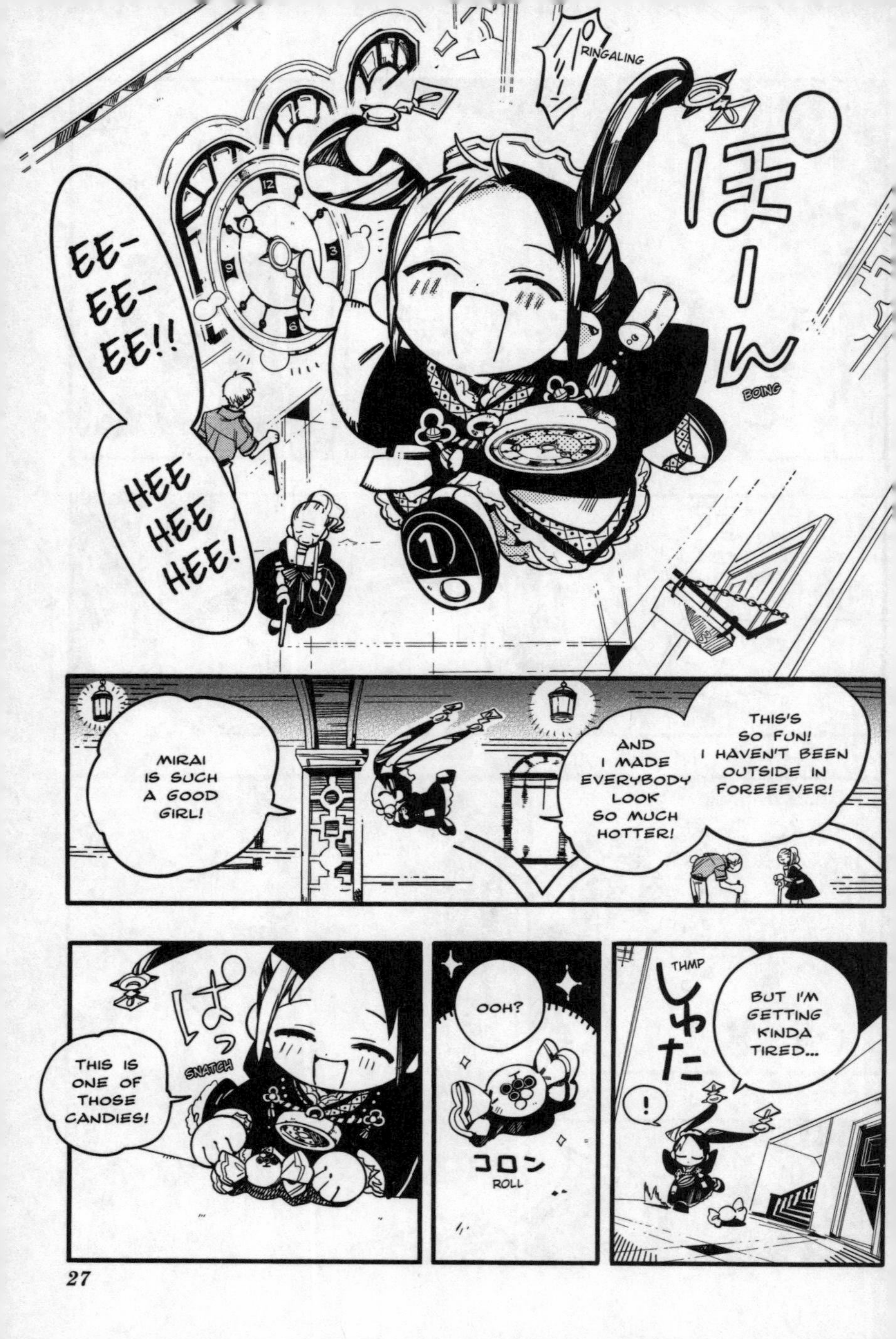

RINGALING
ぽーん
BOING
EE-EE-EE!!
HEE HEE HEE!
THIS'S SO FUN! I HAVEN'T BEEN OUTSIDE IN FOREEEVER!
AND I MADE EVERYBODY LOOK SO MUCH HOTTER!
MIRAI IS SUCH A GOOD GIRL!
しゅた
THMP
BUT I'M GETTING KINDA TIRED...
!
OOH?
コロン
ROLL
ぱっ
SNATCH
THIS IS ONE OF THOSE CANDIES!

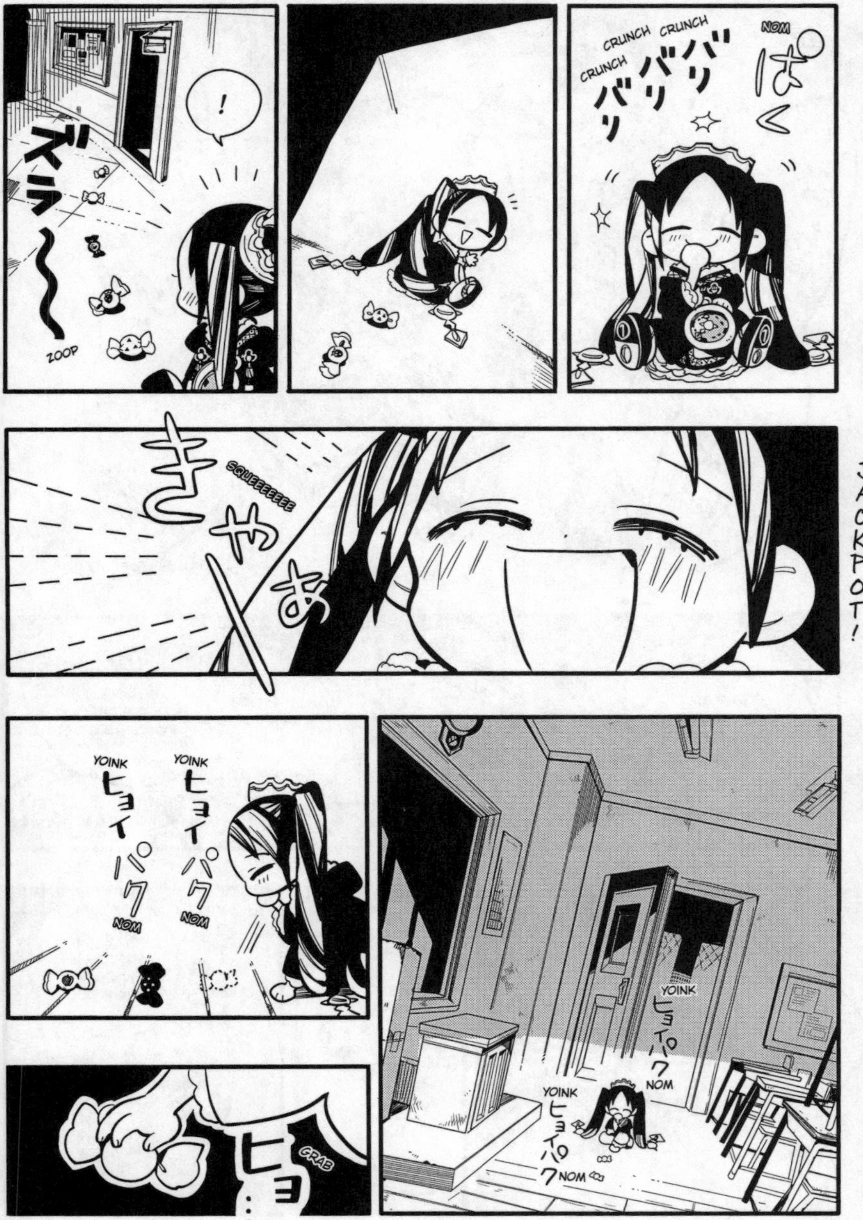
NOM
ぱく
CRUNCH CRUNCH CRUNCH
バリバリバリ
!
ズラ～～
ZOOP
JACKPOT!
きゃぁ～
SQUEEEEEEE
YOINK
ヒョイパク
NOM
YOINK
ヒョイパク
NOM
YOINK
ヒョイパク
NOM
YOINK
ヒョイパク
NOM
ヒョ…
GRAB

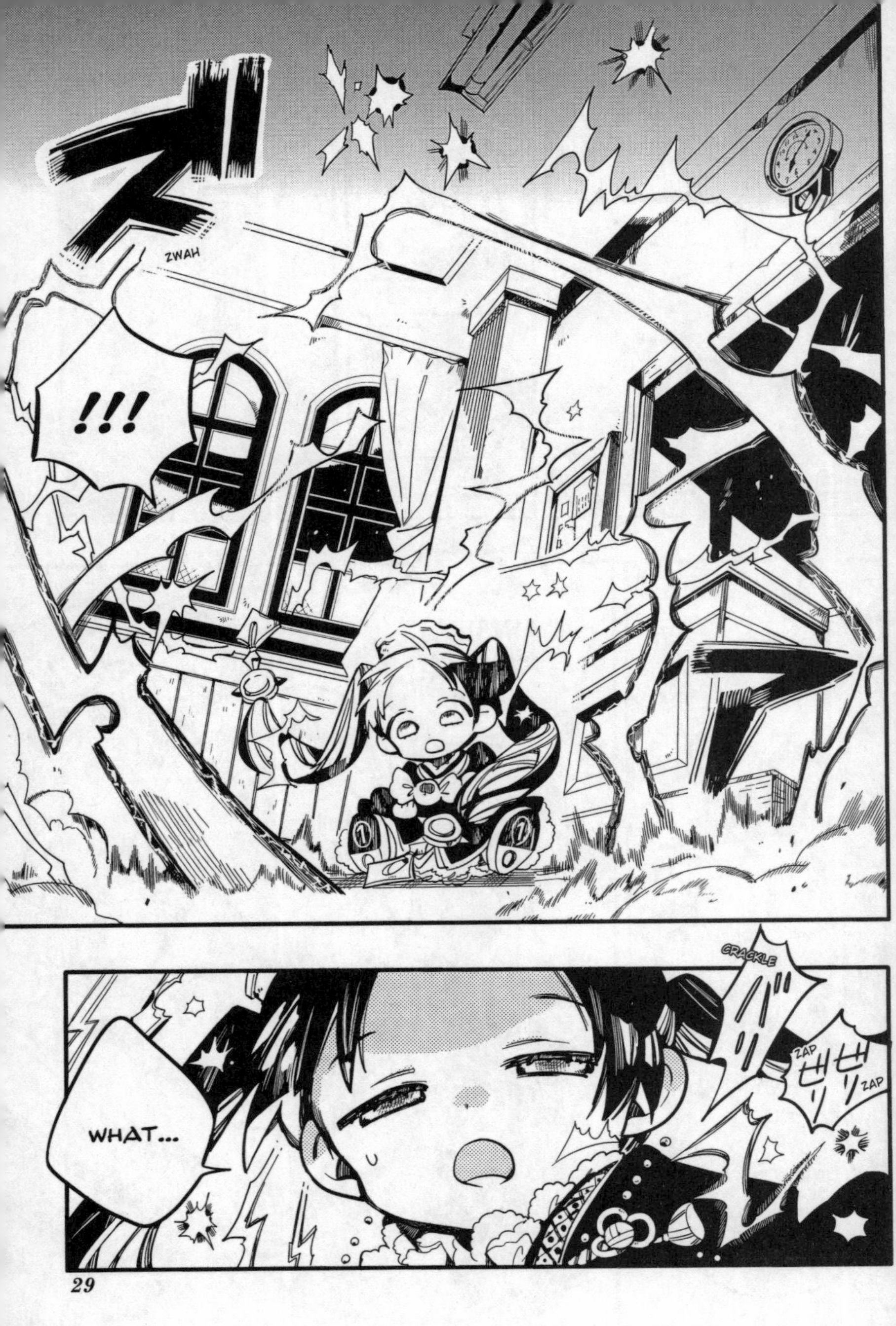
ZWAH
!!!
CRACKLE
ZAP
ビリビリ
ZAP
WHAT...

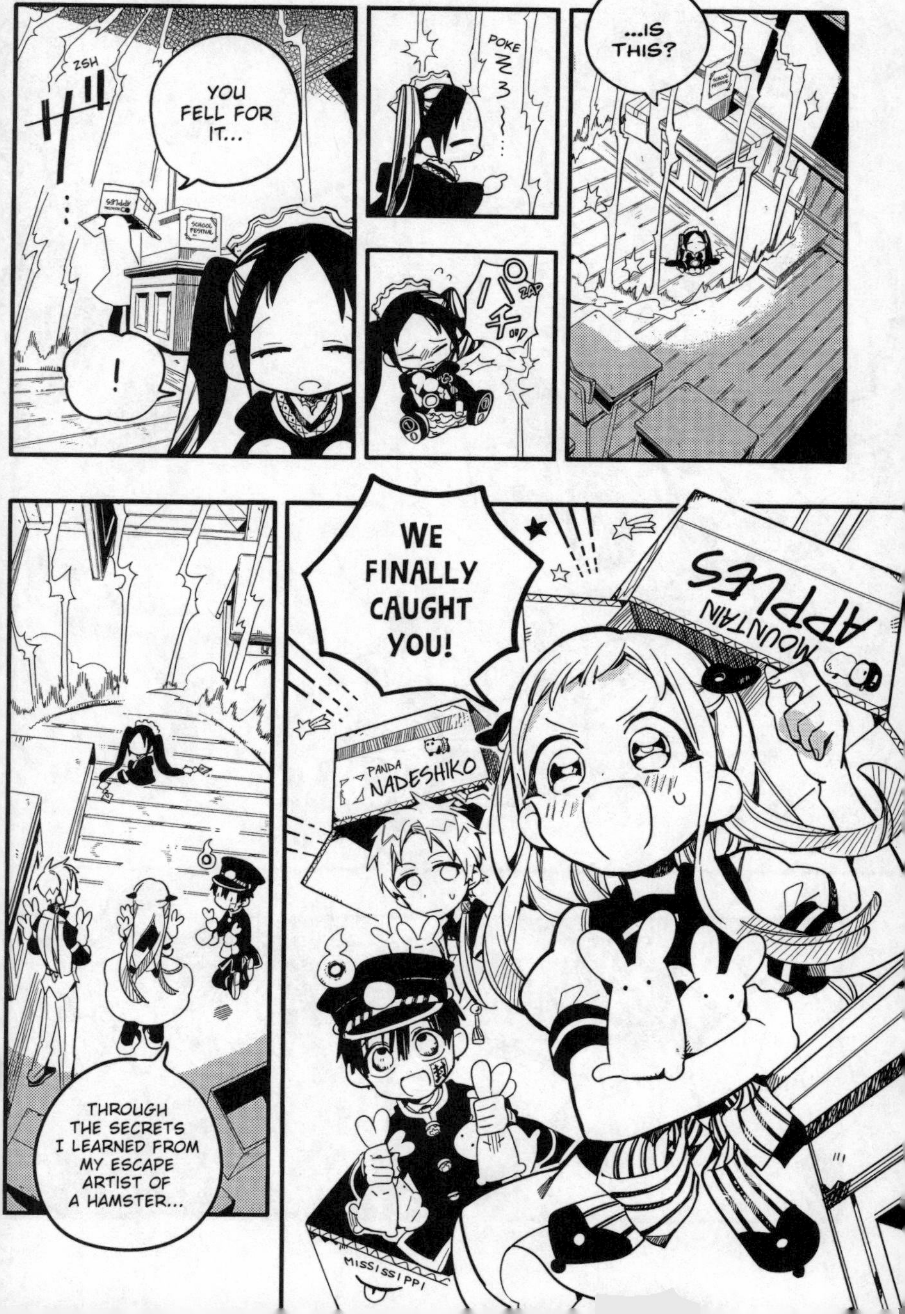
...IS THIS?
SCHOOL FESTIVAL
POKE
パチ
ZAP
ZSH
YOU FELL FOR IT...
SCHOOL FESTIVAL
APPLES
...
!
WE FINALLY CAUGHT YOU!
MOUNTAIN APPLES
PANDA NADESHIKO
MISSISSIPPI
THROUGH THE SECRETS I LEARNED FROM MY ESCAPE ARTIST OF A HAMSTER...

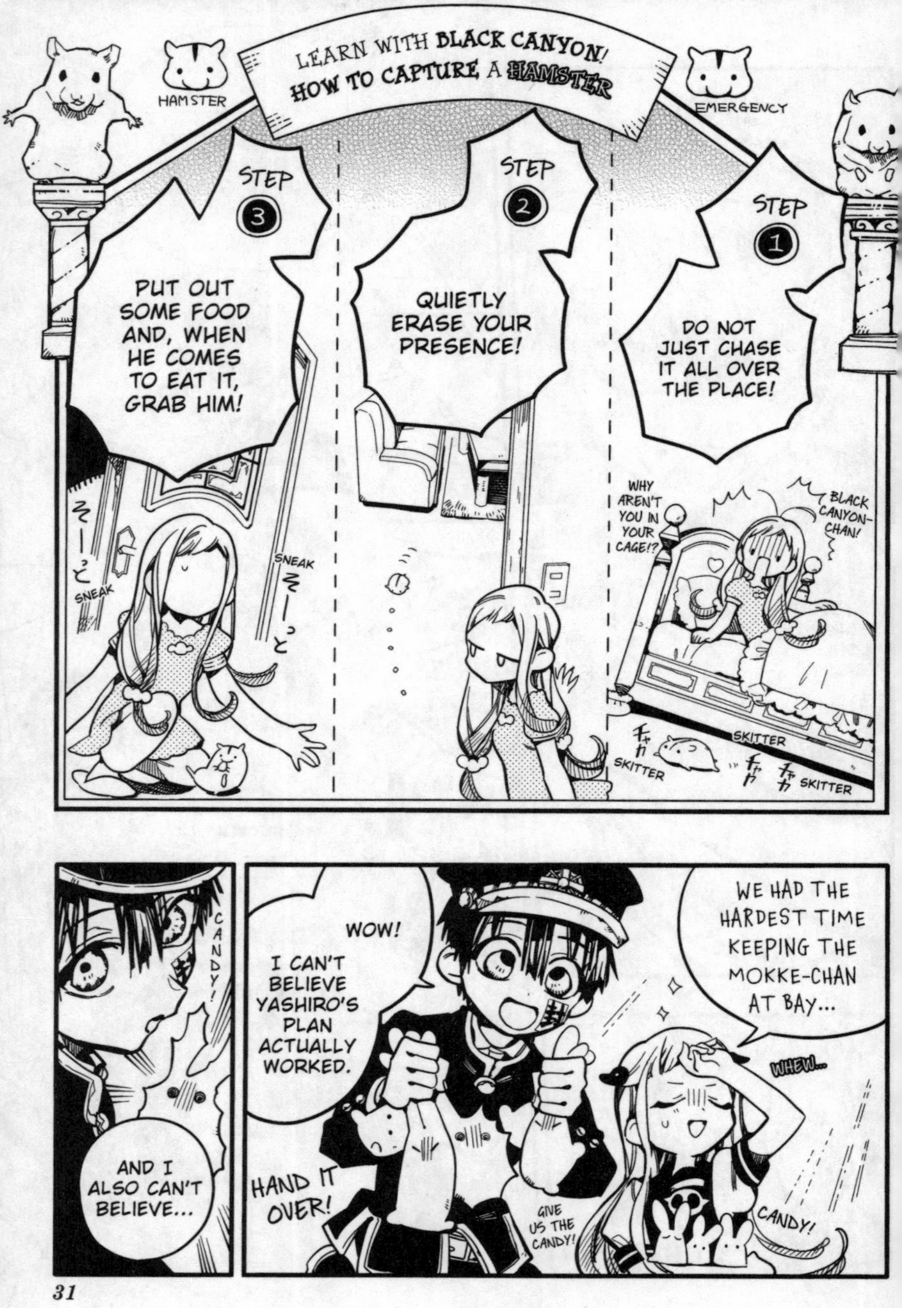
LEARN WITH BLACK CANYON!
HOW TO CAPTURE A HAMSTER
EMERGENCY
HAMSTER
STEP 1
DO NOT JUST CHASE IT ALL OVER THE PLACE!
BLACK CANYON-CHAN!
WHY AREN'T YOU IN YOUR CAGE!?
SKITTER
SKITTER
SKITTER
STEP 2
QUIETLY ERASE YOUR PRESENCE!
STEP 3
PUT OUT SOME FOOD AND, WHEN HE COMES TO EAT IT, GRAB HIM!
SNEAK
SNEAK
WE HAD THE HARDEST TIME KEEPING THE MOKKE-CHAN AT BAY...
WHEW...
CANDY!
GIVE US THE CANDY!
WOW!
I CAN'T BELIEVE YASHIRO'S PLAN ACTUALLY WORKED.
HAND IT OVER!
CANDY!
AND I ALSO CAN'T BELIEVE...

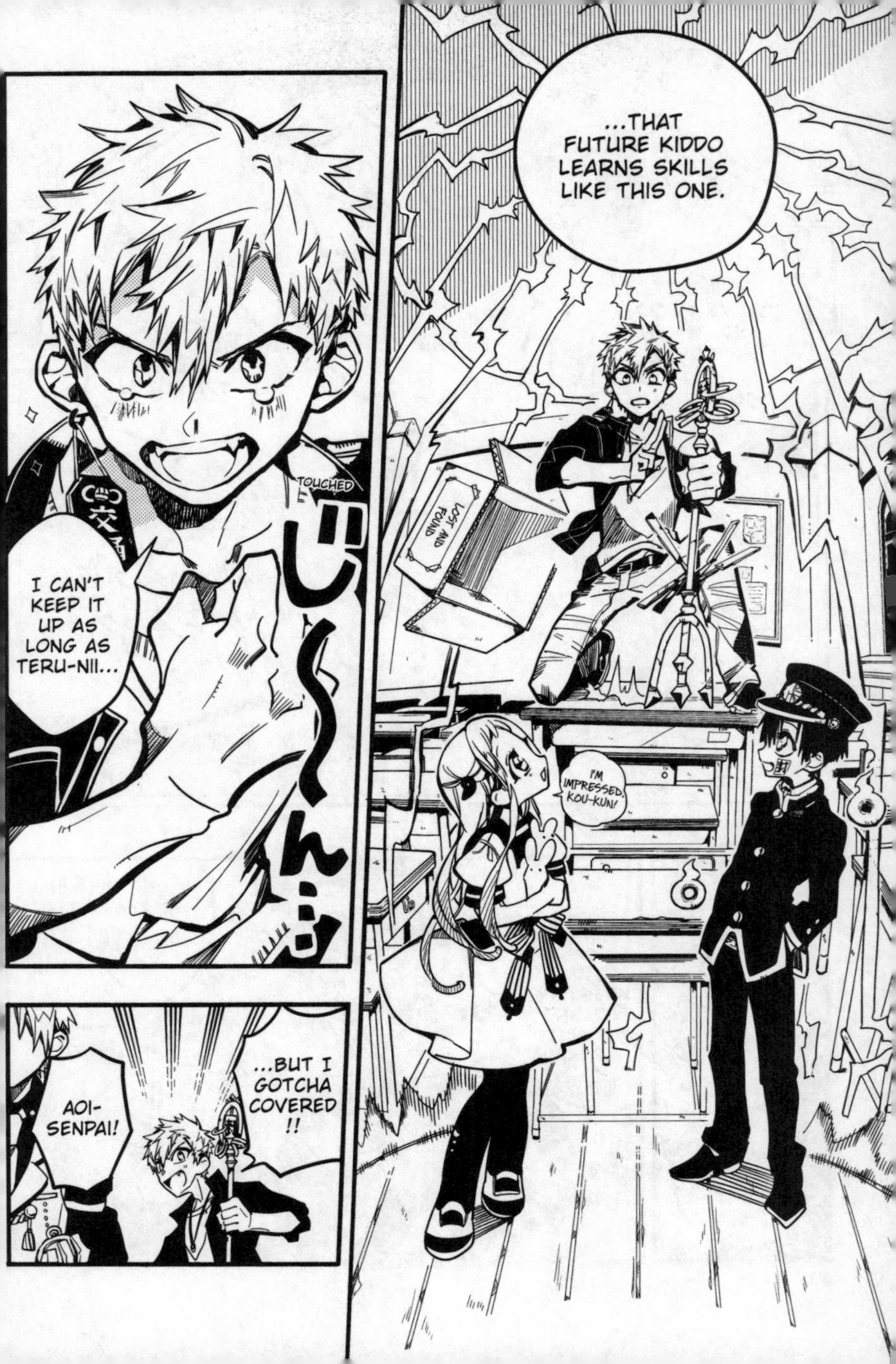
...THAT FUTURE KIDDO LEARNS SKILLS LIKE THIS ONE.
LOST AND FOUND
I'M IMPRESSED, KOU-KUN!
TOUCHED
じ〜ん…
I CAN'T KEEP IT UP AS LONG AS TERU-NII...
...BUT I GOTCHA COVERED!!
AOI-SENPAI!

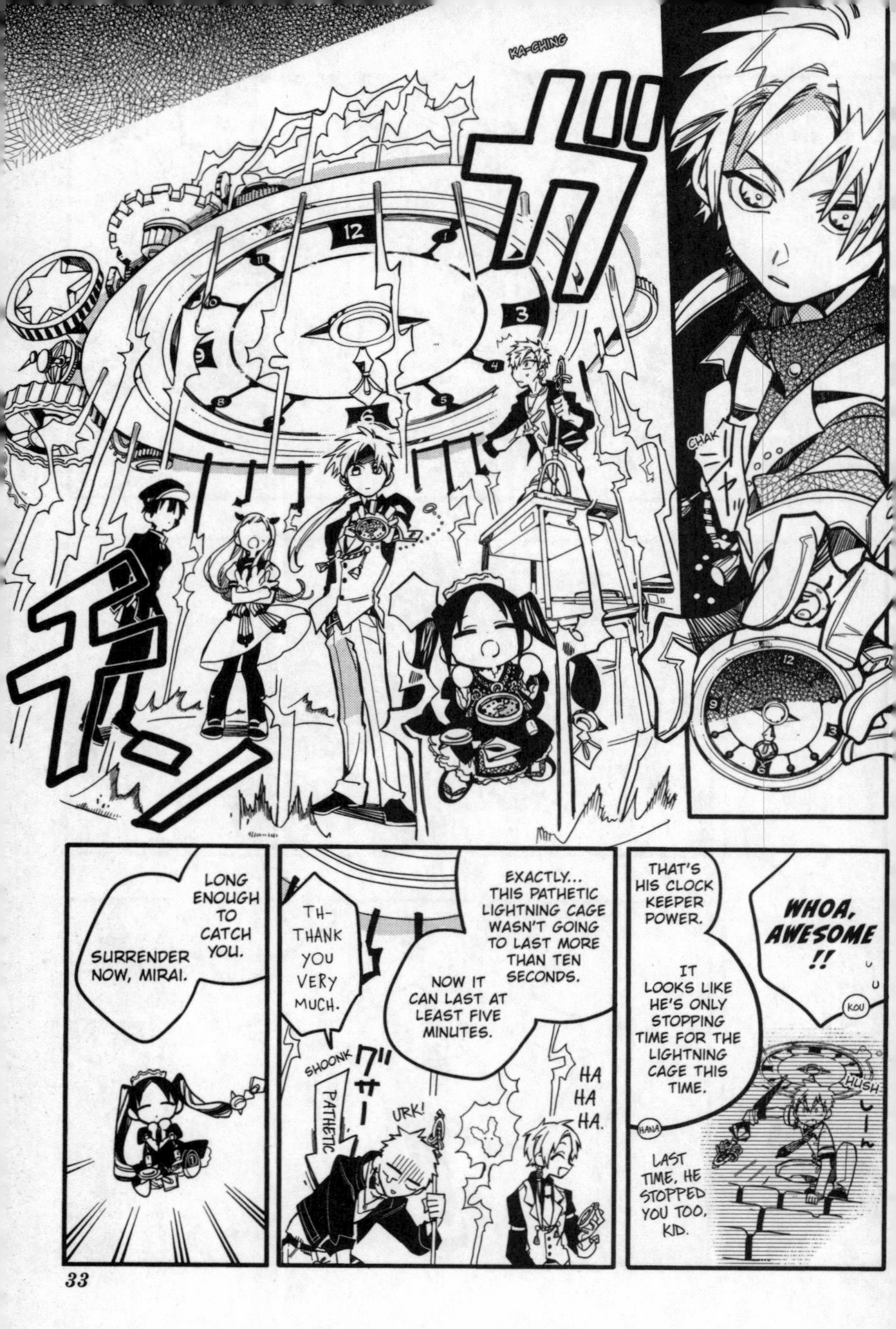
CHAK
KA-CHING
WHOA, AWESOME!!
THAT'S HIS CLOCK KEEPER POWER.
KOU
IT LOOKS LIKE HE'S ONLY STOPPING TIME FOR THE LIGHTNING CAGE THIS TIME.
HUSH
HANA
LAST TIME, HE STOPPED YOU TOO, KID.
EXACTLY... THIS PATHETIC LIGHTNING CAGE WASN'T GOING TO LAST MORE THAN TEN SECONDS.
NOW IT CAN LAST AT LEAST FIVE MINUTES.
TH-THANK YOU VERY MUCH.
HA HA HA.
URK!
SHOONK
グザー
PATHETIC
LONG ENOUGH TO CATCH YOU.
SURRENDER NOW, MIRAI.

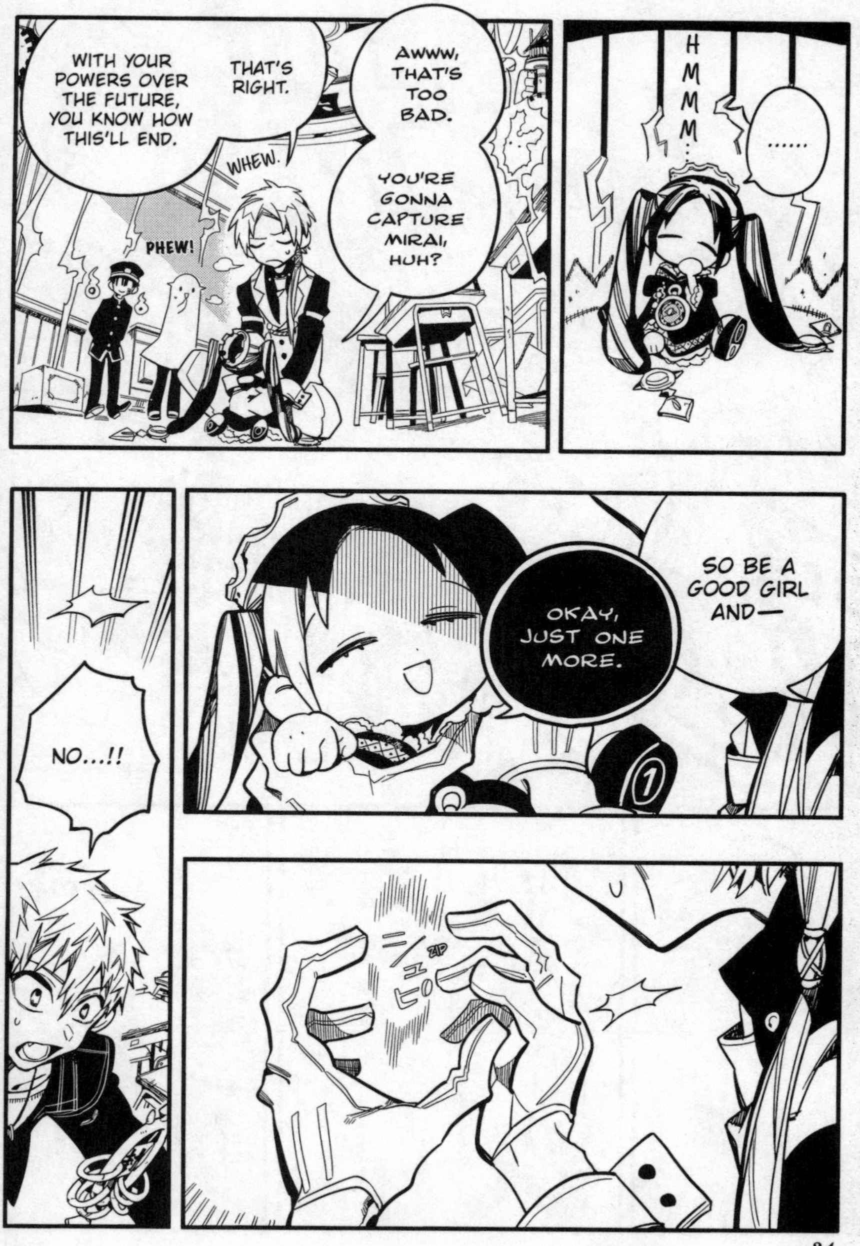
HMMM...
......
AWWW, THAT'S TOO BAD.
YOU'RE GONNA CAPTURE MIRAI, HUH?
THAT'S RIGHT.
WITH YOUR POWERS OVER THE FUTURE, YOU KNOW HOW THIS'LL END.
WHEW.
PHEW!
SO BE A GOOD GIRL AND—
OKAY, JUST ONE MORE.
ZIP
NO...!!

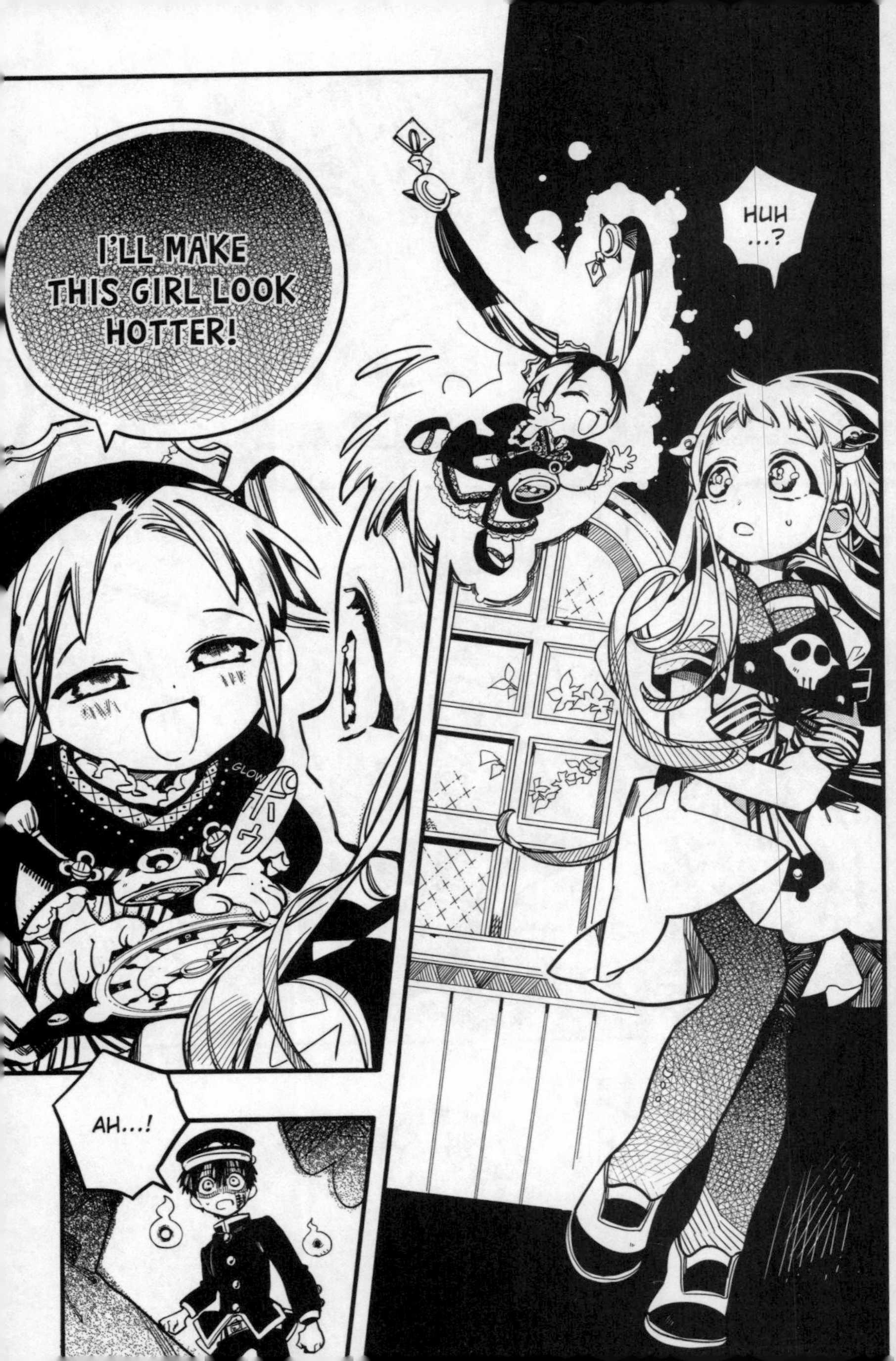
HUH ...?
I'LL MAKE THIS GIRL LOOK HOTTER!
GLOW
AH...!

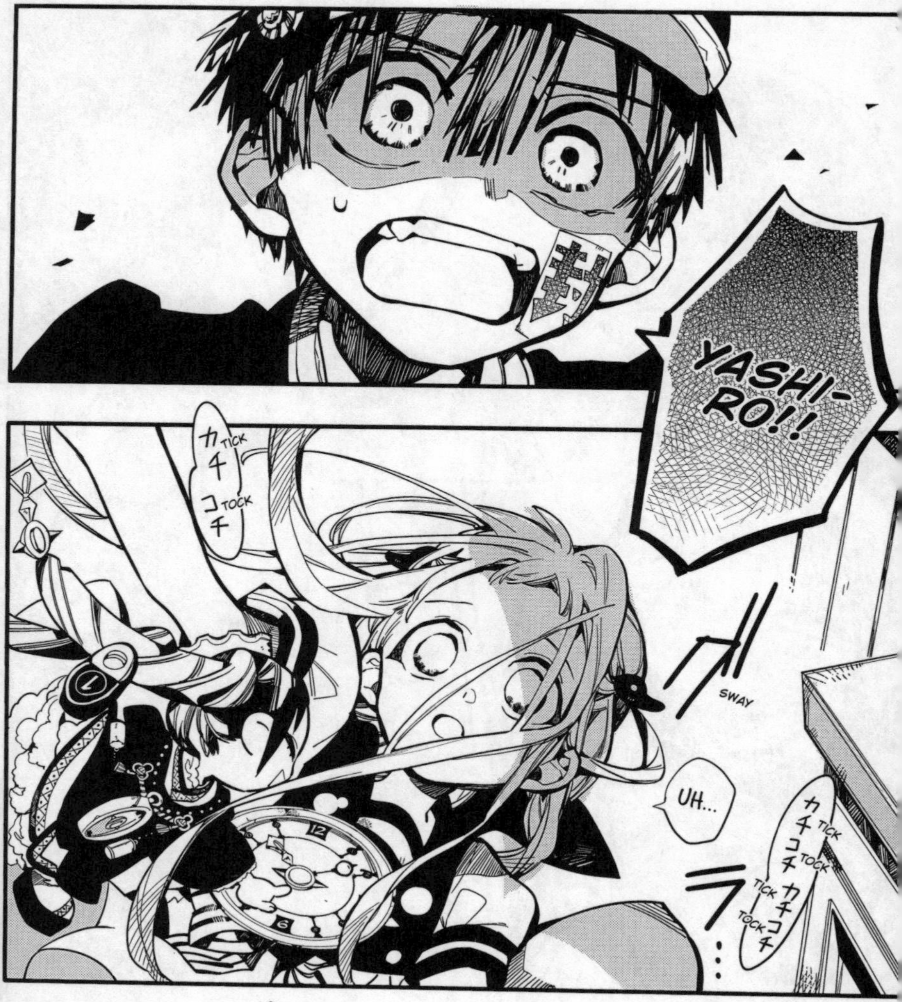
YASHI-RO!!
SWAY
カチコチカチコチ
TICK TOCK TICK TOCK
UH...
カチコチ
TICK TOCK
CRICK

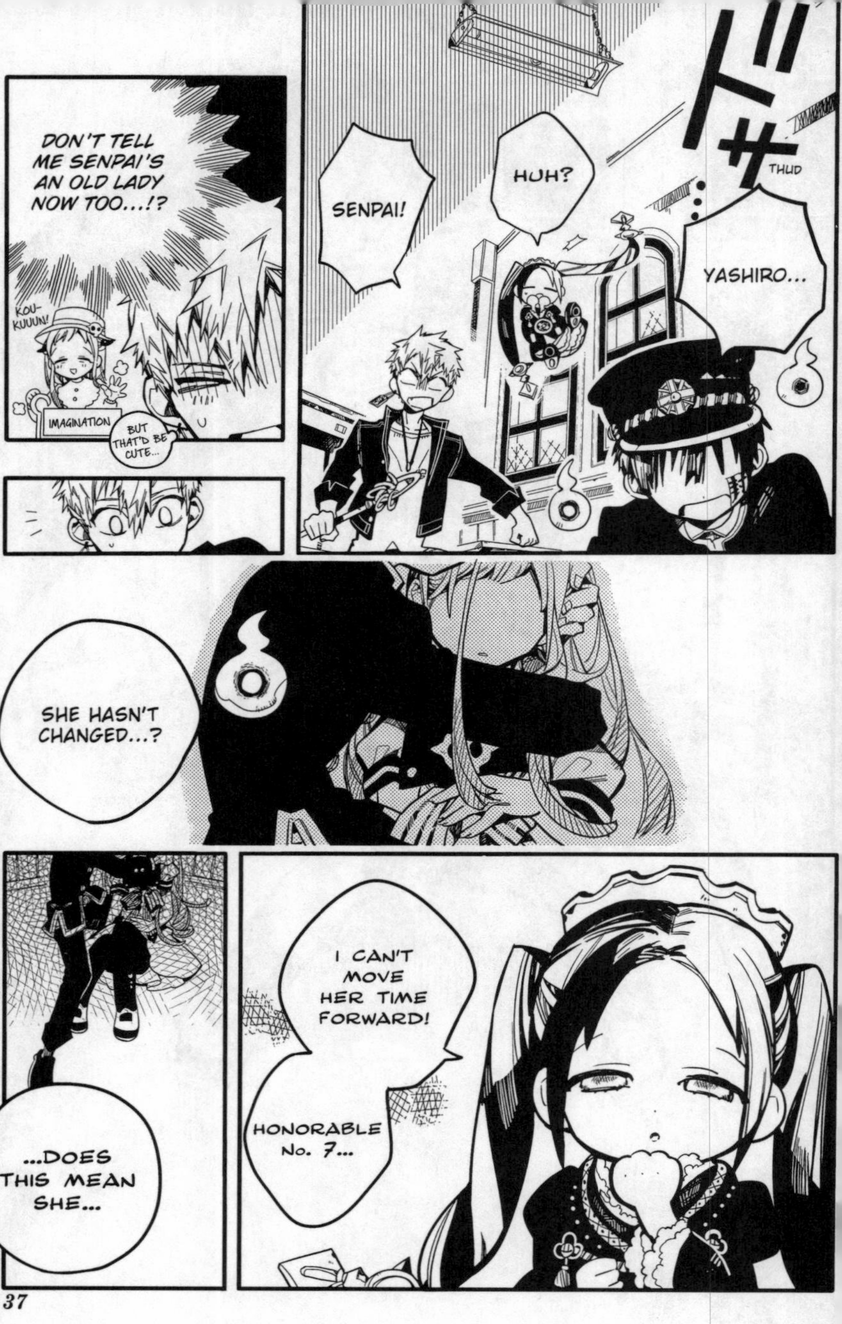

ドザ
THUD
YASHIRO...
HUH?
SENPAI!
DON'T TELL ME SENPAI'S AN OLD LADY NOW TOO...!?
KOU-KUUUN!
IMAGINATION
BUT THAT'D BE CUTE...
SHE HASN'T CHANGED...?
I CAN'T MOVE HER TIME FORWARD!
HONORABLE No. 7...
...DOES THIS MEAN SHE...

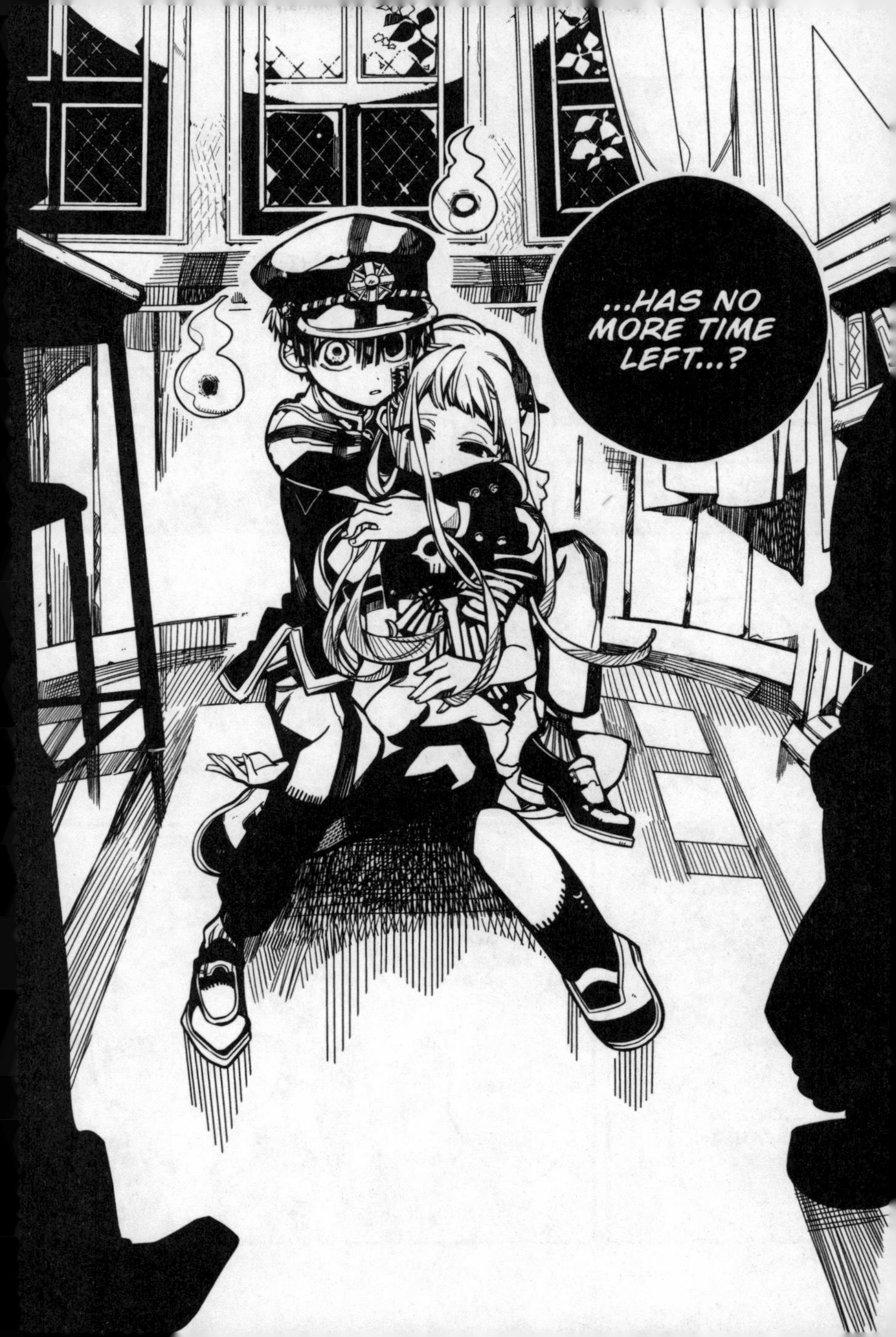
...HAS NO MORE TIME LEFT...?

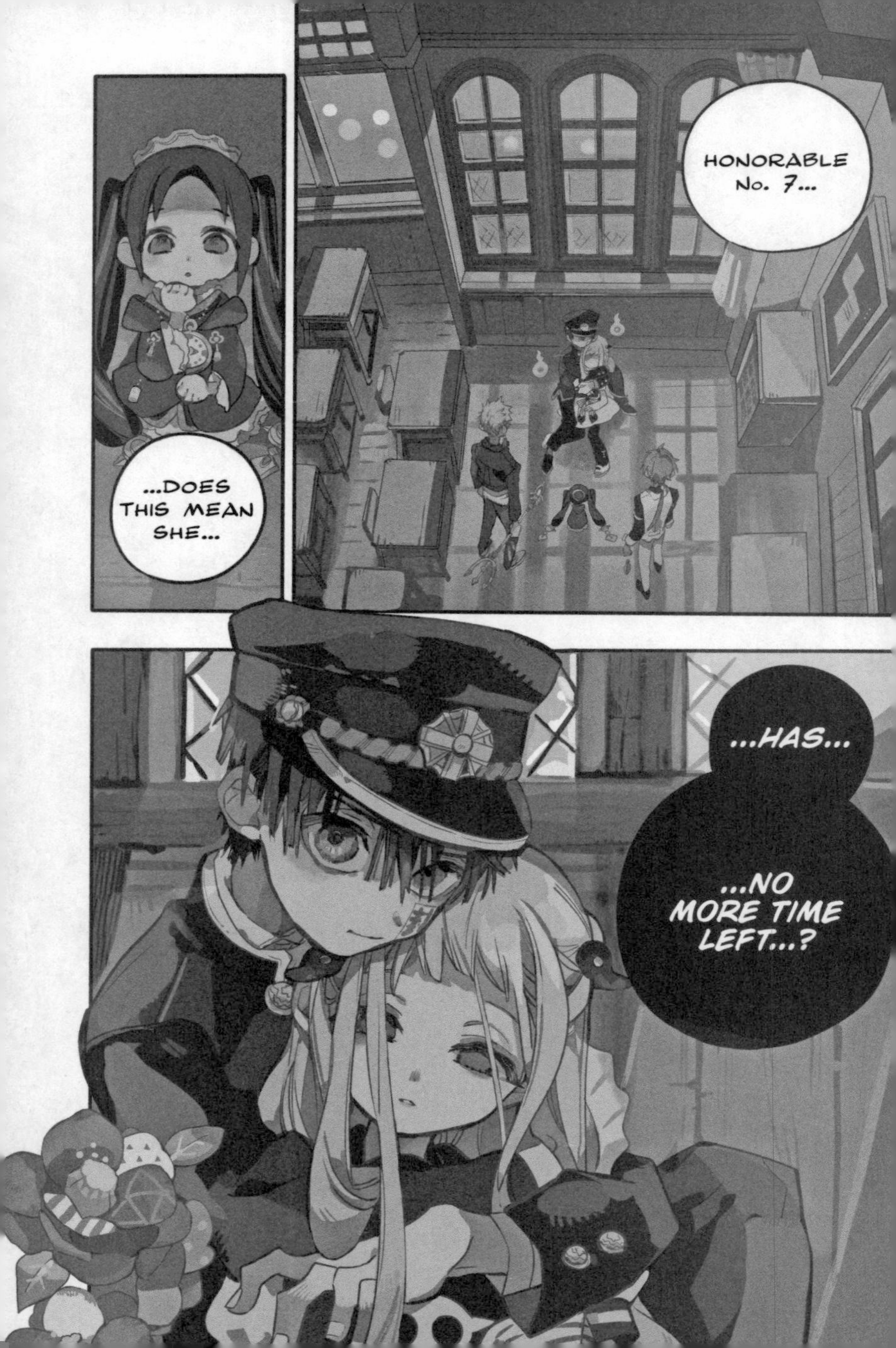
HONORABLE No. 7...
...DOES THIS MEAN SHE...
...HAS...
...NO MORE TIME LEFT...?

SPOOK 27
THE THREE CLOCK KEEPERS (PART 5)

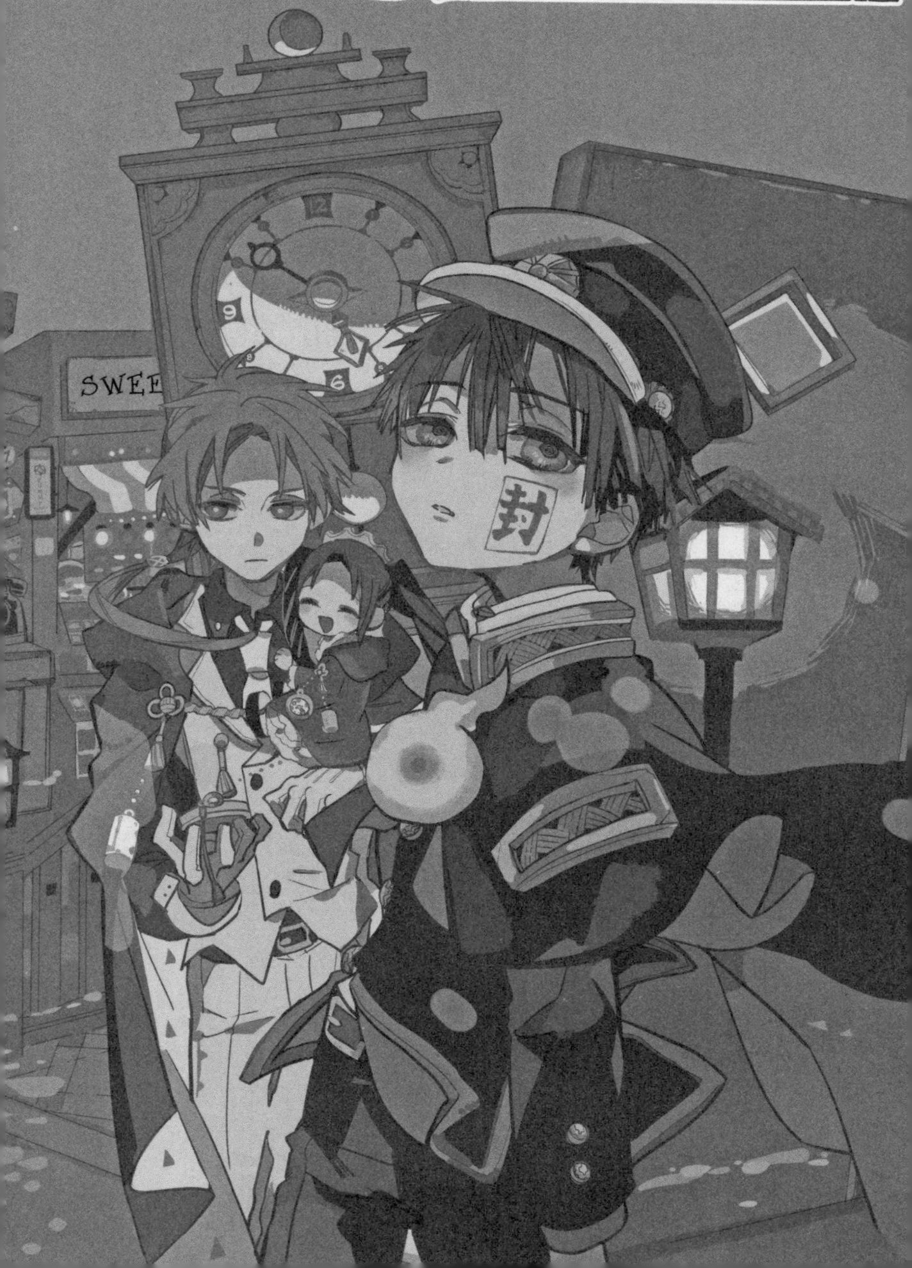
SWEE
封

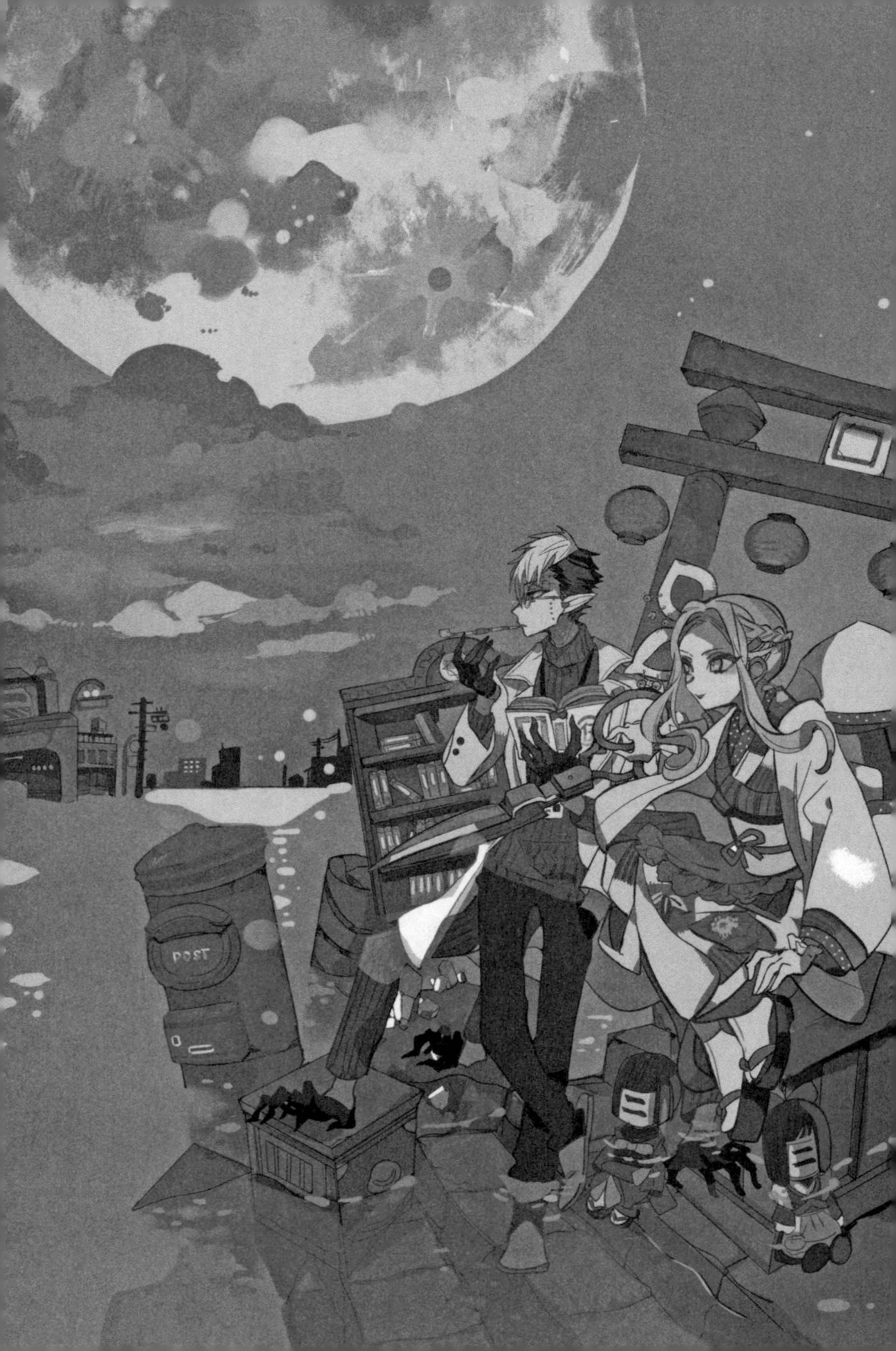
POST

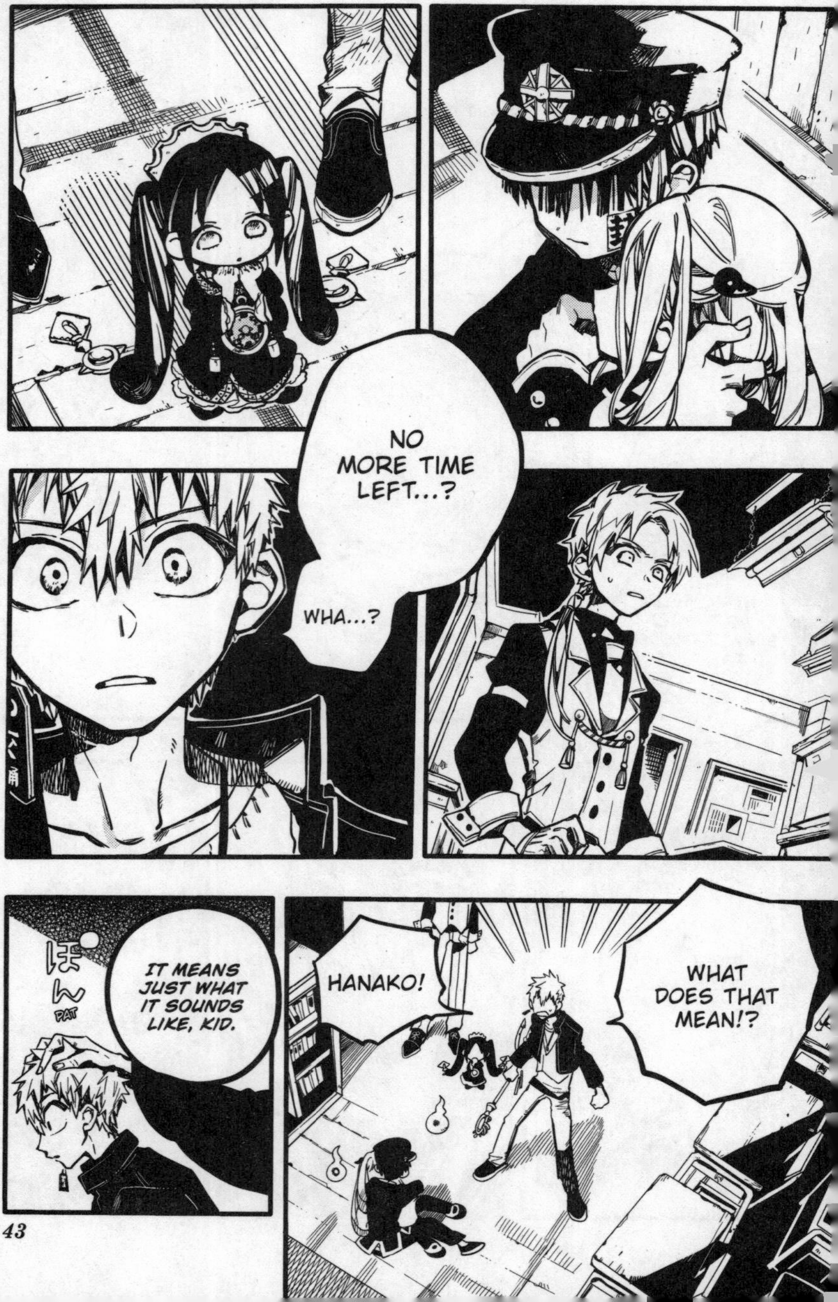
NO MORE TIME LEFT...?
WHA...?
WHAT DOES THAT MEAN!?
HANAKO!
ぽん
PAT
IT MEANS JUST WHAT IT SOUNDS LIKE, KID.

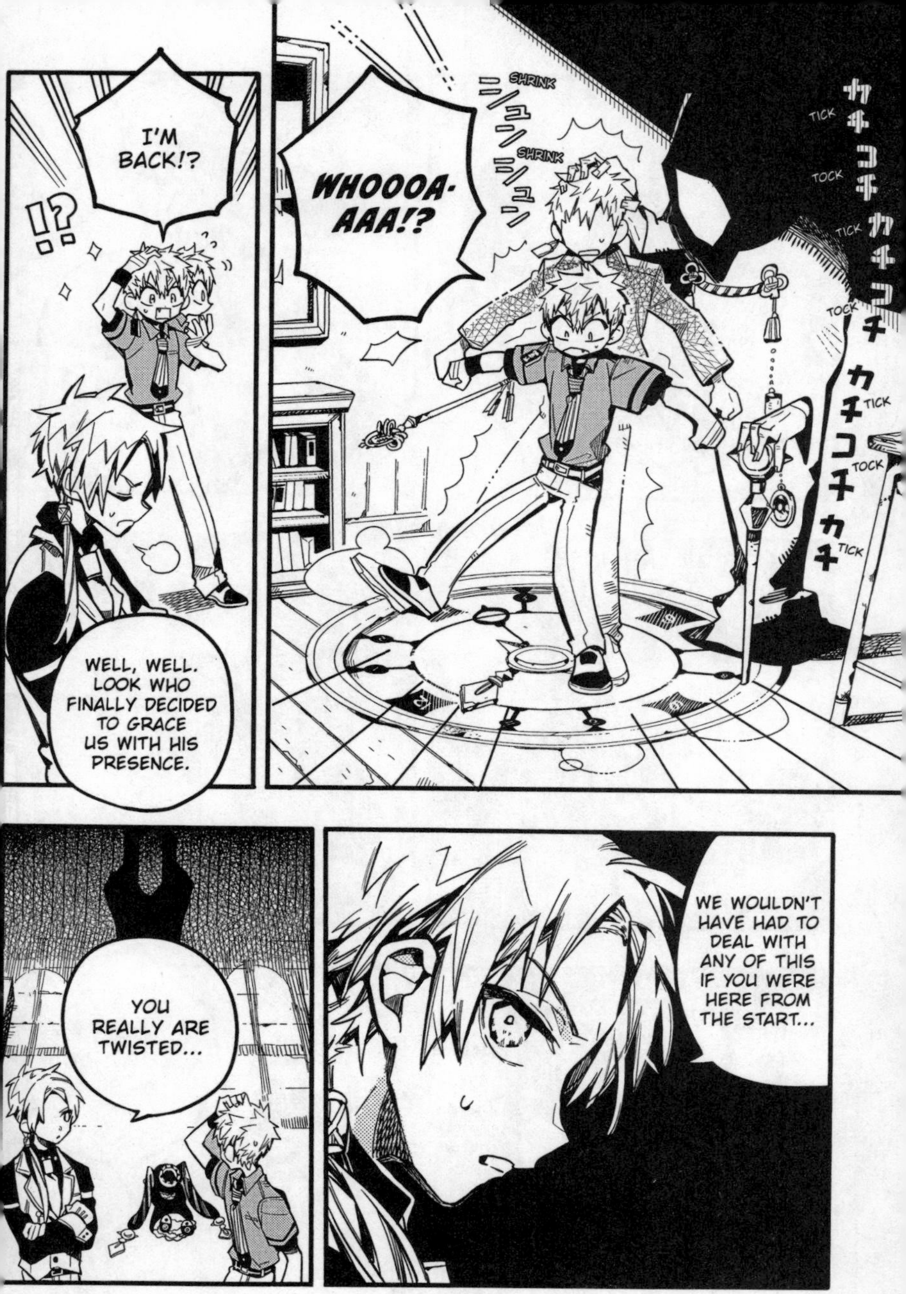
カチコチカチコチ
TICK
TOCK
TICK
TOCK
カチコチカチ
TICK
TOCK
TICK
シュン
SHRINK
シュン
SHRINK
WHOOOA-AAA!?
I'M BACK!?
!?
WELL, WELL. LOOK WHO FINALLY DECIDED TO GRACE US WITH HIS PRESENCE.
WE WOULDN'T HAVE HAD TO DEAL WITH ANY OF THIS IF YOU WERE HERE FROM THE START...
YOU REALLY ARE TWISTED...

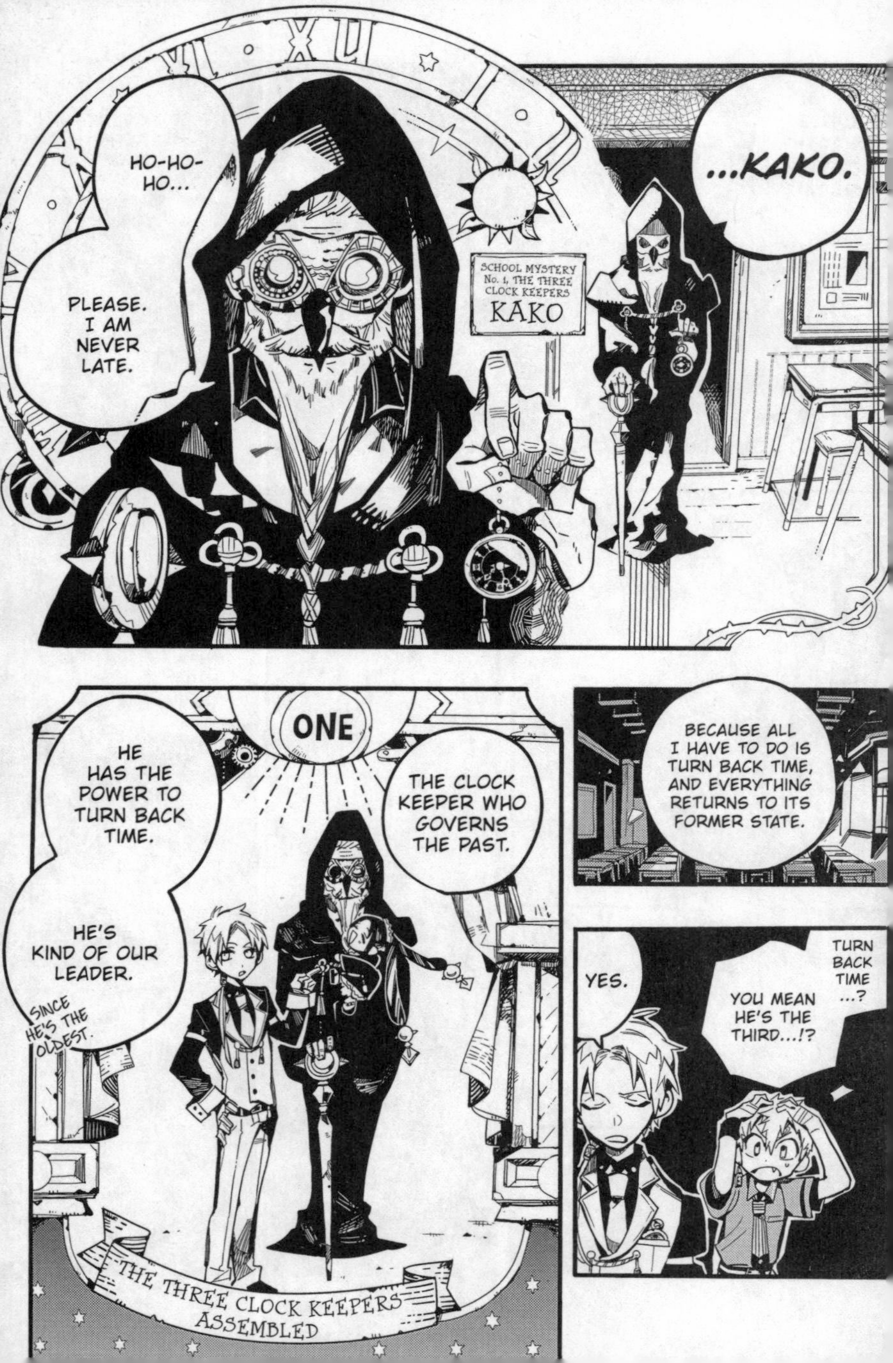
...KAKO.
SCHOOL MYSTERY No. 1, THE THREE CLOCK KEEPERS KAKO
HO-HO-HO...
PLEASE. I AM NEVER LATE.
BECAUSE ALL I HAVE TO DO IS TURN BACK TIME, AND EVERYTHING RETURNS TO ITS FORMER STATE.
TURN BACK TIME ...?
YOU MEAN HE'S THE THIRD...!?
YES.
ONE
THE CLOCK KEEPER WHO GOVERNS THE PAST.
HE HAS THE POWER TO TURN BACK TIME.
HE'S KIND OF OUR LEADER.
SINCE HE'S THE OLDEST.
THE THREE CLOCK KEEPERS ASSEMBLED

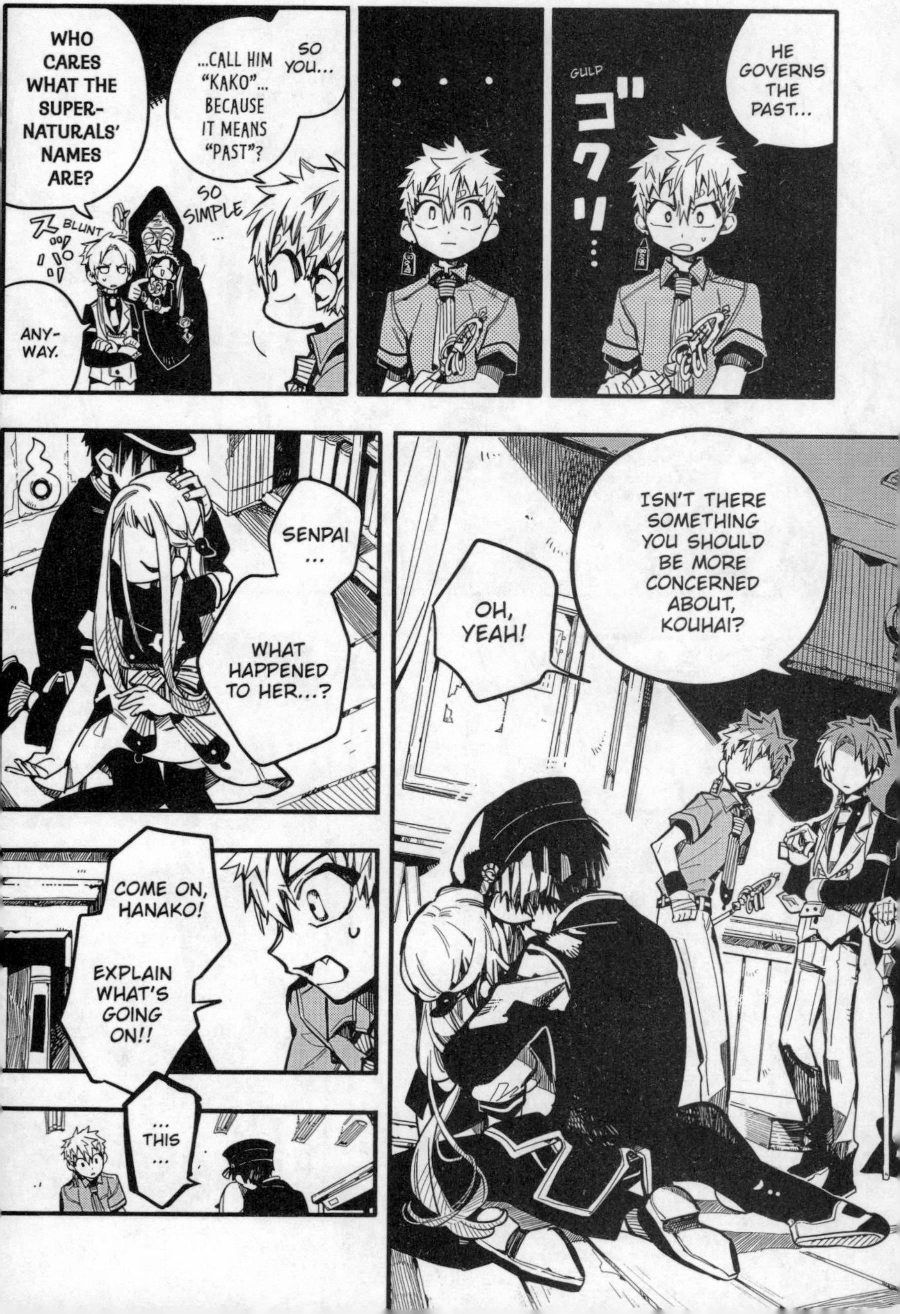
HE GOVERNS THE PAST...
GULP
ゴクリ...
...
SO YOU...
...CALL HIM "KAKO"... BECAUSE IT MEANS "PAST"?
SO SIMPLE...
WHO CARES WHAT THE SUPER-NATURALS' NAMES ARE?
BLUNT
ANY-WAY.
ISN'T THERE SOMETHING YOU SHOULD BE MORE CONCERNED ABOUT, KOUHAI?
OH, YEAH!
SENPAI...
WHAT HAPPENED TO HER...?
COME ON, HANAKO!
EXPLAIN WHAT'S GOING ON!!
... THIS ...

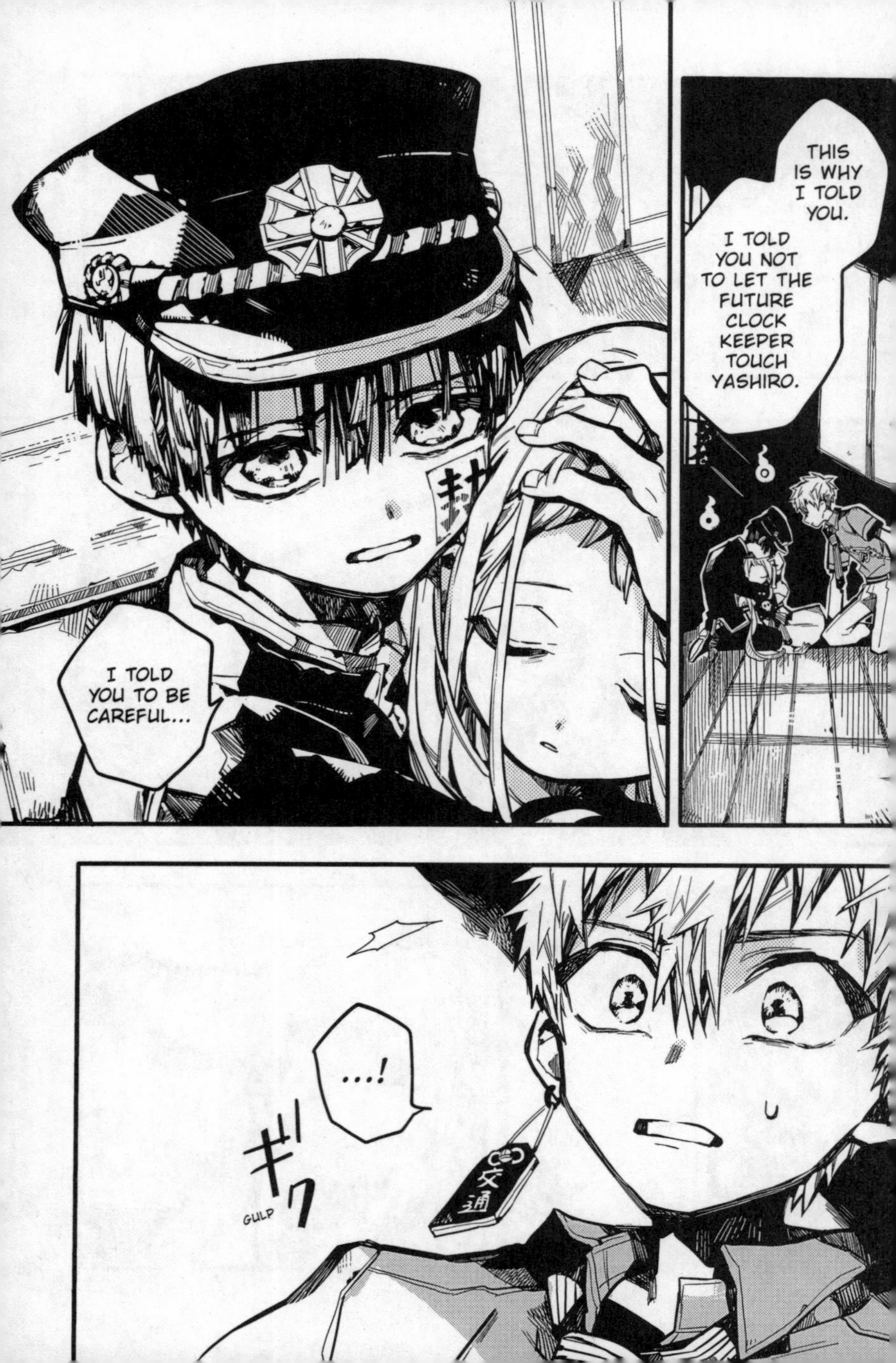
THIS IS WHY I TOLD YOU.
I TOLD YOU NOT TO LET THE FUTURE CLOCK KEEPER TOUCH YASHIRO.
I TOLD YOU TO BE CAREFUL...
...!
ギク
GULP

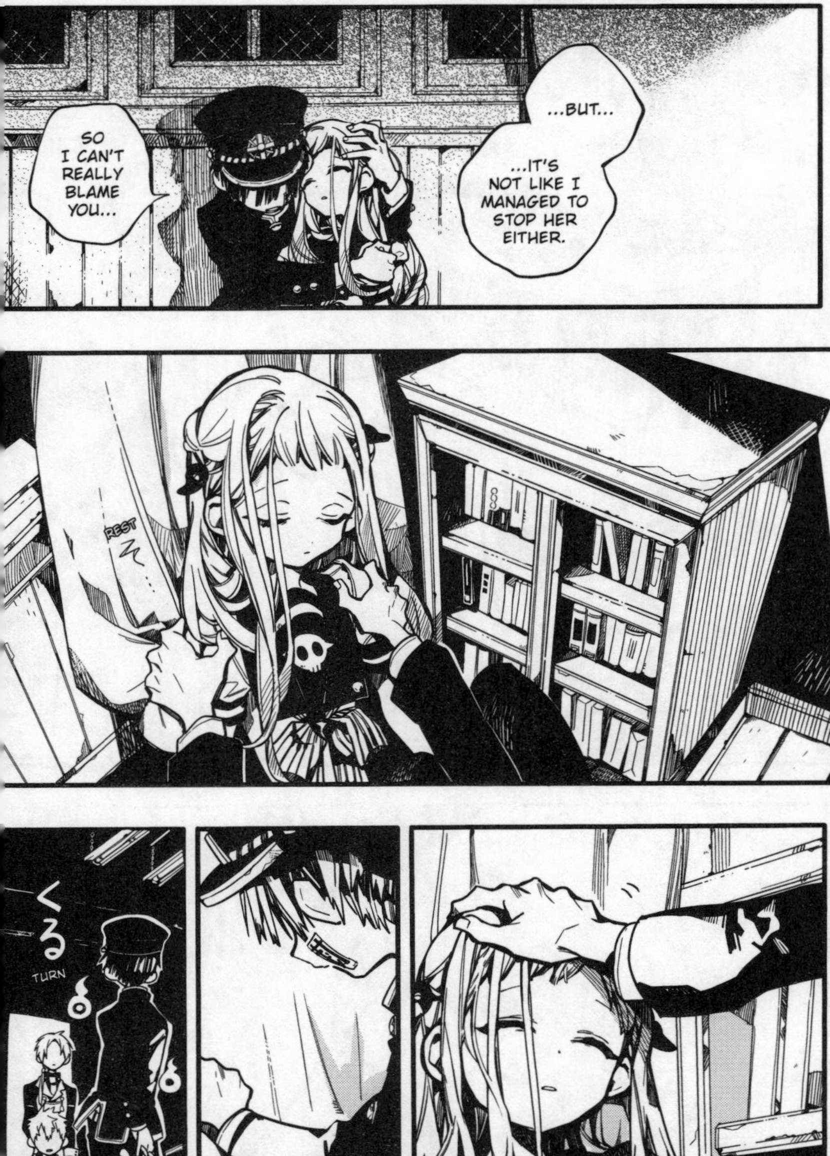
...BUT...
...IT'S NOT LIKE I MANAGED TO STOP HER EITHER.
SO I CAN'T REALLY BLAME YOU...
REST
くる
TURN

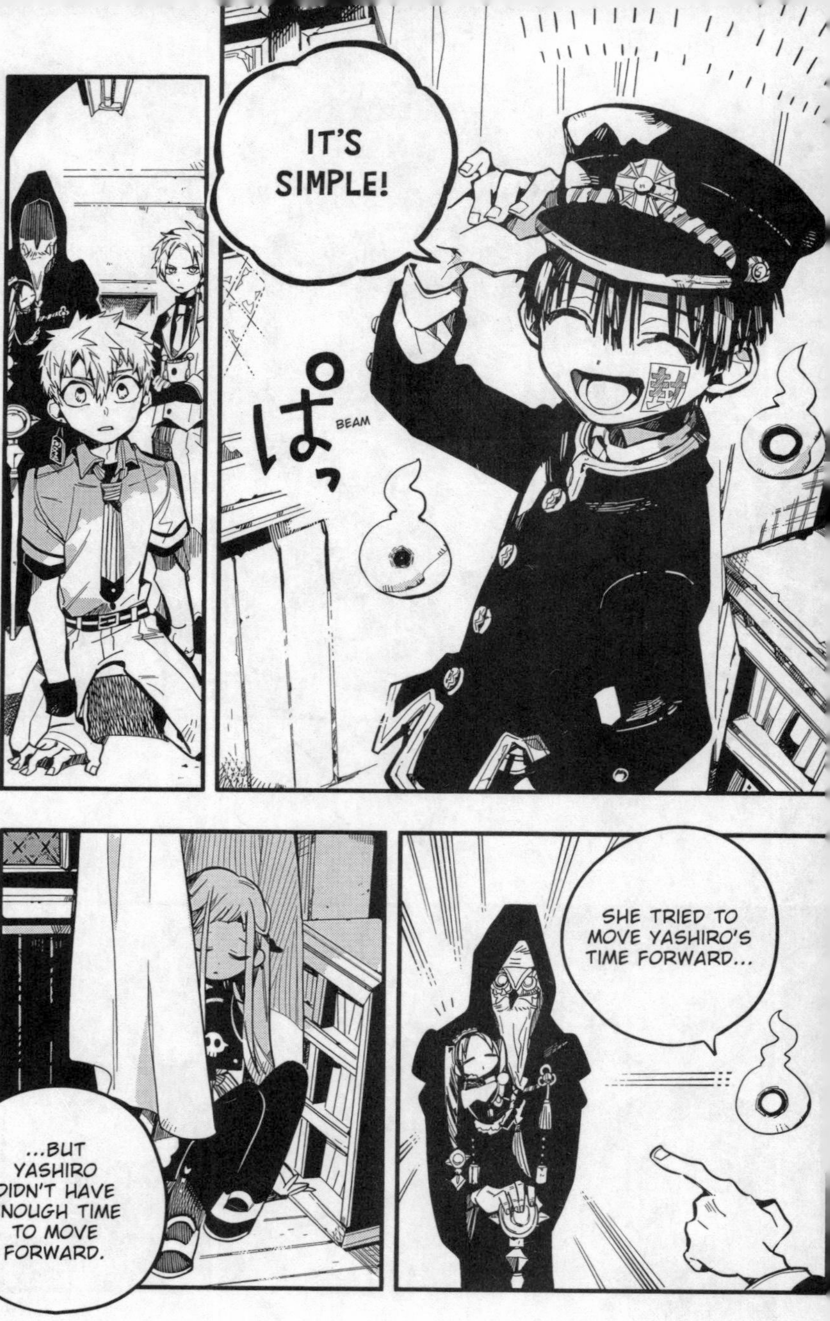
IT'S SIMPLE!
ぱっ
BEAM
SHE TRIED TO MOVE YASHIRO'S TIME FORWARD...
...BUT YASHIRO DIDN'T HAVE ENOUGH TIME TO MOVE FORWARD.

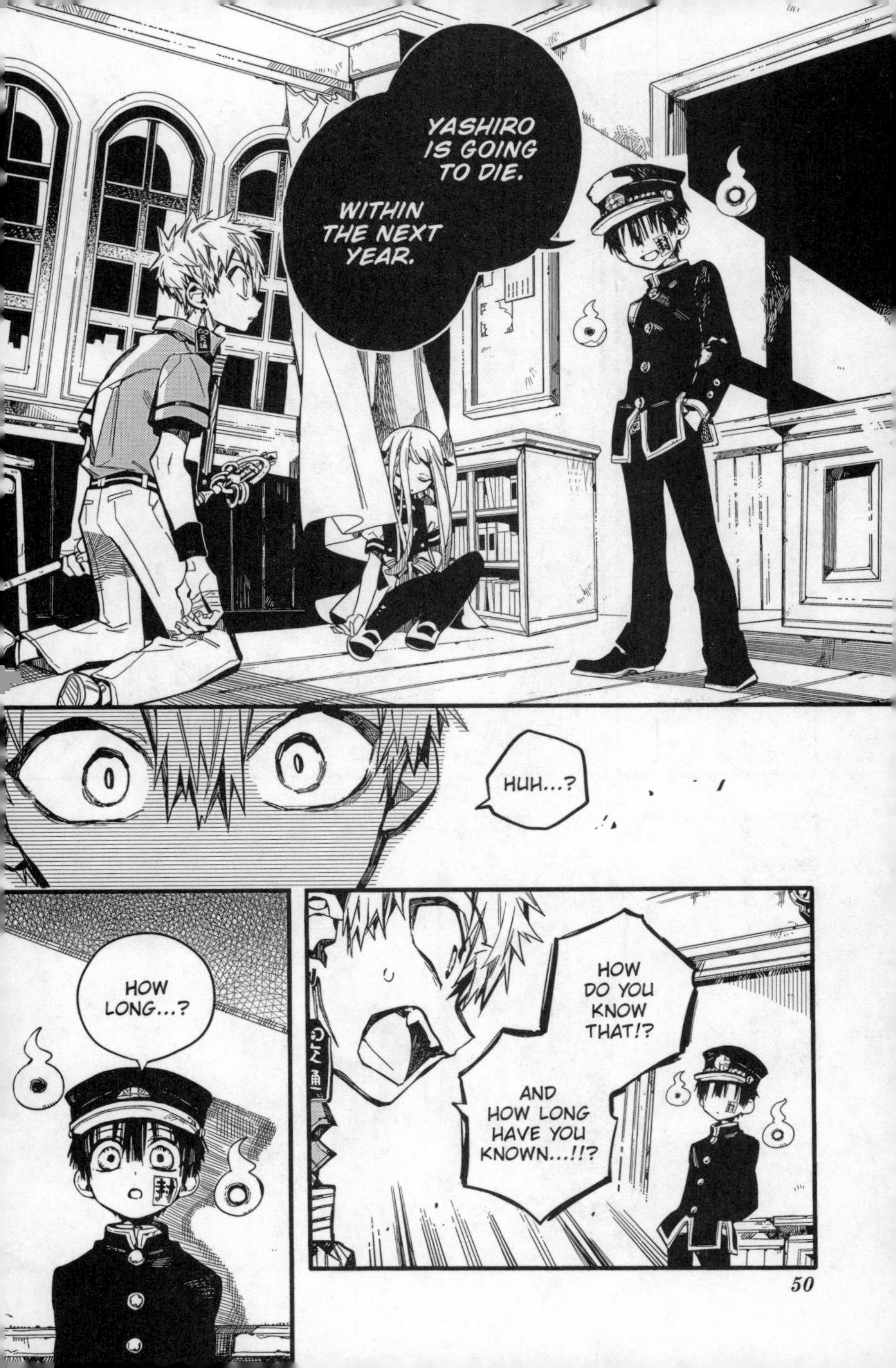
YASHIRO IS GOING TO DIE.
WITHIN THE NEXT YEAR.
HUH...?
HOW DO YOU KNOW THAT!?
AND HOW LONG HAVE YOU KNOWN...!!?
HOW LONG...?

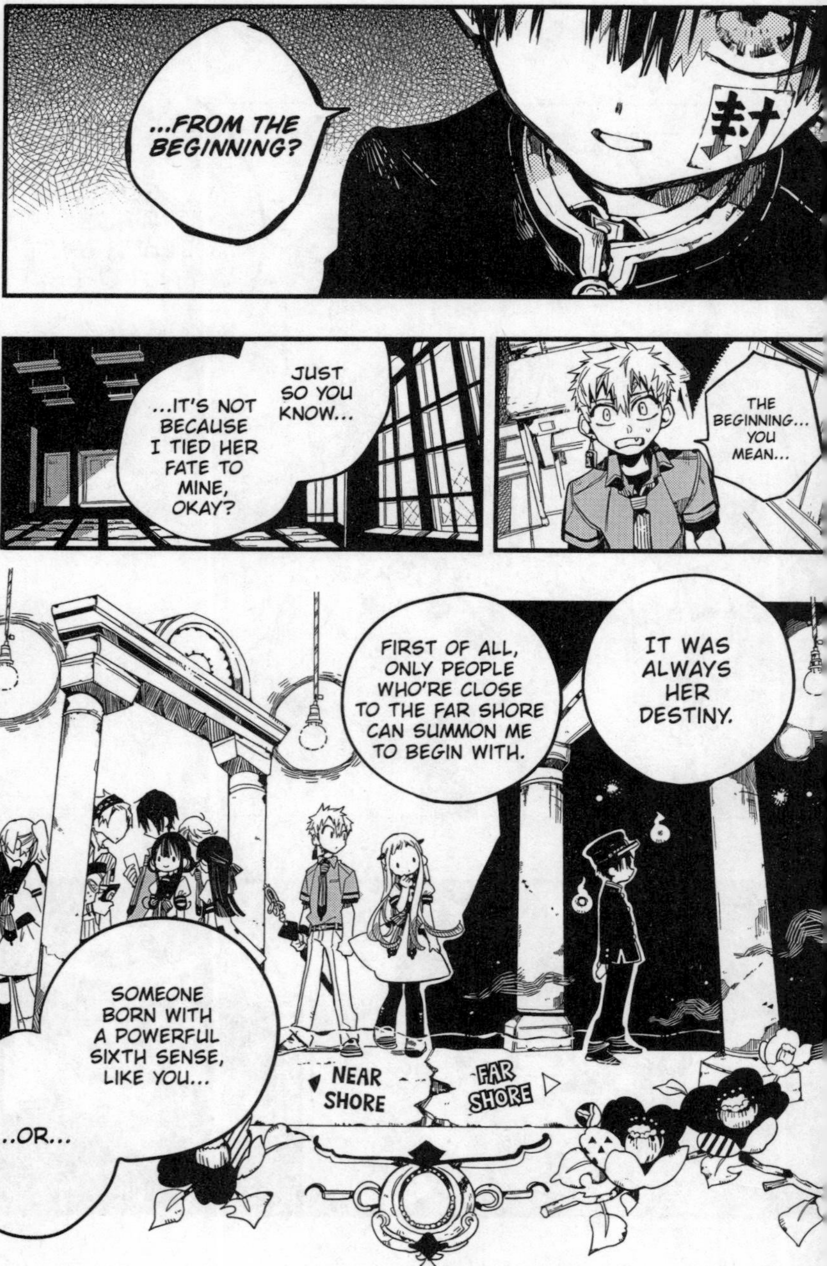
...FROM THE BEGINNING?
THE BEGINNING... YOU MEAN...
JUST SO YOU KNOW...
...IT'S NOT BECAUSE I TIED HER FATE TO MINE, OKAY?
IT WAS ALWAYS HER DESTINY.
FIRST OF ALL, ONLY PEOPLE WHO'RE CLOSE TO THE FAR SHORE CAN SUMMON ME TO BEGIN WITH.
FAR SHORE
NEAR SHORE
SOMEONE BORN WITH A POWERFUL SIXTH SENSE, LIKE YOU...
...OR...

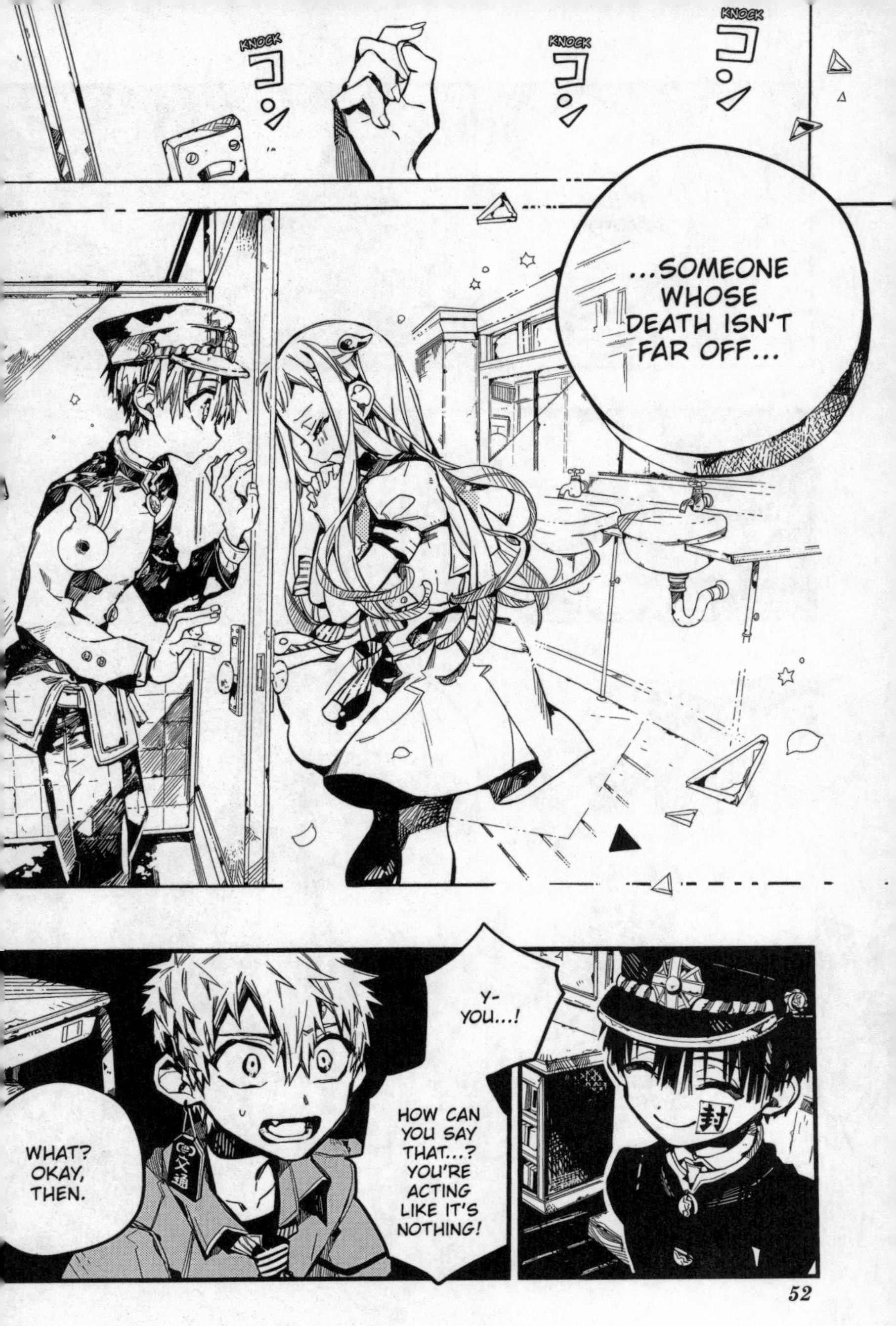
KNOCK
KNOCK
KNOCK
...SOMEONE WHOSE DEATH ISN'T FAR OFF...
Y- YOU...!
HOW CAN YOU SAY THAT...? YOU'RE ACTING LIKE IT'S NOTHING!
WHAT? OKAY, THEN.

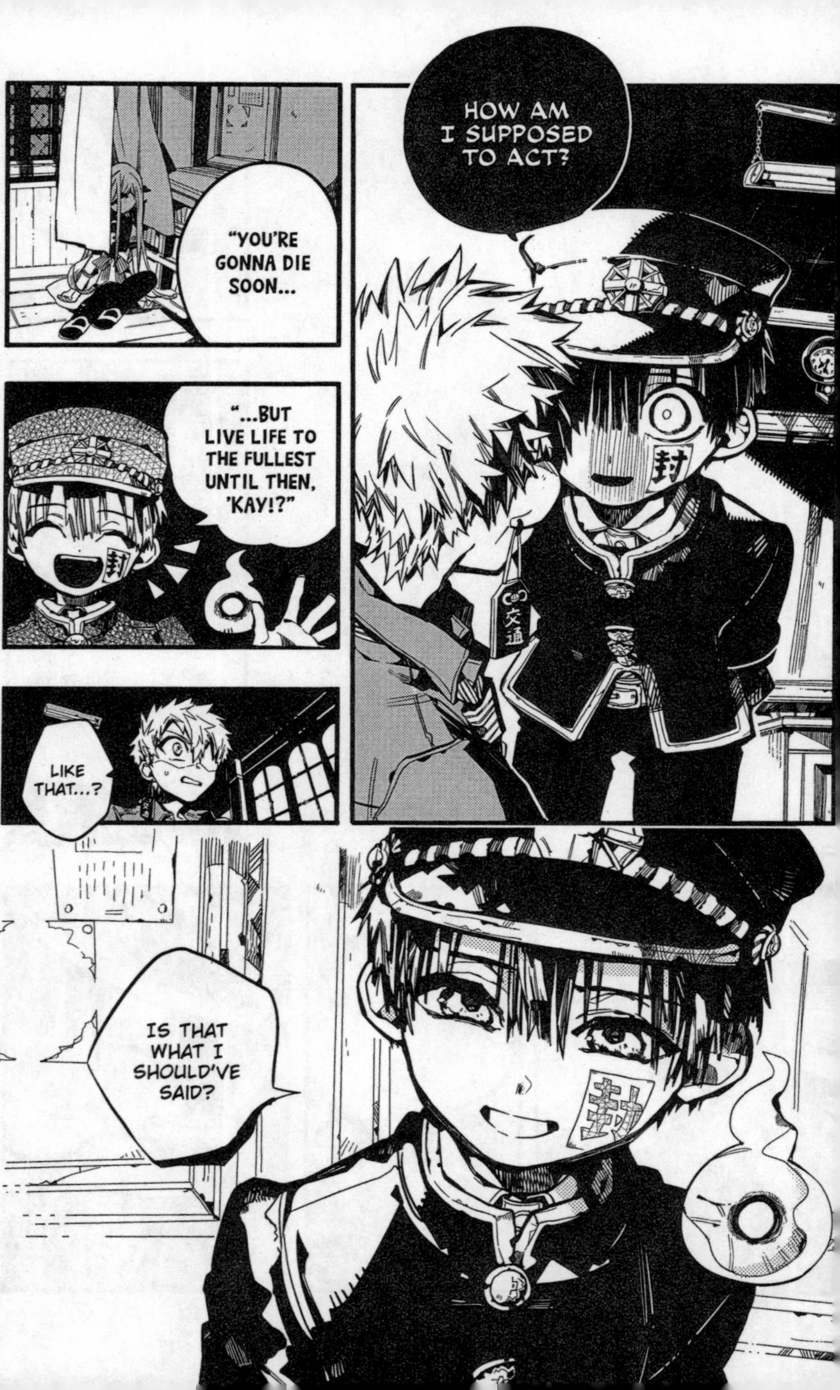
HOW AM I SUPPOSED TO ACT?
"YOU'RE GONNA DIE SOON...
"...BUT LIVE LIFE TO THE FULLEST UNTIL THEN, 'KAY!?"
LIKE THAT...?
IS THAT WHAT I SHOULD'VE SAID?

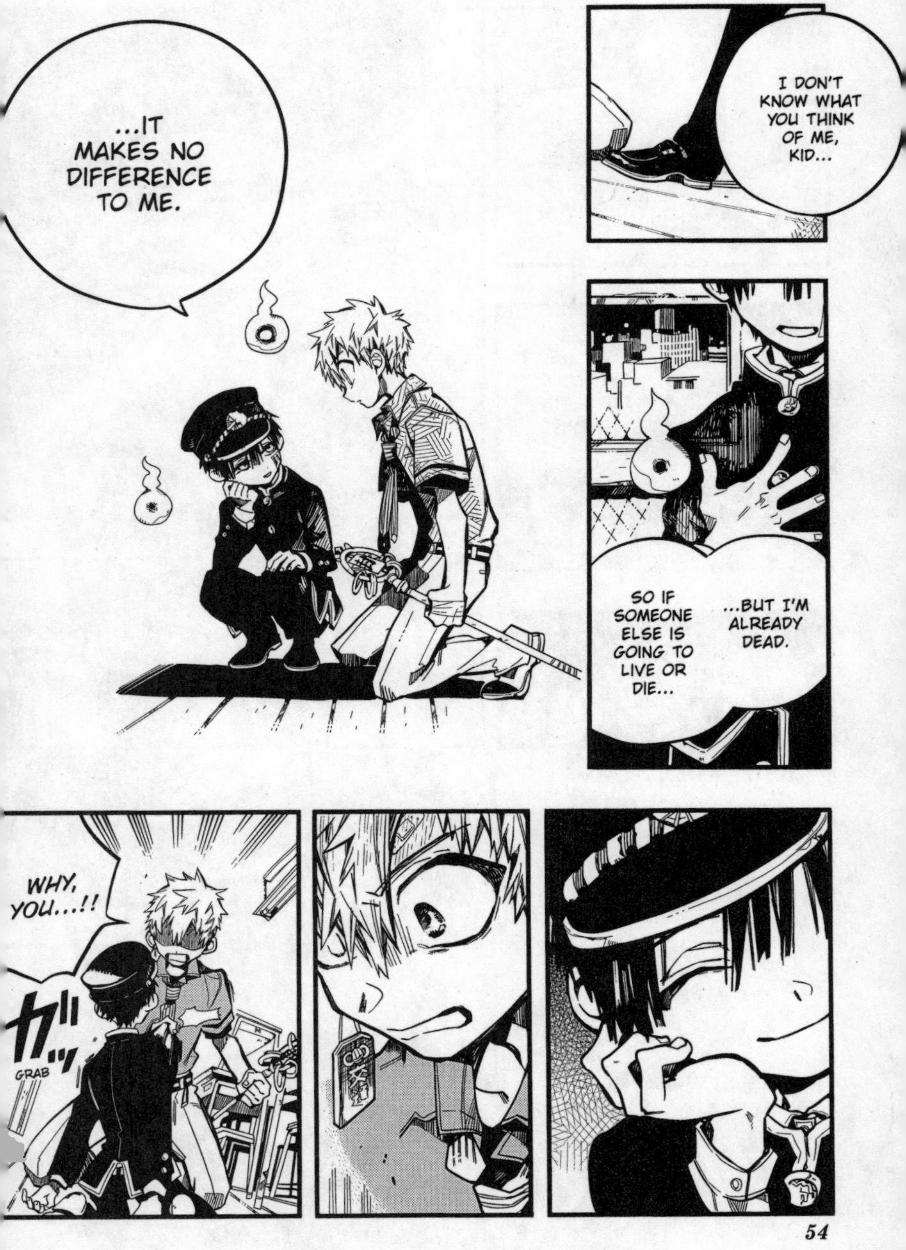

I DON'T KNOW WHAT YOU THINK OF ME, KID...
...BUT I'M ALREADY DEAD.
SO IF SOMEONE ELSE IS GOING TO LIVE OR DIE...
...IT MAKES NO DIFFERENCE TO ME.
WHY, YOU...!!
ガッ
GRAB

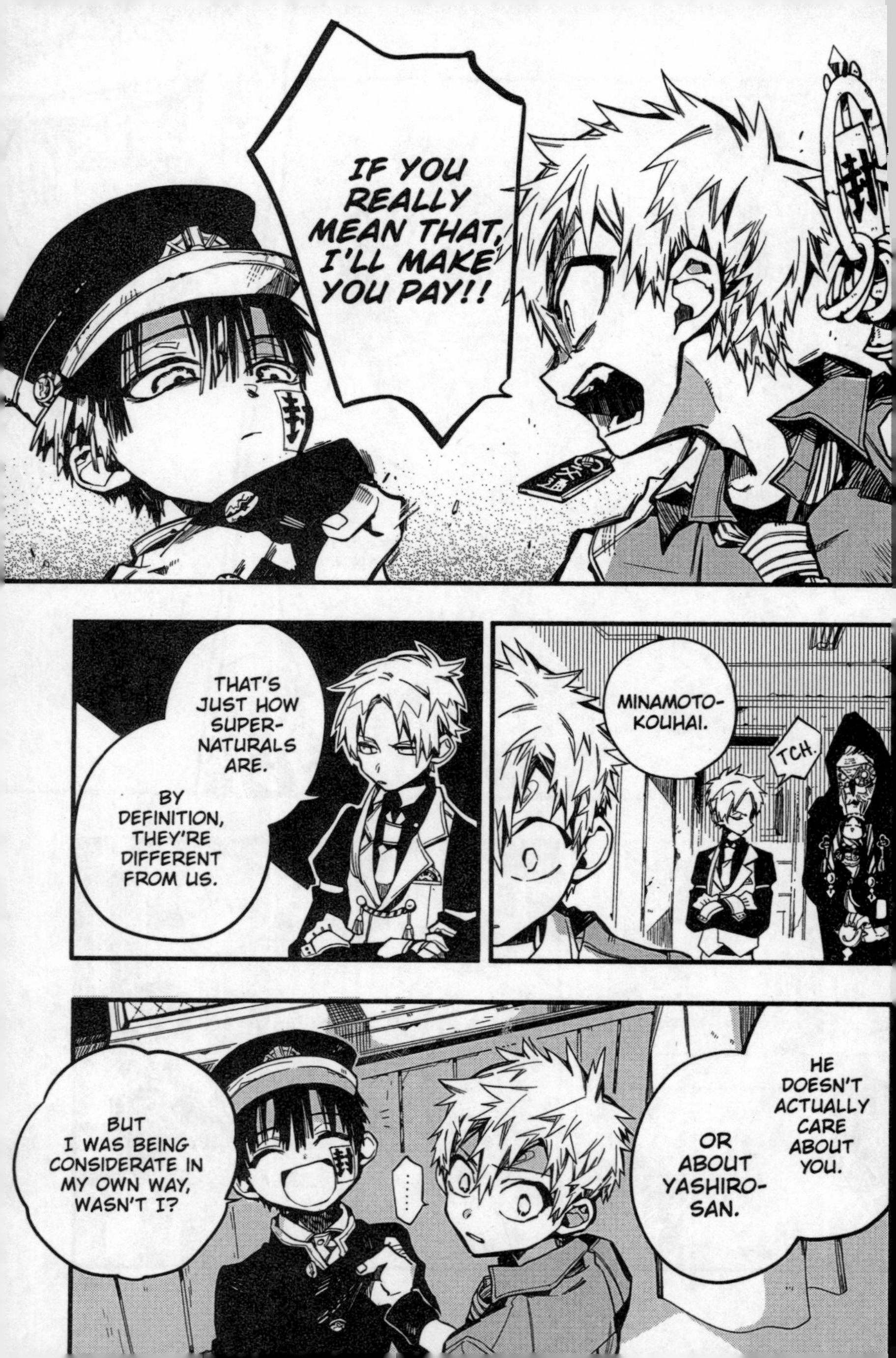
IF YOU REALLY MEAN THAT, I'LL MAKE YOU PAY!!
MINAMOTO-KOUHAI.
TCH.
THAT'S JUST HOW SUPER-NATURALS ARE.
BY DEFINITION, THEY'RE DIFFERENT FROM US.
HE DOESN'T ACTUALLY CARE ABOUT YOU.
OR ABOUT YASHIRO-SAN.
......
BUT I WAS BEING CONSIDERATE IN MY OWN WAY, WASN'T I?

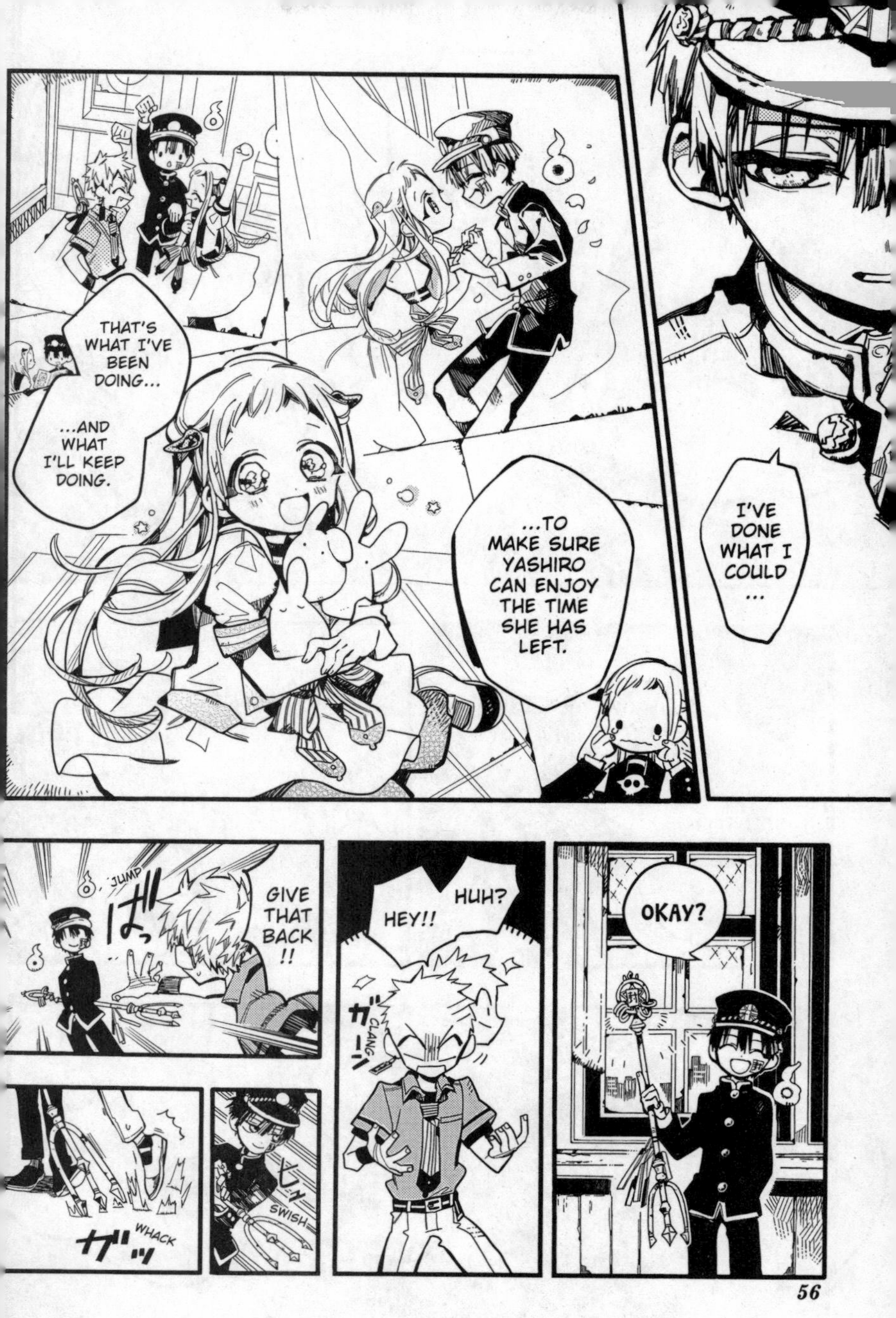
I'VE DONE WHAT I COULD ...
...TO MAKE SURE YASHIRO CAN ENJOY THE TIME SHE HAS LEFT.
THAT'S WHAT I'VE BEEN DOING...
...AND WHAT I'LL KEEP DOING.
OKAY?
HUH?
HEY!!
ガーン
CLANG
ばっ
JUMP
GIVE THAT BACK!!
ヒュ
SWISH
ガッ
WHACK

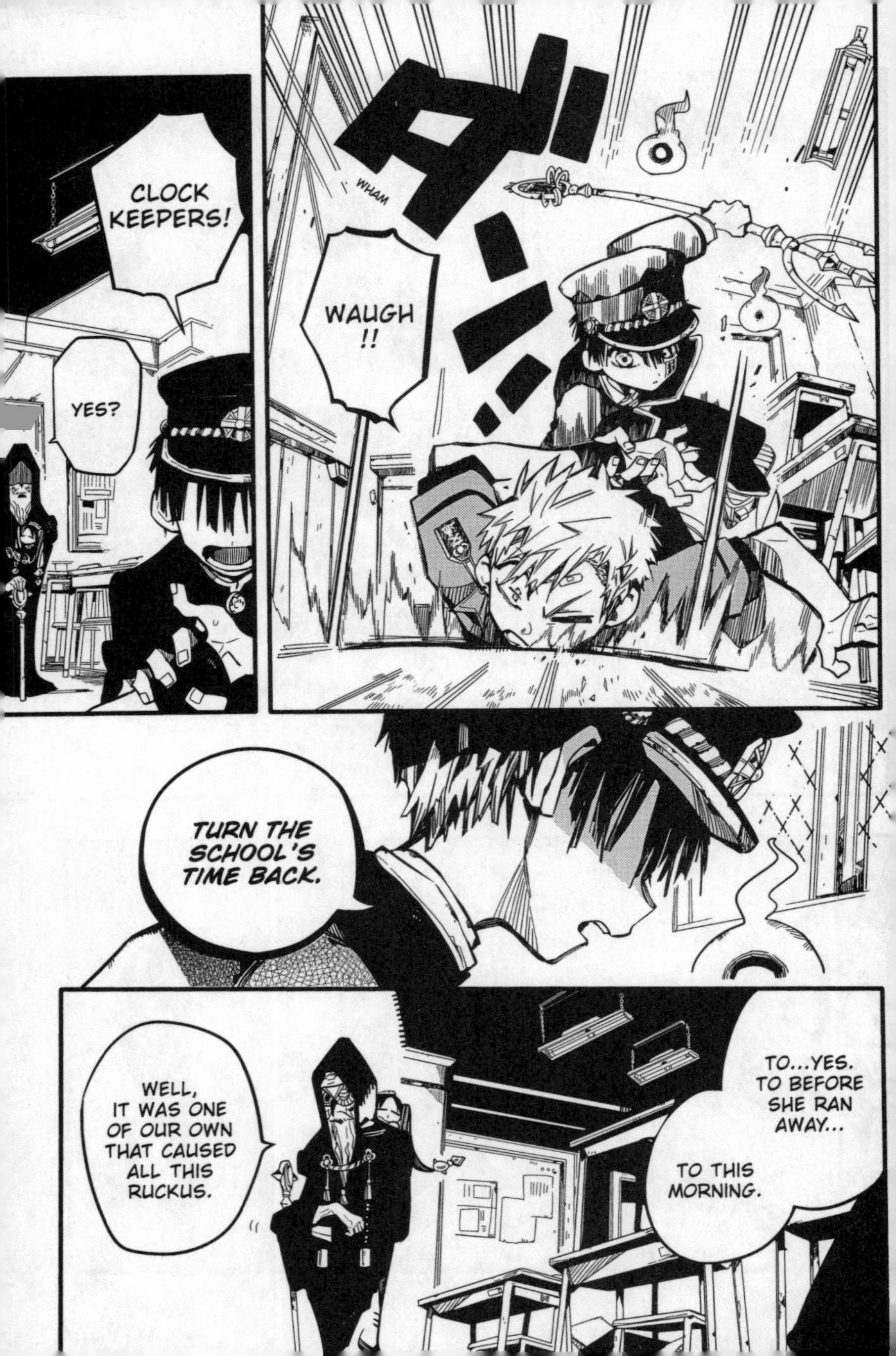
WHAM
WAUGH !!
CLOCK KEEPERS!
YES?
TURN THE SCHOOL'S TIME BACK.
TO...YES. TO BEFORE SHE RAN AWAY...
TO THIS MORNING.
WELL, IT WAS ONE OF OUR OWN THAT CAUSED ALL THIS RUCKUS.

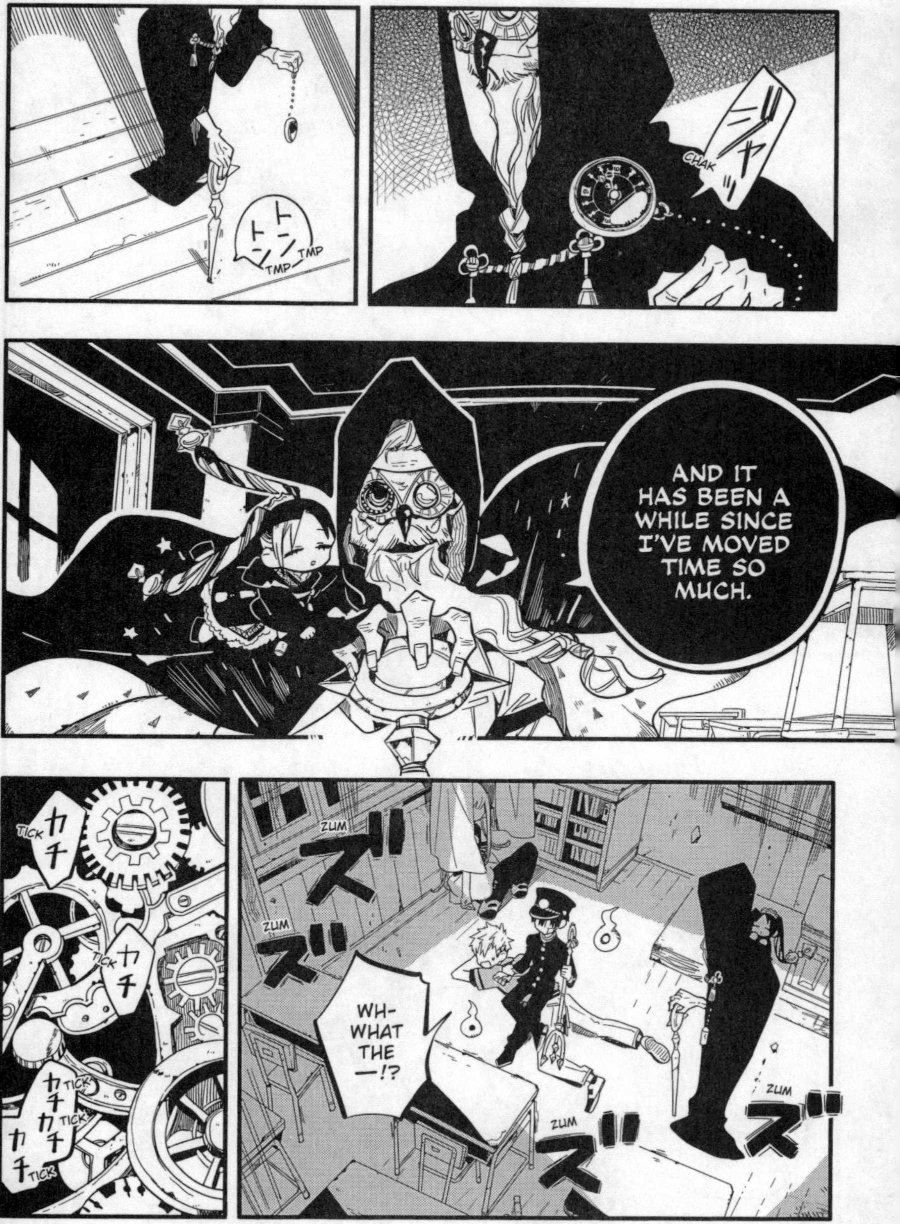
CHAK
トン トン
TMP TMP
AND IT HAS BEEN A WHILE SINCE I'VE MOVED TIME SO MUCH.
ZUM
ZUM
WH- WHAT THE—!?
ZUM
ZUM
カチ
TICK
カチ
TICK
カチ カチ カチ
TICK TICK TICK

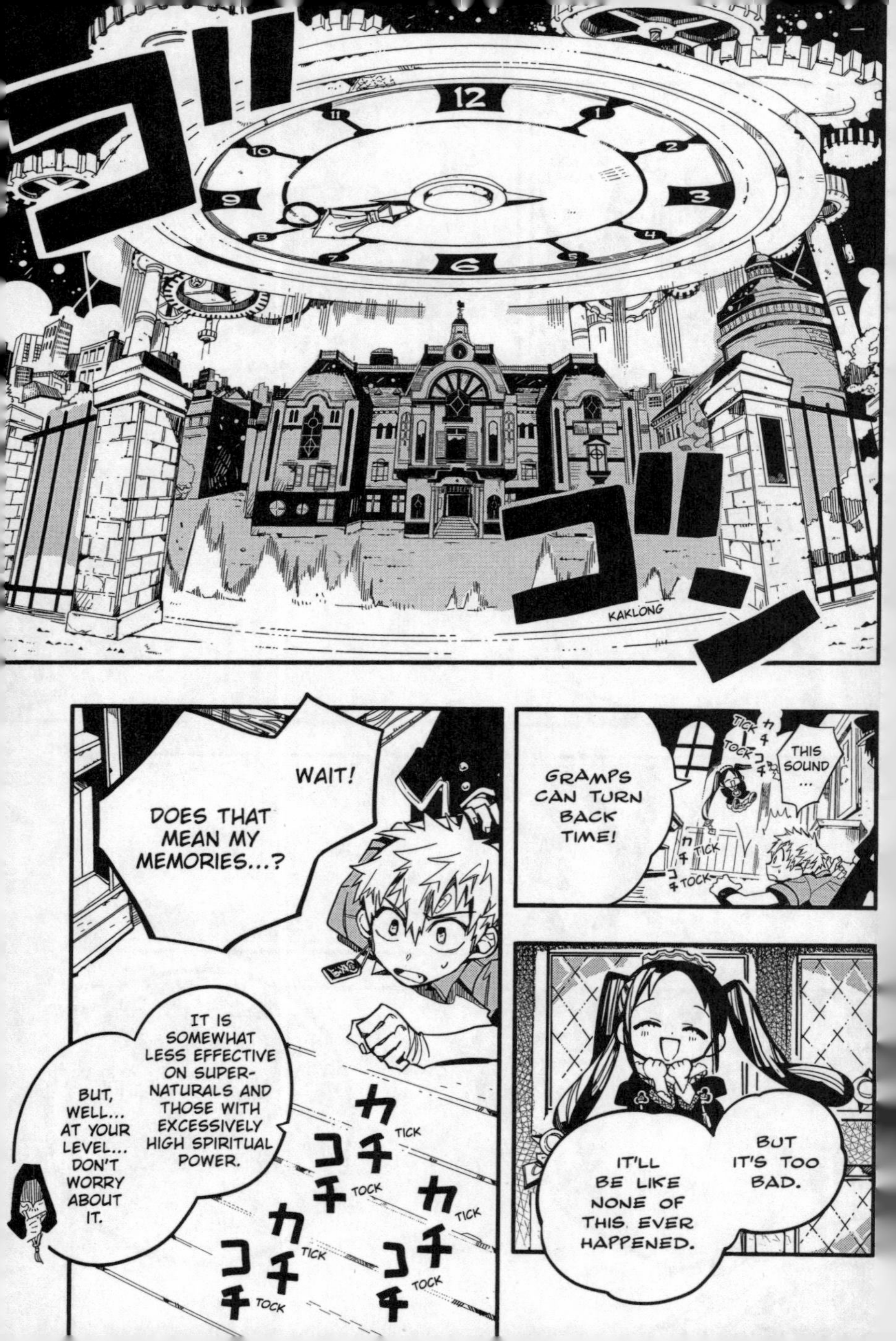
KAKLONG
THIS SOUND ...
カチ TICK
コチ TOCK
GRAMPS CAN TURN BACK TIME!
カチ TICK
コチ TOCK
BUT IT'S TOO BAD.
IT'LL BE LIKE NONE OF THIS EVER HAPPENED.
WAIT!
DOES THAT MEAN MY MEMORIES...?
IT IS SOMEWHAT LESS EFFECTIVE ON SUPER-NATURALS AND THOSE WITH EXCESSIVELY HIGH SPIRITUAL POWER.
BUT, WELL... AT YOUR LEVEL... DON'T WORRY ABOUT IT.
カチ TICK
コチ TOCK
カチ TICK
コチ TOCK
カチ TICK
コチ TOCK

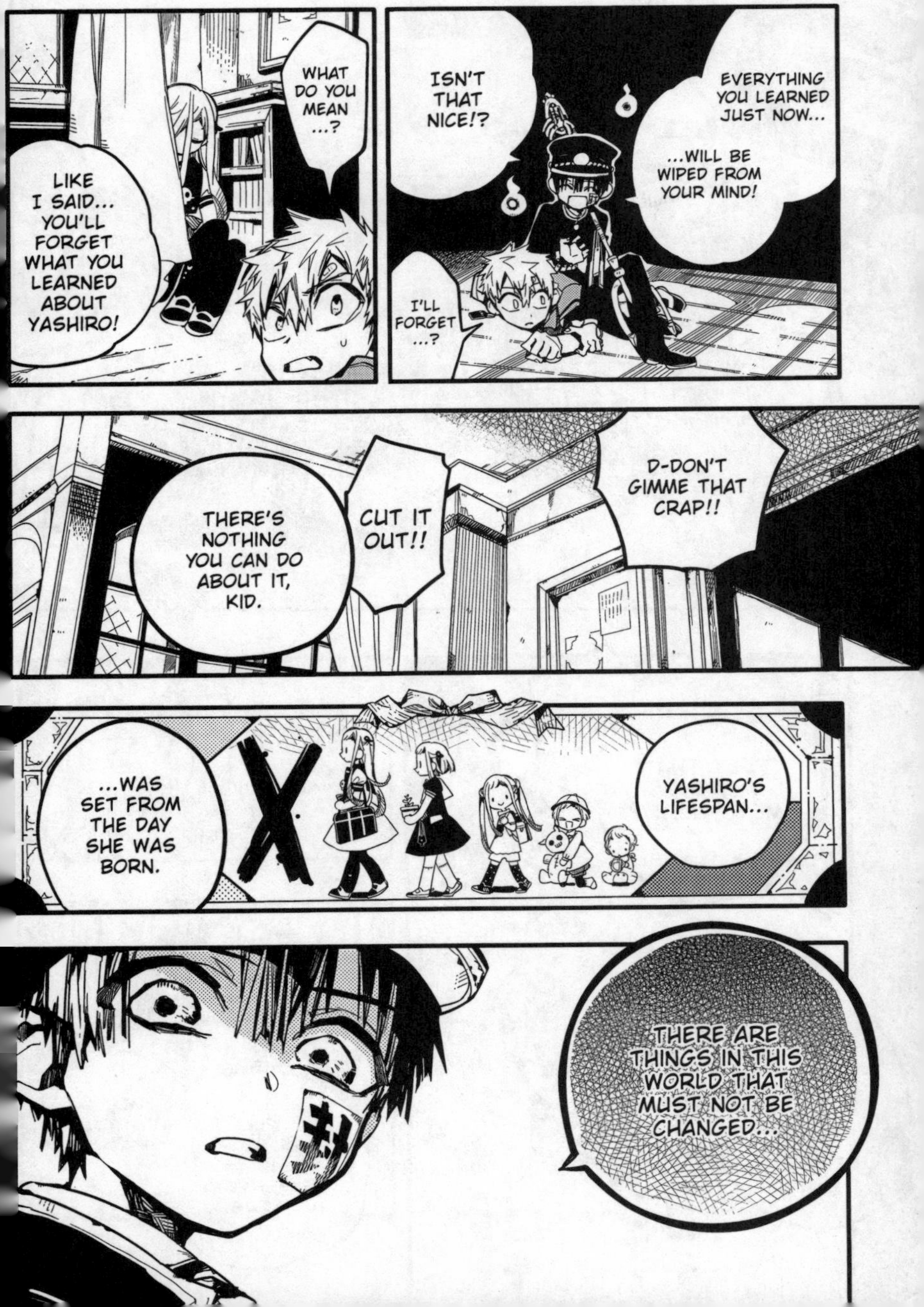
EVERYTHING YOU LEARNED JUST NOW...
...WILL BE WIPED FROM YOUR MIND!
ISN'T THAT NICE!?
I'LL FORGET ...?
WHAT DO YOU MEAN ...?
LIKE I SAID... YOU'LL FORGET WHAT YOU LEARNED ABOUT YASHIRO!
D-DON'T GIMME THAT CRAP!!
CUT IT OUT!!
THERE'S NOTHING YOU CAN DO ABOUT IT, KID.
YASHIRO'S LIFESPAN...
...WAS SET FROM THE DAY SHE WAS BORN.
THERE ARE THINGS IN THIS WORLD THAT MUST NOT BE CHANGED...

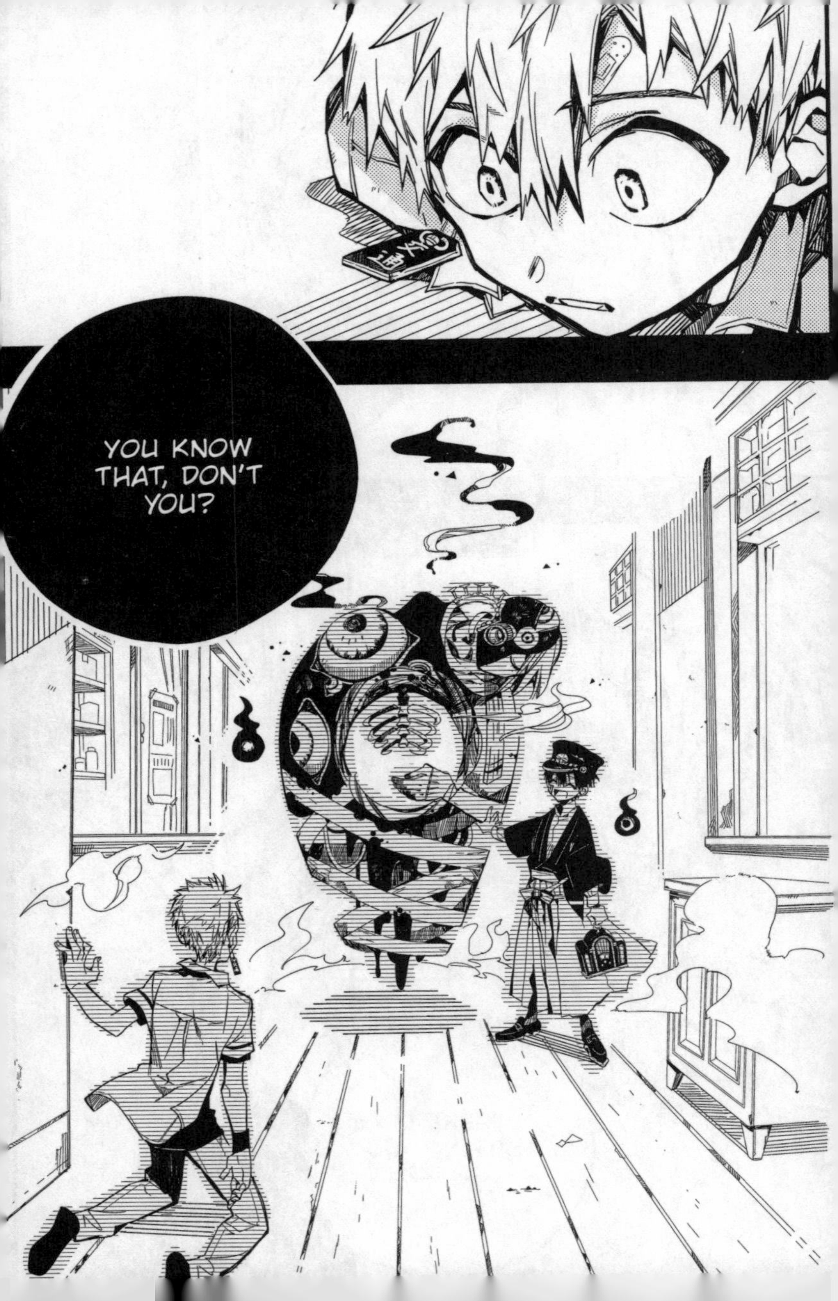
YOU KNOW THAT, DON'T YOU?

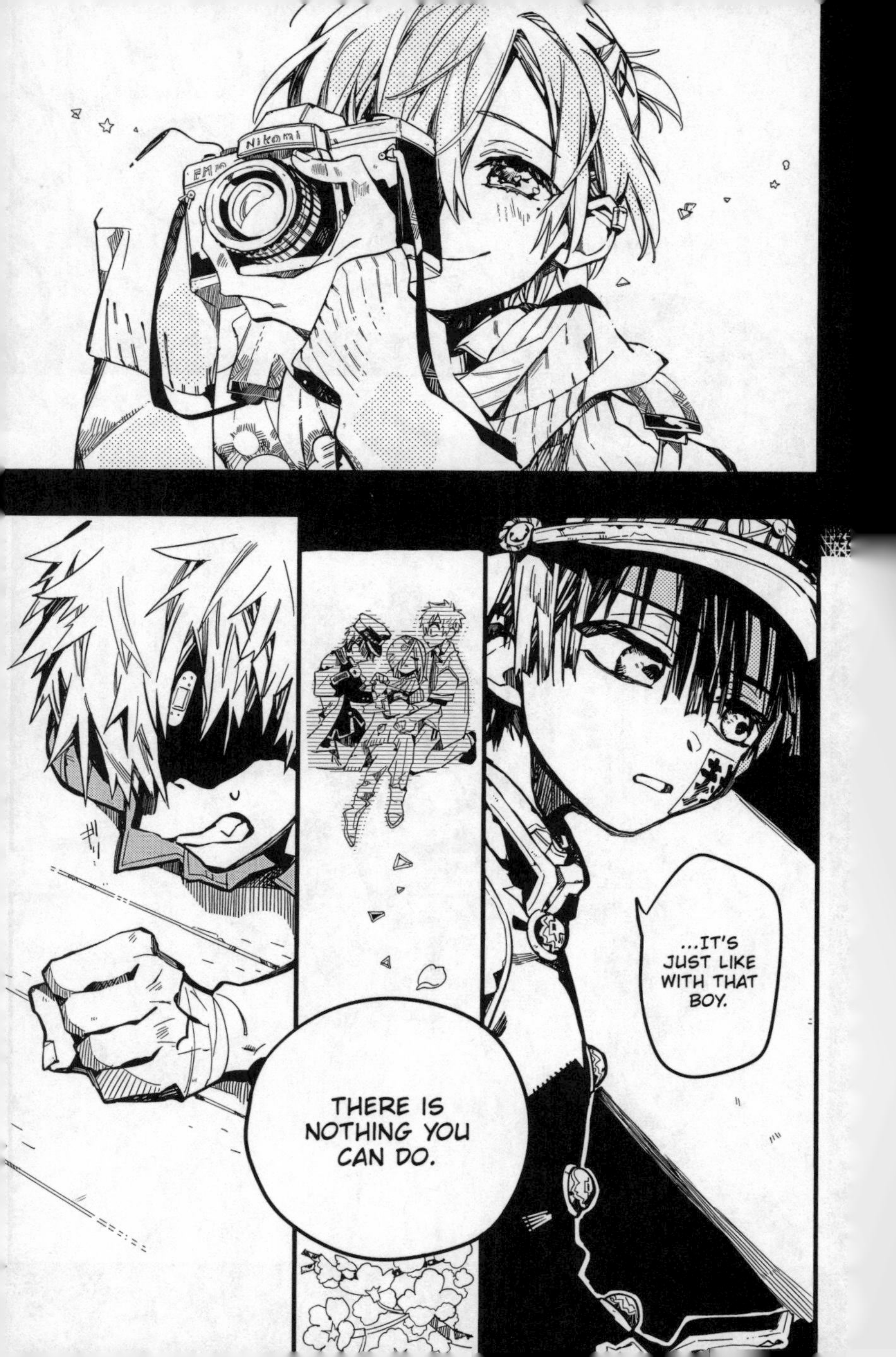

...IT'S JUST LIKE WITH THAT BOY.
THERE IS NOTHING YOU CAN DO.

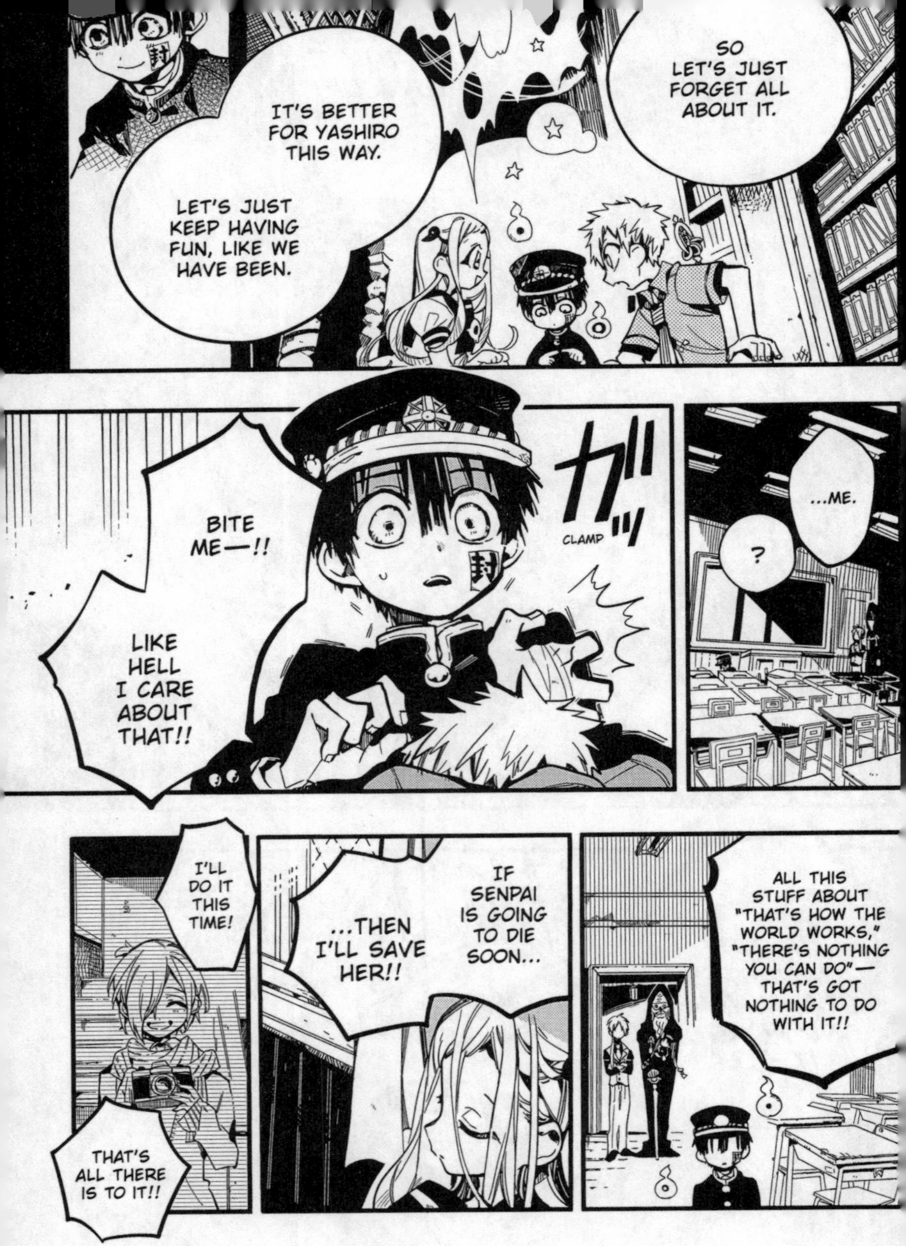
SO LET'S JUST FORGET ALL ABOUT IT.
IT'S BETTER FOR YASHIRO THIS WAY.
LET'S JUST KEEP HAVING FUN, LIKE WE HAVE BEEN.
...ME.
?
ガッ
CLAMP
BITE ME—!!
LIKE HELL I CARE ABOUT THAT!!
ALL THIS STUFF ABOUT "THAT'S HOW THE WORLD WORKS," "THERE'S NOTHING YOU CAN DO"—THAT'S GOT NOTHING TO DO WITH IT!!
IF SENPAI IS GOING TO DIE SOON...
...THEN I'LL SAVE HER!!
I'LL DO IT THIS TIME!
THAT'S ALL THERE IS TO IT!!

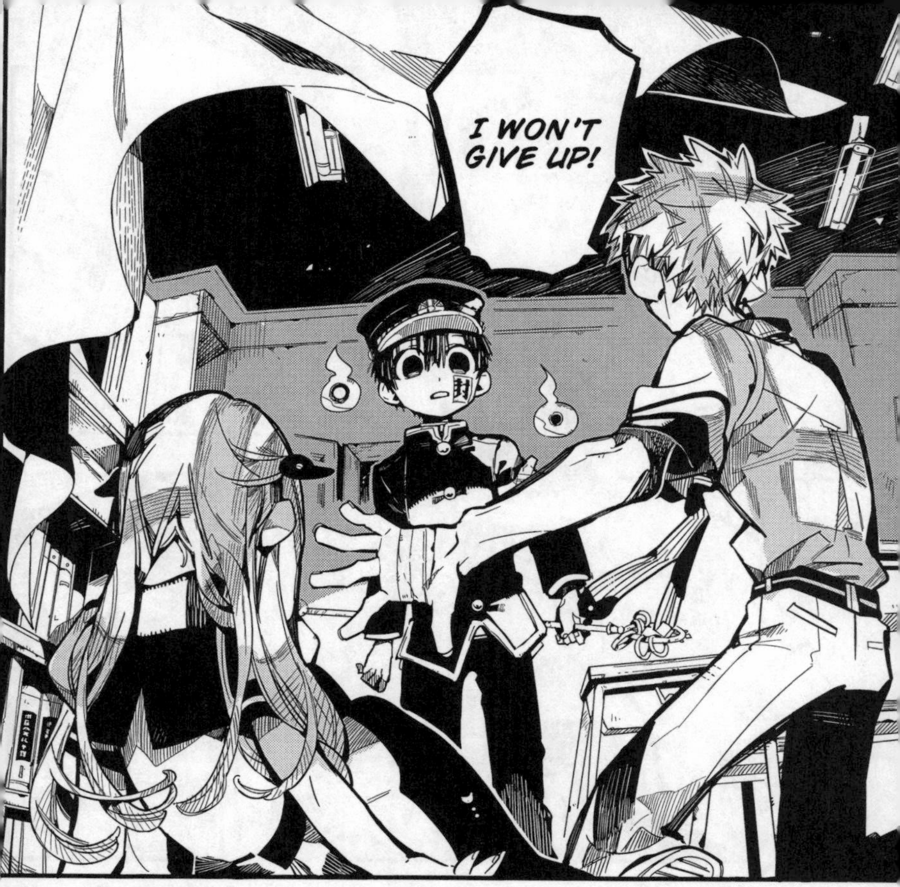
I WON'T GIVE UP!
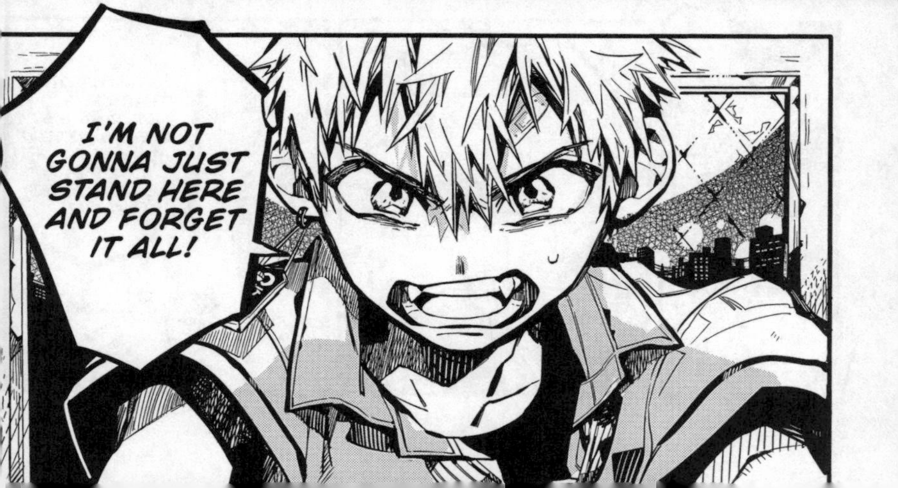
I'M NOT GONNA JUST STAND HERE AND FORGET IT ALL!

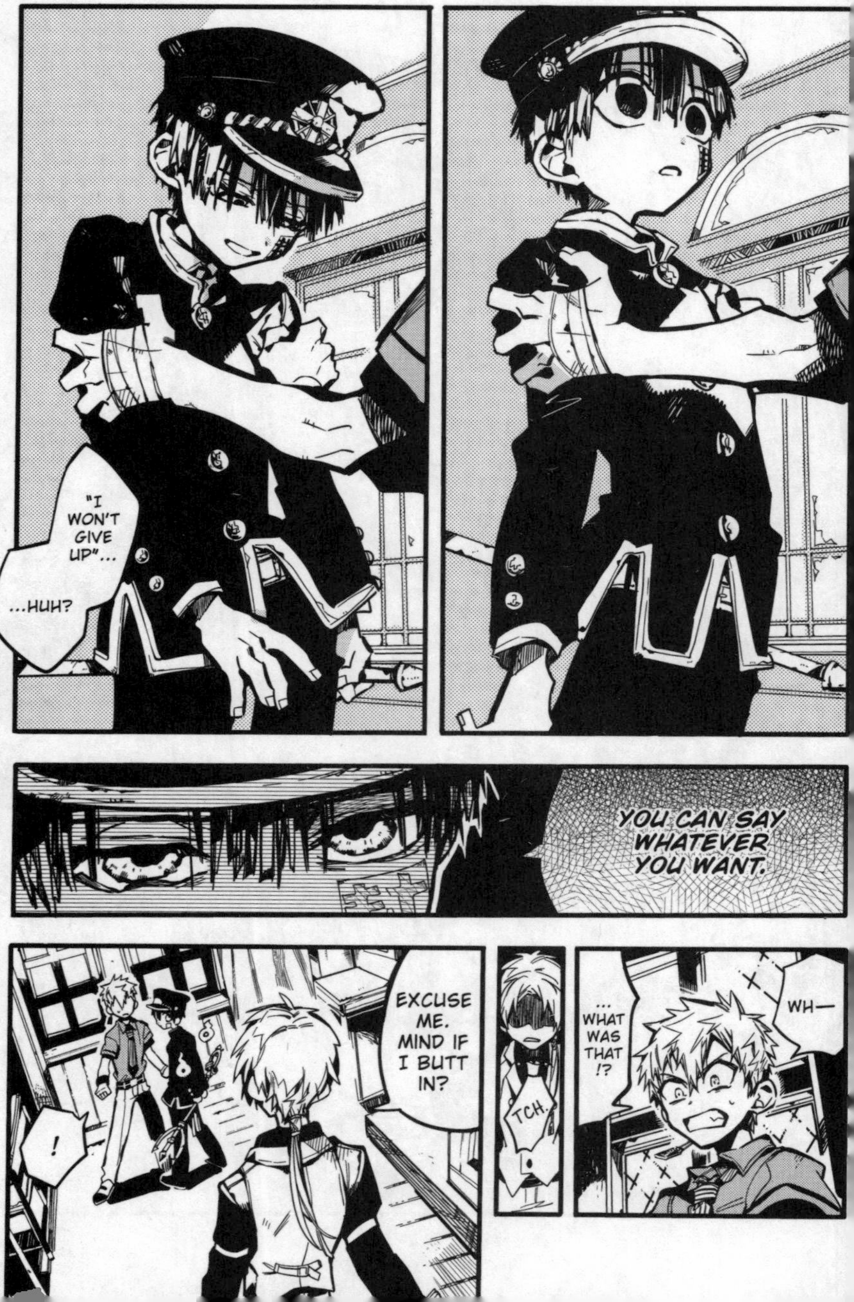
"I WON'T GIVE UP"...
...HUH?
YOU CAN SAY WHATEVER YOU WANT.
WH—
...WHAT WAS THAT!?
TCH.
EXCUSE ME. MIND IF I BUTT IN?
!

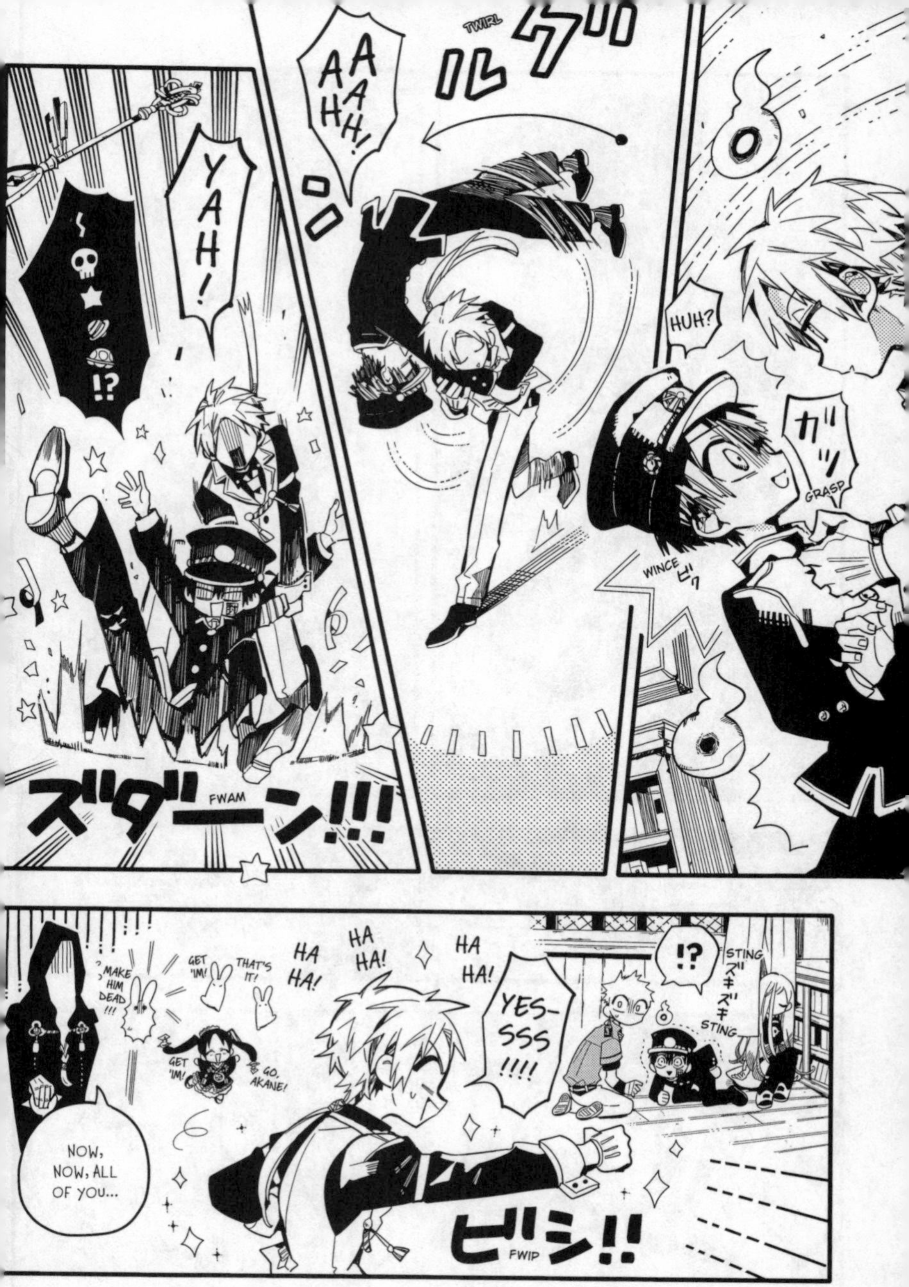
HUH?
ガッ
GRASP
WINCE ビク
TWIRL
AAAHH!
YAH!
!?
ズダーン!!!
FWAM
!?
STING
ズキズキ
STING
YES-SSS!!!!
HA HA!
HA HA!
HA HA!
THAT'S IT!
GET 'IM!
MAKE HIM DEAD!!!
GET 'IM!
GO, AKANE!
NOW, NOW, ALL OF YOU...
ビシ!!
FWIP

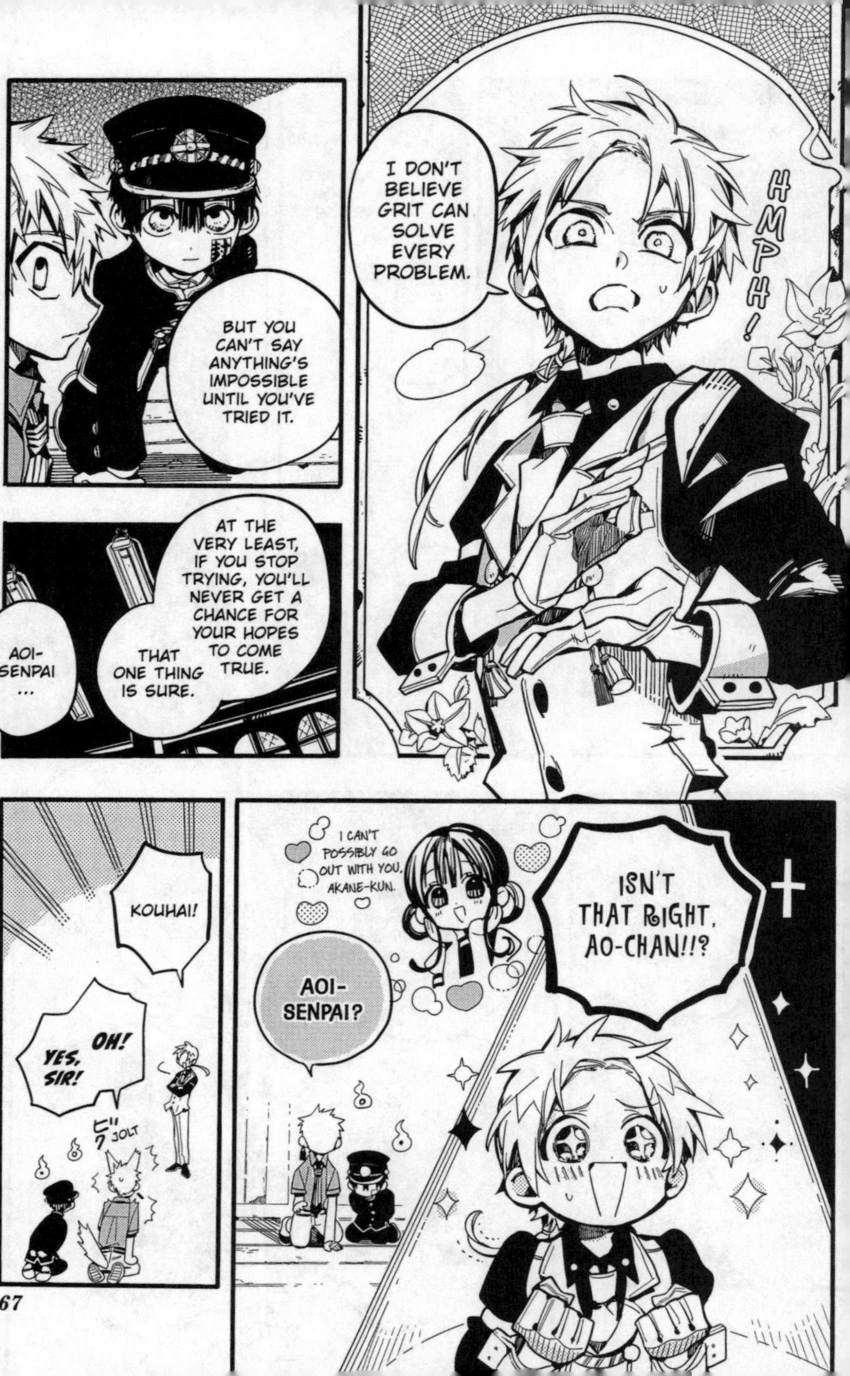
I DON'T BELIEVE GRIT CAN SOLVE EVERY PROBLEM.
HMPH!
BUT YOU CAN'T SAY ANYTHING'S IMPOSSIBLE UNTIL YOU'VE TRIED IT.
AT THE VERY LEAST, IF YOU STOP TRYING, YOU'LL NEVER GET A CHANCE FOR YOUR HOPES TO COME TRUE.
THAT ONE THING IS SURE.
AOI-SENPAI ...
ISN'T THAT RIGHT, AO-CHAN!!?
I CAN'T POSSIBLY GO OUT WITH YOU, AKANE-KUN.
AOI-SENPAI?
KOUHAI!
OH!
YES, SIR!
ビクッ JOLT

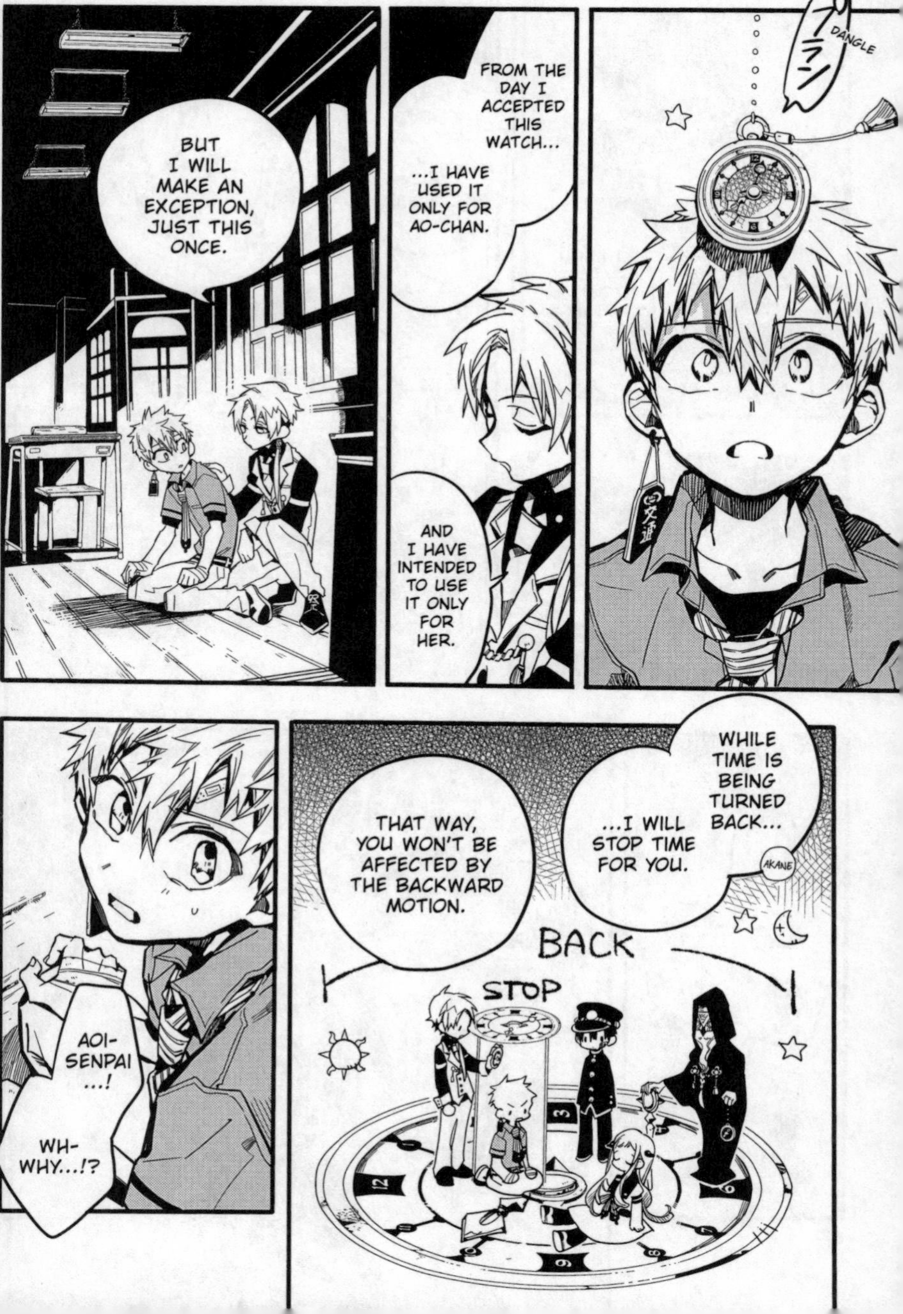
DANGLE
FROM THE DAY I ACCEPTED THIS WATCH...
...I HAVE USED IT ONLY FOR AO-CHAN.
AND I HAVE INTENDED TO USE IT ONLY FOR HER.
BUT I WILL MAKE AN EXCEPTION, JUST THIS ONCE.
WHILE TIME IS BEING TURNED BACK...
...I WILL STOP TIME FOR YOU.
AKANE
THAT WAY, YOU WON'T BE AFFECTED BY THE BACKWARD MOTION.
BACK
STOP
AOI-SENPAI...!
WH-WHY...!?

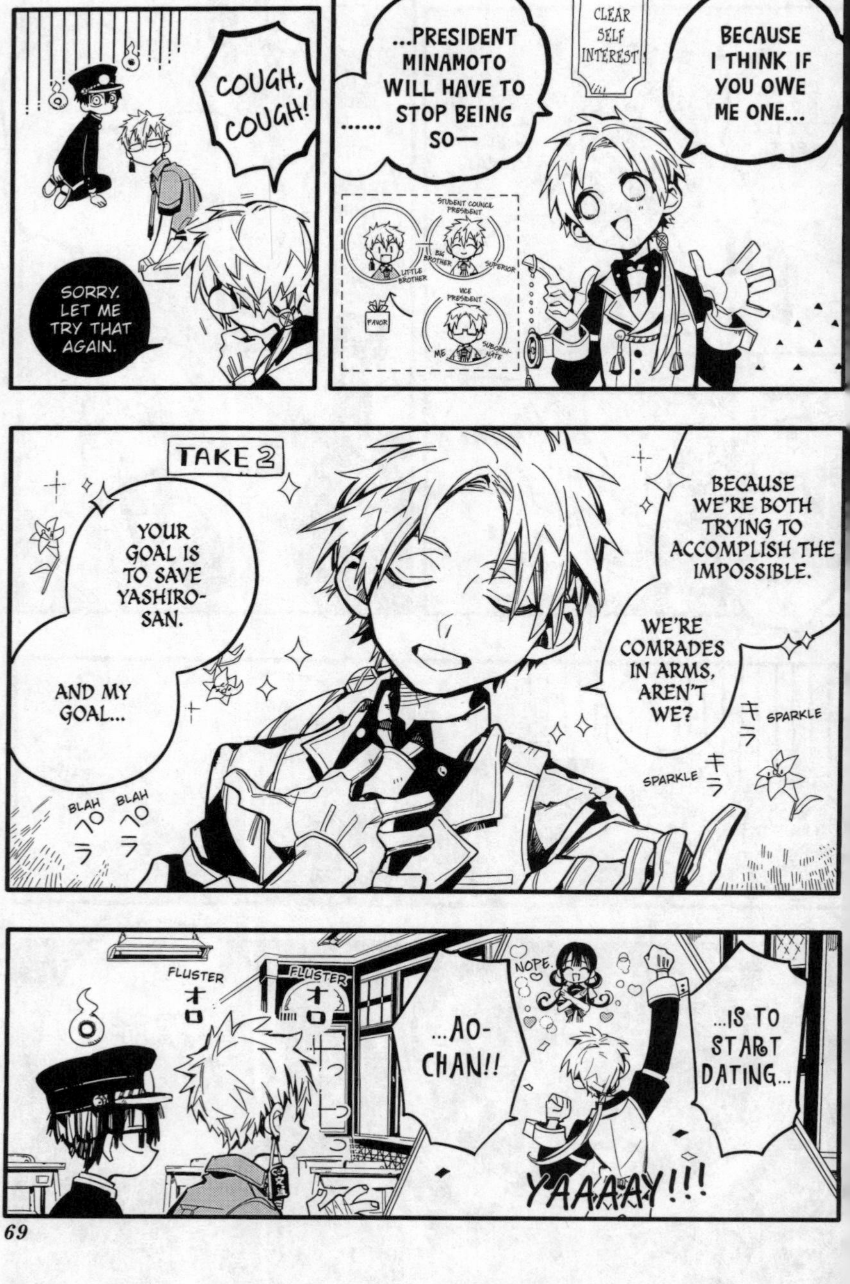
BECAUSE I THINK IF YOU OWE ME ONE...
CLEAR SELF INTEREST
...PRESIDENT MINAMOTO WILL HAVE TO STOP BEING SO—
......
STUDENT COUNCIL PRESIDENT
SUPERIOR
BIG BROTHER
LITTLE BROTHER
VICE PRESIDENT
SUBORDINATE
ME
FAVOR
COUGH, COUGH!
SORRY. LET ME TRY THAT AGAIN.
TAKE 2
BECAUSE WE'RE BOTH TRYING TO ACCOMPLISH THE IMPOSSIBLE.
WE'RE COMRADES IN ARMS, AREN'T WE?
キラ SPARKLE
キラ SPARKLE
YOUR GOAL IS TO SAVE YASHIRO-SAN.
AND MY GOAL...
ヘラ BLAH
ヘラ BLAH
...IS TO START DATING...
YAAAAY!!!
NOPE.
...AO-CHAN!!
オロ FLUSTER
オロ FLUSTER

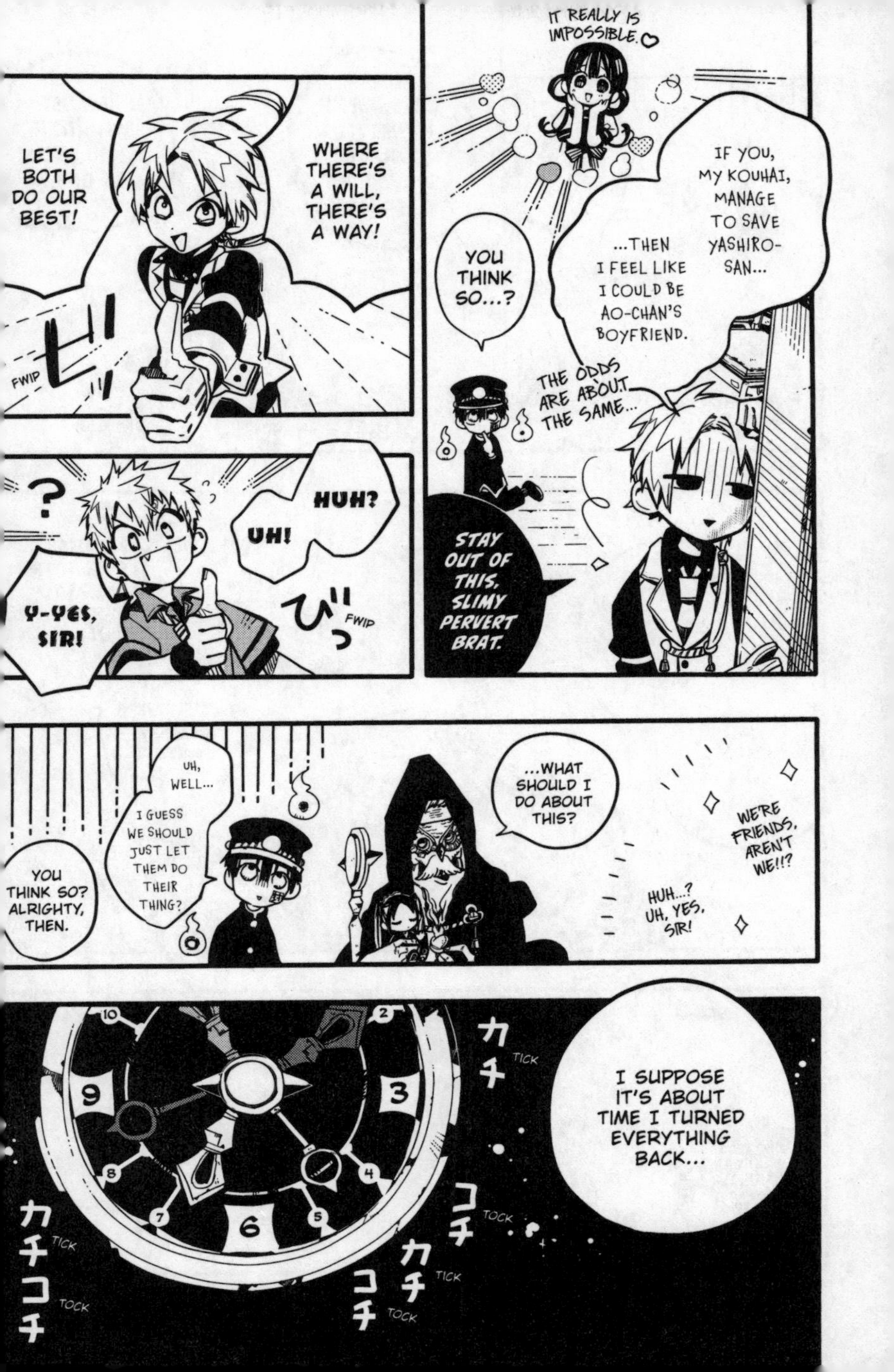
IF YOU, MY KOUHAI, MANAGE TO SAVE YASHIRO-SAN...
...THEN I FEEL LIKE I COULD BE AO-CHAN'S BOYFRIEND.
IT REALLY IS IMPOSSIBLE.♡
YOU THINK SO...?
THE ODDS ARE ABOUT THE SAME...
STAY OUT OF THIS, SLIMY PERVERT BRAT.
WHERE THERE'S A WILL, THERE'S A WAY!
LET'S BOTH DO OUR BEST!
FWIP
HUH?
UH!
FWIP
Y-YES, SIR!
WE'RE FRIENDS, AREN'T WE!!?
HUH...? UH, YES, SIR!
...WHAT SHOULD I DO ABOUT THIS?
UH, WELL...
I GUESS WE SHOULD JUST LET THEM DO THEIR THING?
YOU THINK SO? ALRIGHTY, THEN.
I SUPPOSE IT'S ABOUT TIME I TURNED EVERYTHING BACK...
カチ TICK
コチ TOCK
カチ TICK
コチ TOCK
カチ TICK
コチ TOCK

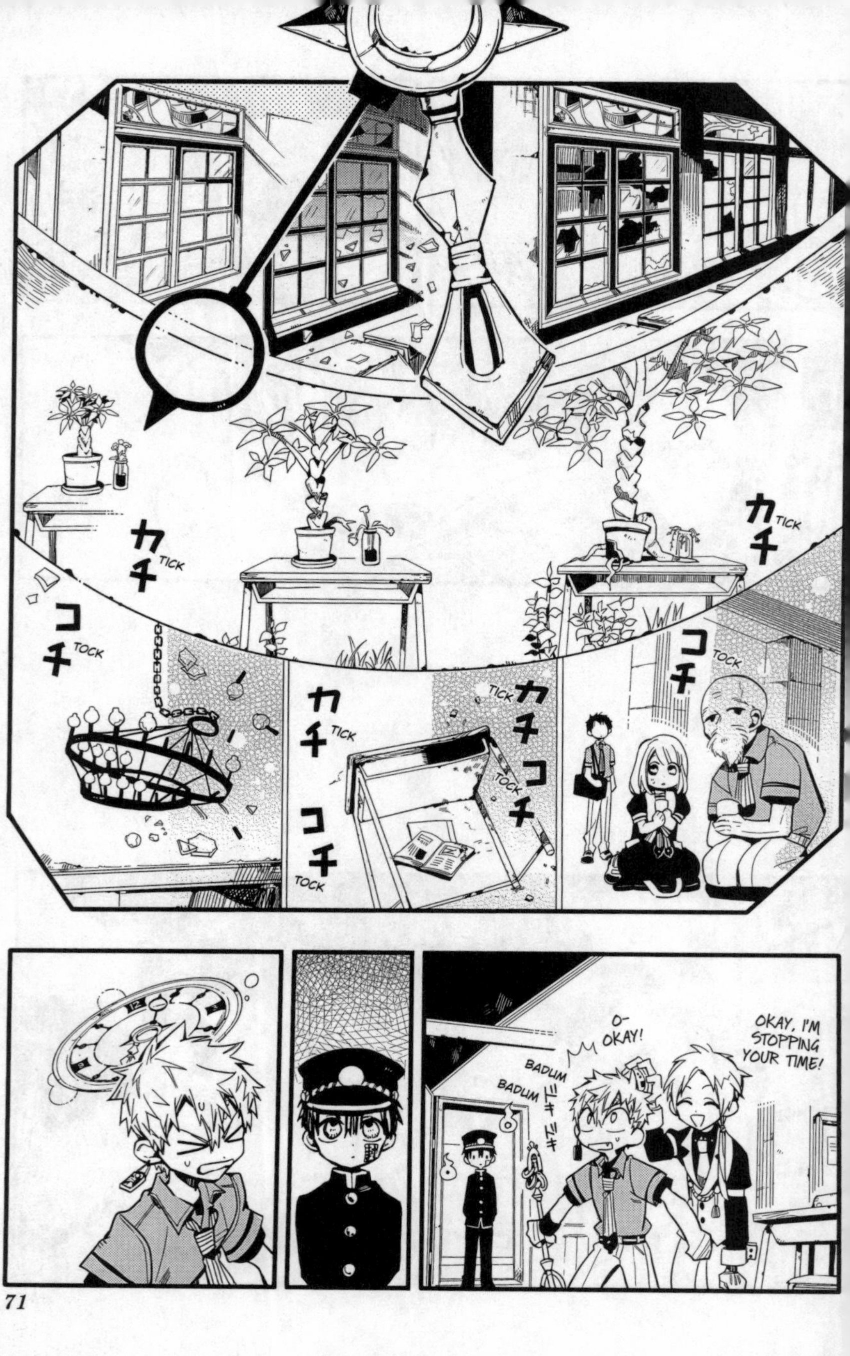
カチ TICK
カチ TICK
コチ TOCK
コチ TOCK
カチ TICK
コチ TOCK
カチ TICK
コチ TOCK
OKAY, I'M STOPPING YOUR TIME!
O- OKAY!
BADUM BADUM ドキドキ

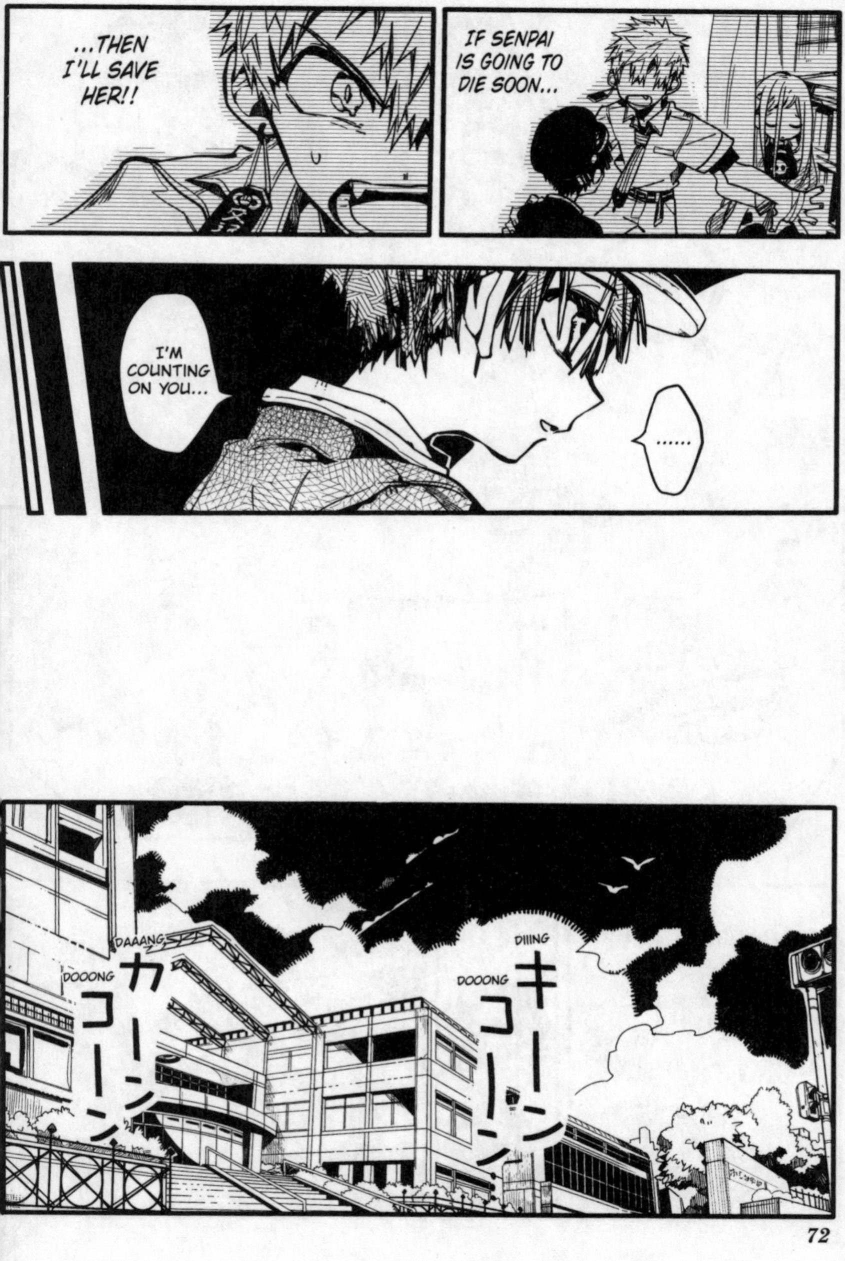
IF SENPAI IS GOING TO DIE SOON...
...THEN I'LL SAVE HER!!
......
I'M COUNTING ON YOU...
DIING
DOOONG
DAAANG
DOOONG

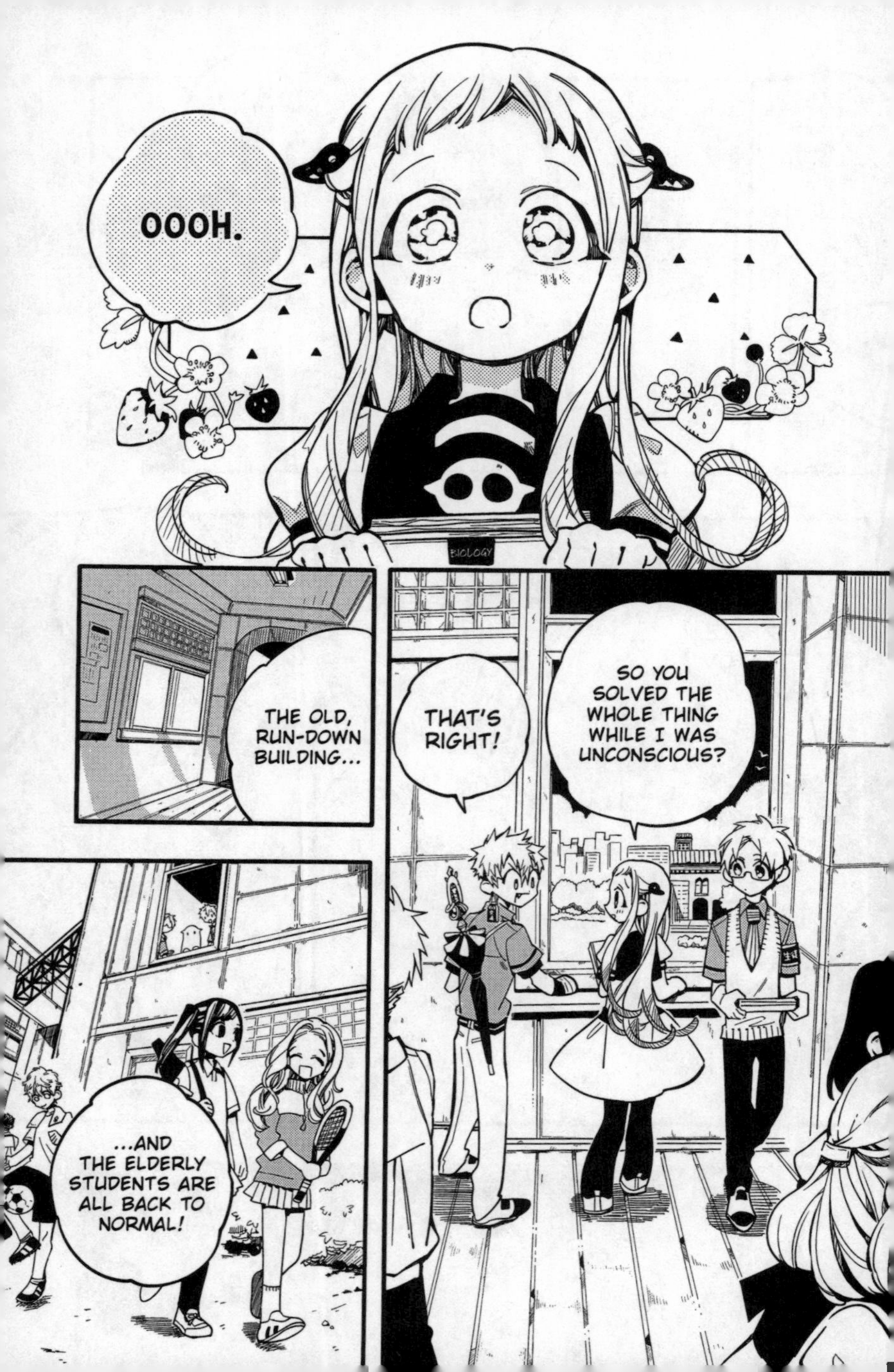
OOOH.
BIOLOGY
SO YOU SOLVED THE WHOLE THING WHILE I WAS UNCONSCIOUS?
THAT'S RIGHT!
THE OLD, RUN-DOWN BUILDING...
...AND THE ELDERLY STUDENTS ARE ALL BACK TO NORMAL!

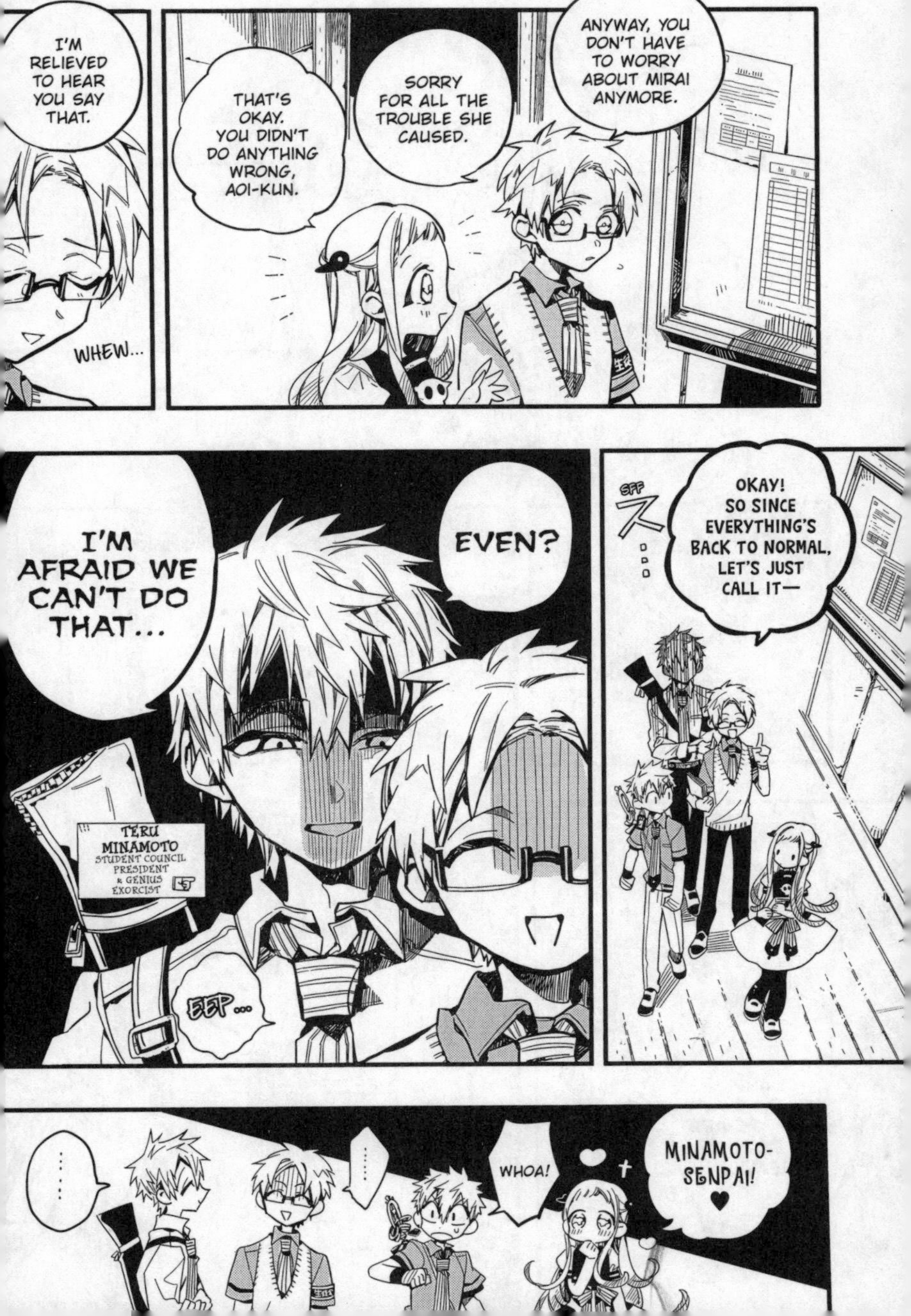
ANYWAY, YOU DON'T HAVE TO WORRY ABOUT MIRAI ANYMORE.
SORRY FOR ALL THE TROUBLE SHE CAUSED.
THAT'S OKAY. YOU DIDN'T DO ANYTHING WRONG, AOI-KUN.
I'M RELIEVED TO HEAR YOU SAY THAT.
WHEW...
SFF
OKAY! SO SINCE EVERYTHING'S BACK TO NORMAL, LET'S JUST CALL IT—
EVEN?
I'M AFRAID WE CAN'T DO THAT...
TERU MINAMOTO STUDENT COUNCIL PRESIDENT & GENIUS EXORCIST
EEP...
MINAMOTO-SENPAI!
WHOA!
......
......

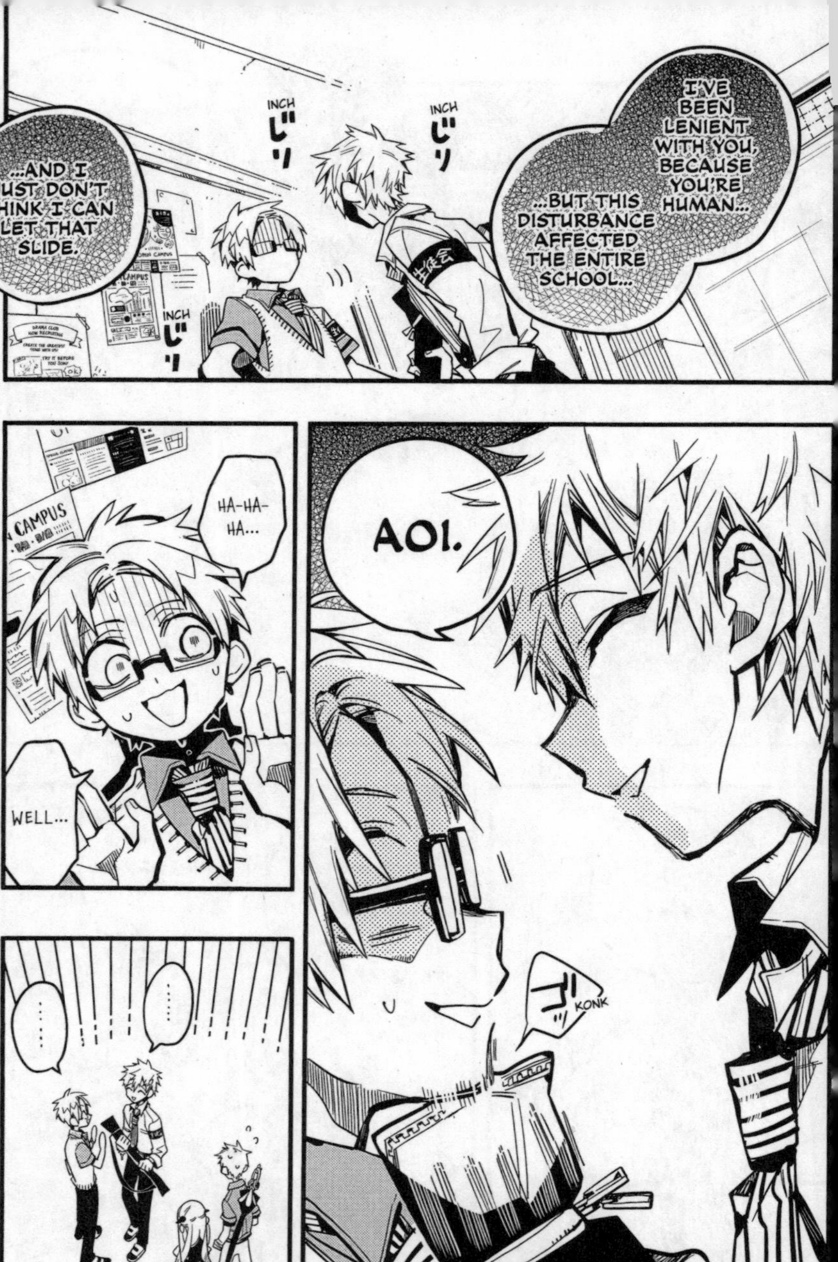
I'VE BEEN LENIENT WITH YOU, BECAUSE YOU'RE HUMAN...
...BUT THIS DISTURBANCE AFFECTED THE ENTIRE SCHOOL...
INCH じり
INCH じり
INCH じり
...AND I JUST DON'T THINK I CAN LET THAT SLIDE.
AOI.
ゴッ KONK
HA-HA-HA...
WELL...
......
......

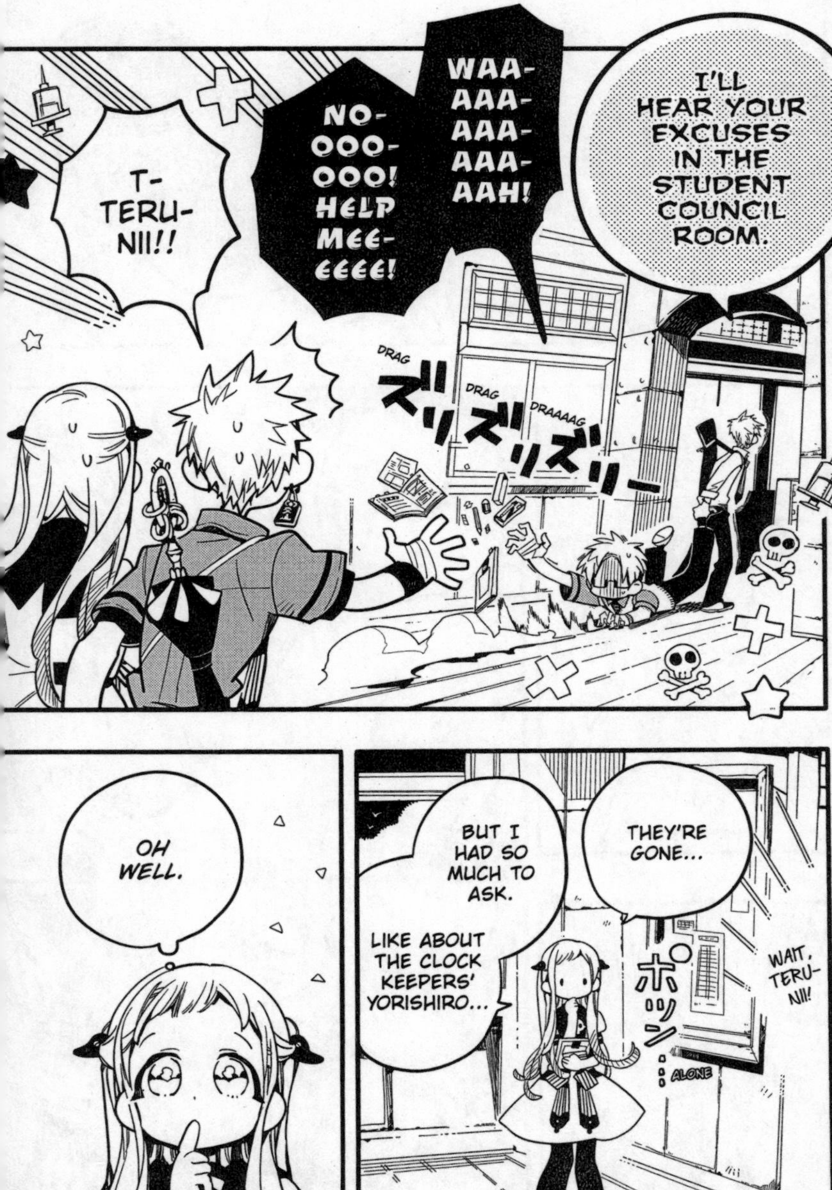
I'LL HEAR YOUR EXCUSES IN THE STUDENT COUNCIL ROOM.
WAA-AAA-AAA-AAA-AAH!
NO-OOO-OOO! HELP MEE-EEEE!
T-TERU-NII!!
DRAG
DRAG
DRAAAAG
THEY'RE GONE...
BUT I HAD SO MUCH TO ASK.
LIKE ABOUT THE CLOCK KEEPERS' YORISHIRO...
WAIT, TERU-NII!
ALONE
OH WELL.

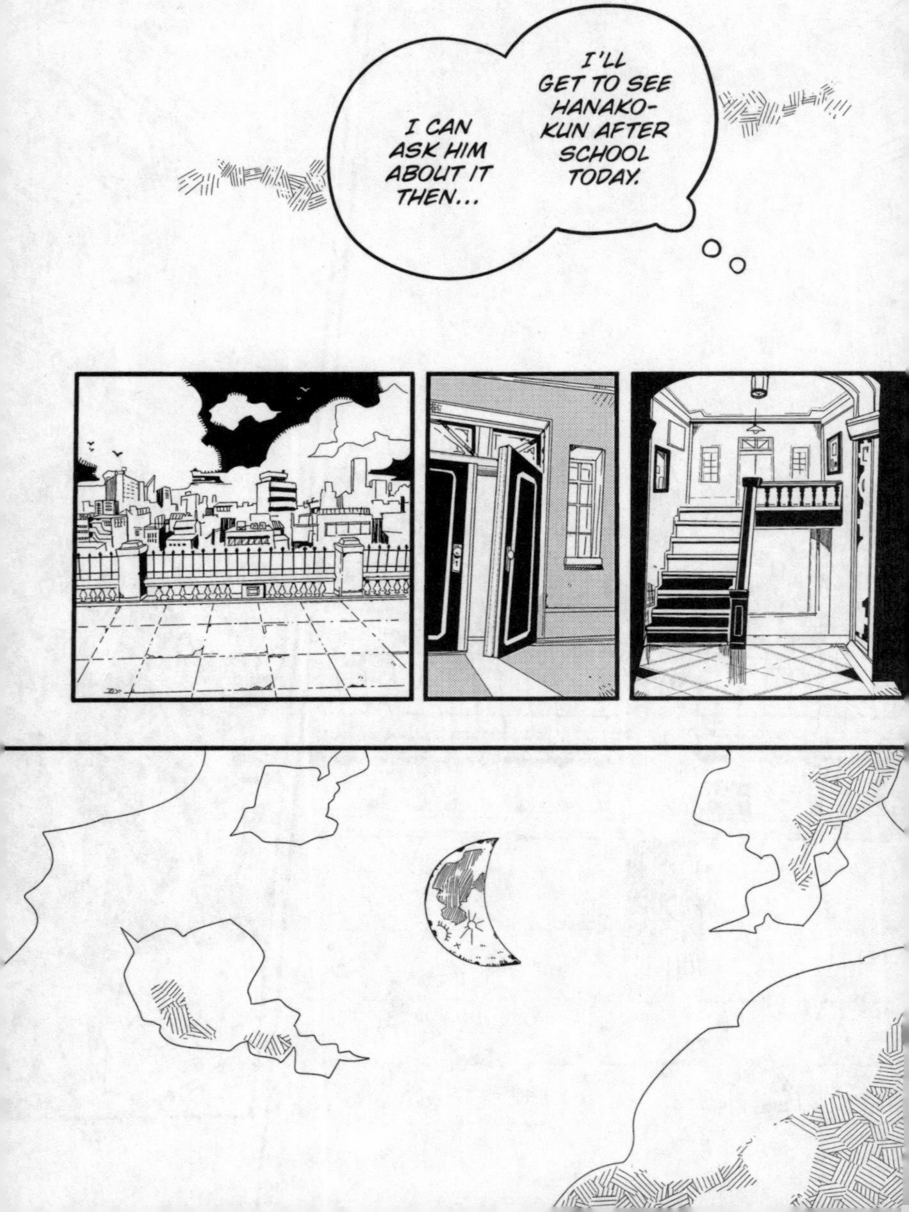
I'LL GET TO SEE HANAKO-KUN AFTER SCHOOL TODAY.
I CAN ASK HIM ABOUT IT THEN...

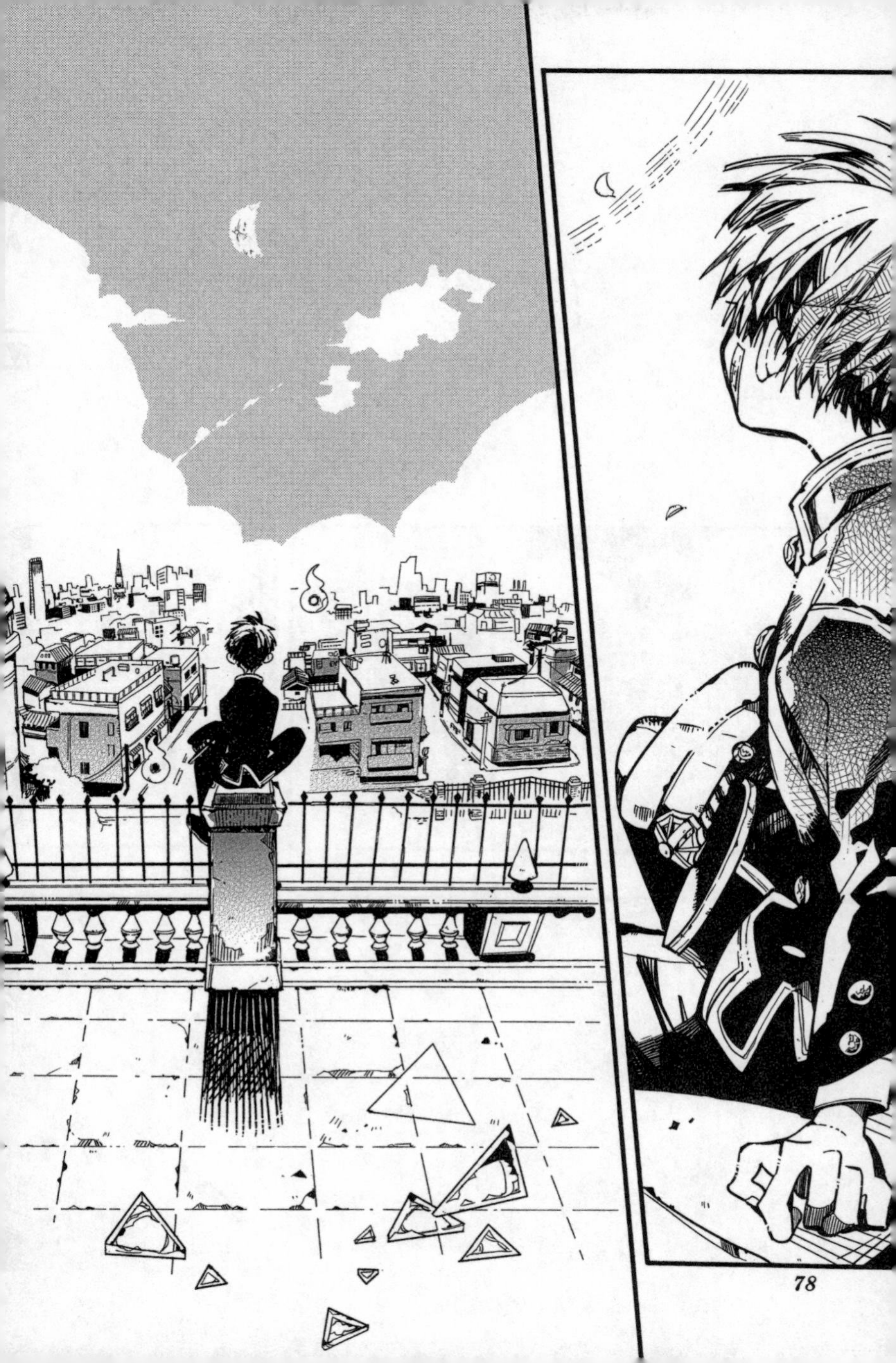

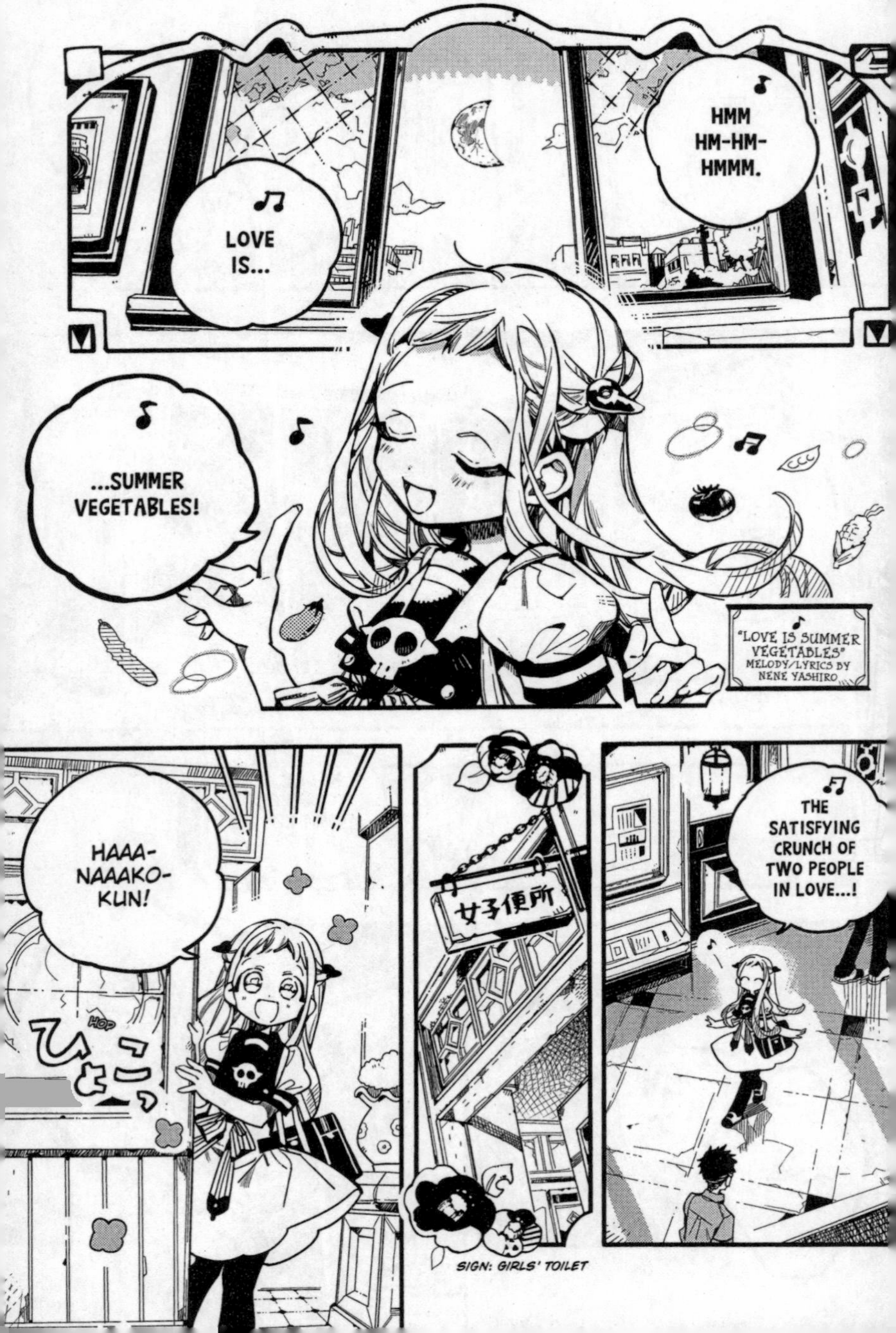
HMM HM-HM-HMMM.
LOVE IS...
...SUMMER VEGETABLES!
"LOVE IS SUMMER VEGETABLES" MELODY/LYRICS BY NENE YASHIRO
THE SATISFYING CRUNCH OF TWO PEOPLE IN LOVE...!
女子便所
SIGN: GIRLS' TOILET
HAAA-NAAAKO-KUN!
HOP
ひょこっ

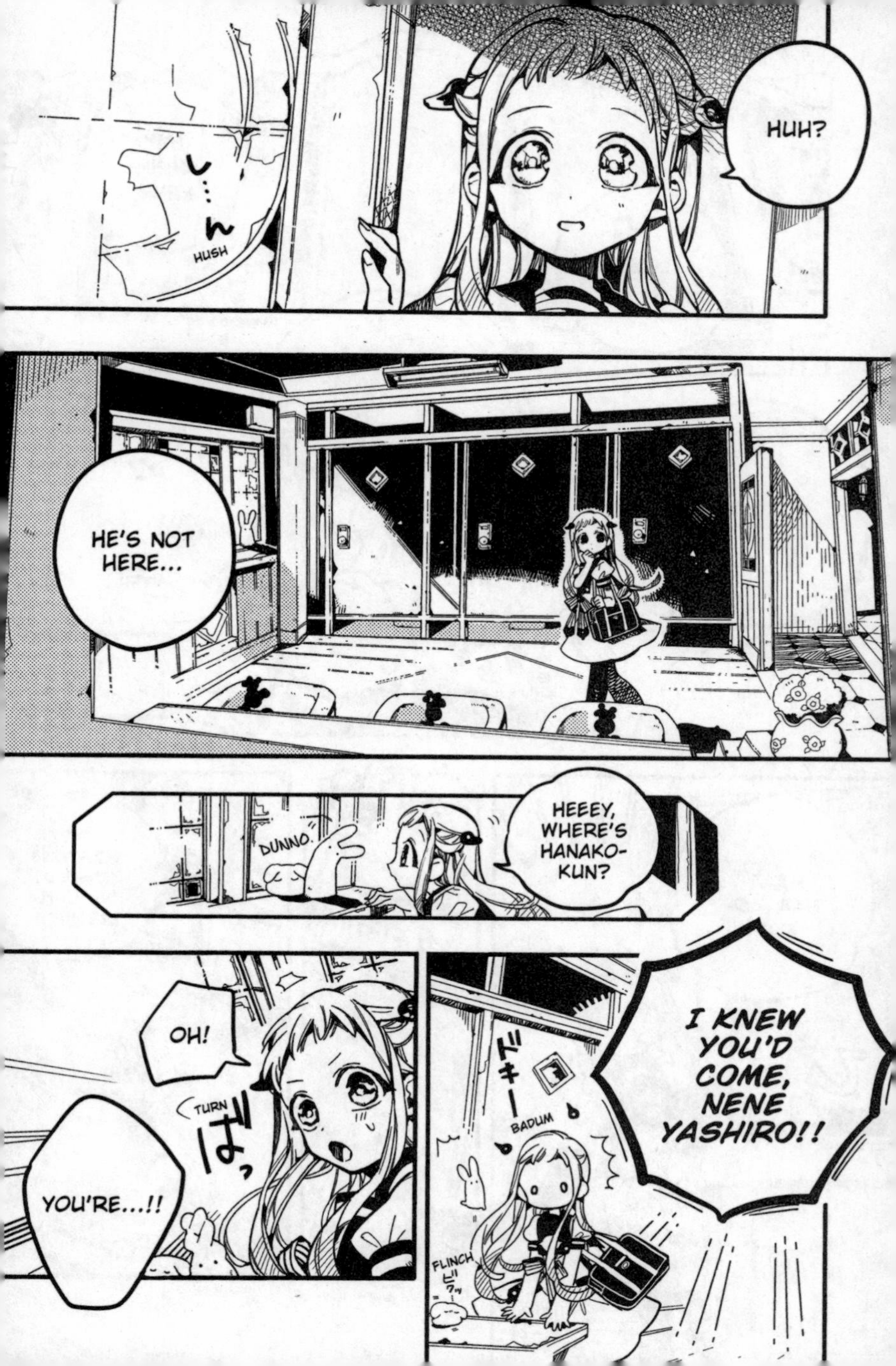
HUH?
し…ん
HUSH
HE'S NOT HERE...
HEEEY, WHERE'S HANAKO-KUN?
DUNNO.
I KNEW YOU'D COME, NENE YASHIRO!!
ドキー
BADUM
FLINCH
ビクッ
OH!
TURN
ぱっ
YOU'RE...!!

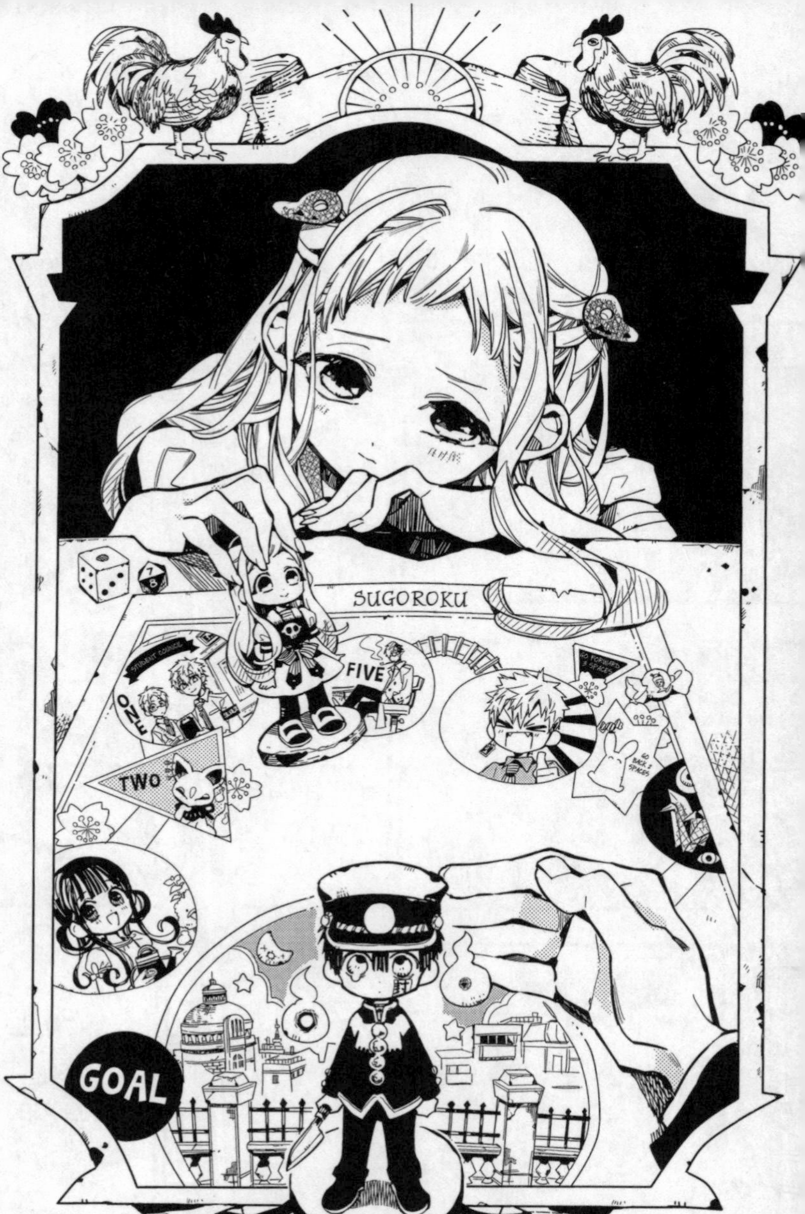
SUGOROKU
GO FORWARD 3 SPACES
FIVE
STUDENT COUNCIL
ONE
GO BACK 2 SPACES
TWO
GOAL

SPOOK 28

SEARCHING (PART 1)

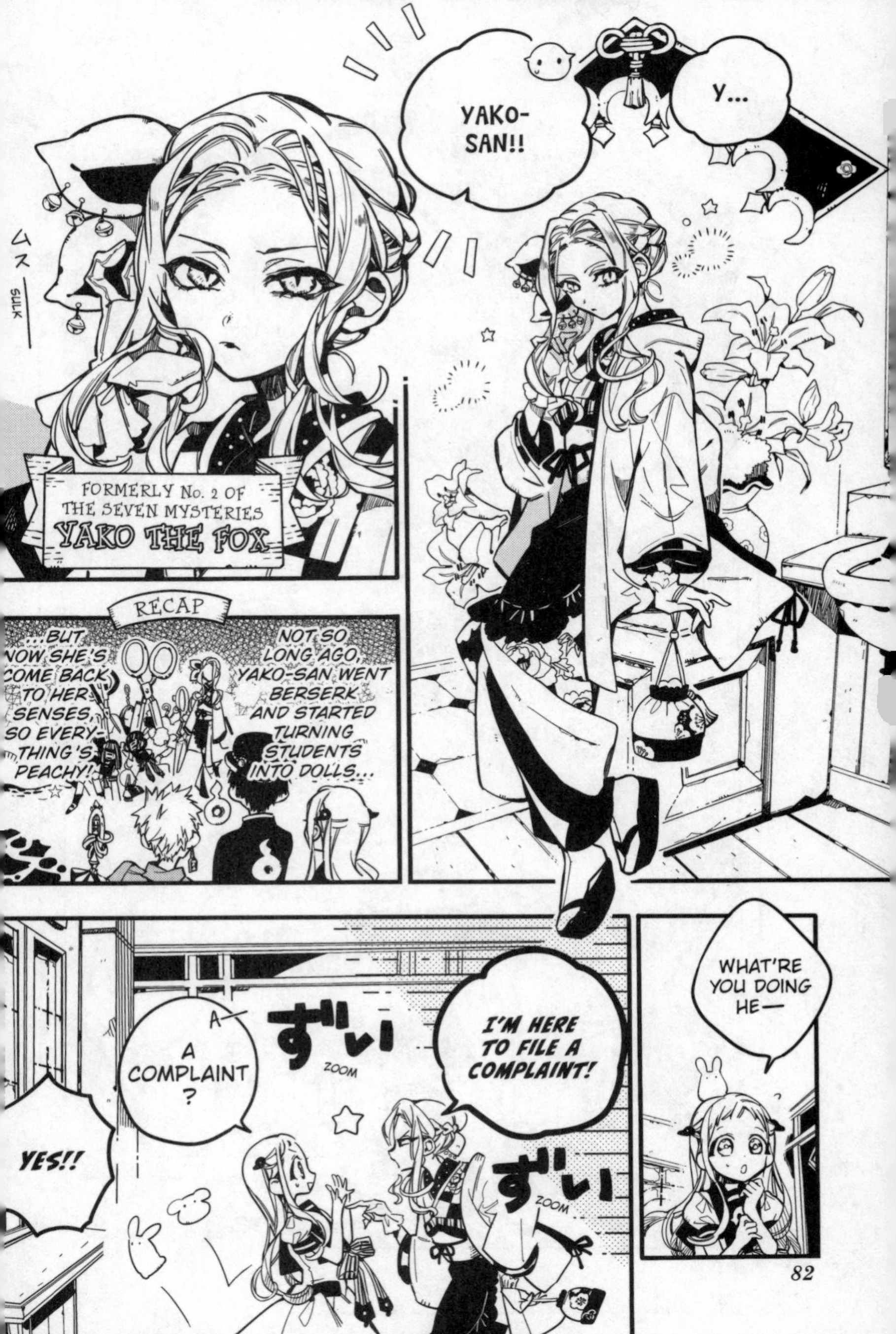
Y...
YAKO-SAN!!
ムス
SULK
FORMERLY No. 2 OF THE SEVEN MYSTERIES
YAKO THE FOX
RECAP
NOT SO LONG AGO, YAKO-SAN WENT BERSERK AND STARTED TURNING STUDENTS INTO DOLLS...
...BUT NOW SHE'S COME BACK TO HER SENSES, SO EVERYTHING'S PEACHY!
WHAT'RE YOU DOING HE—
I'M HERE TO FILE A COMPLAINT!
ずい
ZOOM
ずい
ZOOM
A—
A COMPLAINT?
YES!!

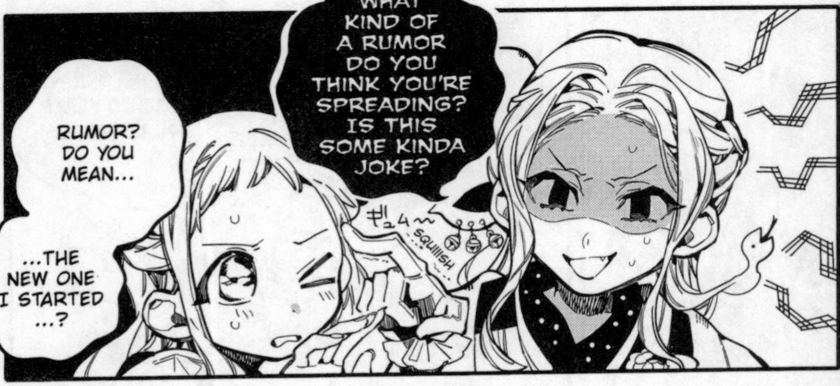
WHAT KIND OF A RUMOR DO YOU THINK YOU'RE SPREADING? IS THIS SOME KINDA JOKE?
SQUIIISH
RUMOR? DO YOU MEAN...
...THE NEW ONE I STARTED ...?

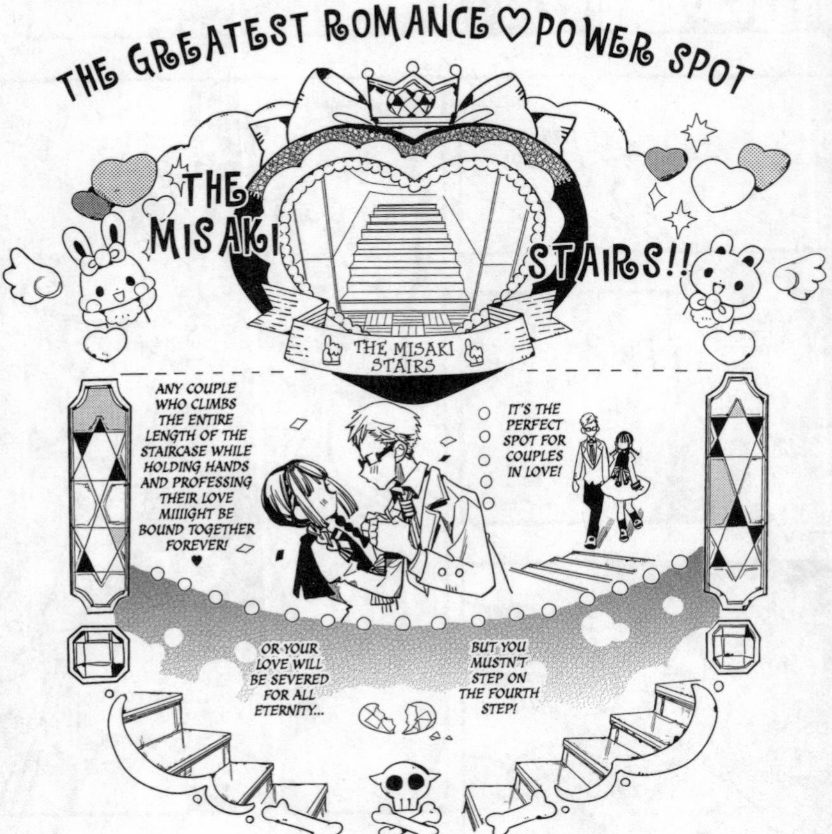
THE GREATEST ROMANCE ♡ POWER SPOT
THE MISAKI STAIRS!!
THE MISAKI STAIRS
IT'S THE PERFECT SPOT FOR COUPLES IN LOVE!
ANY COUPLE WHO CLIMBS THE ENTIRE LENGTH OF THE STAIRCASE WHILE HOLDING HANDS AND PROFESSING THEIR LOVE MIIIGHT BE BOUND TOGETHER FOREVER! ♥
BUT YOU MUSTN'T STEP ON THE FOURTH STEP!
OR YOUR LOVE WILL BE SEVERED FOR ALL ETERNITY...

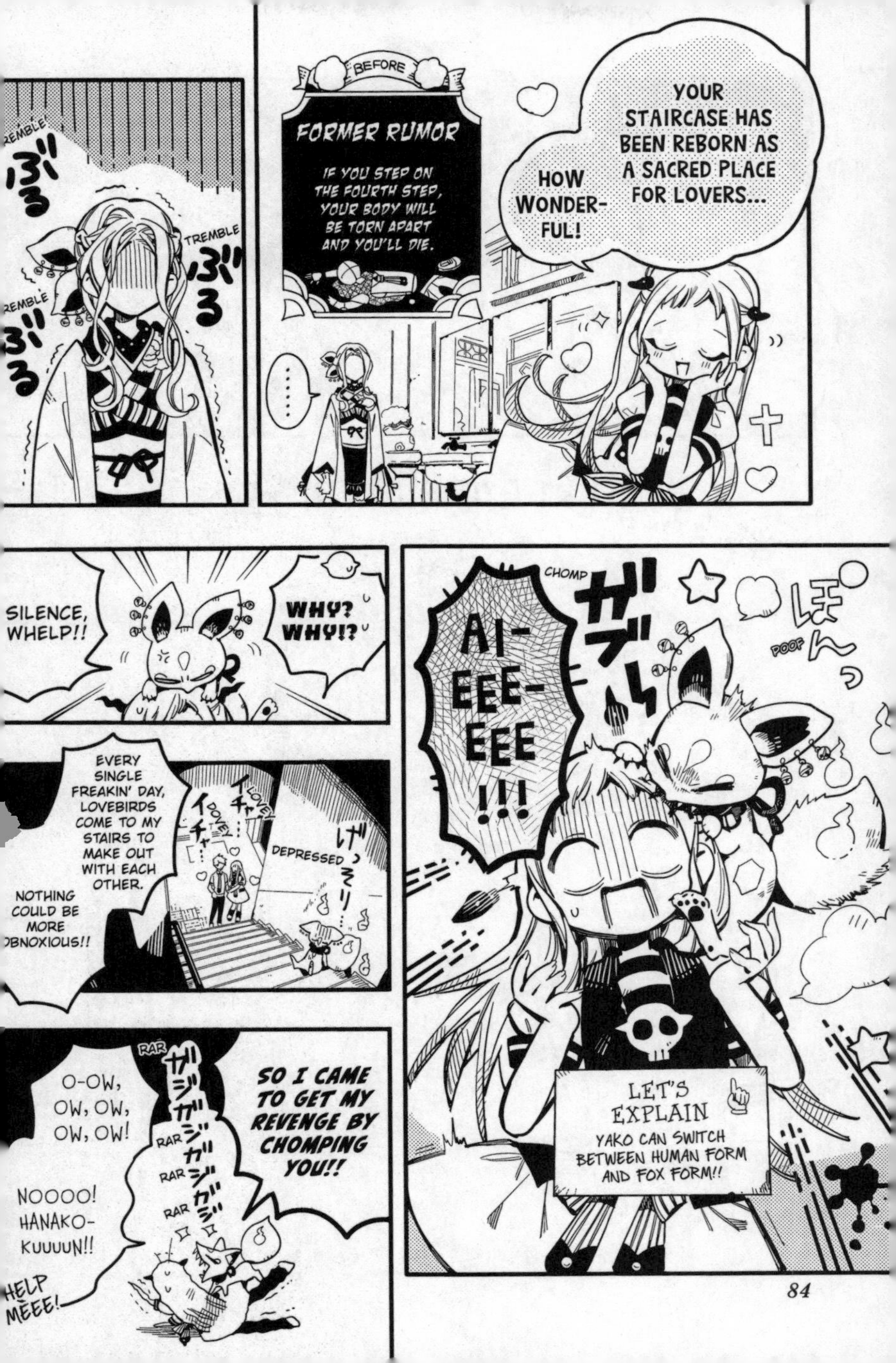
YOUR STAIRCASE HAS BEEN REBORN AS A SACRED PLACE FOR LOVERS...
HOW WONDER-FUL!
BEFORE
FORMER RUMOR
IF YOU STEP ON THE FOURTH STEP, YOUR BODY WILL BE TORN APART AND YOU'LL DIE.
......
TREMBLE
ぶる
TREMBLE!
ぶる
TREMBLE
ぶる
ぽんっ
POOF
CHOMP
ガブッ
AI-EEE-EEE!!!
LET'S EXPLAIN
YAKO CAN SWITCH BETWEEN HUMAN FORM AND FOX FORM!!
WHY? WHY!?
SILENCE, WHELP!!
LOVEY DOVEY
イチャイチャ
DEPRESSED
げっそり...
EVERY SINGLE FREAKIN' DAY, LOVEBIRDS COME TO MY STAIRS TO MAKE OUT WITH EACH OTHER.
NOTHING COULD BE MORE OBNOXIOUS!!
SO I CAME TO GET MY REVENGE BY CHOMPING YOU!!
RAR
ガジガジガジガジ
RAR
RAR
RAR
O-OW, OW, OW, OW, OW!
NOOOO! HANAKO-KUUUUN!!
HELP MEEE!

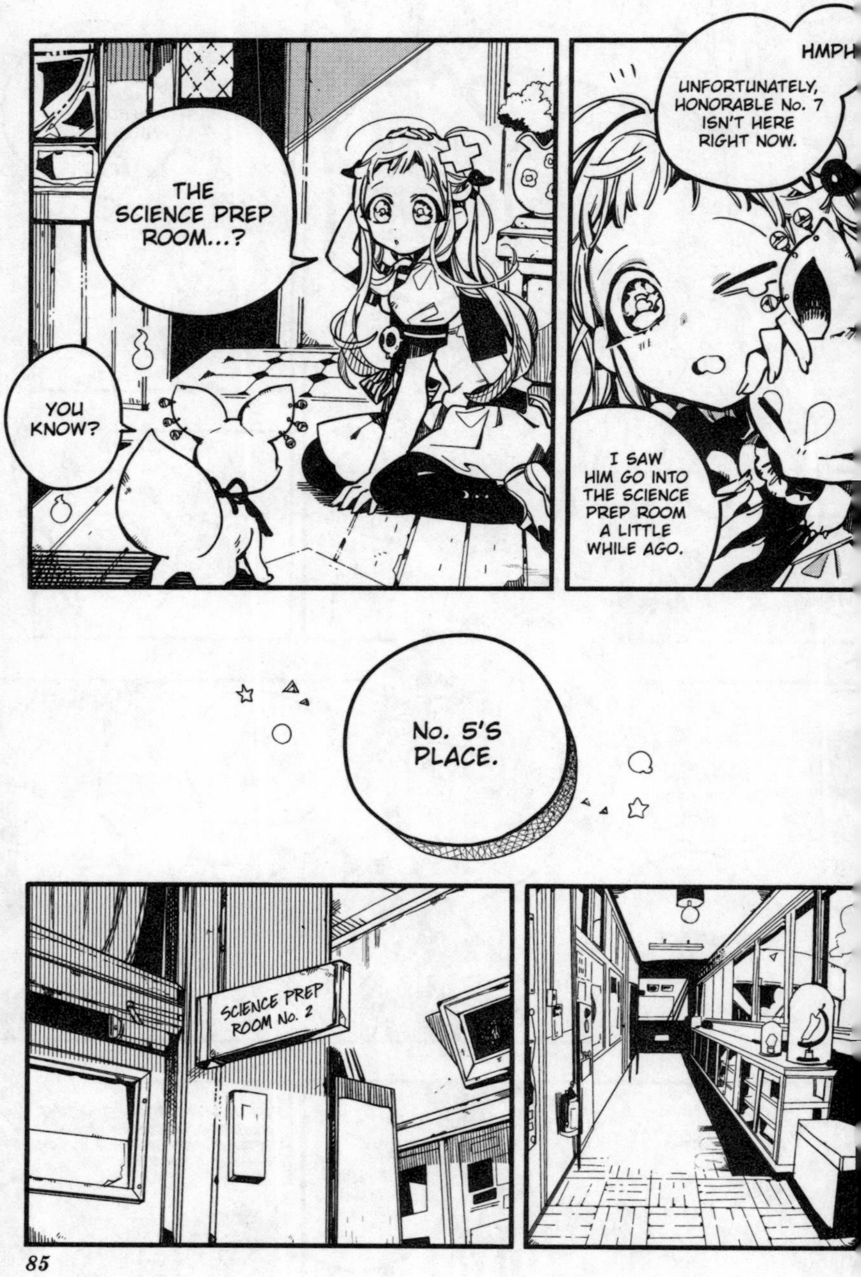
HMPH
UNFORTUNATELY, HONORABLE No. 7 ISN'T HERE RIGHT NOW.
I SAW HIM GO INTO THE SCIENCE PREP ROOM A LITTLE WHILE AGO.
THE SCIENCE PREP ROOM...?
YOU KNOW?
No. 5'S PLACE.
SCIENCE PREP ROOM No. 2

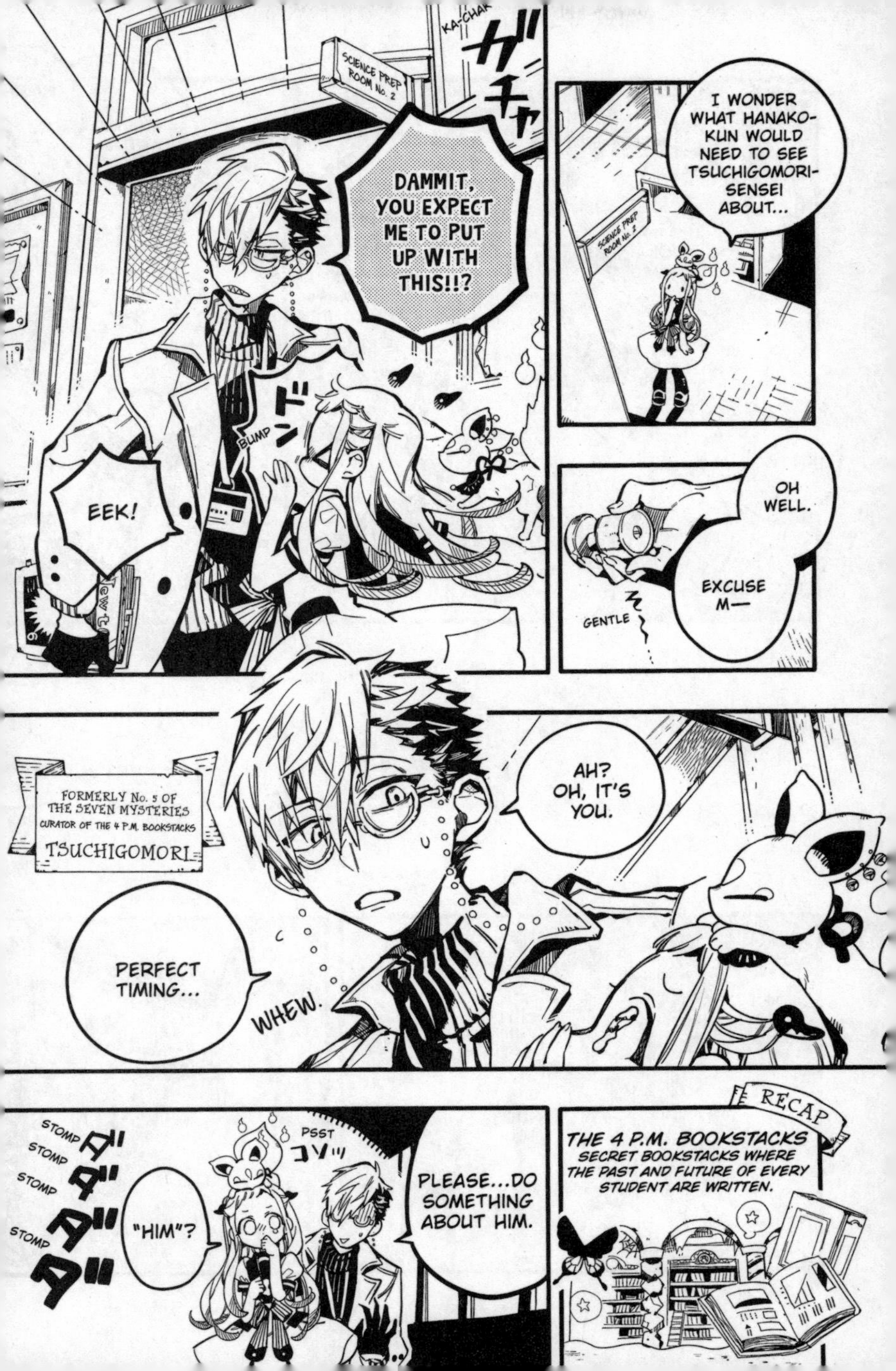

I WONDER WHAT HANAKO-KUN WOULD NEED TO SEE TSUCHIGOMORI-SENSEI ABOUT...
SCIENCE PREP ROOM No. 2
OH WELL.
EXCUSE M—
GENTLE
KA-CHAK
ガチャ
SCIENCE PREP ROOM No. 2
DAMMIT, YOU EXPECT ME TO PUT UP WITH THIS!!?
ドン
BUMP
EEK!
AH? OH, IT'S YOU.
FORMERLY No. 5 OF THE SEVEN MYSTERIES
CURATOR OF THE 4 P.M. BOOKSTACKS
TSUCHIGOMORI
PERFECT TIMING...
WHEW.
RECAP
THE 4 P.M. BOOKSTACKS
SECRET BOOKSTACKS WHERE THE PAST AND FUTURE OF EVERY STUDENT ARE WRITTEN.
PLEASE...DO SOMETHING ABOUT HIM.
PSST
コソッ
"HIM"?
STOMP
STOMP
STOMP
STOMP
ダダダダ

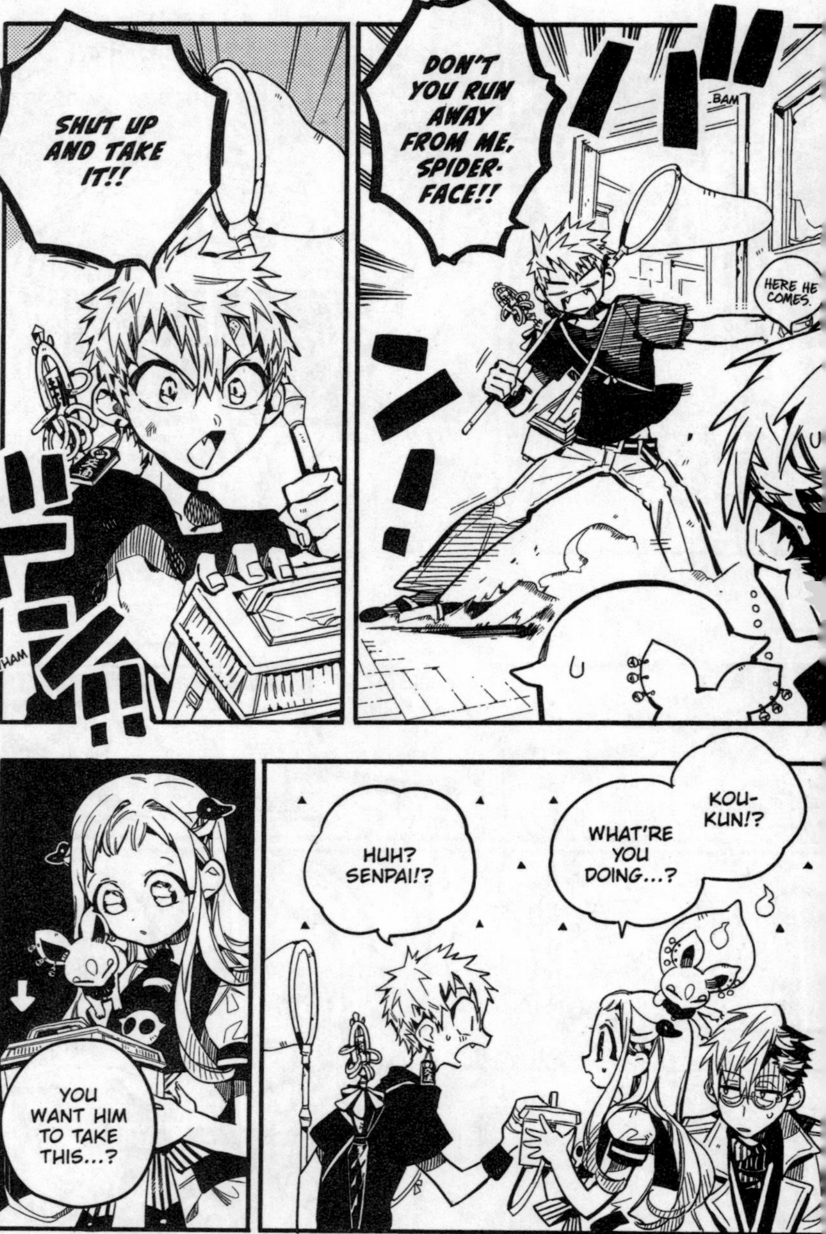
DON'T YOU RUN AWAY FROM ME, SPIDER-FACE!!
BAM
HERE HE COMES.
SHUT UP AND TAKE IT!!
WHAM
KOU-KUN!?
WHAT'RE YOU DOING...?
HUH? SENPAI!?
YOU WANT HIM TO TAKE THIS...?

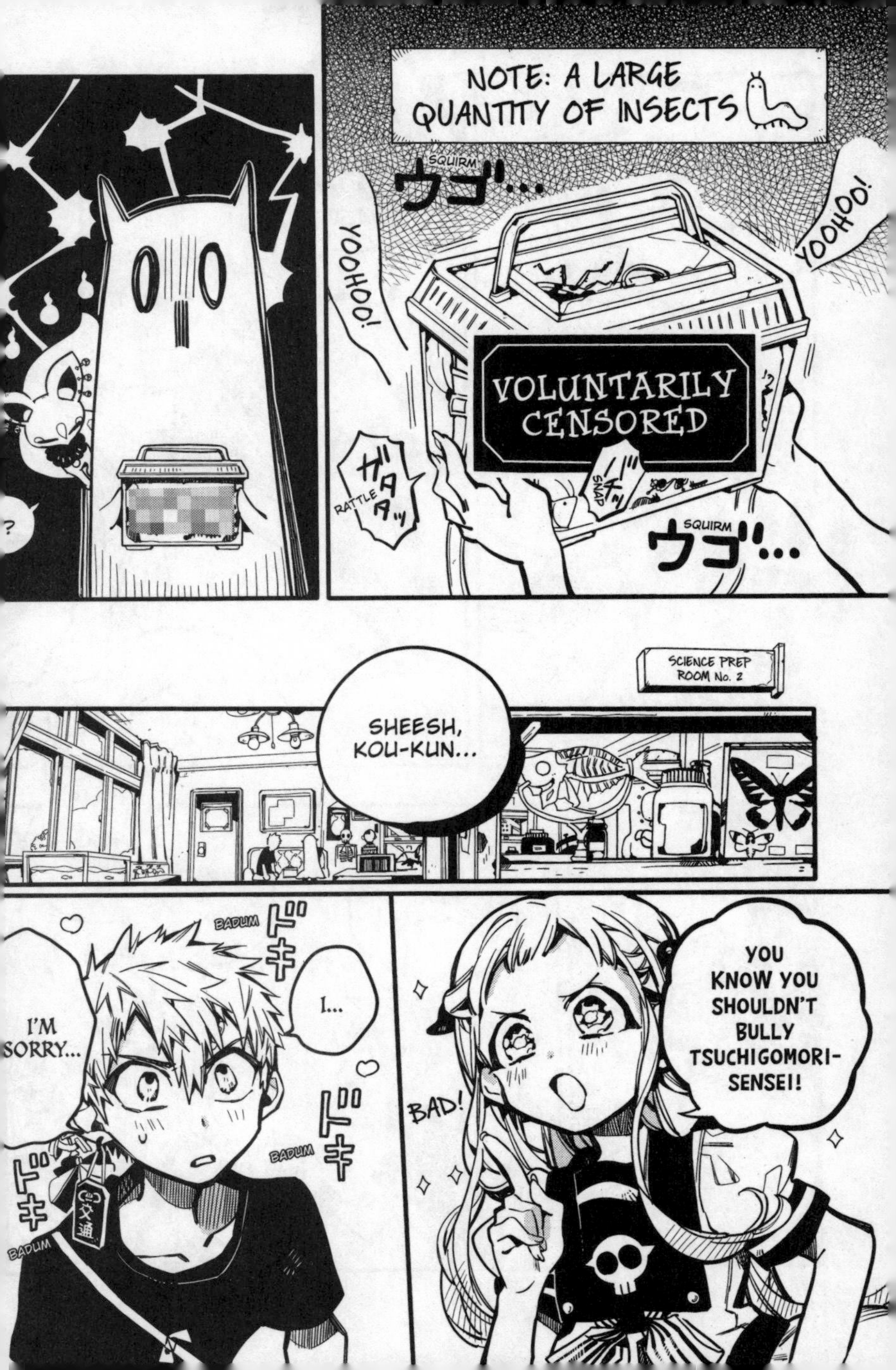

NOTE: A LARGE QUANTITY OF INSECTS
SQUIRM
ウゴ…
YOOHOO!
YOOHOO!
VOLUNTARILY CENSORED
SNAP
RATTLE
ガタタッ
SQUIRM
ウゴ…
?
SCIENCE PREP ROOM No. 2
SHEESH, KOU-KUN...
YOU KNOW YOU SHOULDN'T BULLY TSUCHIGOMORI-SENSEI!
BAD!
BADUM
ドキ
I...
I'M SORRY...
BADUM
ドキ
BADUM
ドキ

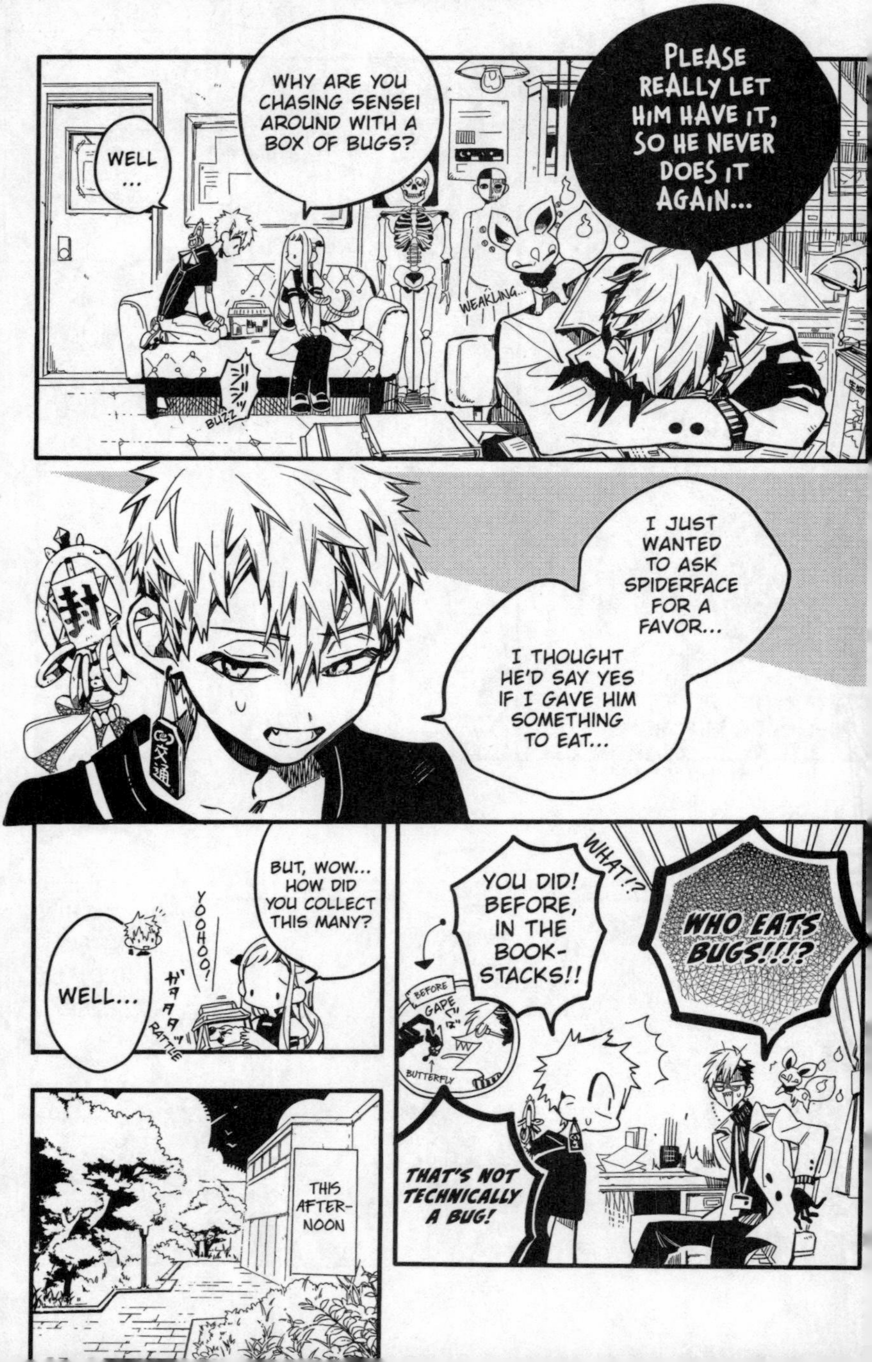
PLEASE REALLY LET HIM HAVE IT, SO HE NEVER DOES IT AGAIN...
WEAKLING...
WHY ARE YOU CHASING SENSEI AROUND WITH A BOX OF BUGS?
WELL ...
BUZZ
I JUST WANTED TO ASK SPIDERFACE FOR A FAVOR...
I THOUGHT HE'D SAY YES IF I GAVE HIM SOMETHING TO EAT...
WHO EATS BUGS!!!?
WHAT!?
YOU DID! BEFORE, IN THE BOOK-STACKS!!
BEFORE
GAPE
BUTTERFLY
THAT'S NOT TECHNICALLY A BUG!
BUT, WOW... HOW DID YOU COLLECT THIS MANY?
YOOHOO!
RATTLE
WELL...
THIS AFTER-NOON

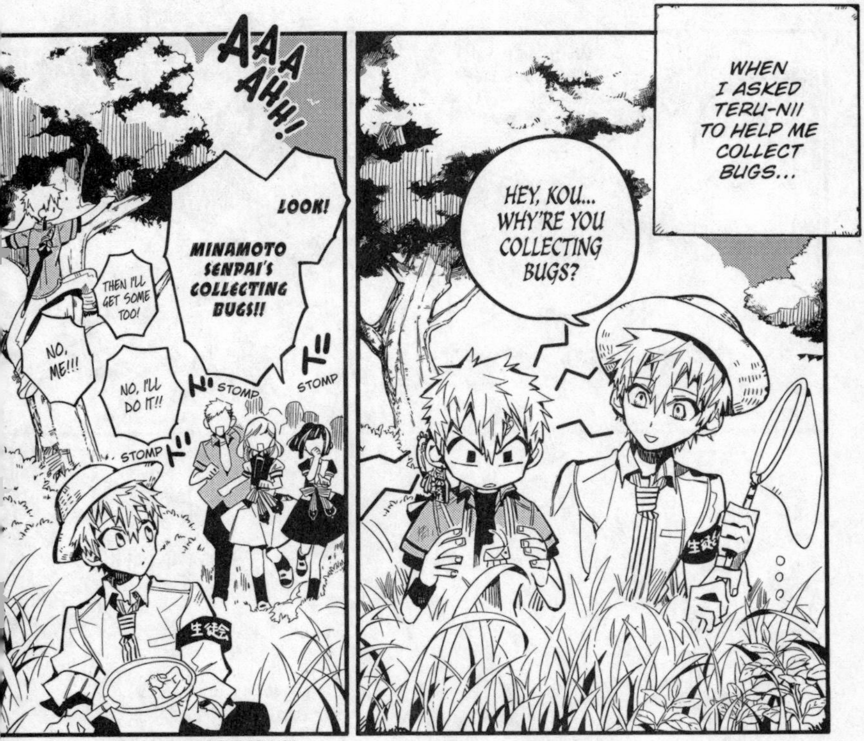
WHEN I ASKED TERU-NII TO HELP ME COLLECT BUGS...
HEY, KOU... WHY'RE YOU COLLECTING BUGS?
AAAAHH!
LOOK!
MINAMOTO SENPAI's COLLECTING BUGS!!
THEN I'LL GET SOME TOO!
NO, ME!!!
NO, I'LL DO IT!!
ド STOMP
ド STOMP
ド STOMP

ARMBAND: STUDENT COUNCIL

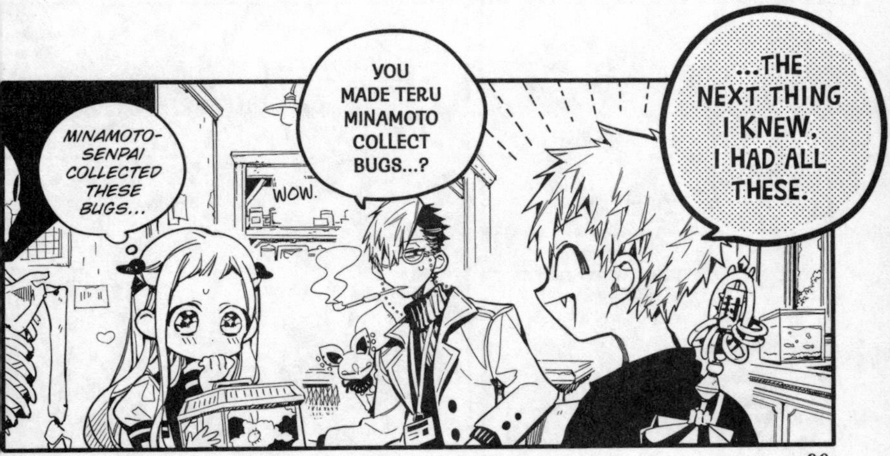
...THE NEXT THING I KNEW, I HAD ALL THESE.
YOU MADE TERU MINAMOTO COLLECT BUGS...?
WOW.
MINAMOTO-SENPAI COLLECTED THESE BUGS...

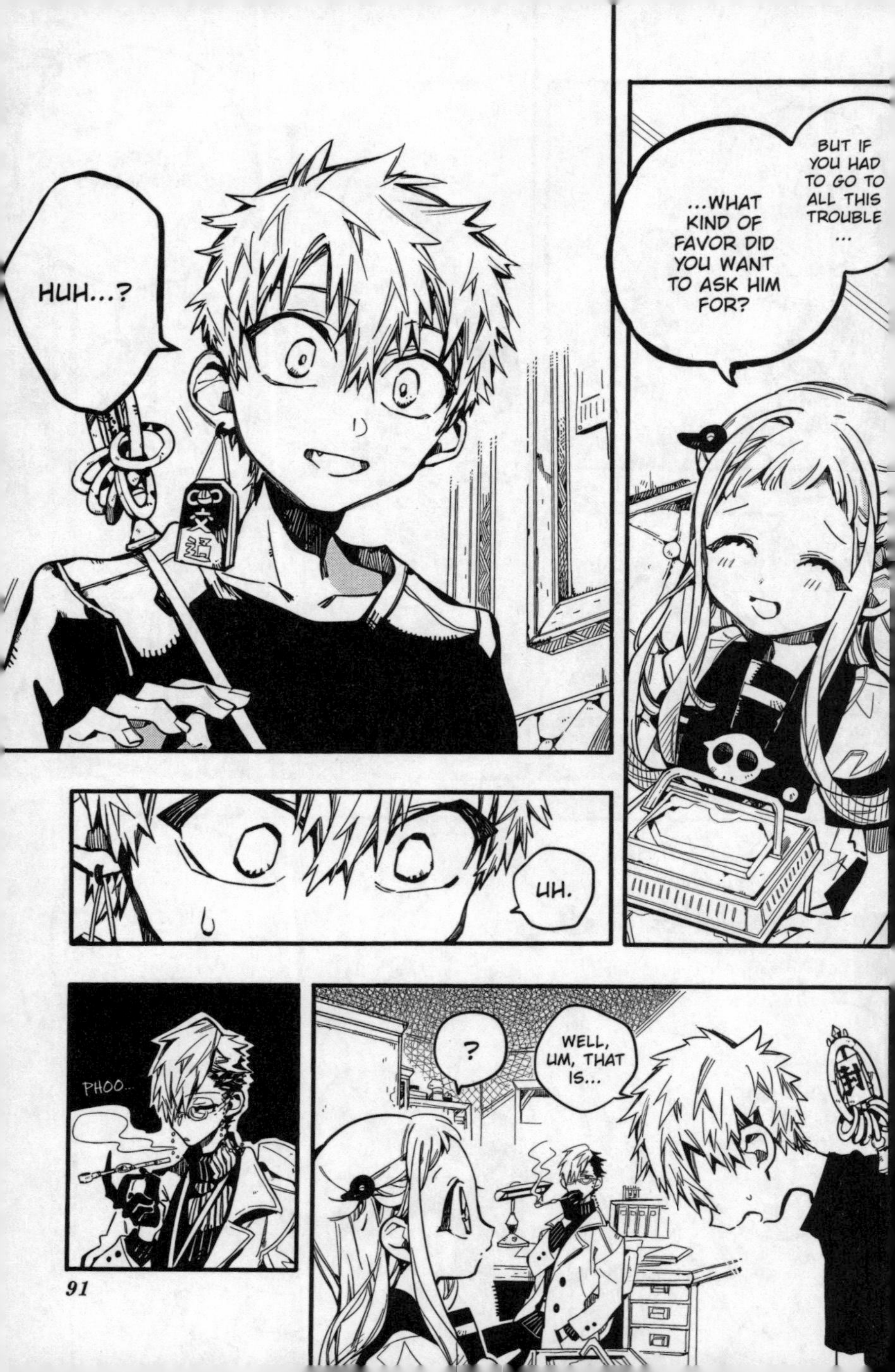
BUT IF YOU HAD TO GO TO ALL THIS TROUBLE...
...WHAT KIND OF FAVOR DID YOU WANT TO ASK HIM FOR?
HUH...?
UH.
WELL, UM, THAT IS...
?
PHOO...

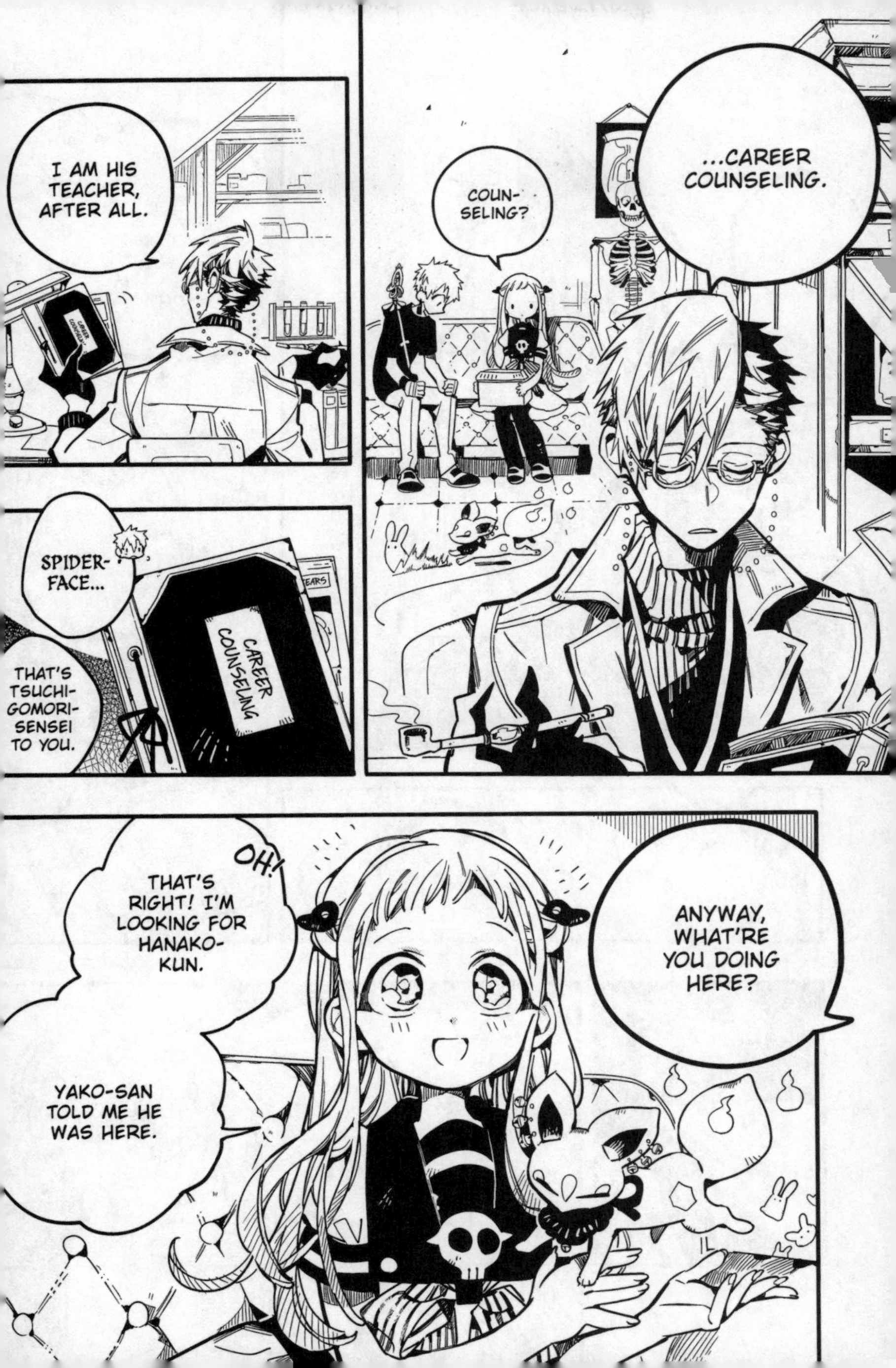

...CAREER COUNSELING.
COUN-SELING?
I AM HIS TEACHER, AFTER ALL.
SPIDER-FACE...
CAREER COUNSELING
THAT'S TSUCHIGOMORI-SENSEI TO YOU.
ANYWAY, WHAT'RE YOU DOING HERE?
OH!
THAT'S RIGHT! I'M LOOKING FOR HANAKO-KUN.
YAKO-SAN TOLD ME HE WAS HERE.

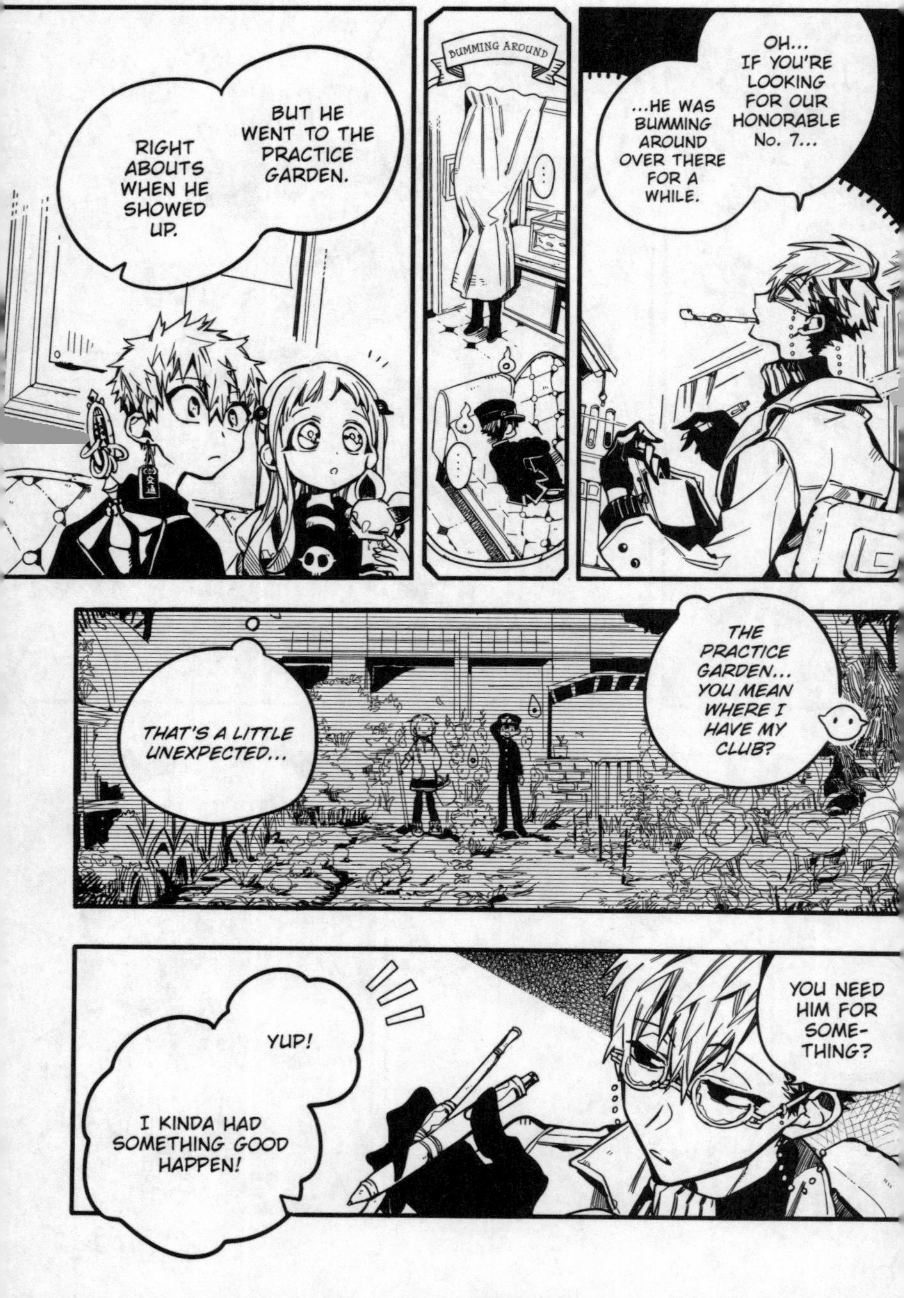
OH... IF YOU'RE LOOKING FOR OUR HONORABLE No. 7...
...HE WAS BUMMING AROUND OVER THERE FOR A WHILE.
BUMMING AROUND
BUT HE WENT TO THE PRACTICE GARDEN.
RIGHT ABOUTS WHEN HE SHOWED UP.
THE PRACTICE GARDEN... YOU MEAN WHERE I HAVE MY CLUB?
THAT'S A LITTLE UNEXPECTED...
YOU NEED HIM FOR SOME-THING?
YUP!
I KINDA HAD SOMETHING GOOD HAPPEN!

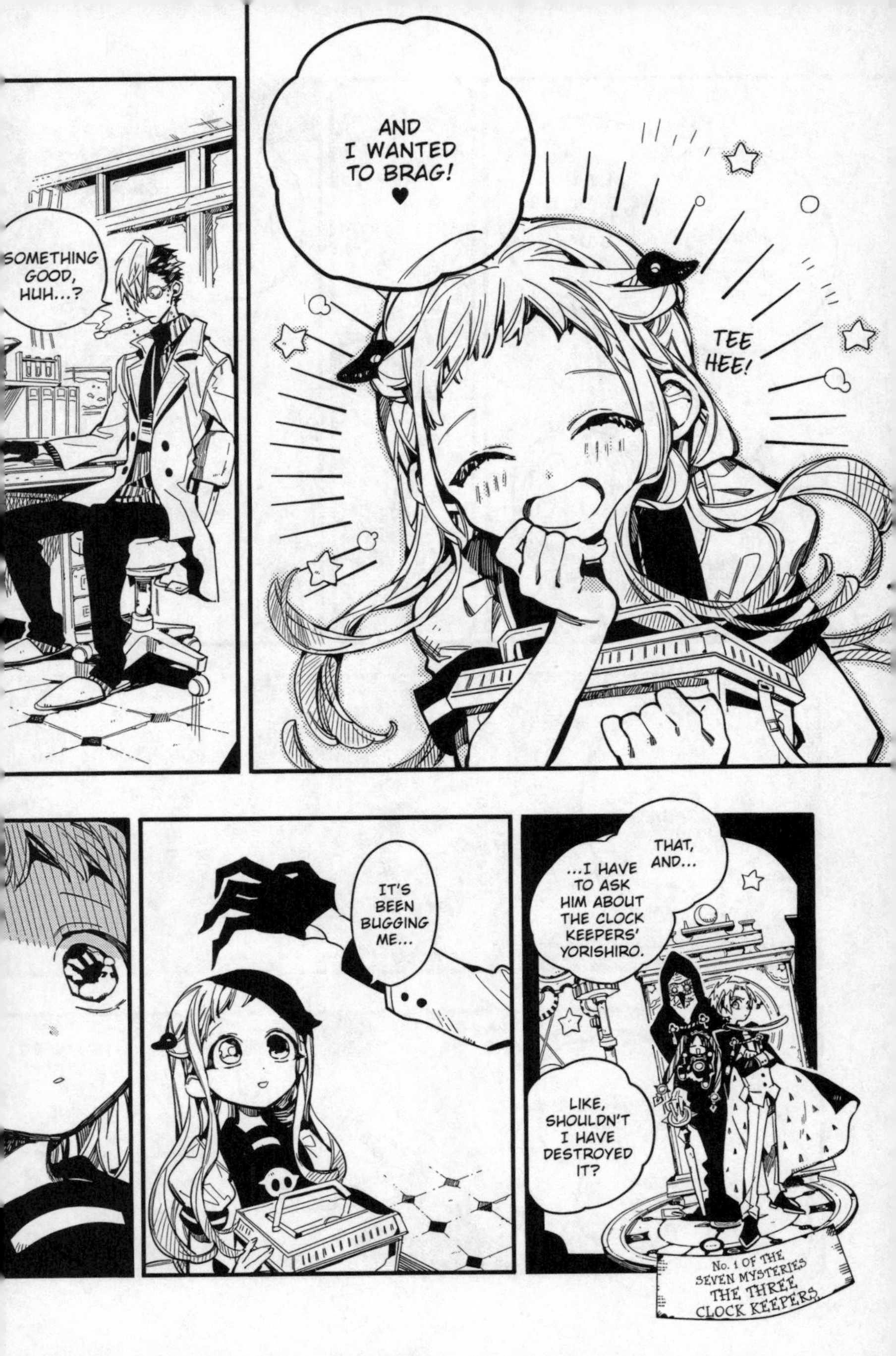
AND I WANTED TO BRAG! ♥
TEE HEE!
SOMETHING GOOD, HUH...?
THAT, AND...
...I HAVE TO ASK HIM ABOUT THE CLOCK KEEPERS' YORISHIRO.
LIKE, SHOULDN'T I HAVE DESTROYED IT?
No. 1 OF THE SEVEN MYSTERIES THE THREE CLOCK KEEPERS
IT'S BEEN BUGGING ME...

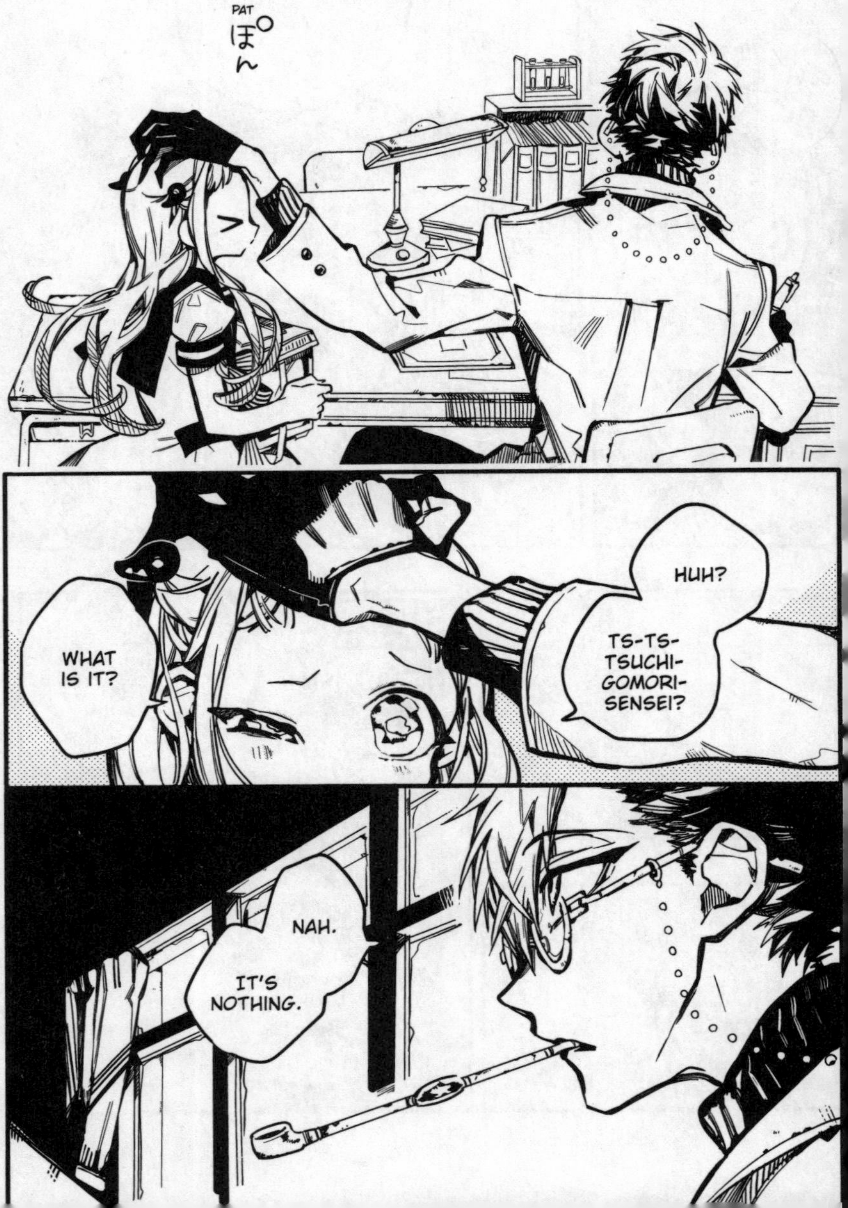
PAT
ぽん
HUH?
TS-TS-TSUCHIGOMORI-SENSEI?
WHAT IS IT?
NAH.
IT'S NOTHING.

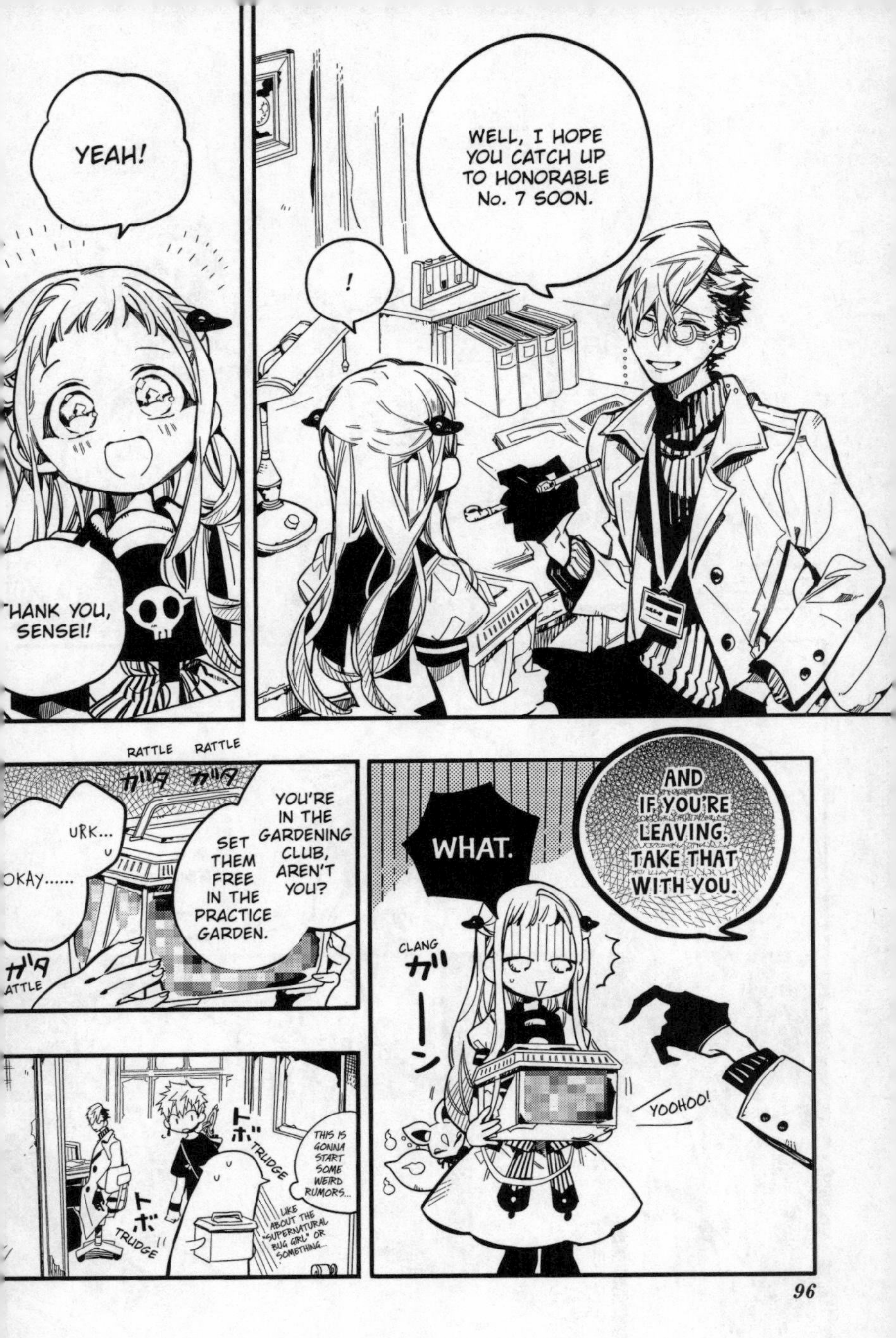
WELL, I HOPE YOU CATCH UP TO HONORABLE No. 7 SOON.
!
YEAH!
THANK YOU, SENSEI!
AND IF YOU'RE LEAVING, TAKE THAT WITH YOU.
WHAT.
CLANG
YOOHOO!
RATTLE RATTLE
YOU'RE IN THE GARDENING CLUB, AREN'T YOU?
SET THEM FREE IN THE PRACTICE GARDEN.
URK...
OKAY......
RATTLE
TRUDGE
THIS IS GONNA START SOME WEIRD RUMORS...
LIKE ABOUT THE "SUPERNATURAL BUG GIRL" OR SOMETHING...
TRUDGE

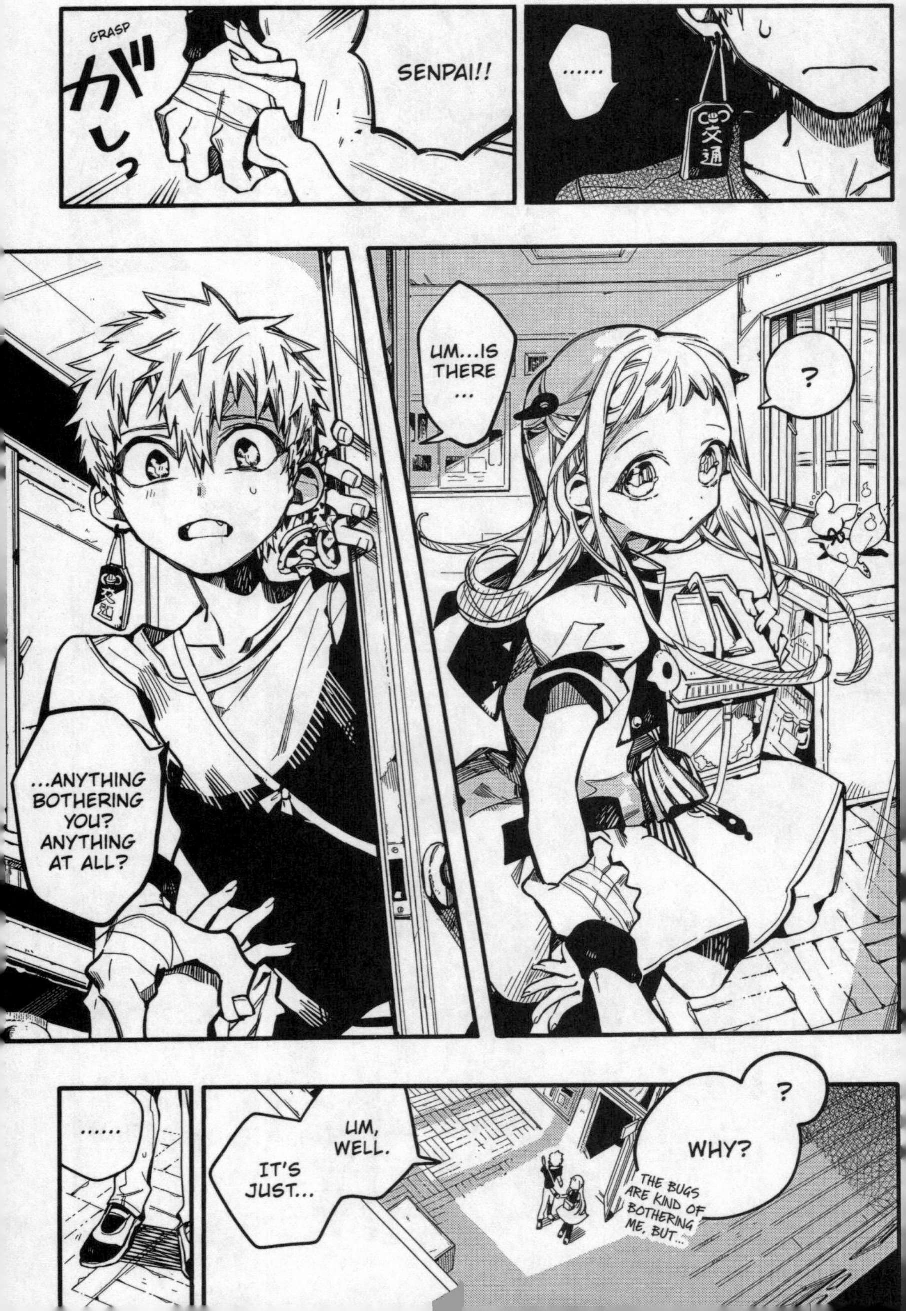
......
SENPAI!!
GRASP
ガしっ
?
UM...IS THERE ...
...ANYTHING BOTHERING YOU? ANYTHING AT ALL?
?
WHY?
THE BUGS ARE KIND OF BOTHERING ME, BUT...
UM, WELL.
IT'S JUST...
......

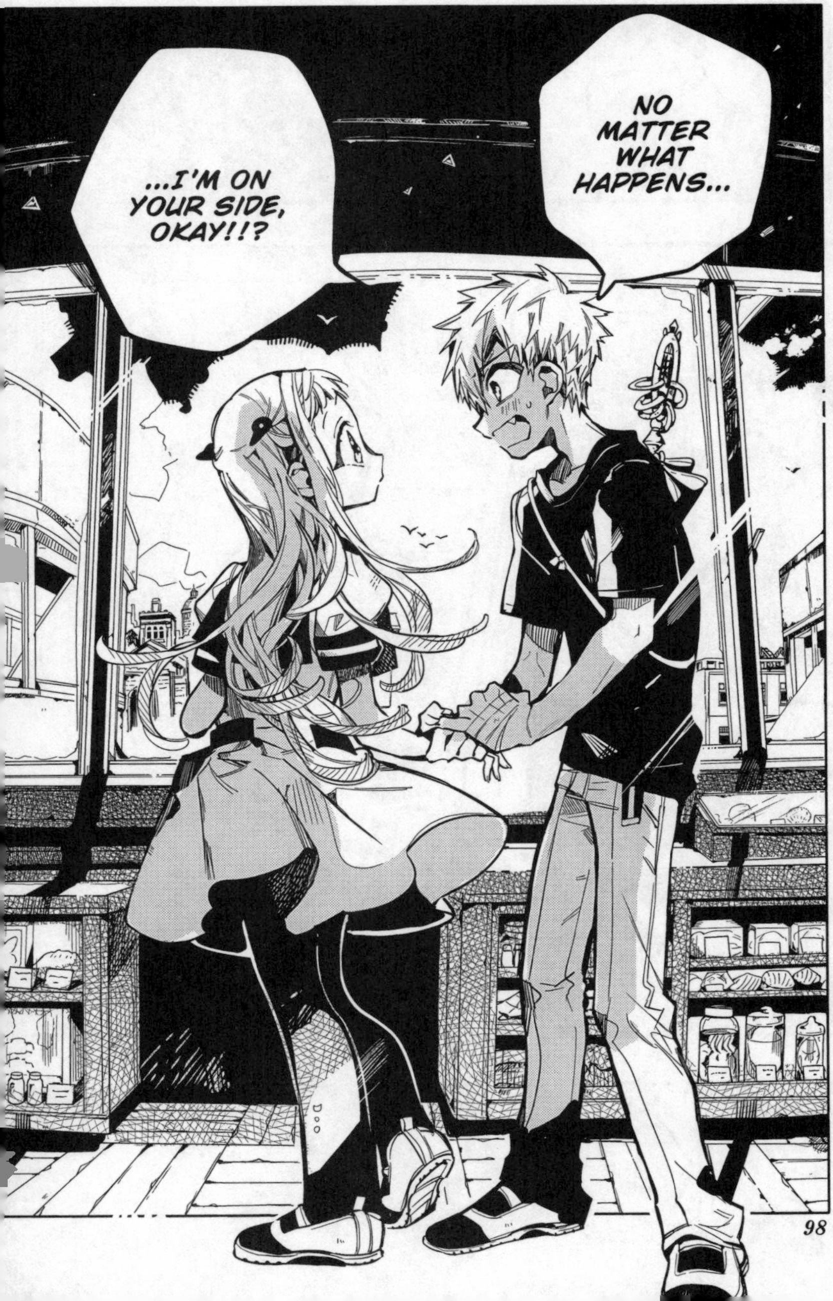
NO MATTER WHAT HAPPENS...
...I'M ON YOUR SIDE, OKAY!!?

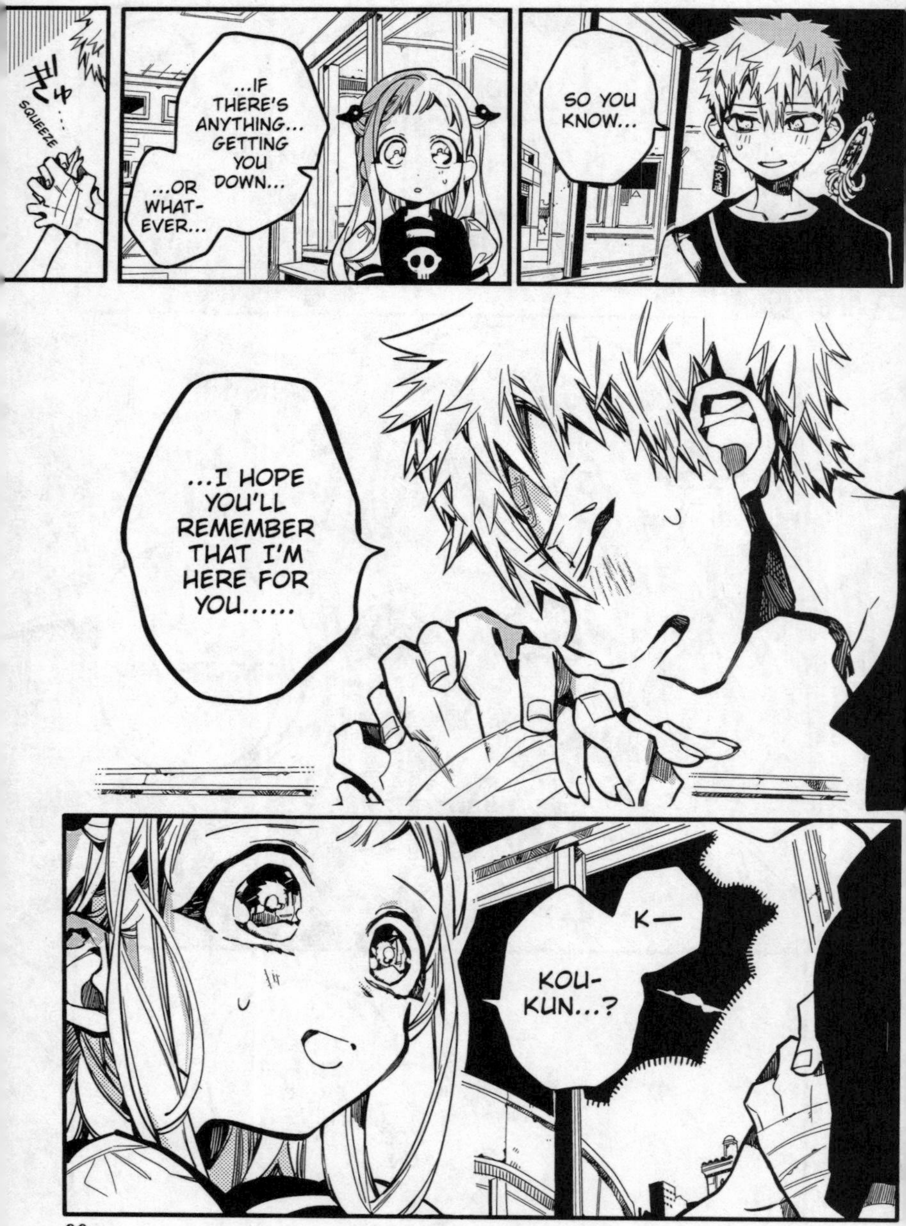
SO YOU KNOW...
...IF THERE'S ANYTHING... GETTING YOU DOWN...
...OR WHATEVER...
ぎゅ…
SQUEEZE
...I HOPE YOU'LL REMEMBER THAT I'M HERE FOR YOU......
K—
KOU-KUN...?

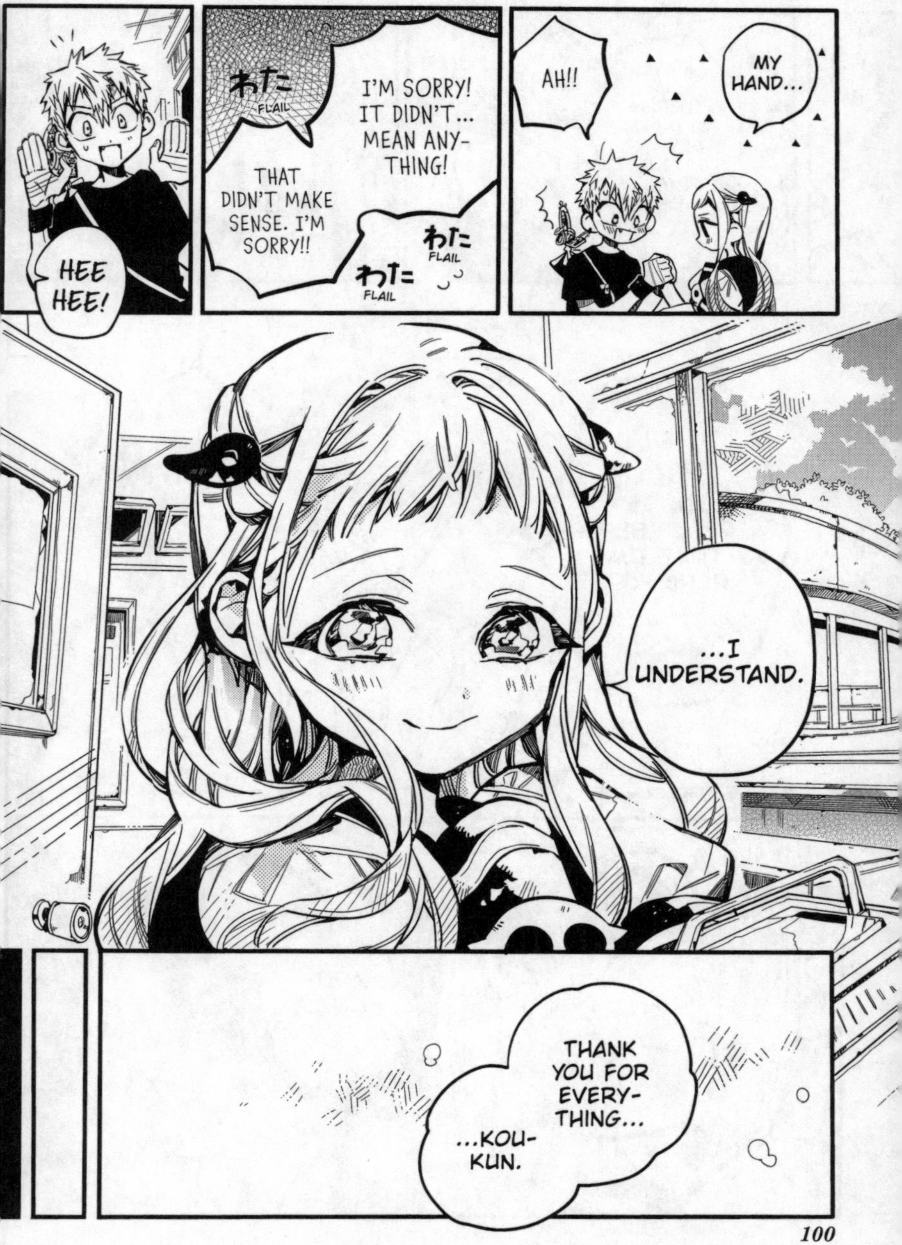
MY HAND...
AH!!
I'M SORRY! IT DIDN'T... MEAN ANY-THING!
わた FLAIL
THAT DIDN'T MAKE SENSE. I'M SORRY!!
わた FLAIL
わた FLAIL
HEE HEE!
...I UNDERSTAND.
THANK YOU FOR EVERY-THING...
...KOU-KUN.

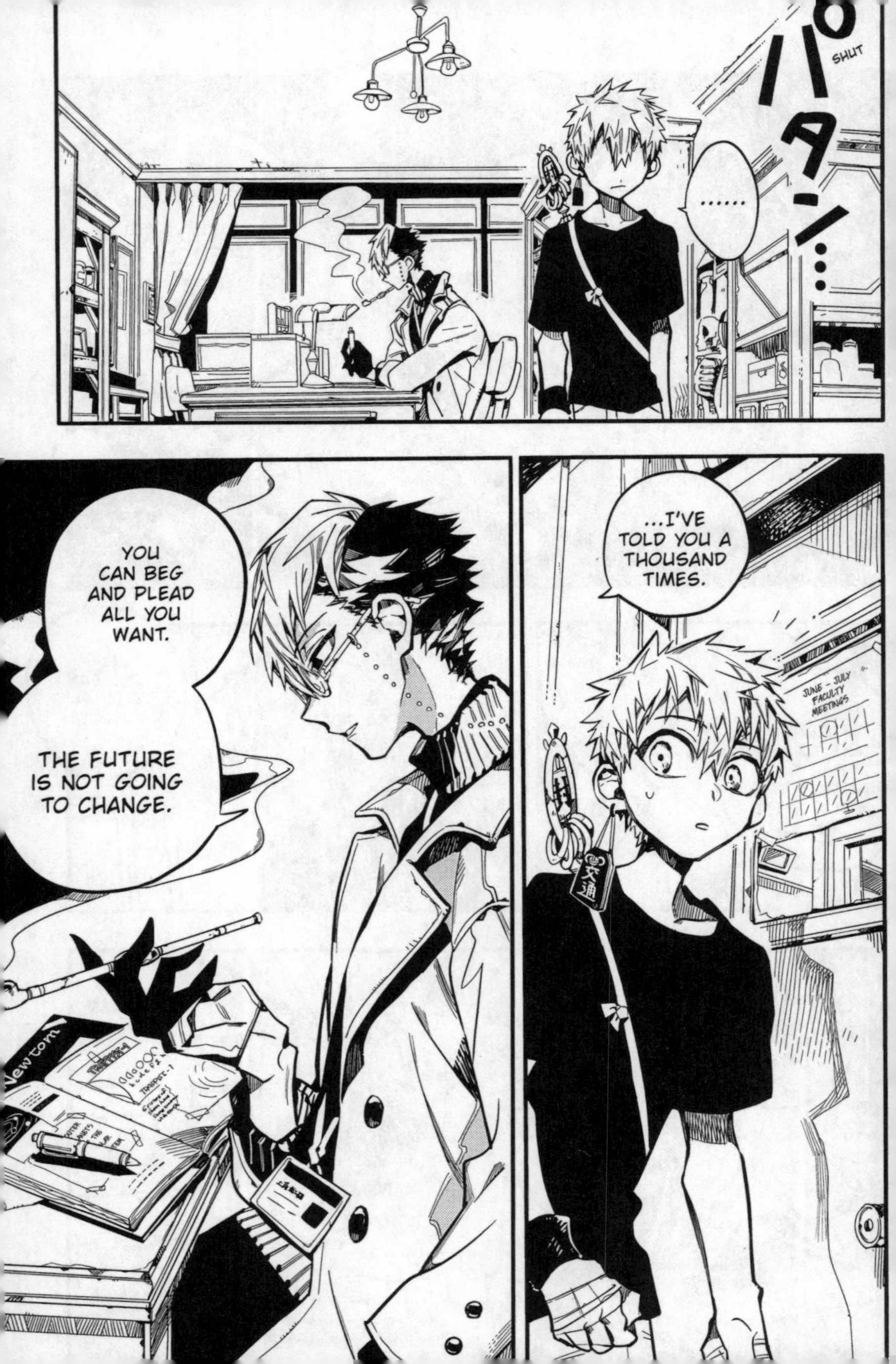

SHUT
......
...I'VE TOLD YOU A THOUSAND TIMES.
JUNE - JULY FACULTY MEETINGS
YOU CAN BEG AND PLEAD ALL YOU WANT.
THE FUTURE IS NOT GOING TO CHANGE.
Newton

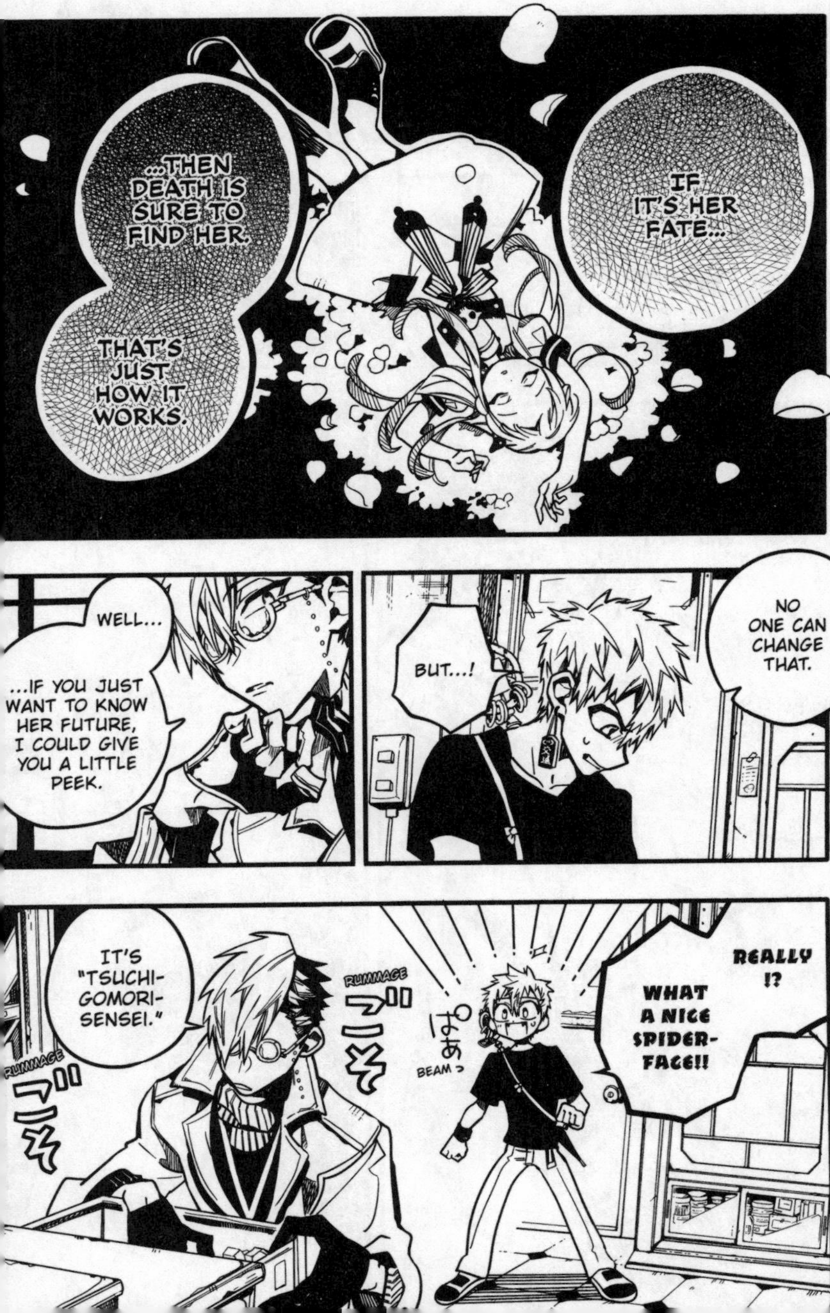
IF IT'S HER FATE...
...THEN DEATH IS SURE TO FIND HER.
THAT'S JUST HOW IT WORKS.
NO ONE CAN CHANGE THAT.
BUT...!
WELL...
...IF YOU JUST WANT TO KNOW HER FUTURE, I COULD GIVE YOU A LITTLE PEEK.
REALLY!?
WHAT A NICE SPIDER-FACE!!
ぱあ
BEAM
RUMMAGE
IT'S "TSUCHI-GOMORI-SENSEI."
RUMMAGE

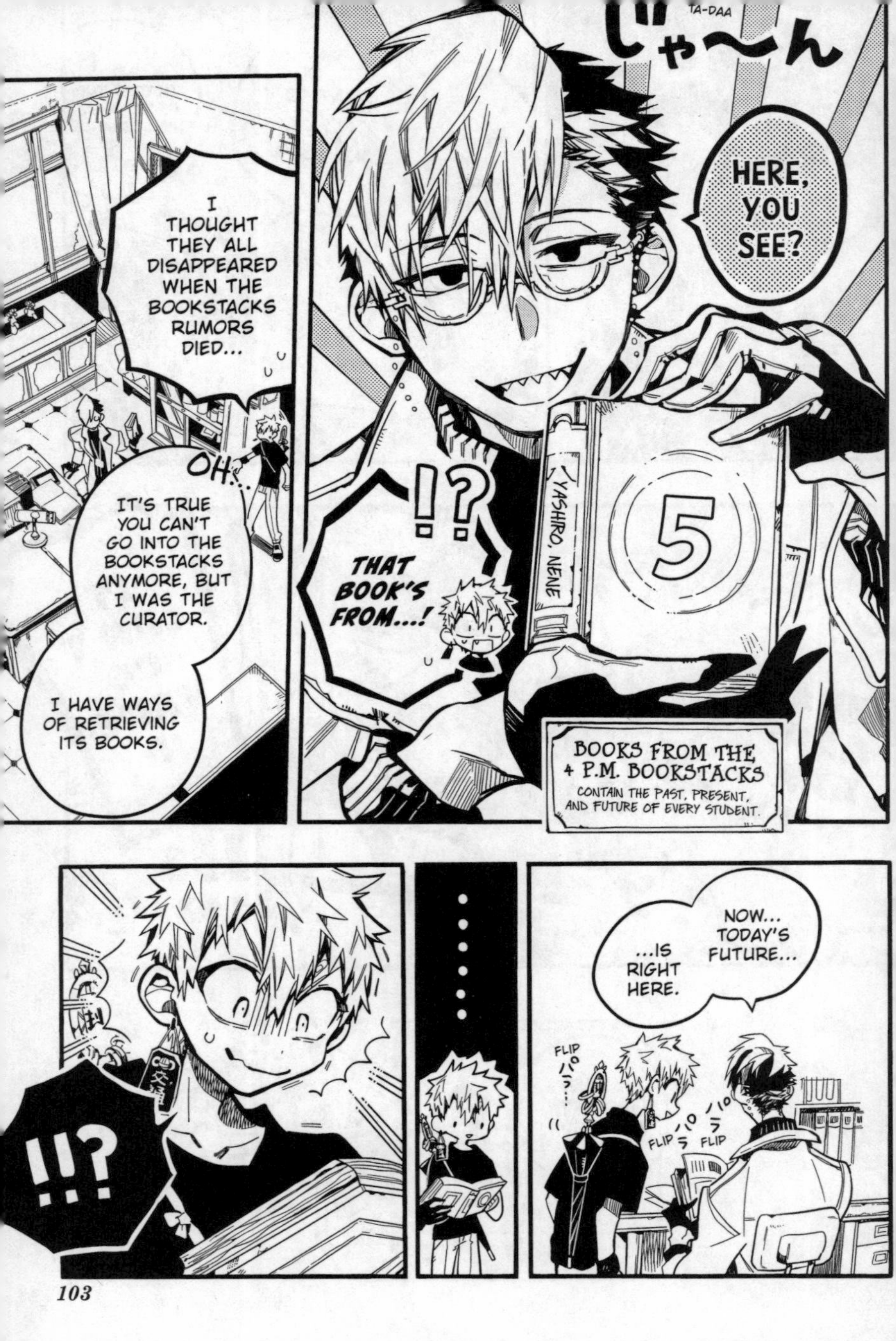
TA-DAA
じゃ〜ん
HERE, YOU SEE?
!?
THAT BOOK'S FROM...!
YASHIRO, NENE
5
BOOKS FROM THE 4 P.M. BOOKSTACKS CONTAIN THE PAST, PRESENT, AND FUTURE OF EVERY STUDENT.
I THOUGHT THEY ALL DISAPPEARED WHEN THE BOOKSTACKS RUMORS DIED...
OH...
IT'S TRUE YOU CAN'T GO INTO THE BOOKSTACKS ANYMORE, BUT I WAS THE CURATOR.
I HAVE WAYS OF RETRIEVING ITS BOOKS.
NOW... TODAY'S FUTURE...
...IS RIGHT HERE.
FLIP パラ...
パラ FLIP
パラ FLIP
......
!!?

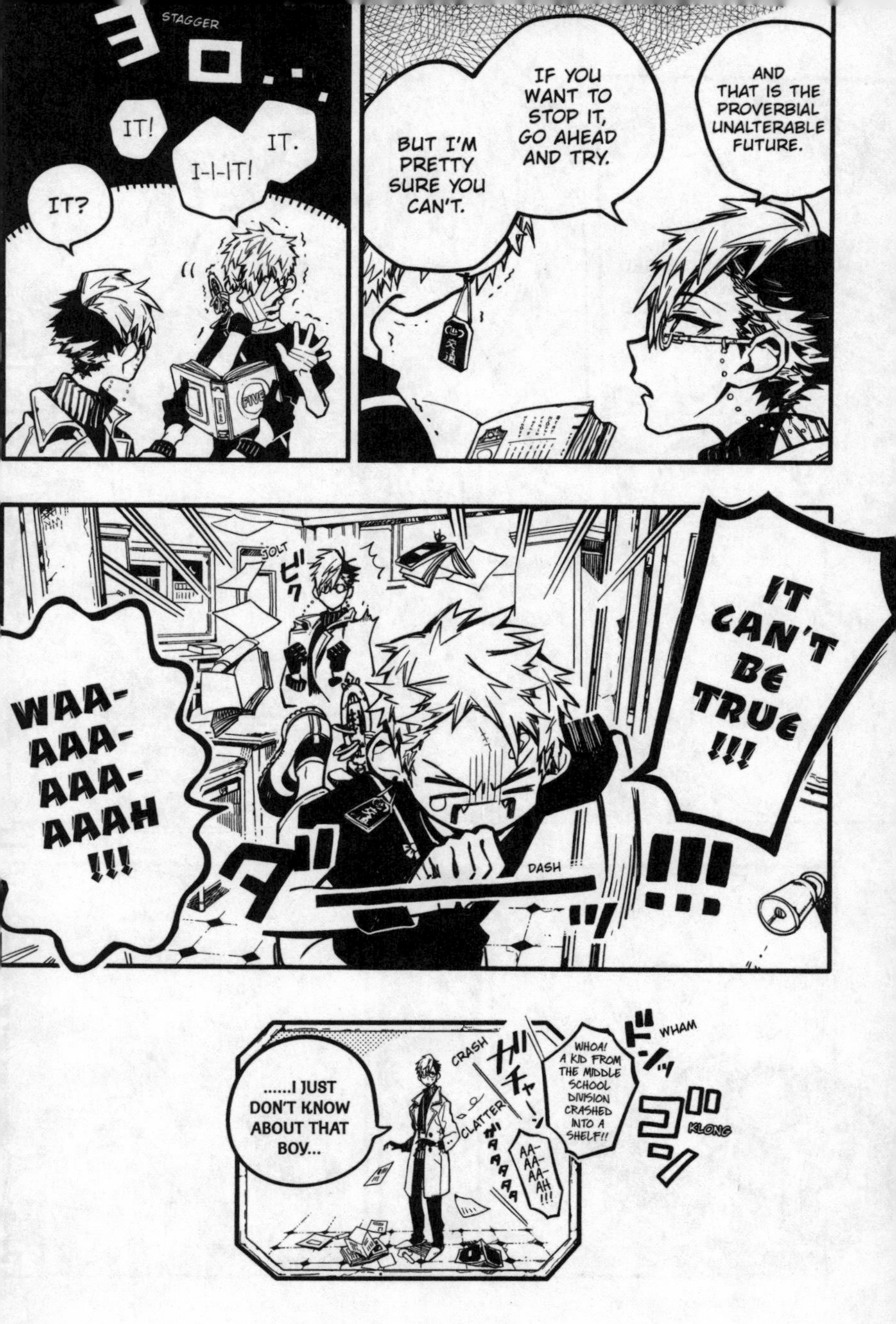
AND THAT IS THE PROVERBIAL UNALTERABLE FUTURE.
IF YOU WANT TO STOP IT, GO AHEAD AND TRY.
BUT I'M PRETTY SURE YOU CAN'T.
STAGGER
IT.
I-I-IT!
IT!
IT?
IT CAN'T BE TRUE!!!
DASH
JOLT
WAA-AAA-AAA-AAAH!!!
WHAM
KLONG
WHOA! A KID FROM THE MIDDLE SCHOOL DIVISION CRASHED INTO A SHELF!!
AA-AA-AA-AH!!!
CRASH
CLATTER
......I JUST DON'T KNOW ABOUT THAT BOY...

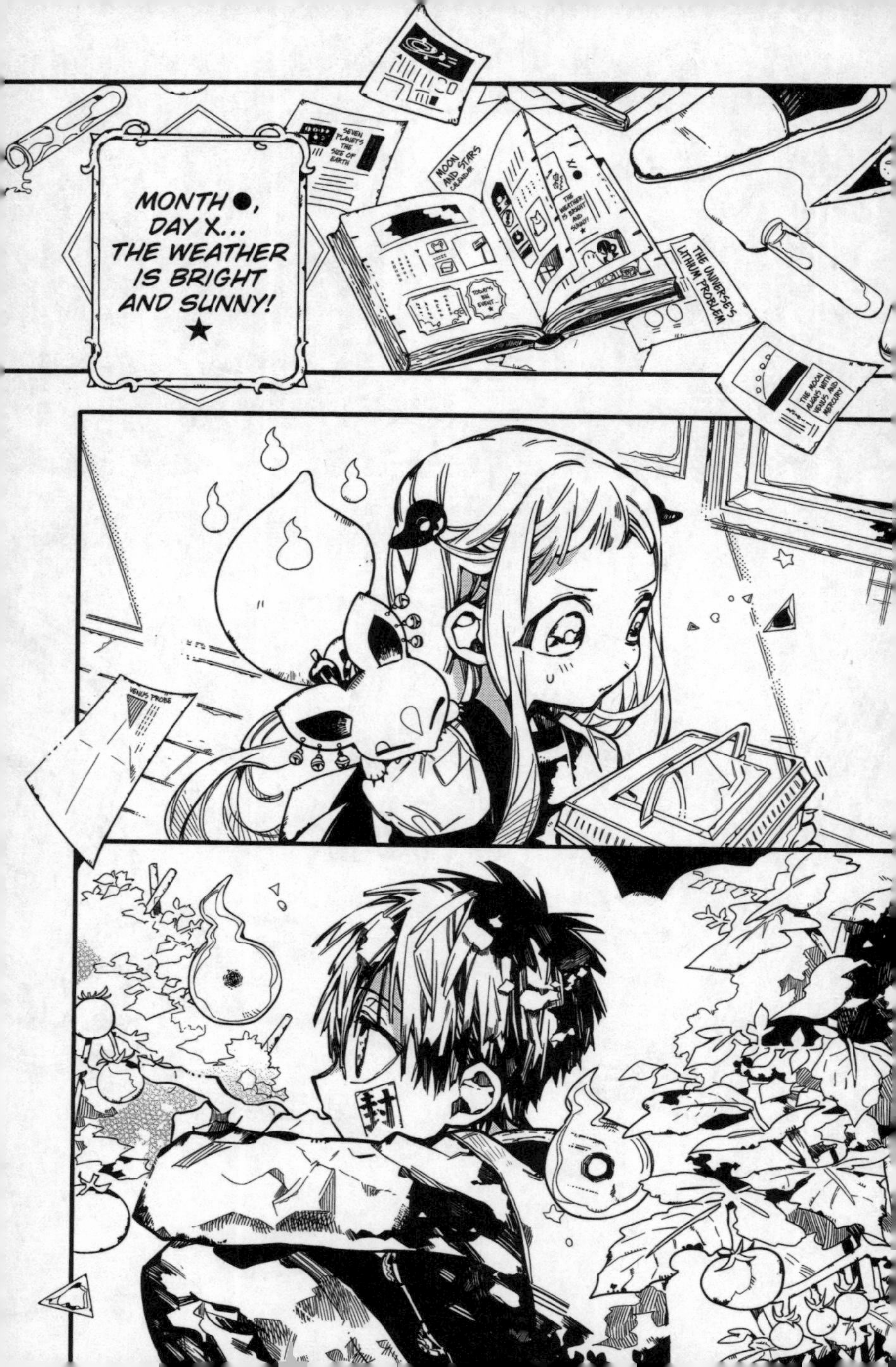
THE MOON ALIGNS WITH VENUS AND MERCURY
THE UNIVERSE'S LITHIUM PROBLEM
THE WEATHER IS BRIGHT AND SUNNY! ★
MOON AND STARS CALENDAR
TODAY'S BIG EVENT... ★
SEVEN PLANETS THE SIZE OF EARTH
MONTH ●, DAY X... THE WEATHER IS BRIGHT AND SUNNY! ★
VENUS PROBE

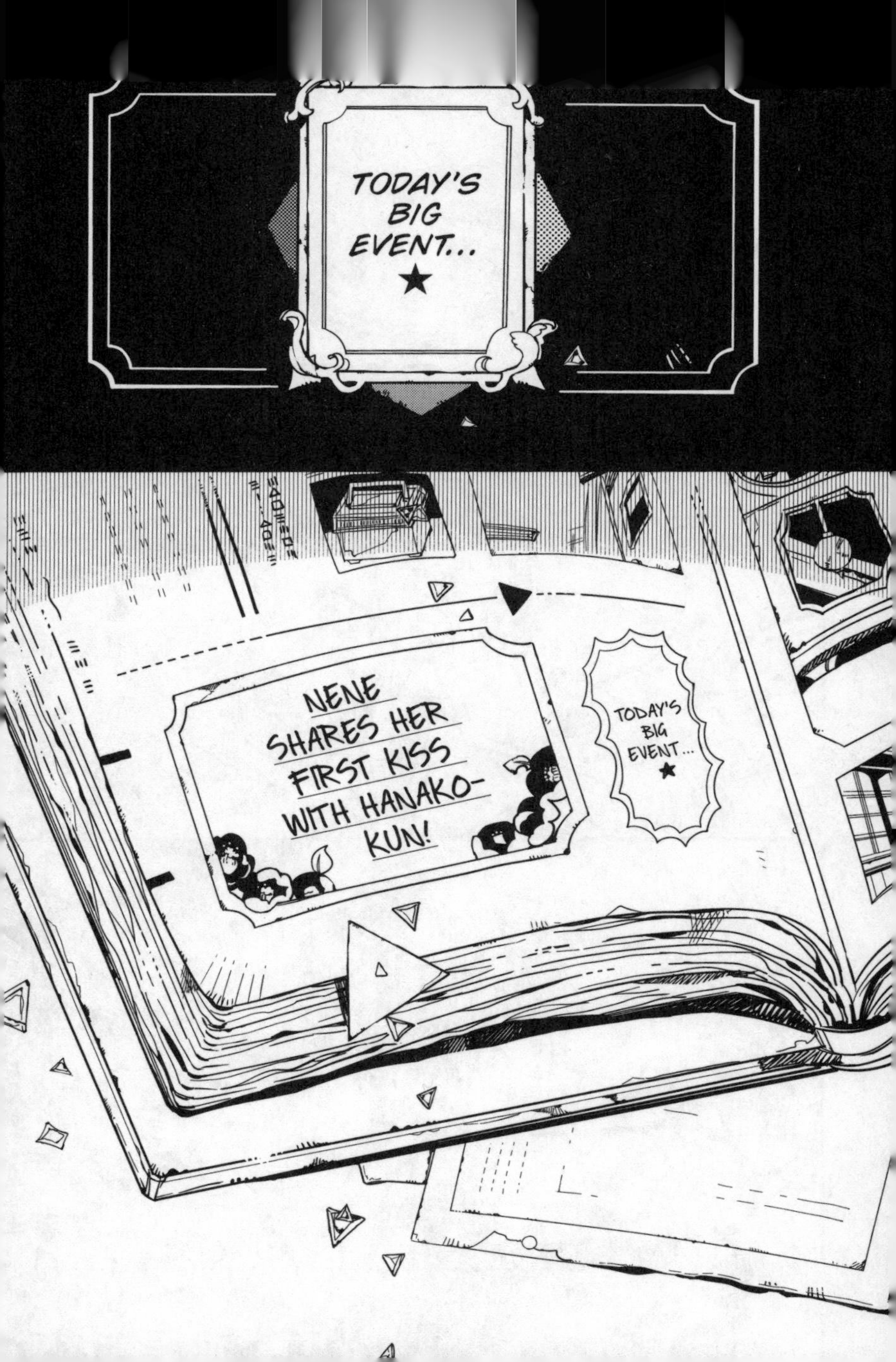

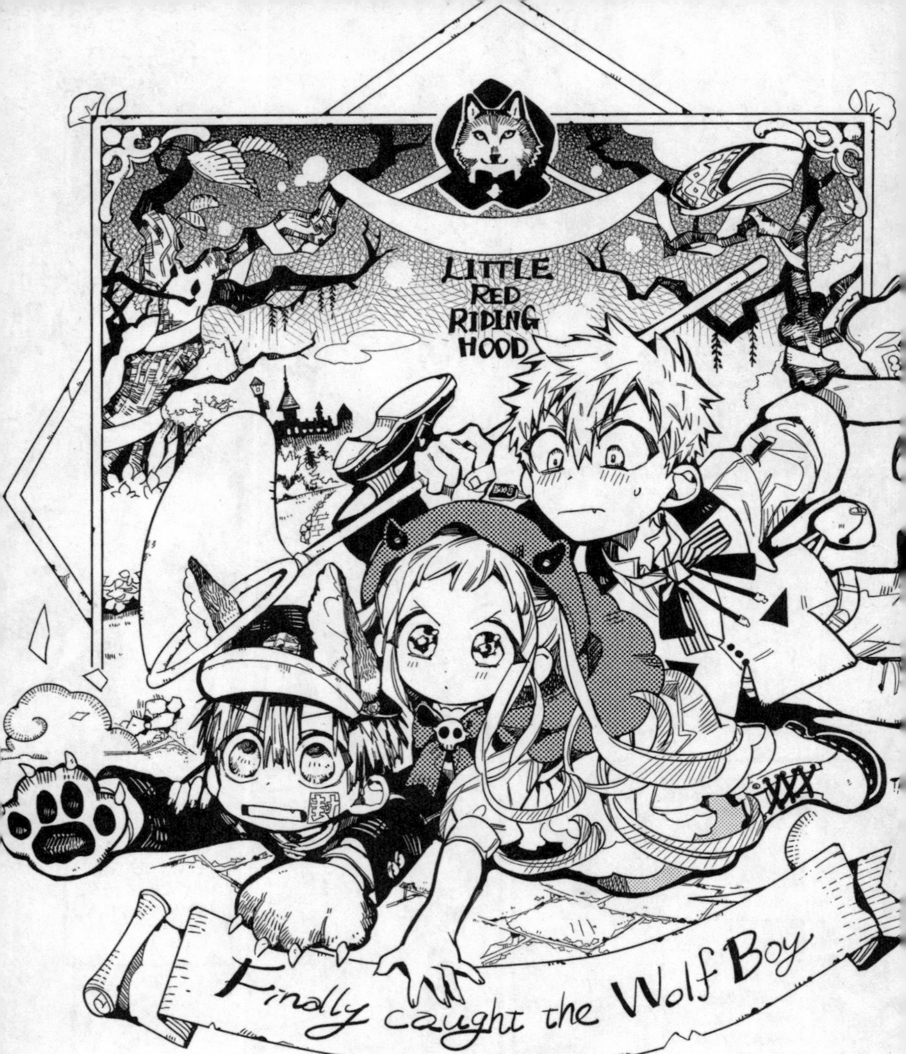
LITTLE RED RIDING HOOD
Finally caught the Wolf Boy

SPOOK 29

SEARCHING (PART 2)

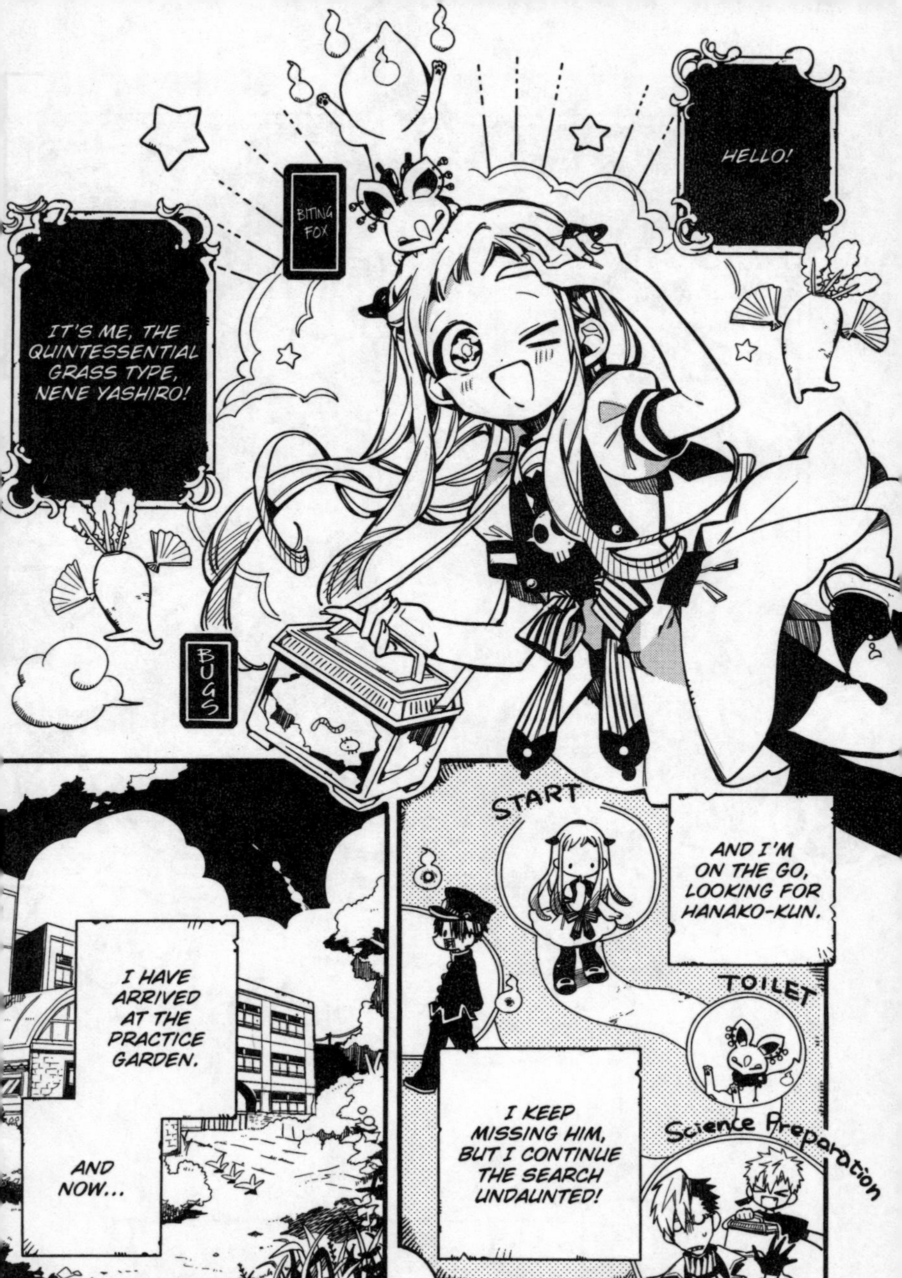
HELLO!
BITING FOX
IT'S ME, THE QUINTESSENTIAL GRASS TYPE, NENE YASHIRO!
BUGS
START
AND I'M ON THE GO, LOOKING FOR HANAKO-KUN.
TOILET
Science Preparation Room
I KEEP MISSING HIM, BUT I CONTINUE THE SEARCH UNDAUNTED!
I HAVE ARRIVED AT THE PRACTICE GARDEN.
AND NOW...

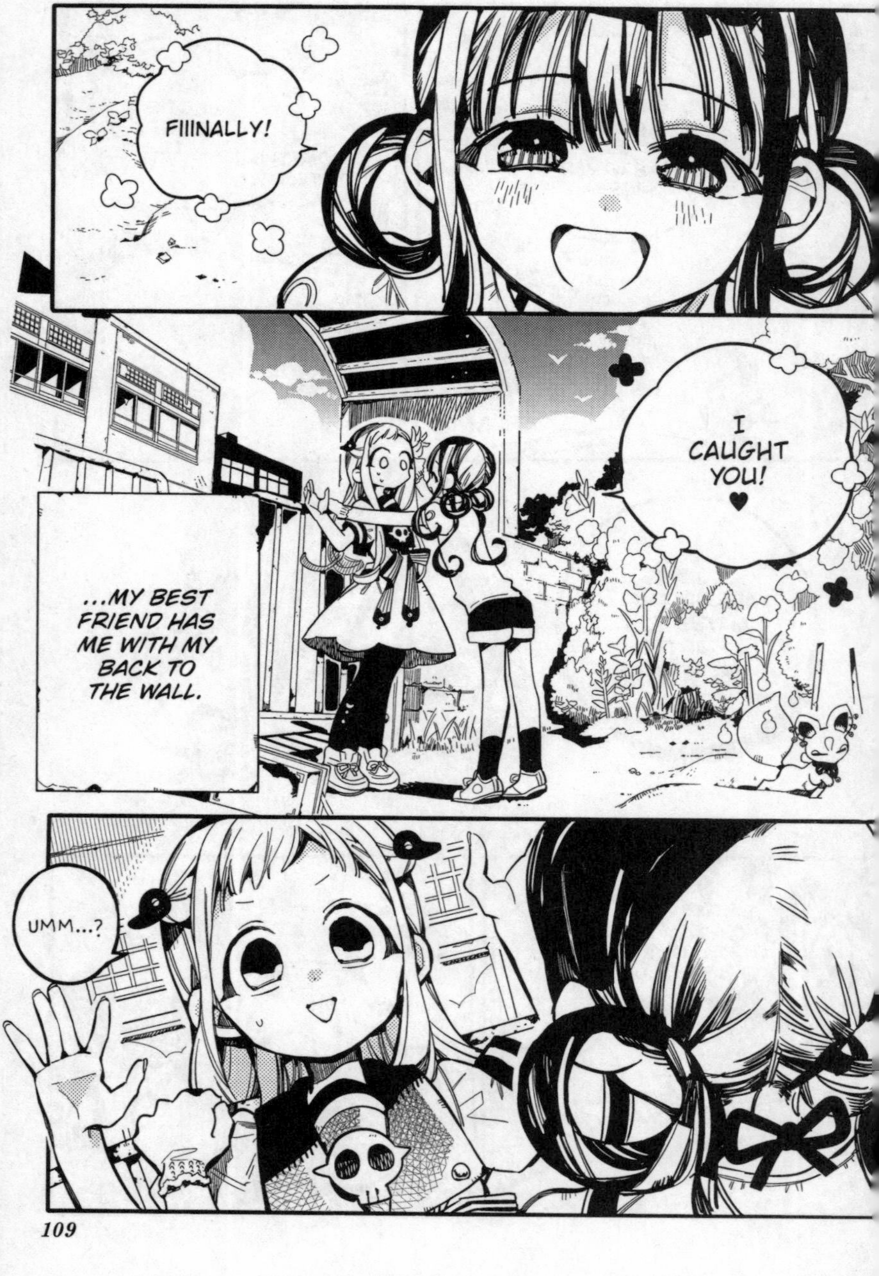
FIIINALLY!
I CAUGHT YOU! ♥
...MY BEST FRIEND HAS ME WITH MY BACK TO THE WALL.
UMM...?

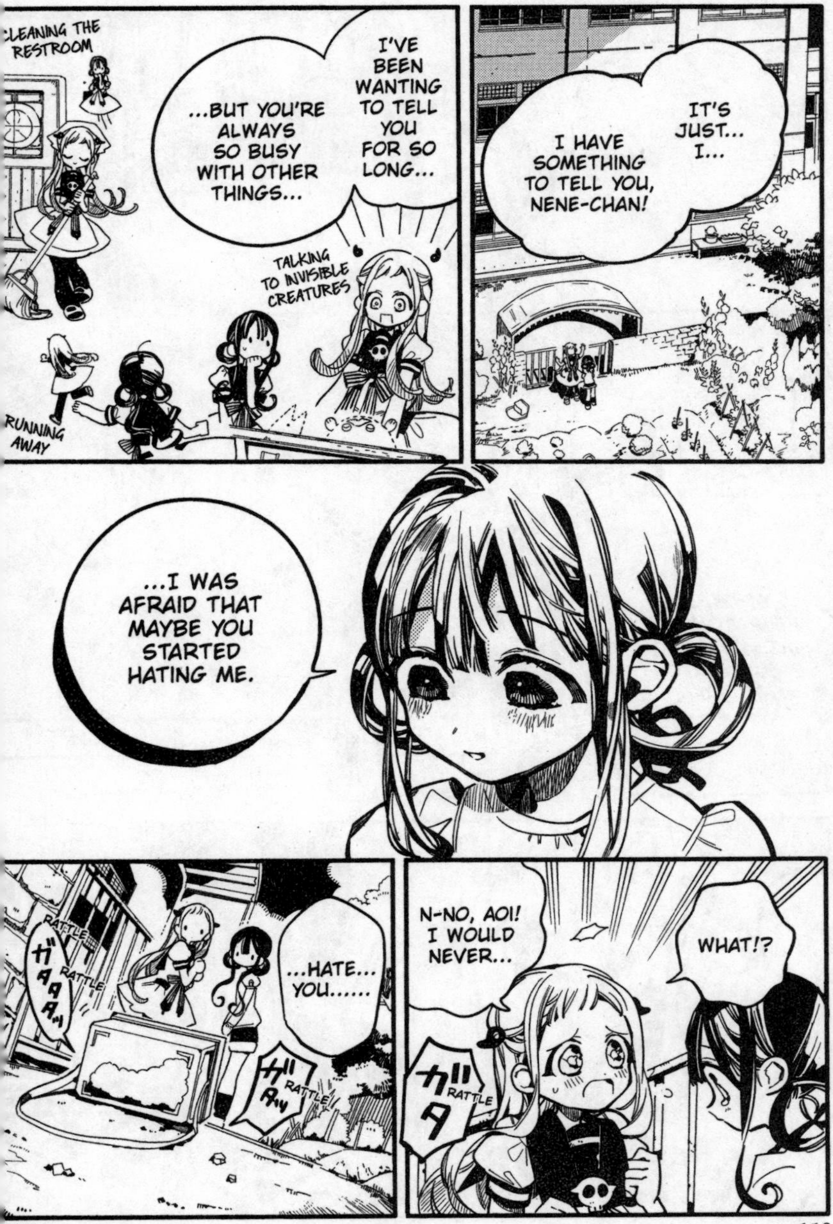
IT'S JUST... I...
I HAVE SOMETHING TO TELL YOU, NENE-CHAN!
I'VE BEEN WANTING TO TELL YOU FOR SO LONG...
...BUT YOU'RE ALWAYS SO BUSY WITH OTHER THINGS...
CLEANING THE RESTROOM
TALKING TO INVISIBLE CREATURES
RUNNING AWAY
...I WAS AFRAID THAT MAYBE YOU STARTED HATING ME.
WHAT!?
N-NO, AOI! I WOULD NEVER...
カタ
RATTLE
...HATE... YOU......
ガタタタッ
RATTLE
RATTLE
ガタッ
RATTLE

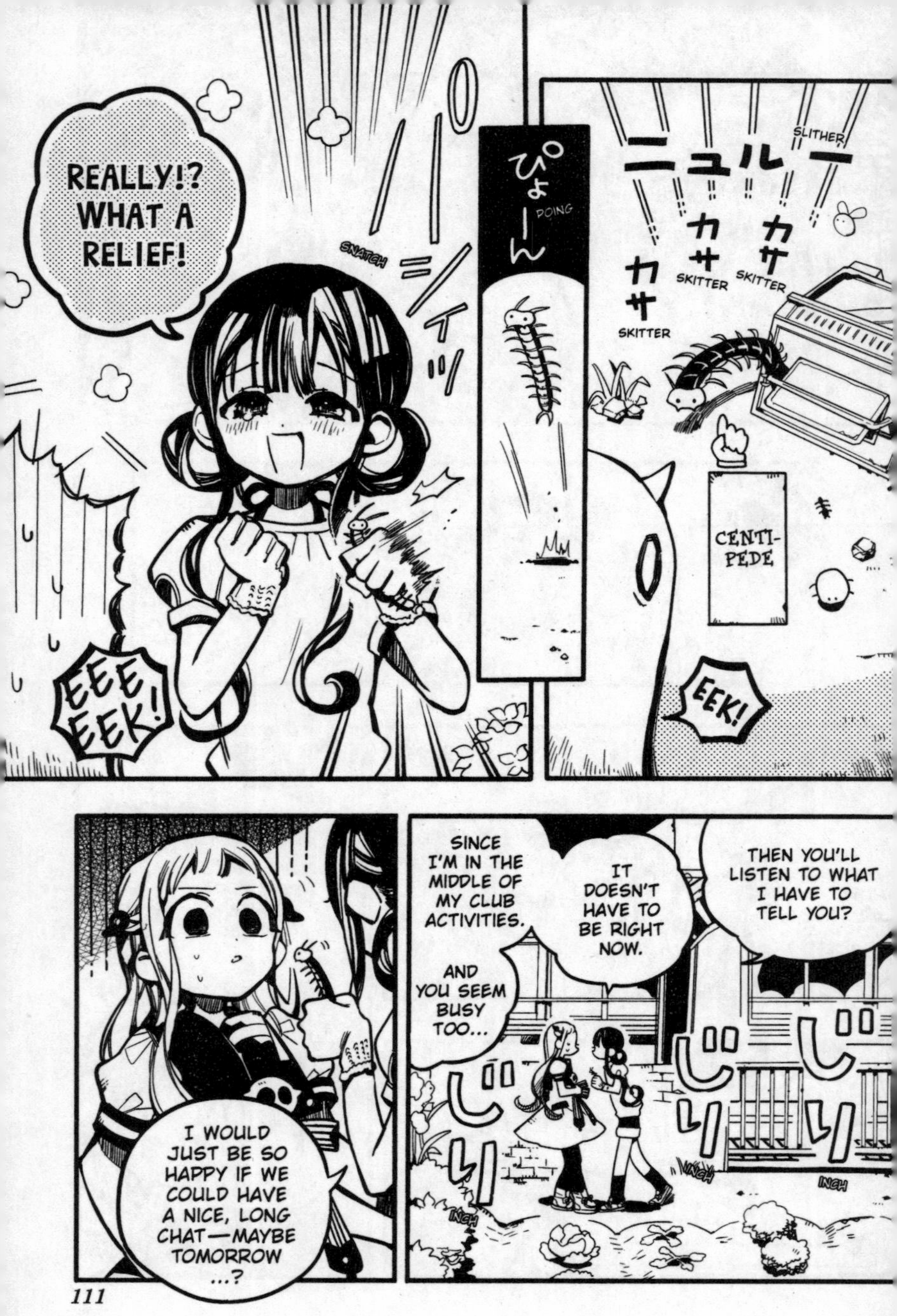

ニュルー
SLITHER
カサ
SKITTER
カサ
SKITTER
カサ
SKITTER
CENTI-PEDE
EEK!
ぴょーん
POING
SNATCH
REALLY!? WHAT A RELIEF!
EEEEEK!
THEN YOU'LL LISTEN TO WHAT I HAVE TO TELL YOU?
IT DOESN'T HAVE TO BE RIGHT NOW.
SINCE I'M IN THE MIDDLE OF MY CLUB ACTIVITIES.
AND YOU SEEM BUSY TOO...
INCH
INCH
INCH
I WOULD JUST BE SO HAPPY IF WE COULD HAVE A NICE, LONG CHAT—MAYBE TOMORROW ...?

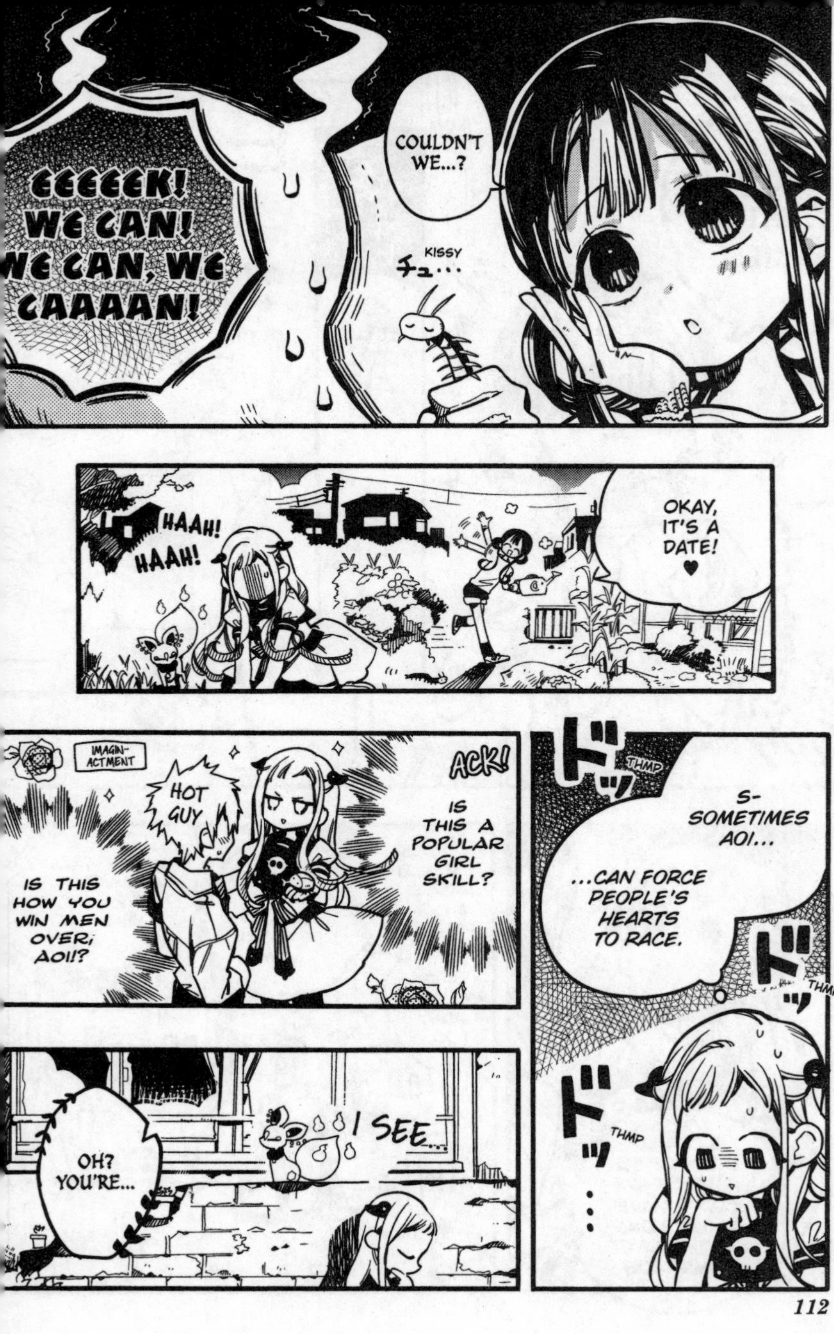
COULDN'T WE...?
KISSY
チュ…
EEEEEK! WE CAN! WE CAN, WE CAAAAN!
OKAY, IT'S A DATE! ♥
HAAH! HAAH!
ドッ
THMP
S-SOMETIMES AOI...
...CAN FORCE PEOPLE'S HEARTS TO RACE.
ドッ
THMP
ドッ
THMP
...
ACK!
IS THIS A POPULAR GIRL SKILL?
HOT GUY
IMAGIN-ACTMENT
IS THIS HOW YOU WIN MEN OVER, AOI!?
I SEE...
OH? YOU'RE...

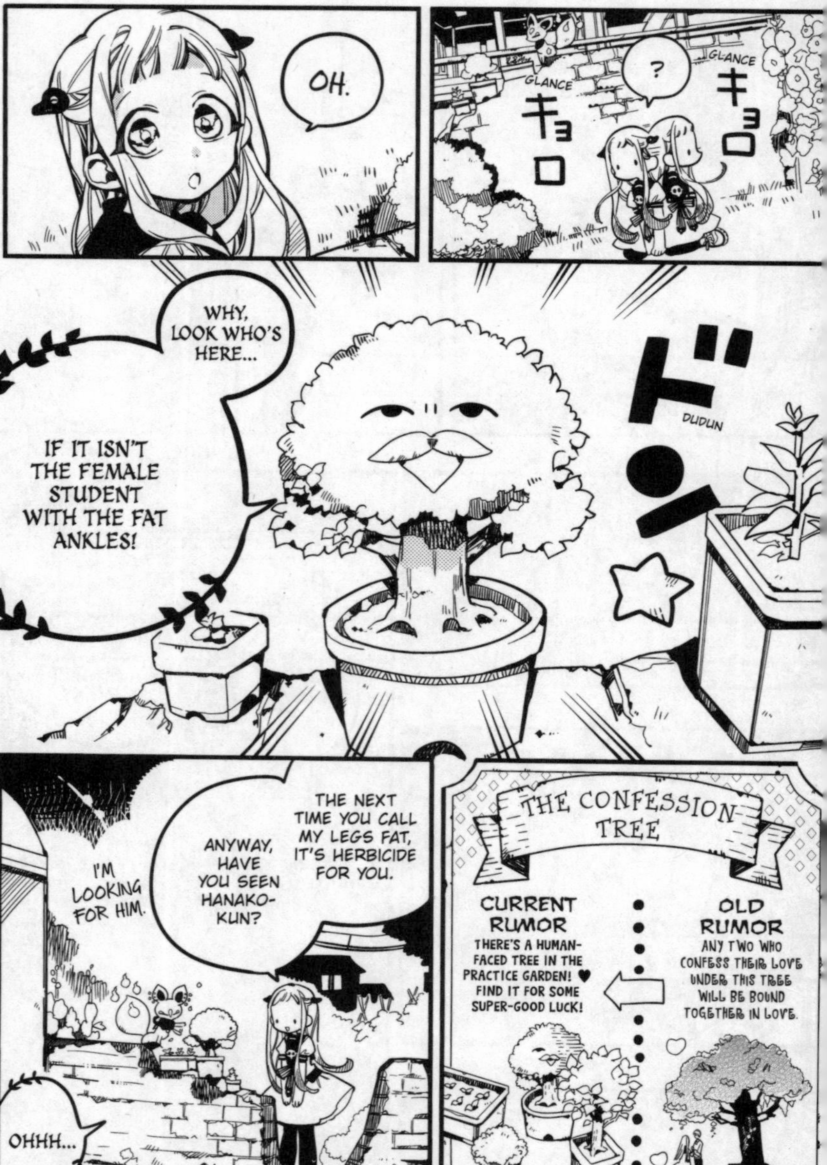
GLANCE
キョロ
?
GLANCE
キョロ
OH.
DUDUN
ドン
WHY, LOOK WHO'S HERE...
IF IT ISN'T THE FEMALE STUDENT WITH THE FAT ANKLES!
THE CONFESSION TREE
OLD RUMOR
ANY TWO WHO CONFESS THEIR LOVE UNDER THIS TREE WILL BE BOUND TOGETHER IN LOVE.
CURRENT RUMOR
THERE'S A HUMAN-FACED TREE IN THE PRACTICE GARDEN! ♥ FIND IT FOR SOME SUPER-GOOD LUCK!
THE NEXT TIME YOU CALL MY LEGS FAT, IT'S HERBICIDE FOR YOU.
ANYWAY, HAVE YOU SEEN HANAKO-KUN?
I'M LOOKING FOR HIM.
OHHH...

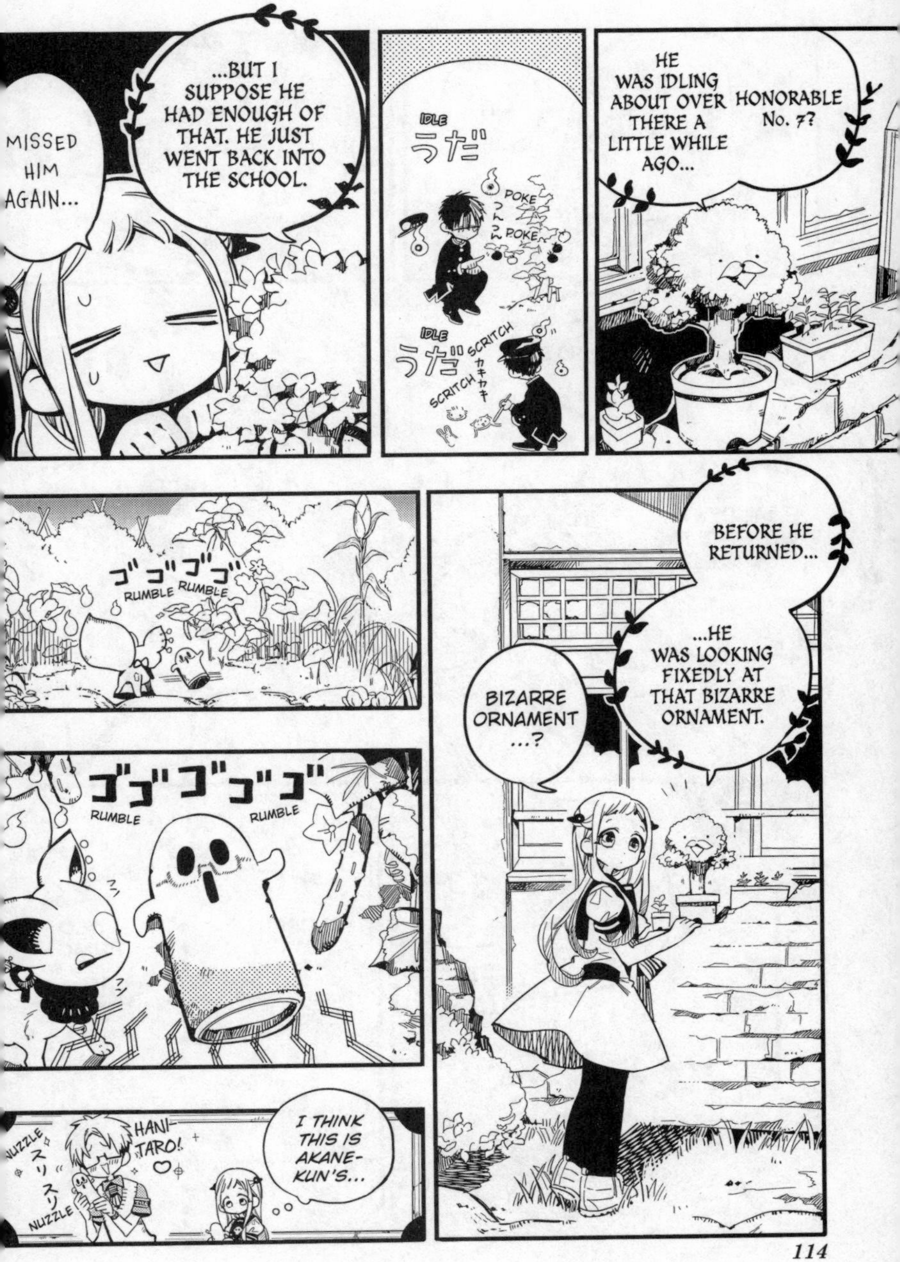
HONORABLE No. 7?
HE WAS IDLING ABOUT OVER THERE A LITTLE WHILE AGO...
IDLE
うだ
POKE
つんつん
POKE
IDLE
うだ
SCRITCH
カキカキ
SCRITCH
...BUT I SUPPOSE HE HAD ENOUGH OF THAT. HE JUST WENT BACK INTO THE SCHOOL.
MISSED HIM AGAIN...
BEFORE HE RETURNED...
...HE WAS LOOKING FIXEDLY AT THAT BIZARRE ORNAMENT.
BIZARRE ORNAMENT...?
ゴゴゴゴ
RUMBLE RUMBLE
ゴゴゴゴ
RUMBLE RUMBLE
I THINK THIS IS AKANE-KUN'S...
HANI-TARO!
NUZZLE
スリスリ
NUZZLE

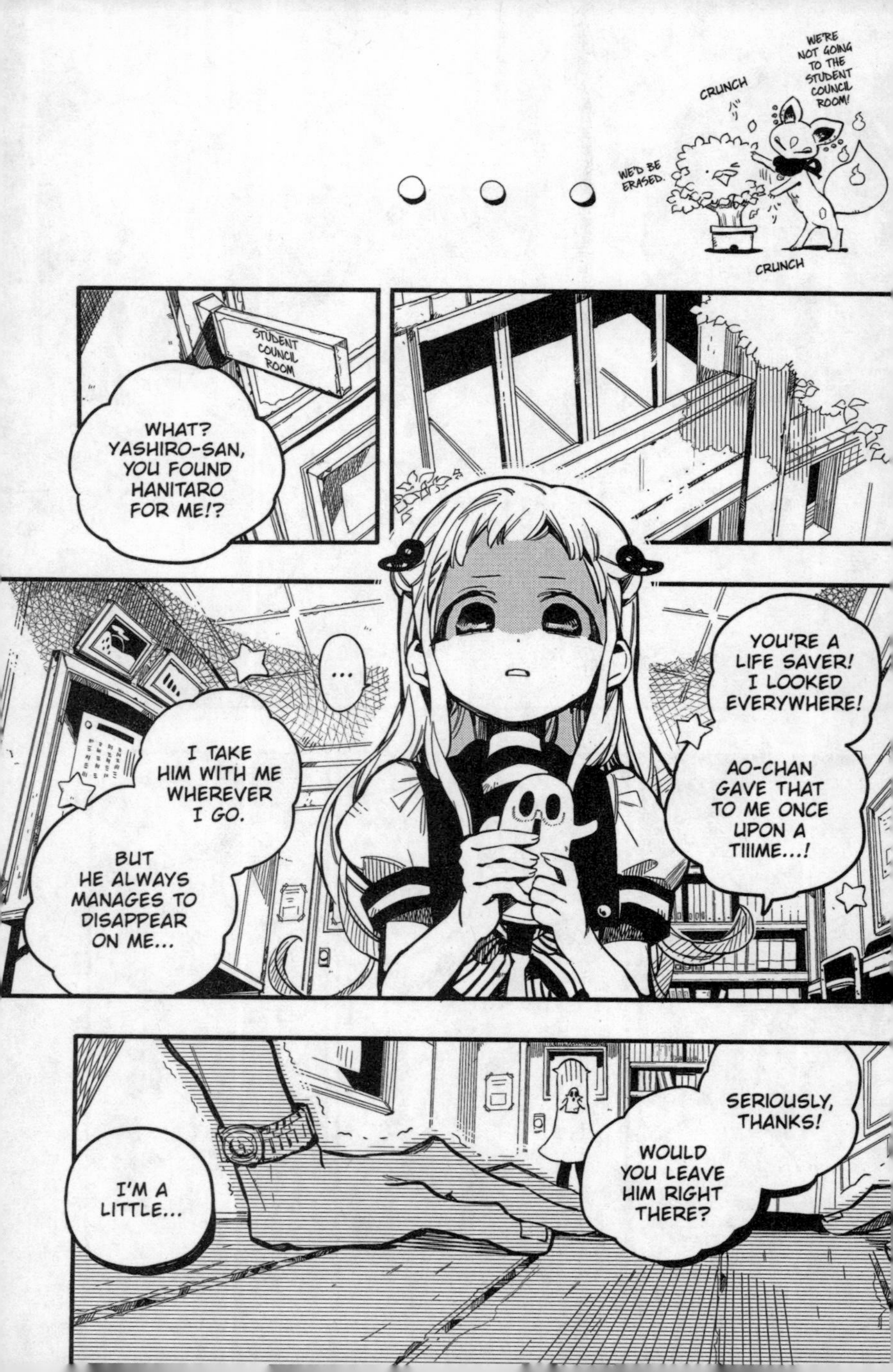
WE'RE NOT GOING TO THE STUDENT COUNCIL ROOM!
CRUNCH
WE'D BE ERASED.
CRUNCH
STUDENT COUNCIL ROOM
WHAT? YASHIRO-SAN, YOU FOUND HANITARO FOR ME!?
YOU'RE A LIFE SAVER! I LOOKED EVERYWHERE!
AO-CHAN GAVE THAT TO ME ONCE UPON A TIIIME...!
...
I TAKE HIM WITH ME WHEREVER I GO.
BUT HE ALWAYS MANAGES TO DISAPPEAR ON ME...
SERIOUSLY, THANKS!
WOULD YOU LEAVE HIM RIGHT THERE?
I'M A LITTLE...

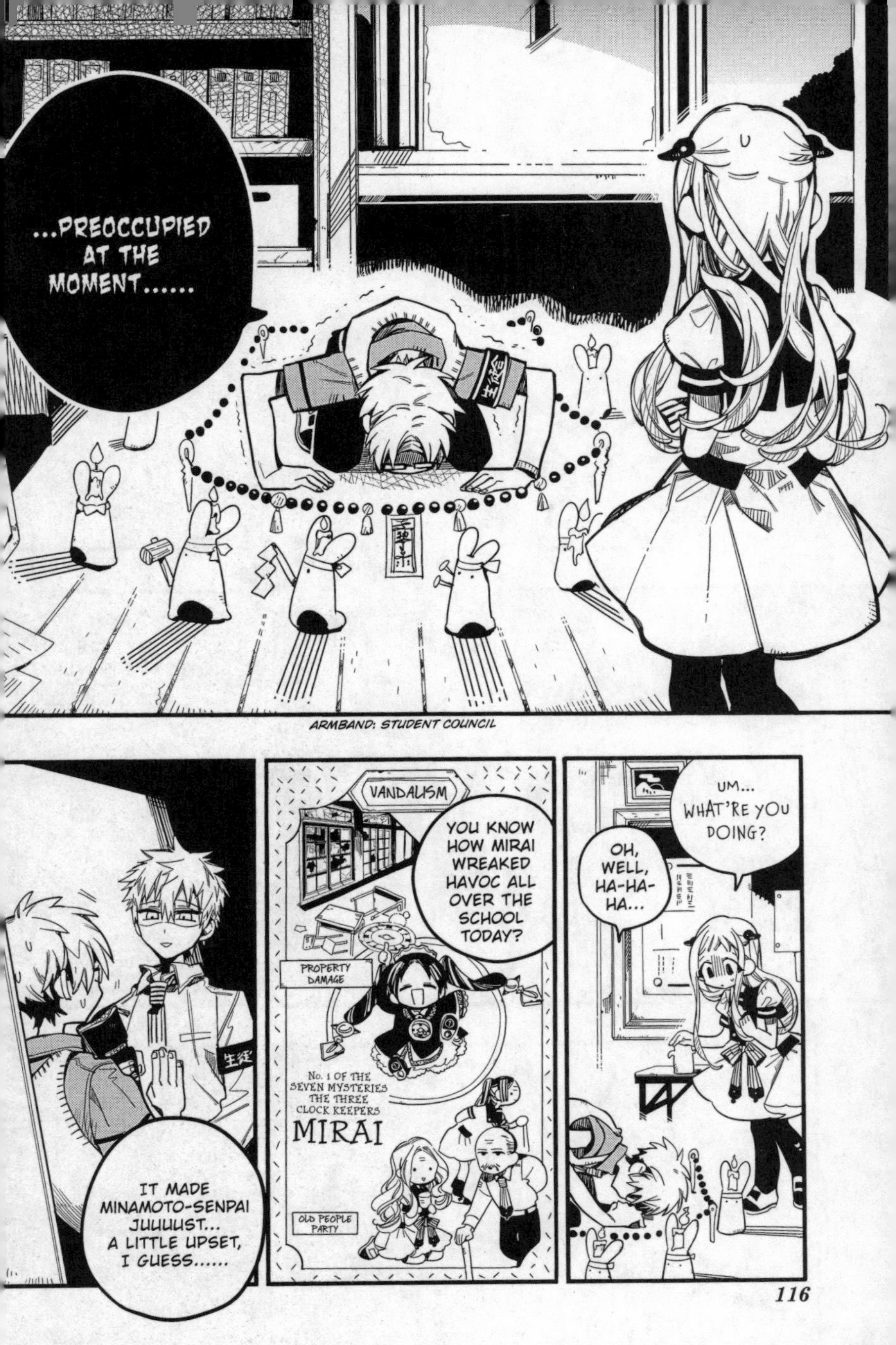
...PREOCCUPIED AT THE MOMENT......
ARMBAND: STUDENT COUNCIL
UM... WHAT'RE YOU DOING?
OH, WELL, HA-HA-HA...
VANDALISM
YOU KNOW HOW MIRAI WREAKED HAVOC ALL OVER THE SCHOOL TODAY?
PROPERTY DAMAGE
No. 1 OF THE SEVEN MYSTERIES THE THREE CLOCK KEEPERS
MIRAI
OLD PEOPLE PARTY
IT MADE MINAMOTO-SENPAI JUUUUST... A LITTLE UPSET, I GUESS......

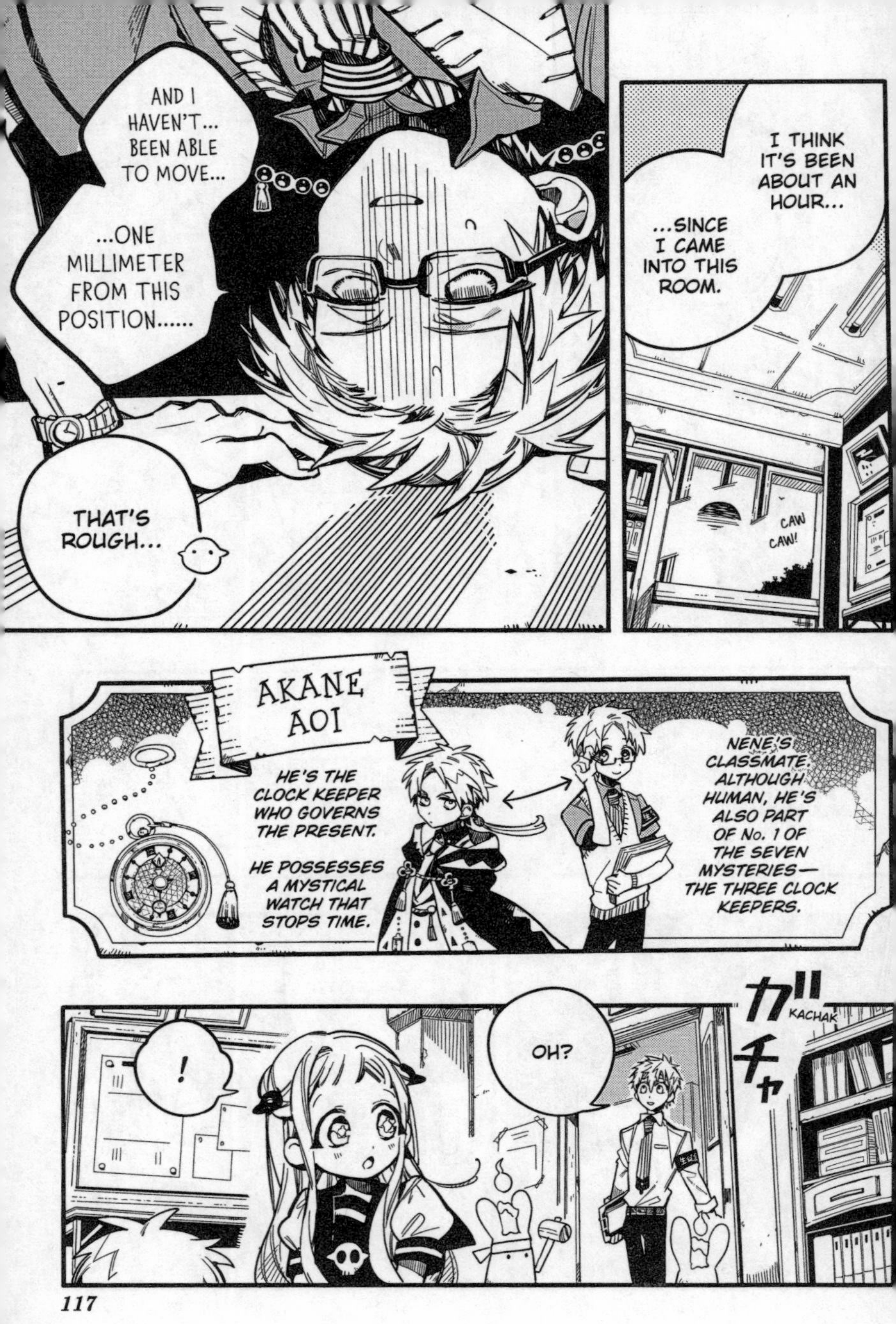

I THINK IT'S BEEN ABOUT AN HOUR...
...SINCE I CAME INTO THIS ROOM.
CAW CAW!
AND I HAVEN'T... BEEN ABLE TO MOVE...
...ONE MILLIMETER FROM THIS POSITION......
THAT'S ROUGH...
AKANE AOI
NENE'S CLASSMATE. ALTHOUGH HUMAN, HE'S ALSO PART OF No. 1 OF THE SEVEN MYSTERIES—THE THREE CLOCK KEEPERS.
HE'S THE CLOCK KEEPER WHO GOVERNS THE PRESENT.
HE POSSESSES A MYSTICAL WATCH THAT STOPS TIME.
ガチャ
KACHAK
OH?
!

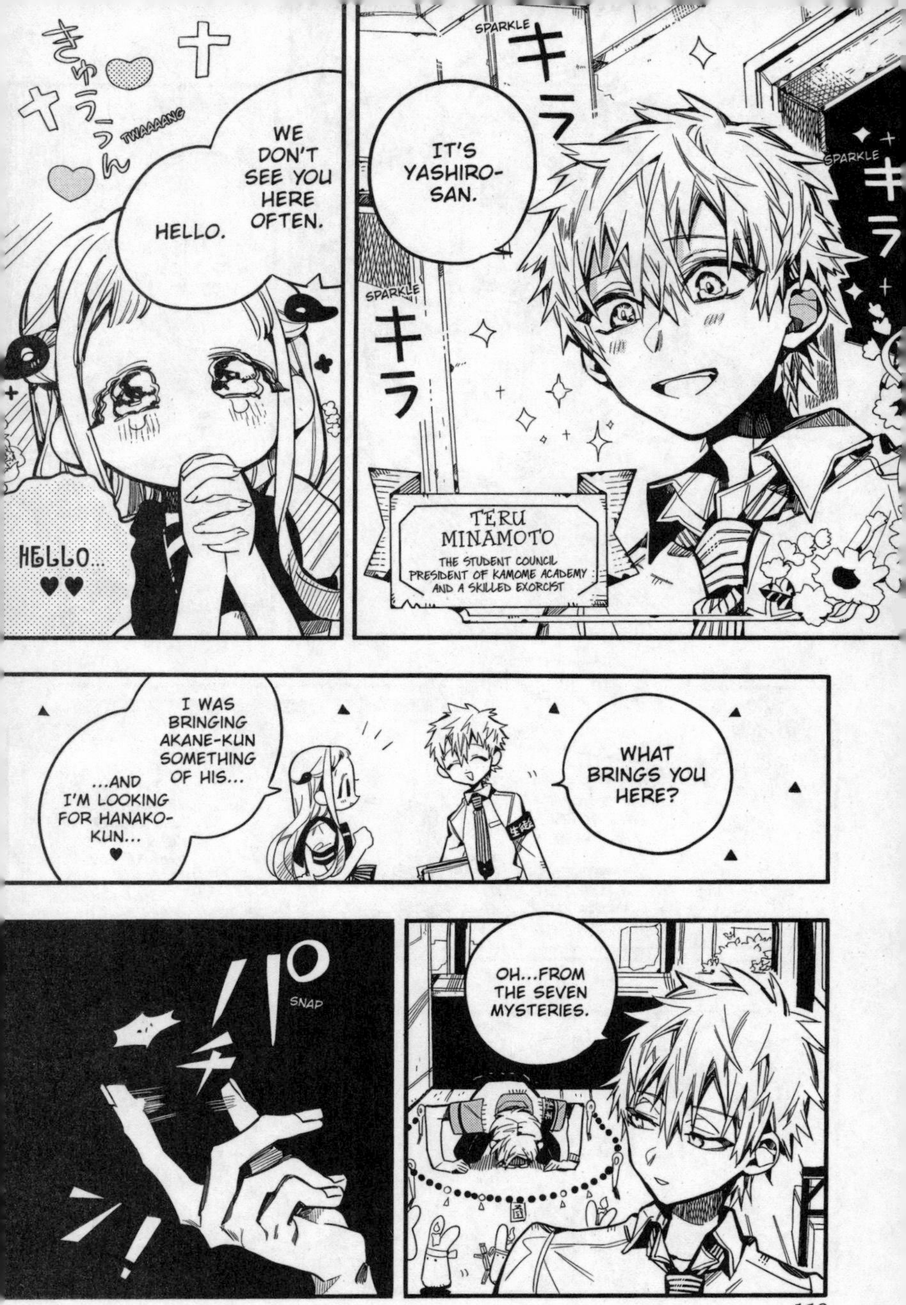
SPARKLE
キラ
IT'S YASHIRO-SAN.
SPARKLE
キラ
SPARKLE
キラ
TERU MINAMOTO
THE STUDENT COUNCIL PRESIDENT OF KAMOME ACADEMY AND A SKILLED EXORCIST
WE DON'T SEE YOU HERE OFTEN.
HELLO.
きゅらーん
TWAAAANG
HELLO...
WHAT BRINGS YOU HERE?
I WAS BRINGING AKANE-KUN SOMETHING OF HIS...
...AND I'M LOOKING FOR HANAKO-KUN...
OH...FROM THE SEVEN MYSTERIES.
パチ
SNAP

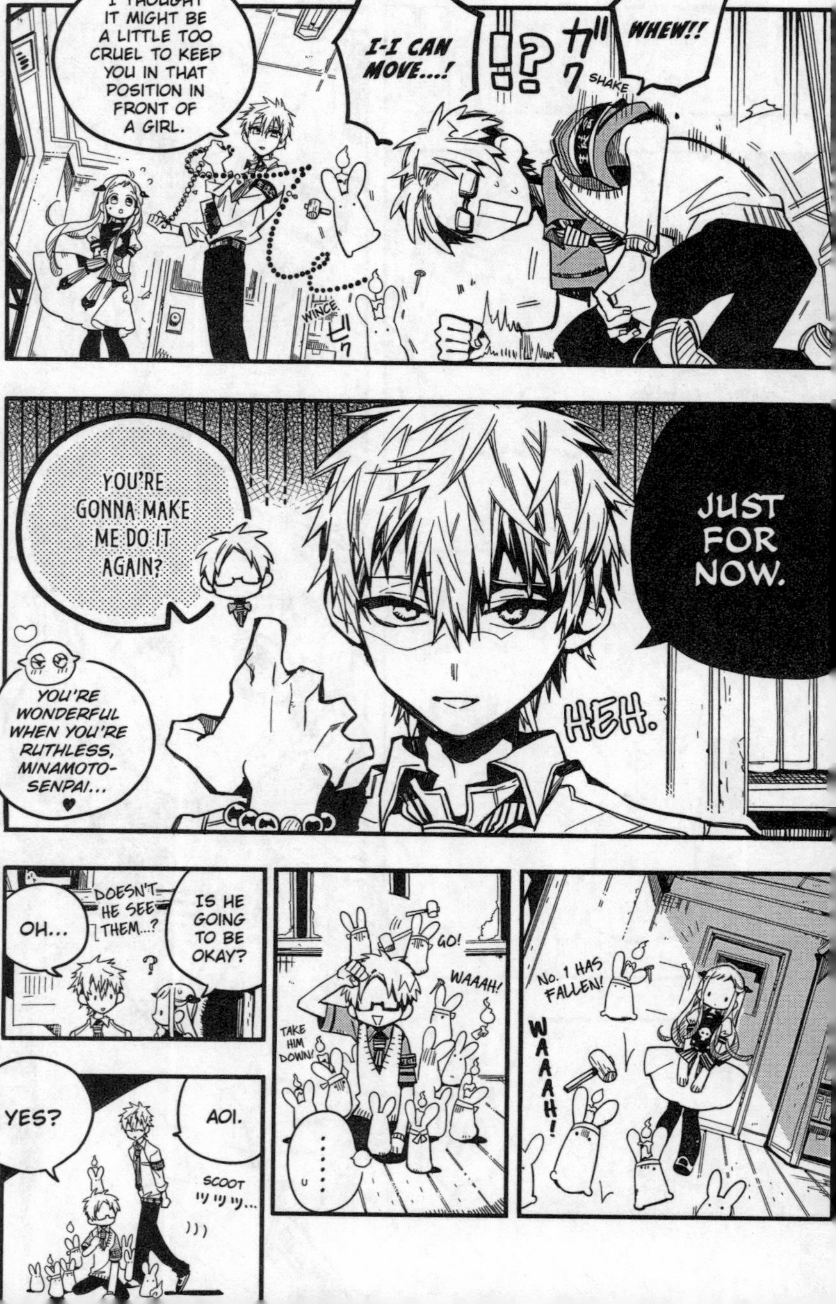
WHEW!!
SHAKE
!?
I-I CAN MOVE...!
I THOUGHT IT MIGHT BE A LITTLE TOO CRUEL TO KEEP YOU IN THAT POSITION IN FRONT OF A GIRL.
WINCE
JUST FOR NOW.
HEH.
YOU'RE GONNA MAKE ME DO IT AGAIN?
YOU'RE WONDERFUL WHEN YOU'RE RUTHLESS, MINAMOTO-SENPAI...
No. 1 HAS FALLEN!
WAAAAH!
GO!
WAAAH!
TAKE HIM DOWN!
......
IS HE GOING TO BE OKAY?
DOESN'T HE SEE THEM...?
OH...
AOI.
YES?
SCOOT

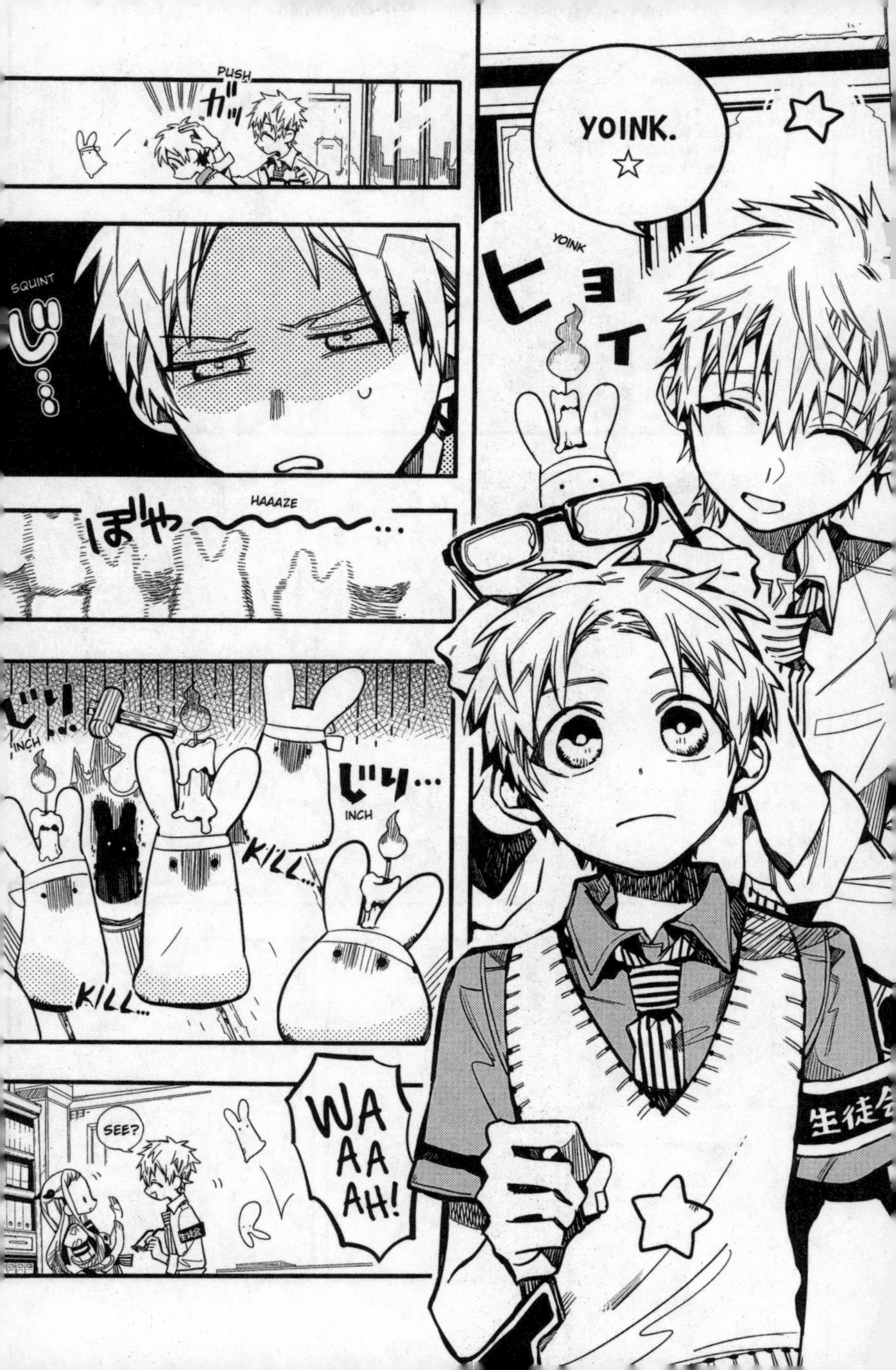

YOINK.
YOINK
ヒョイ
生徒会
WAAAAAH!
PUSH
ガッ
SQUINT
じ…
HAAAZE
ぼや〜〜〜…
じり…
INCH
じり…
INCH
KILL…
KILL…
SEE?

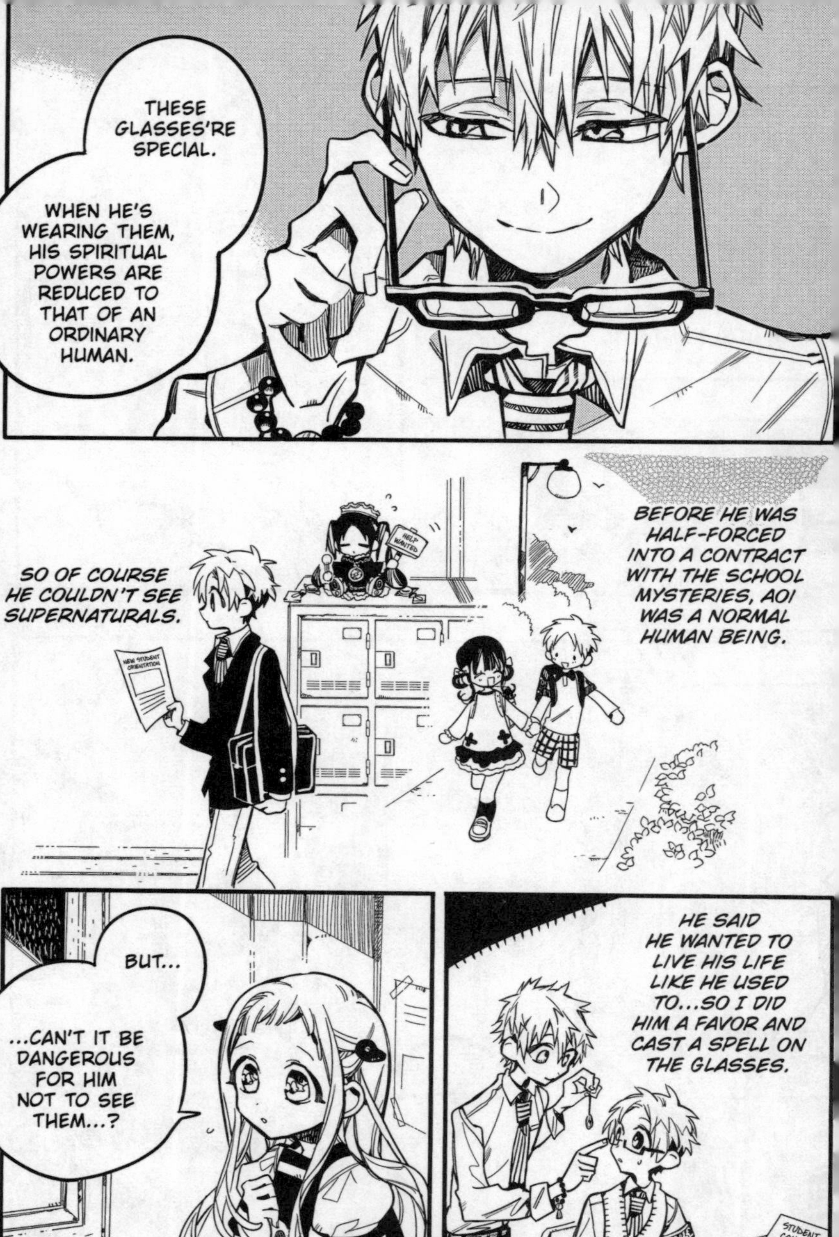
THESE GLASSES'RE SPECIAL.
WHEN HE'S WEARING THEM, HIS SPIRITUAL POWERS ARE REDUCED TO THAT OF AN ORDINARY HUMAN.
BEFORE HE WAS HALF-FORCED INTO A CONTRACT WITH THE SCHOOL MYSTERIES, AOI WAS A NORMAL HUMAN BEING.
HELP WANTED
SO OF COURSE HE COULDN'T SEE SUPERNATURALS.
NEW STUDENT ORIENTATION
HE SAID HE WANTED TO LIVE HIS LIFE LIKE HE USED TO...SO I DID HIM A FAVOR AND CAST A SPELL ON THE GLASSES.
STUDENT COUNCIL
BUT...
...CAN'T IT BE DANGEROUS FOR HIM NOT TO SEE THEM...?

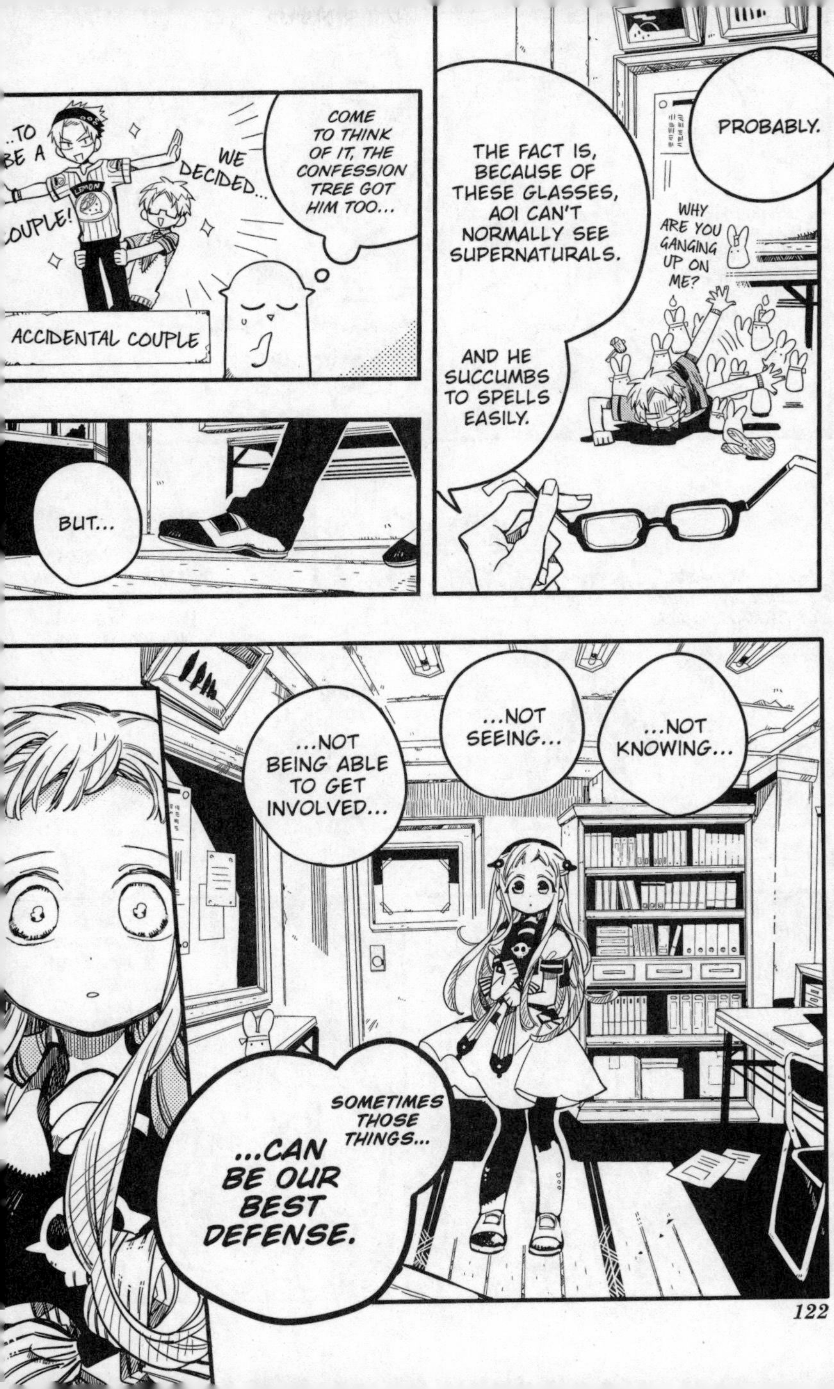
PROBABLY.
THE FACT IS, BECAUSE OF THESE GLASSES, AOI CAN'T NORMALLY SEE SUPERNATURALS.
WHY ARE YOU GANGING UP ON ME?
AND HE SUCCUMBS TO SPELLS EASILY.
COME TO THINK OF IT, THE CONFESSION TREE GOT HIM TOO...
WE DECIDED...
..TO BE A COUPLE!
ACCIDENTAL COUPLE
BUT...
...NOT KNOWING...
...NOT SEEING...
...NOT BEING ABLE TO GET INVOLVED...
SOMETIMES THOSE THINGS...
...CAN BE OUR BEST DEFENSE.

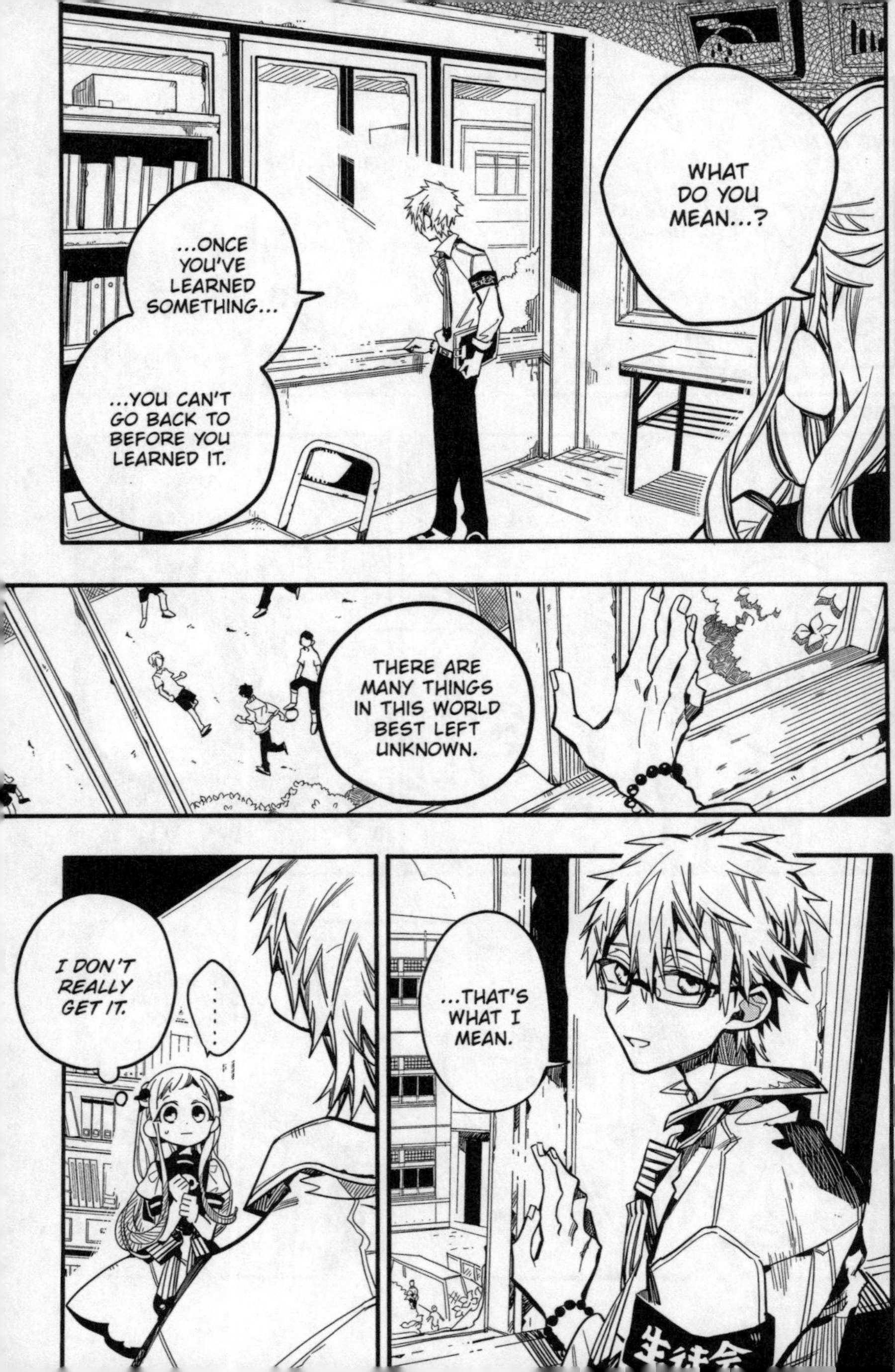
WHAT DO YOU MEAN...?
...ONCE YOU'VE LEARNED SOMETHING...
...YOU CAN'T GO BACK TO BEFORE YOU LEARNED IT.
THERE ARE MANY THINGS IN THIS WORLD BEST LEFT UNKNOWN.
...THAT'S WHAT I MEAN.
......
I DON'T REALLY GET IT.

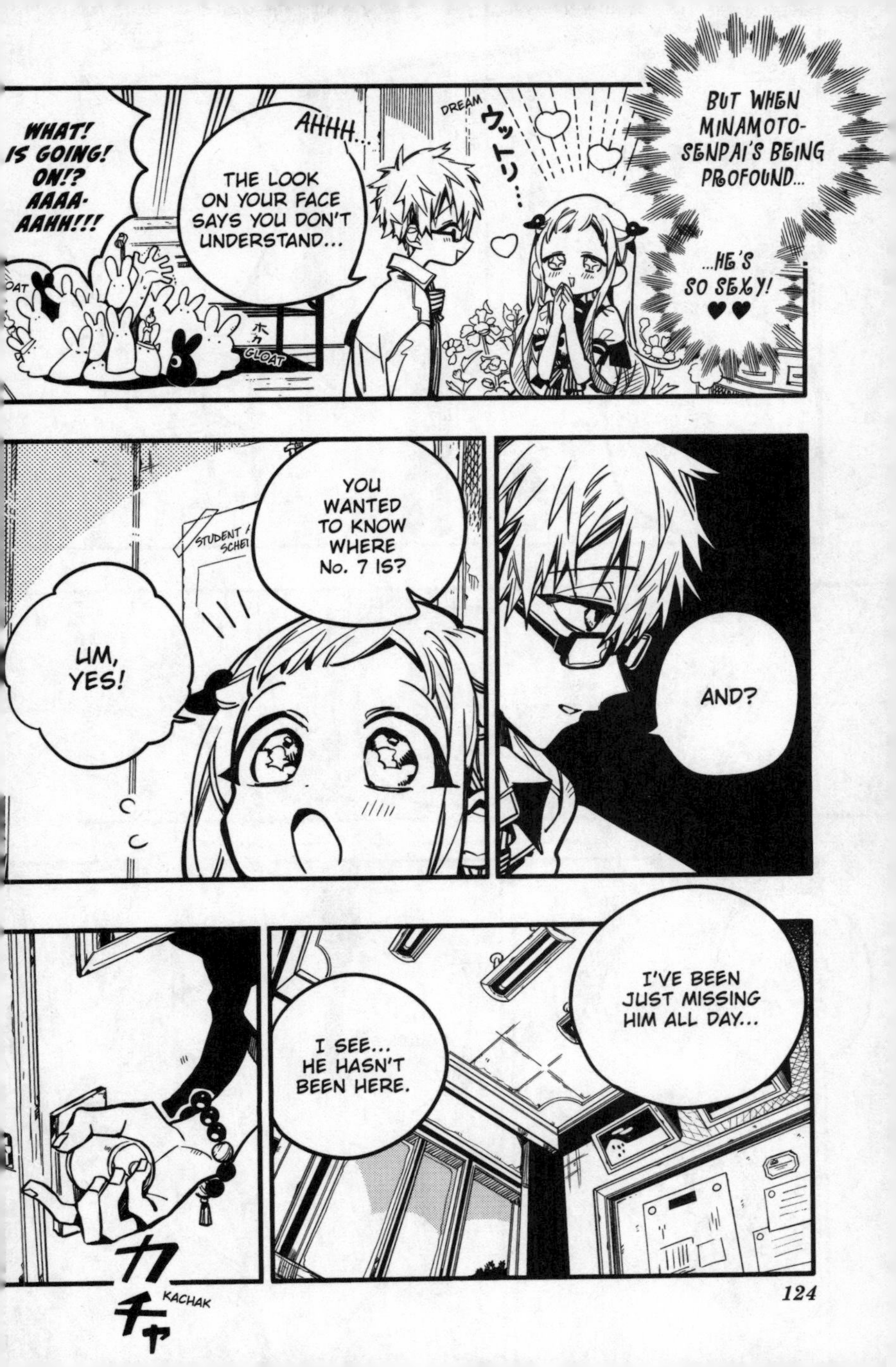
BUT WHEN MINAMOTO-SENPAI'S BEING PROFOUND...
...HE'S SO SEXY! ♥♥
ウットリ…
DREAM
AHHH...
THE LOOK ON YOUR FACE SAYS YOU DON'T UNDERSTAND...
WHAT! IS GOING! ON!? AAAA-AAHH!!!
ホカ
GLOAT
AND?
YOU WANTED TO KNOW WHERE No. 7 IS?
UM, YES!
I'VE BEEN JUST MISSING HIM ALL DAY...
I SEE... HE HASN'T BEEN HERE.
カチャ
KACHAK

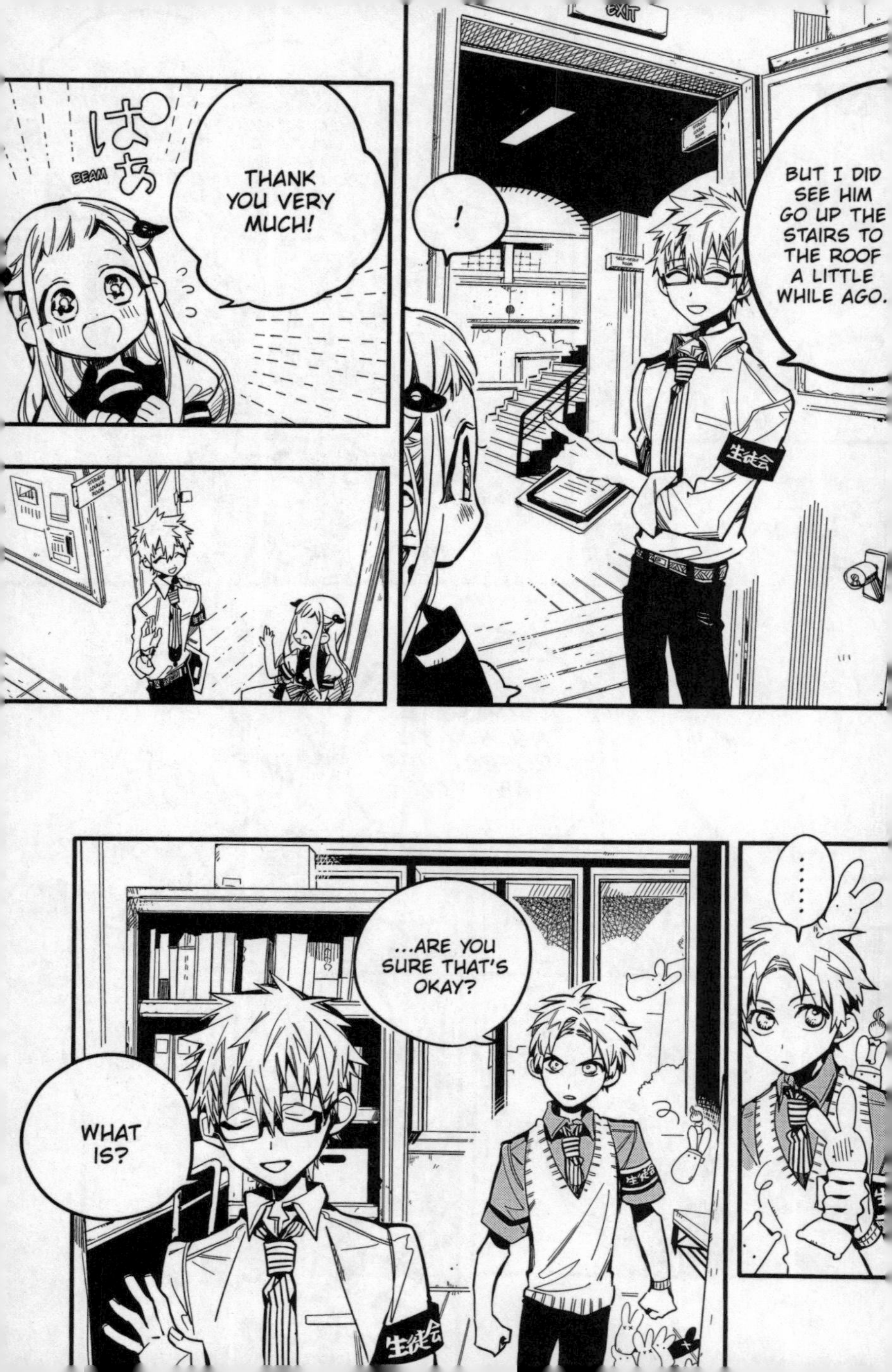
EXIT
BUT I DID SEE HIM GO UP THE STAIRS TO THE ROOF A LITTLE WHILE AGO.
!
ぱぁ
BEAM
THANK YOU VERY MUCH!
......
...ARE YOU SURE THAT'S OKAY?
WHAT IS?

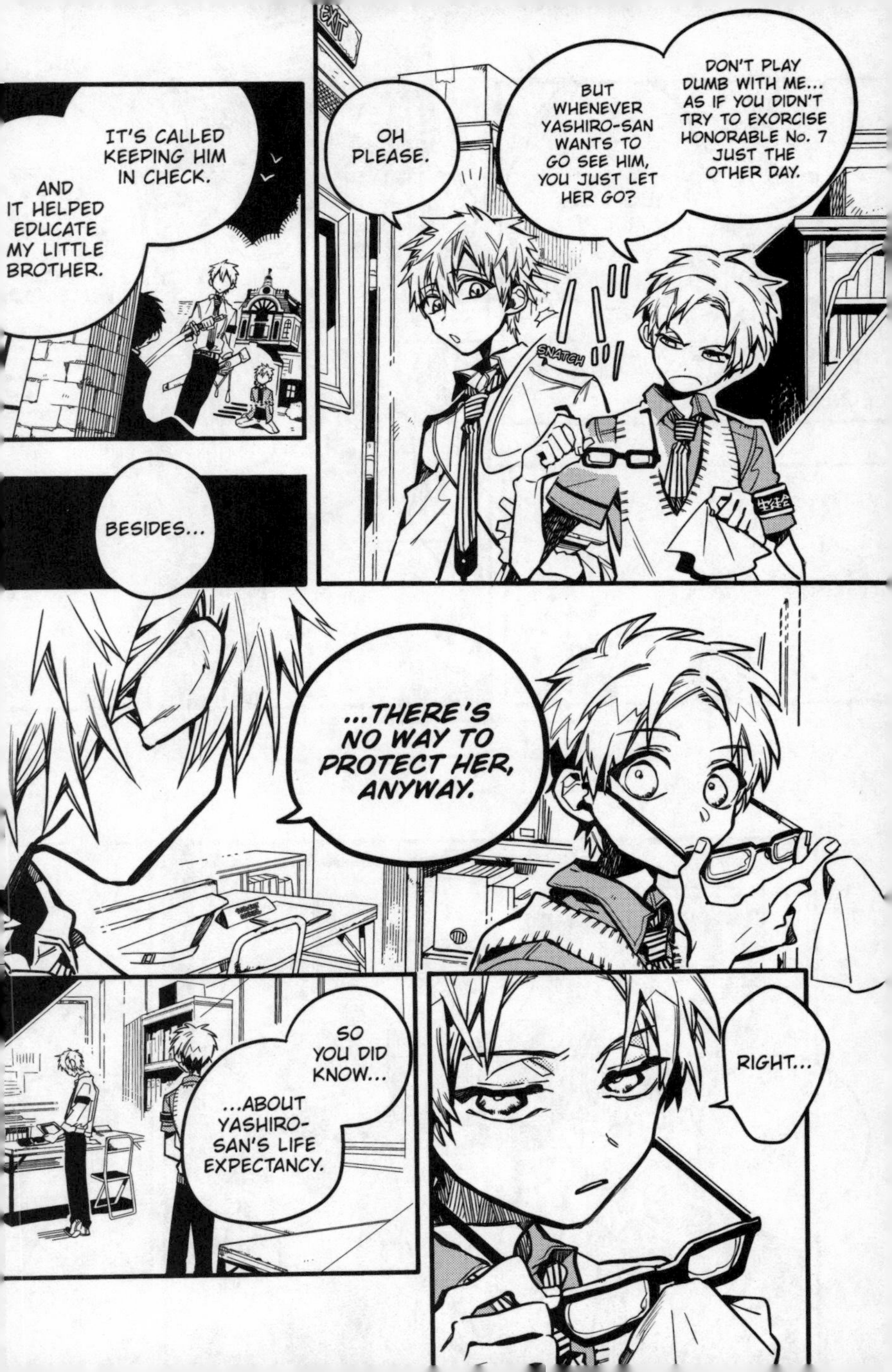
DON'T PLAY DUMB WITH ME... AS IF YOU DIDN'T TRY TO EXORCISE HONORABLE No. 7 JUST THE OTHER DAY.
BUT WHENEVER YASHIRO-SAN WANTS TO GO SEE HIM, YOU JUST LET HER GO?
OH PLEASE.
SNATCH
IT'S CALLED KEEPING HIM IN CHECK.
AND IT HELPED EDUCATE MY LITTLE BROTHER.
BESIDES...
...THERE'S NO WAY TO PROTECT HER, ANYWAY.
RIGHT...
SO YOU DID KNOW...
...ABOUT YASHIRO-SAN'S LIFE EXPECTANCY.

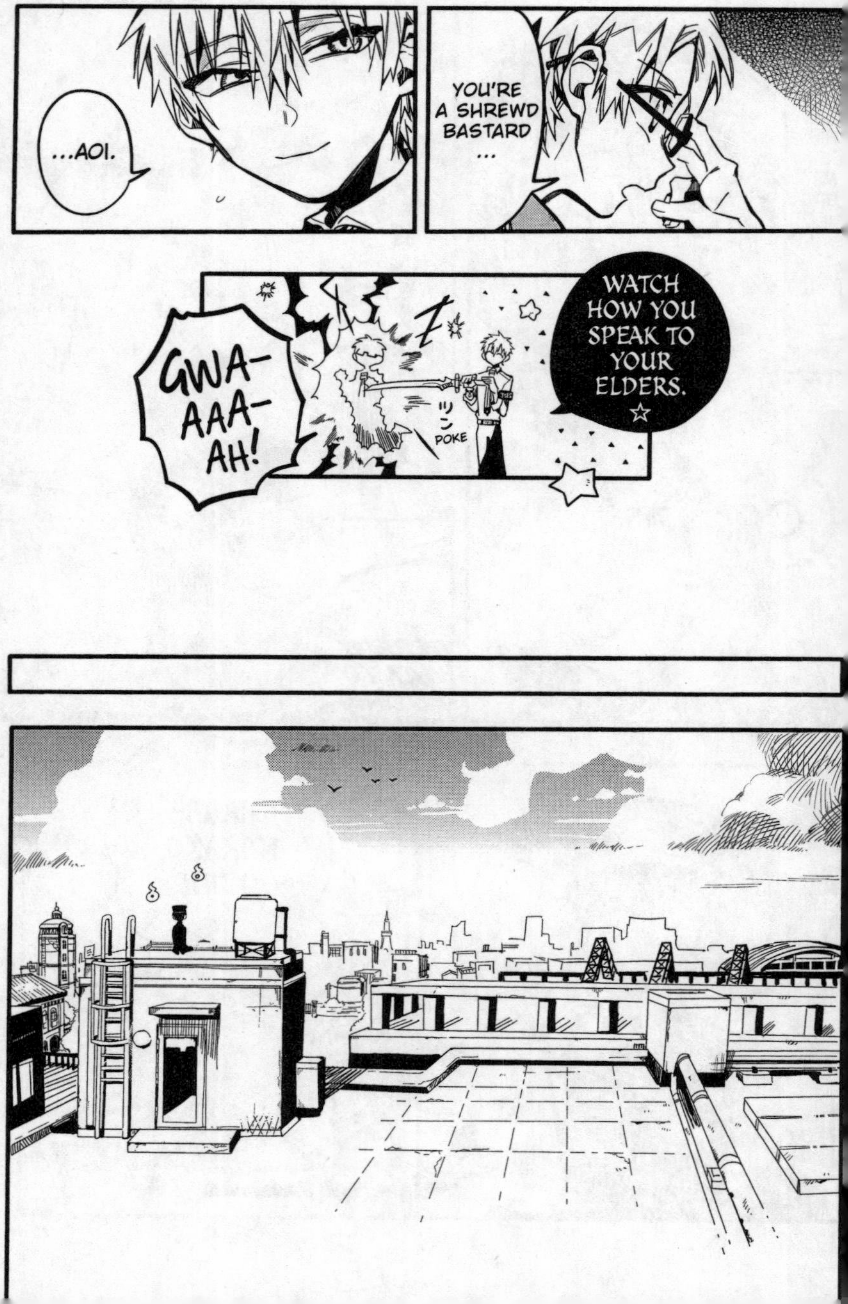
YOU'RE A SHREWD BASTARD ...
...AOI.
WATCH HOW YOU SPEAK TO YOUR ELDERS. ☆
ツン
POKE
GWA-AAA-AH!

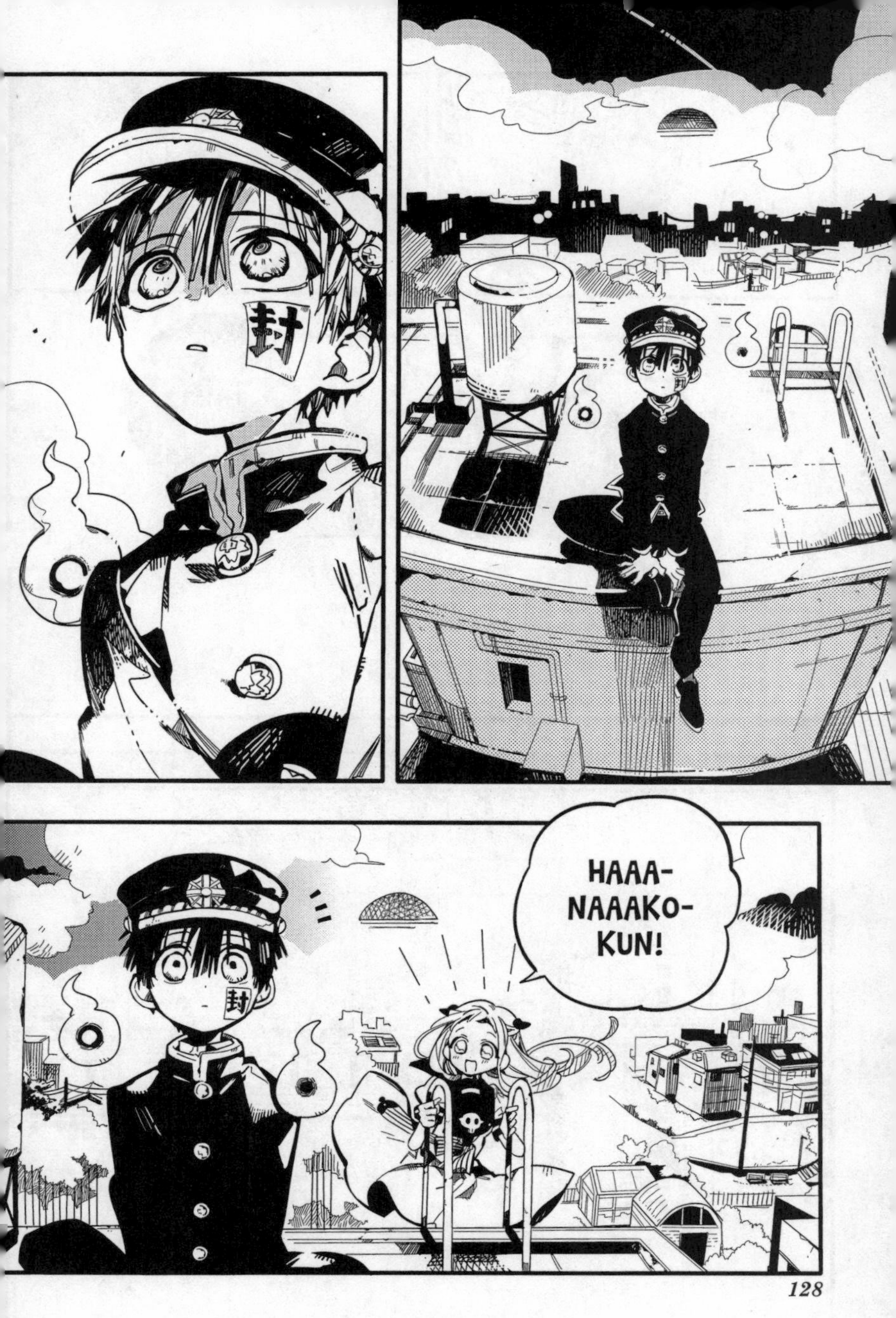
HAAA-NAAAKO-KUN!

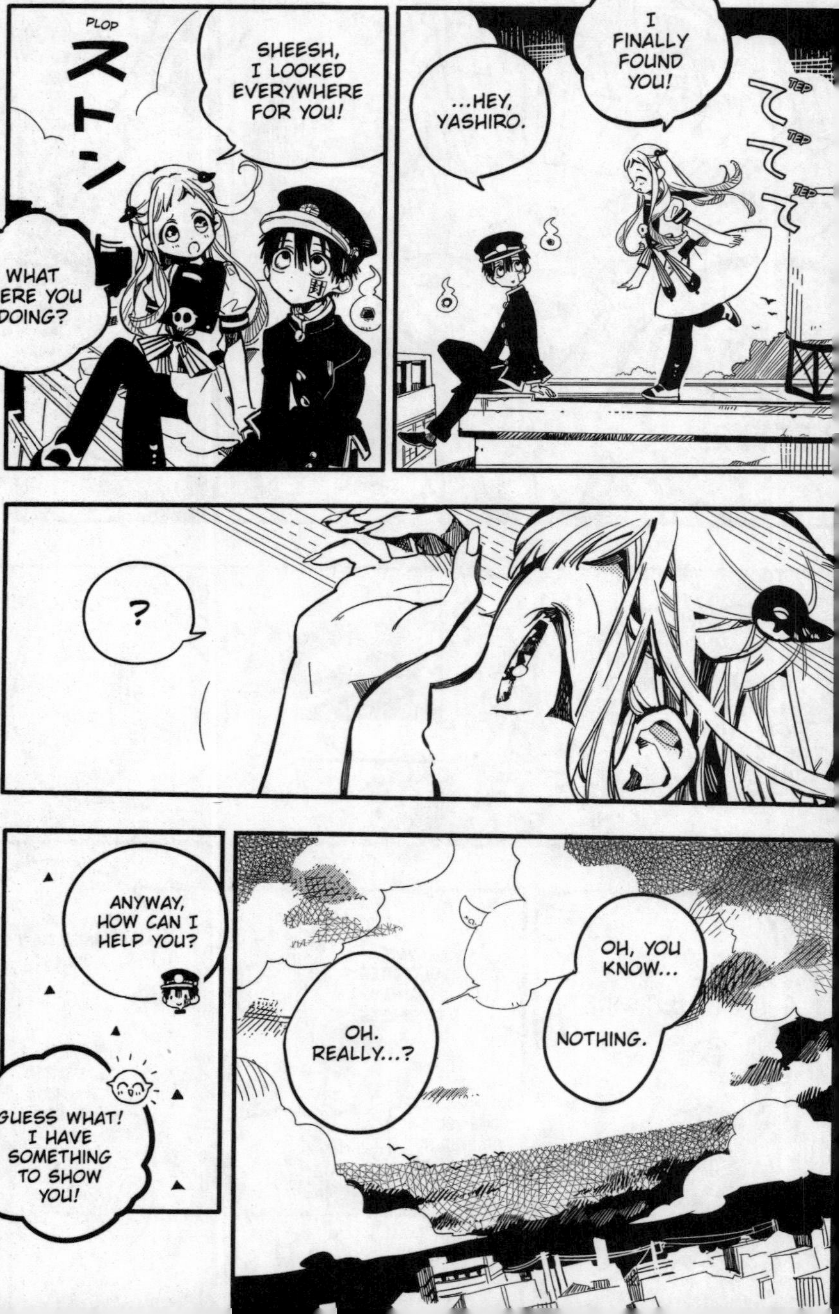
I FINALLY FOUND YOU!
TEP
て
TEP
て
TEP
て
...HEY, YASHIRO.
SHEESH, I LOOKED EVERYWHERE FOR YOU!
PLOP
ストン
WHAT WERE YOU DOING?
?
OH, YOU KNOW...
NOTHING.
OH. REALLY...?
ANYWAY, HOW CAN I HELP YOU?
GUESS WHAT! I HAVE SOMETHING TO SHOW YOU!

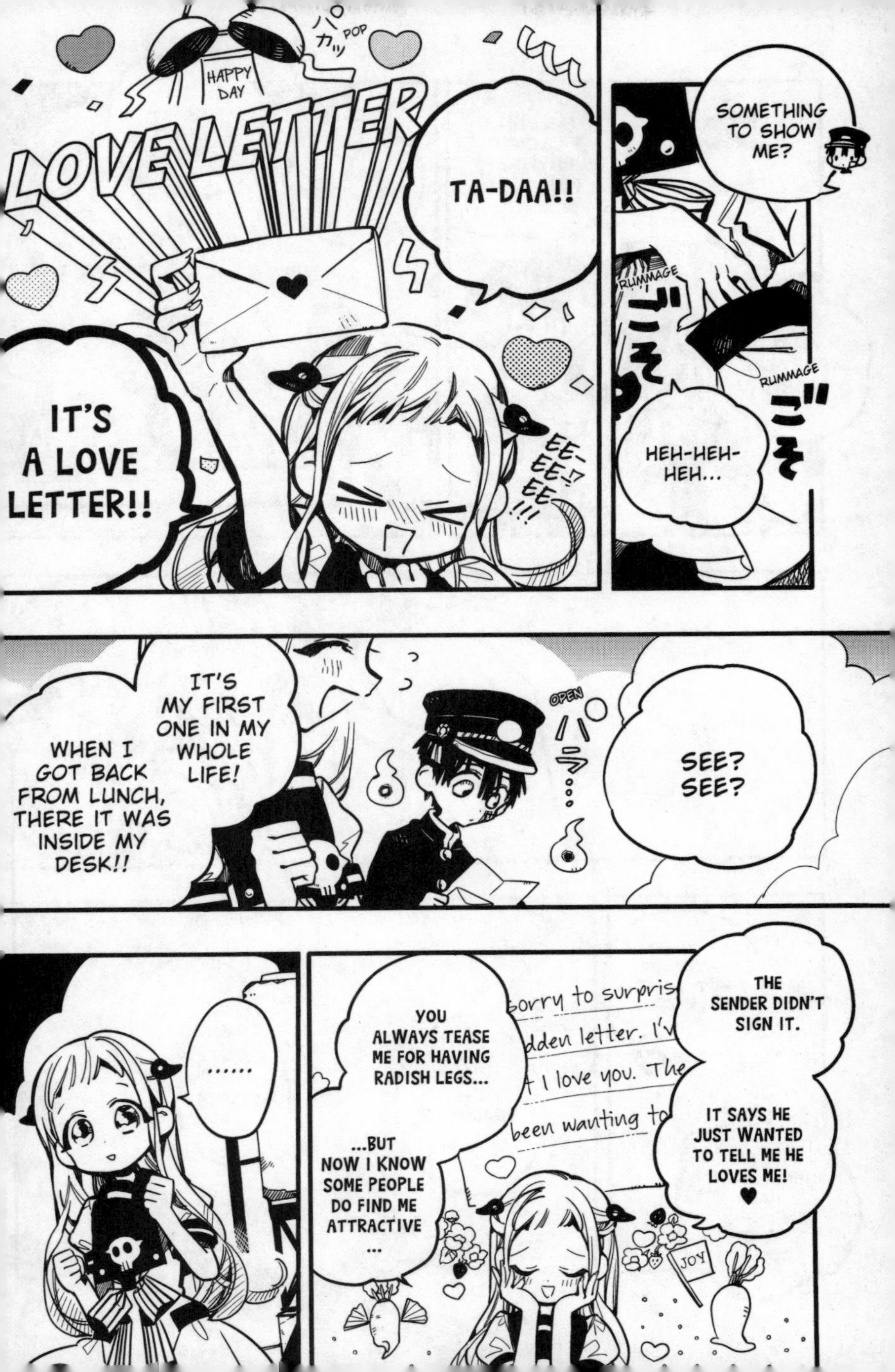
SOMETHING TO SHOW ME?
RUMMAGE ごそ
RUMMAGE ごそ
HEH-HEH-HEH...
パカッ POP
HAPPY DAY
LOVE LETTER
TA-DAA!!
IT'S A LOVE LETTER!!
EE-EE-!? EE-!!!
SEE? SEE?
OPEN パラ...
IT'S MY FIRST ONE IN MY WHOLE LIFE!
WHEN I GOT BACK FROM LUNCH, THERE IT WAS INSIDE MY DESK!!
THE SENDER DIDN'T SIGN IT.
IT SAYS HE JUST WANTED TO TELL ME HE LOVES ME! ♥
sorry to surpris
dden letter. I'v
l love you. The
been wanting to
YOU ALWAYS TEASE ME FOR HAVING RADISH LEGS...
...BUT NOW I KNOW SOME PEOPLE DO FIND ME ATTRACTIVE ...
JOY
......

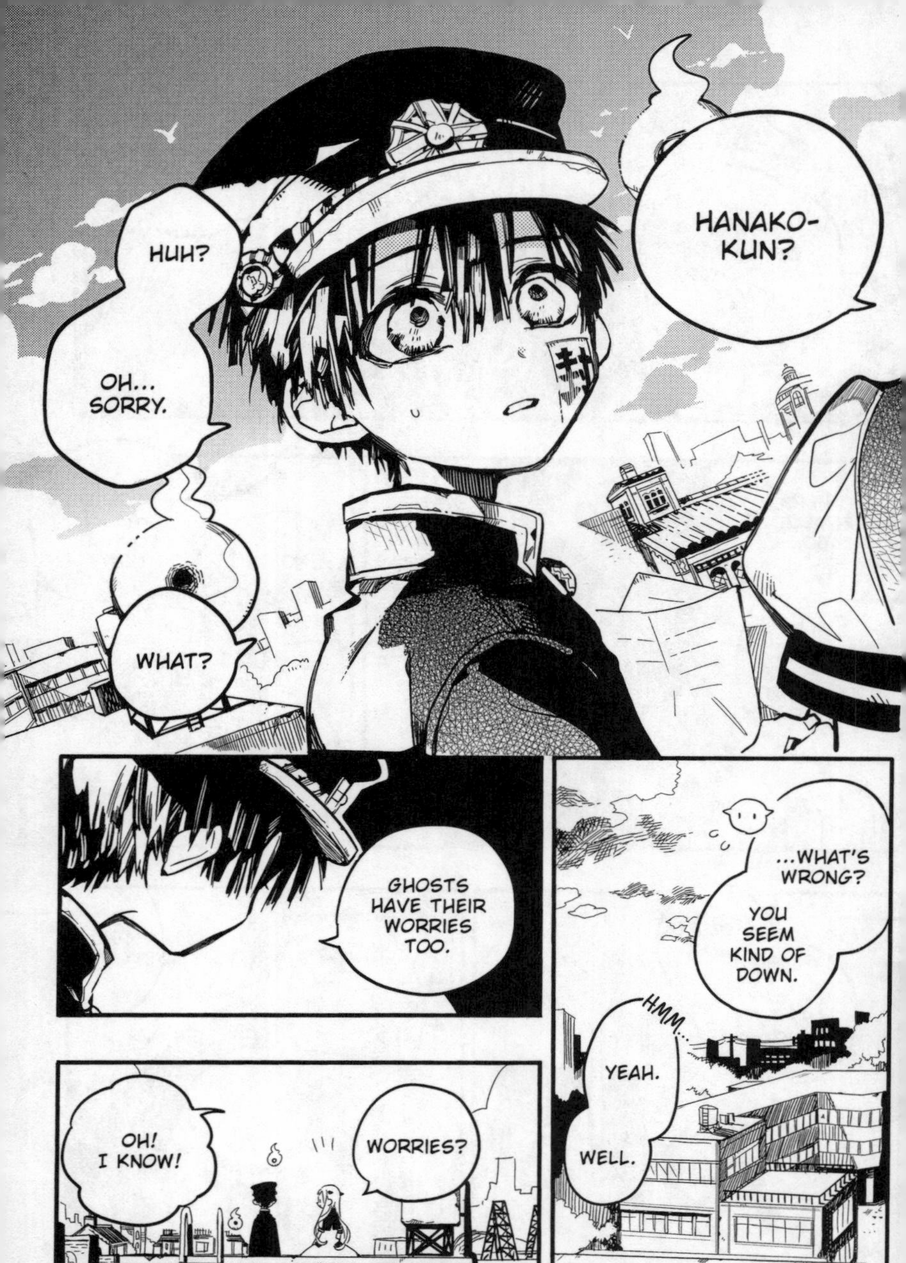
HANAKO-KUN?
HUH?
OH... SORRY.
WHAT?
...WHAT'S WRONG?
YOU SEEM KIND OF DOWN.
HMM...
YEAH.
WELL.
GHOSTS HAVE THEIR WORRIES TOO.
WORRIES?
OH! I KNOW!

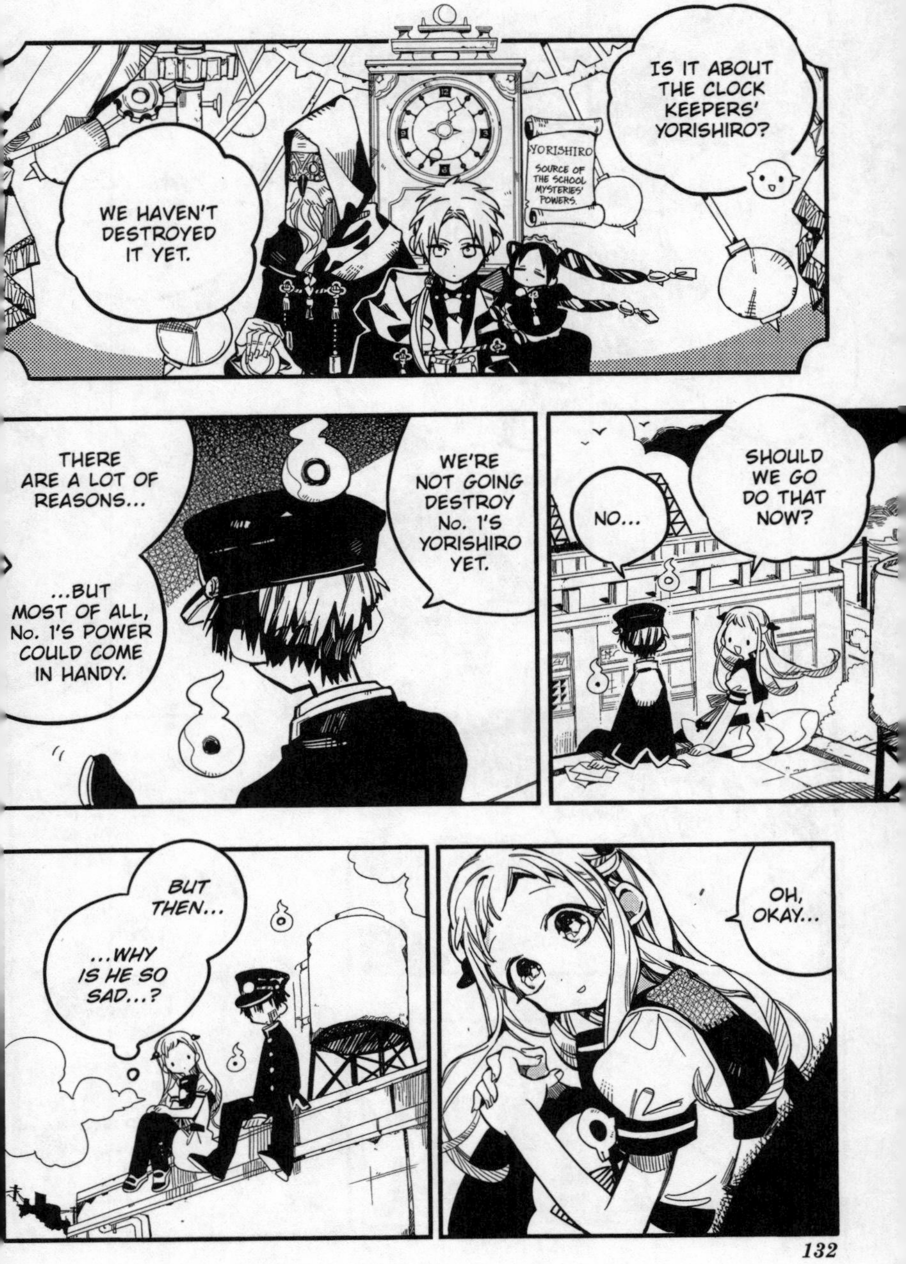
IS IT ABOUT THE CLOCK KEEPERS' YORISHIRO?
YORISHIRO
SOURCE OF THE SCHOOL MYSTERIES' POWERS.
WE HAVEN'T DESTROYED IT YET.
SHOULD WE GO DO THAT NOW?
NO...
WE'RE NOT GOING DESTROY No. 1'S YORISHIRO YET.
THERE ARE A LOT OF REASONS...
...BUT MOST OF ALL, No. 1'S POWER COULD COME IN HANDY.
OH, OKAY...
BUT THEN...
...WHY IS HE SO SAD...?

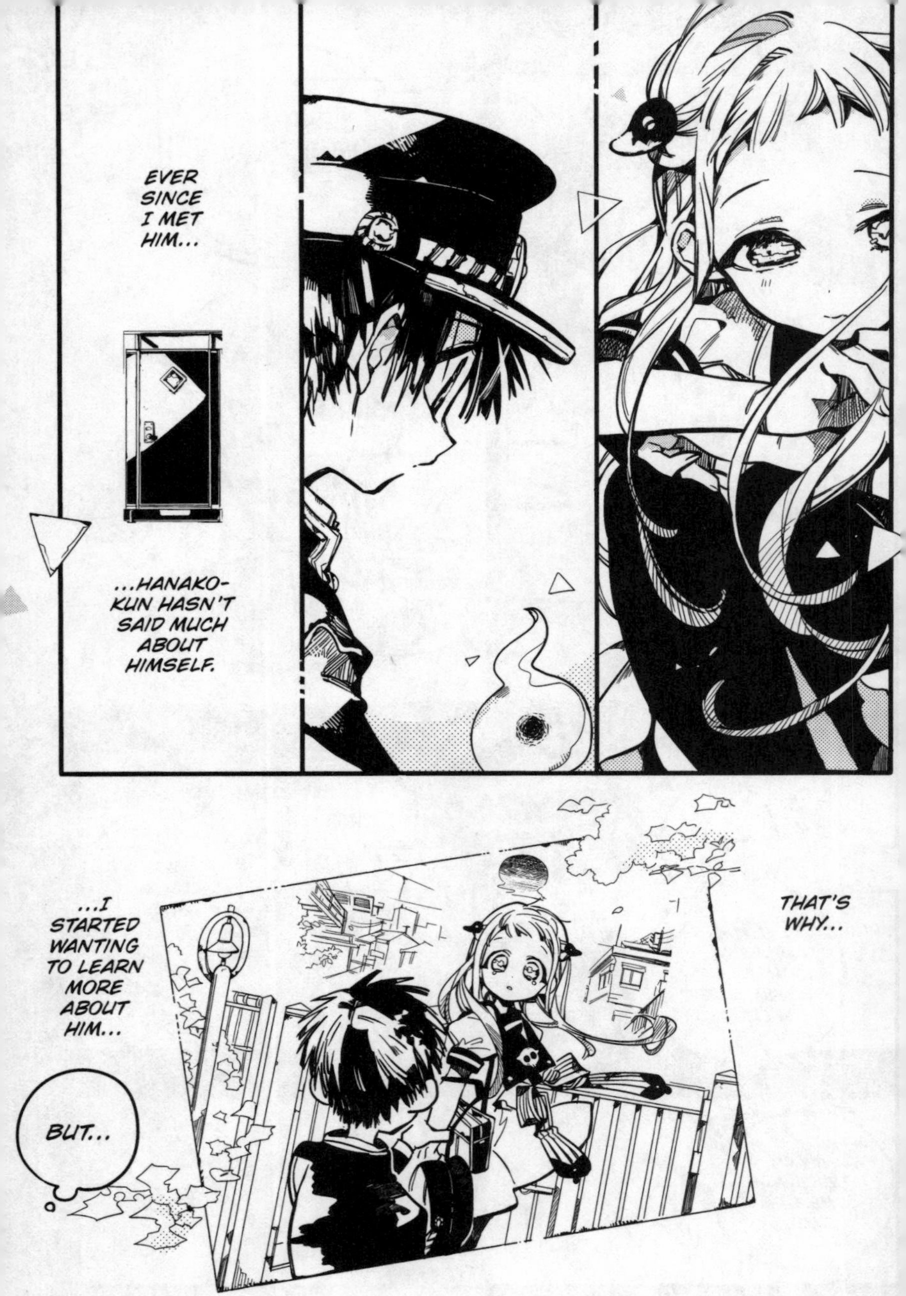
EVER SINCE I MET HIM...
...HANAKO-KUN HASN'T SAID MUCH ABOUT HIMSELF.
THAT'S WHY...
...I STARTED WANTING TO LEARN MORE ABOUT HIM...
BUT...

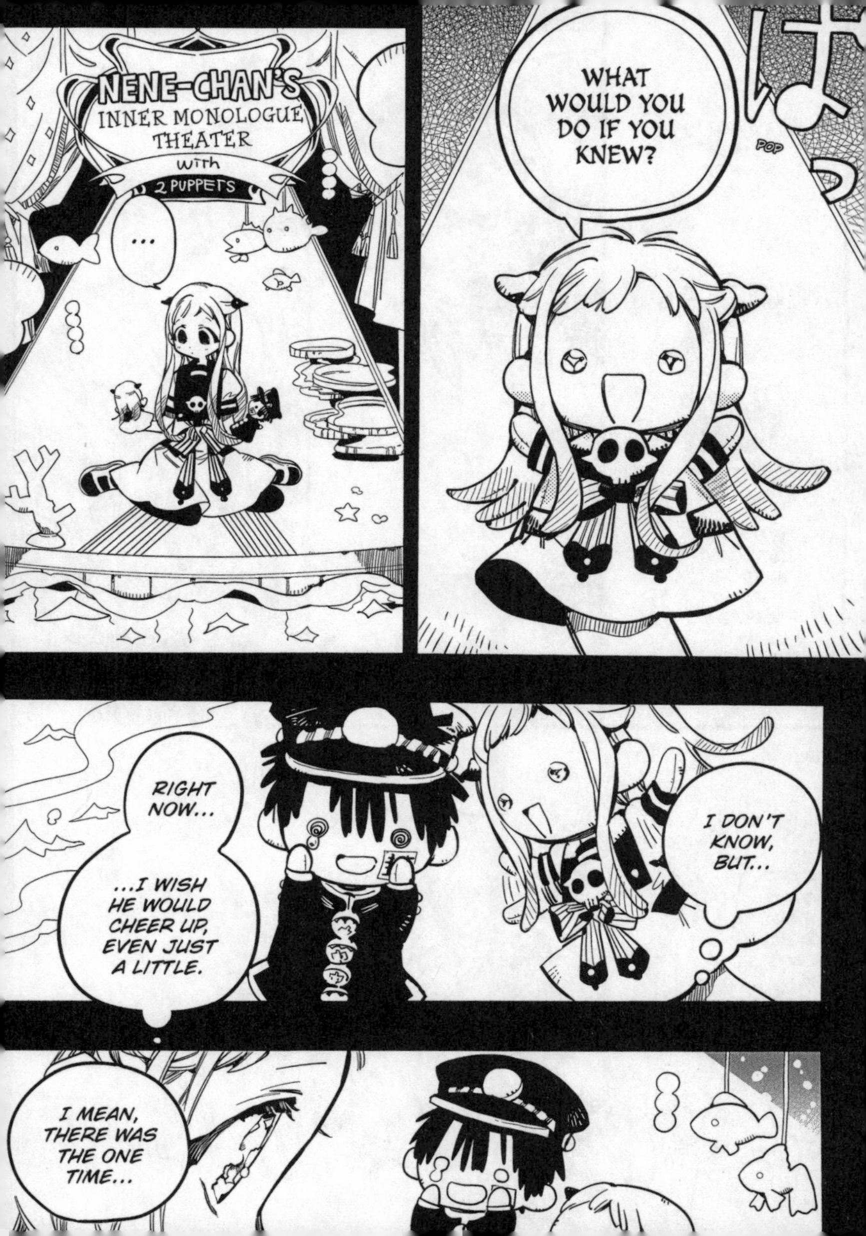

ぽっ
POP
WHAT WOULD YOU DO IF YOU KNEW?
NENE-CHAN'S INNER MONOLOGUE THEATER with 2 PUPPETS
...
I DON'T KNOW, BUT...
RIGHT NOW...
...I WISH HE WOULD CHEER UP, EVEN JUST A LITTLE.
I MEAN, THERE WAS THE ONE TIME...

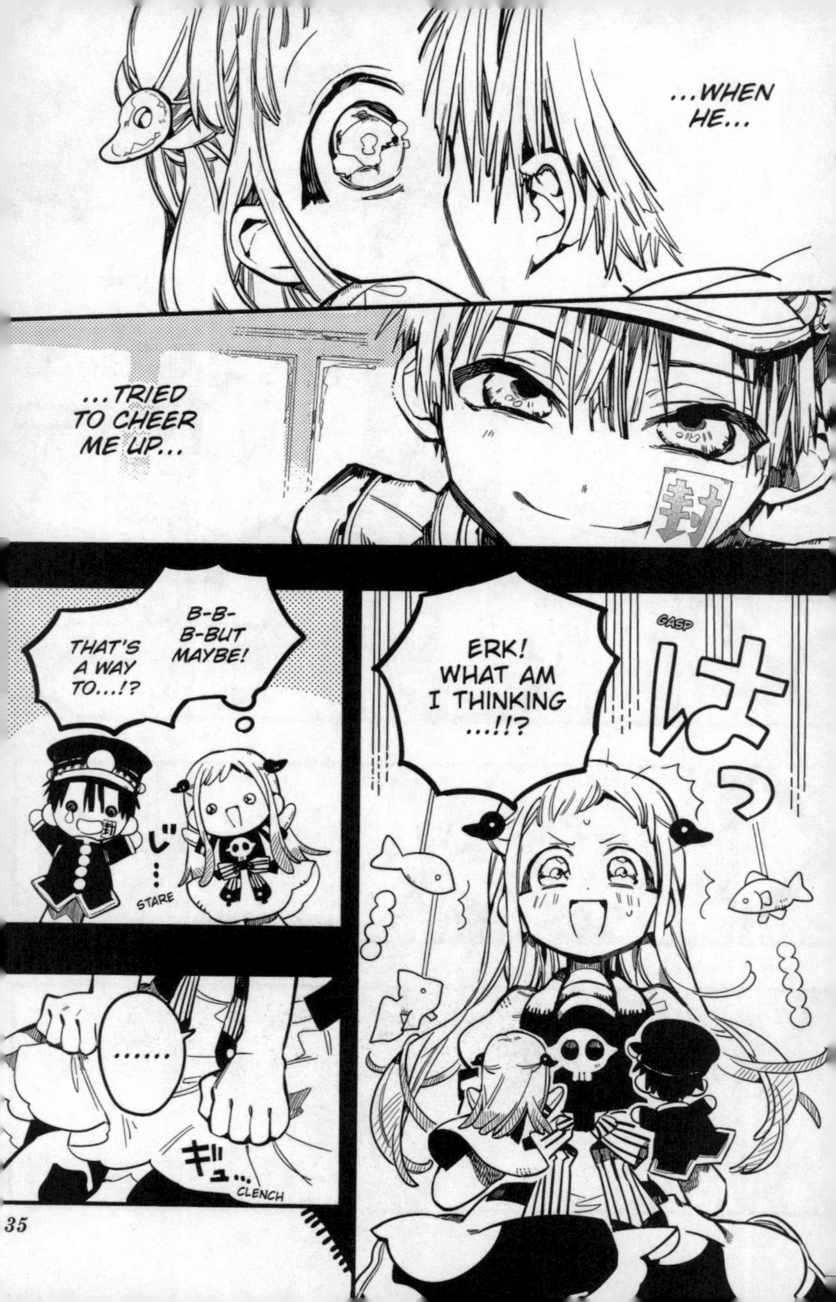

...WHEN HE...
...TRIED TO CHEER ME UP...
GASP
はっ
ERK! WHAT AM I THINKING ...!!?
B-B-B-BUT MAYBE!
THAT'S A WAY TO...!?
じ...
STARE
......
ギュ...
CLENCH

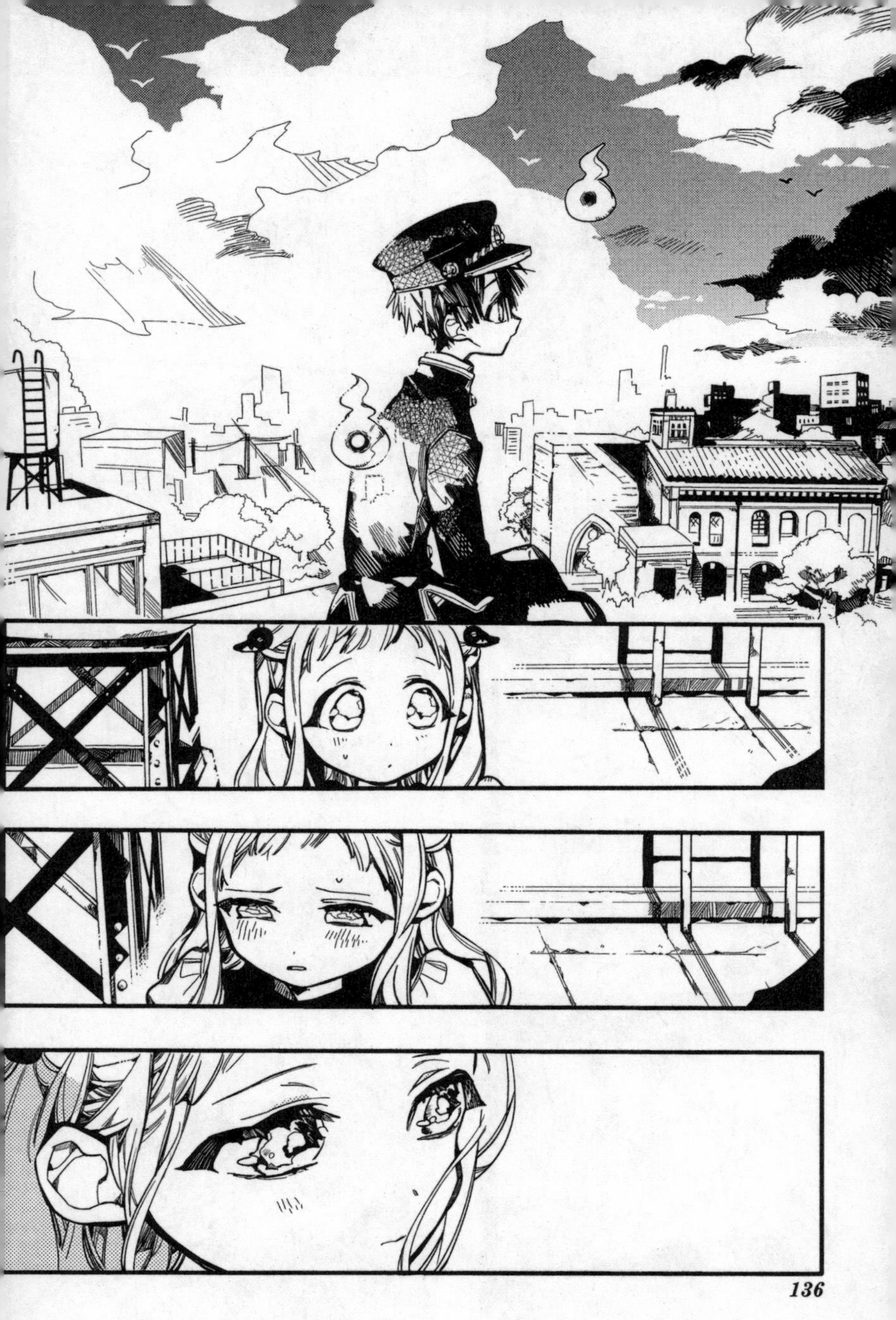

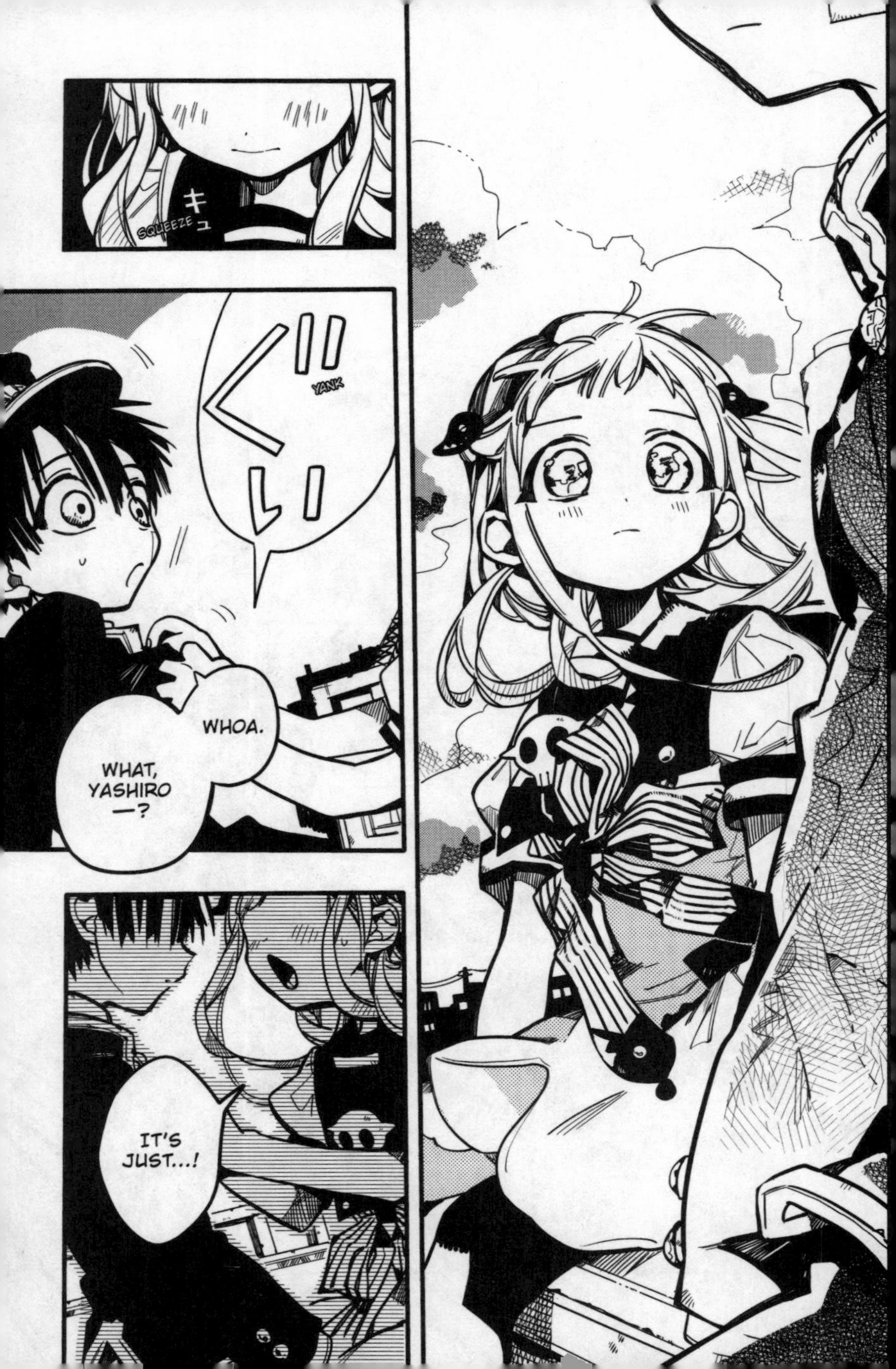
キュ
SQUEEZE
ぐい
YANK
WHOA.
WHAT, YASHIRO—?
IT'S JUST...!

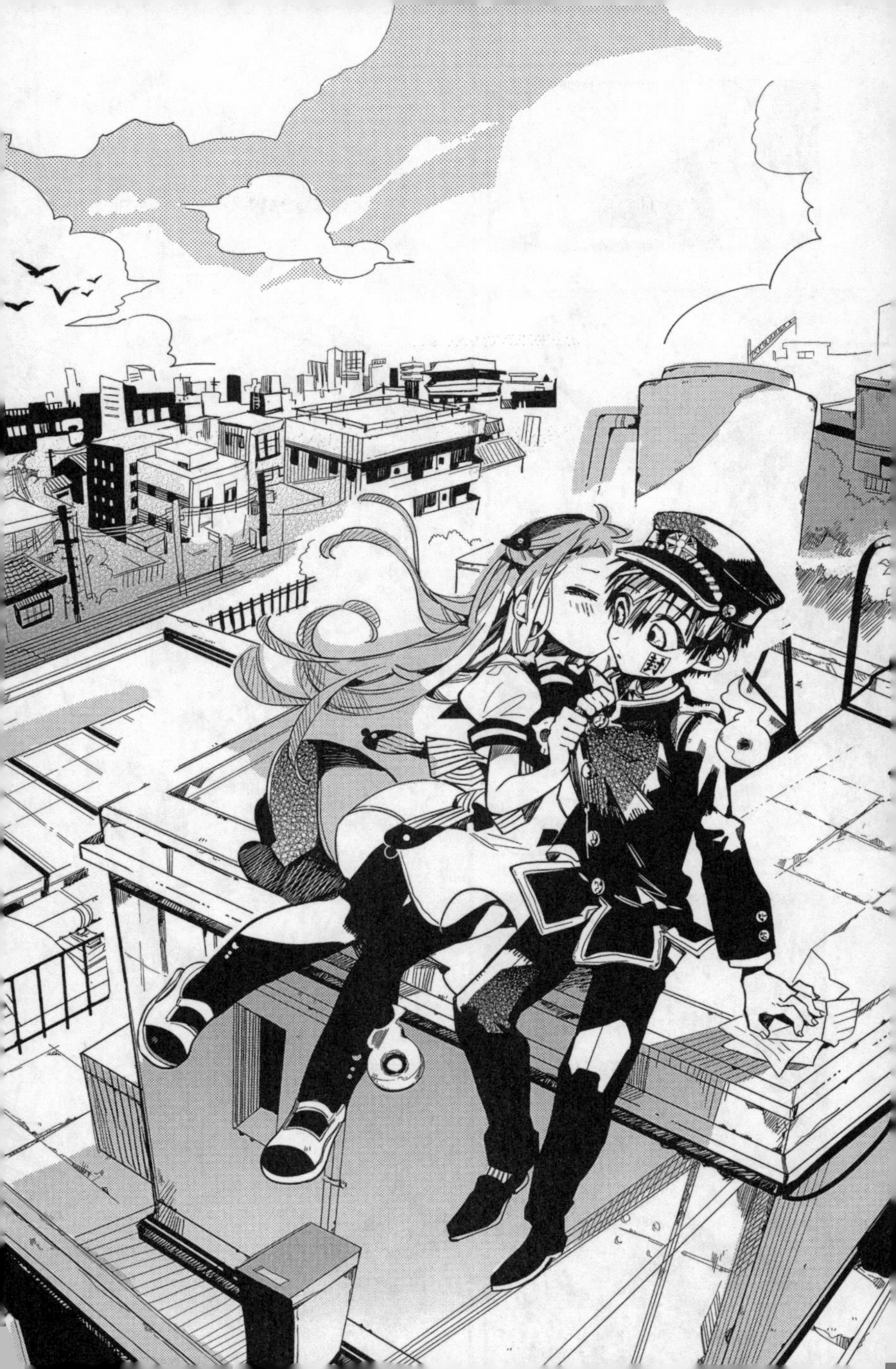

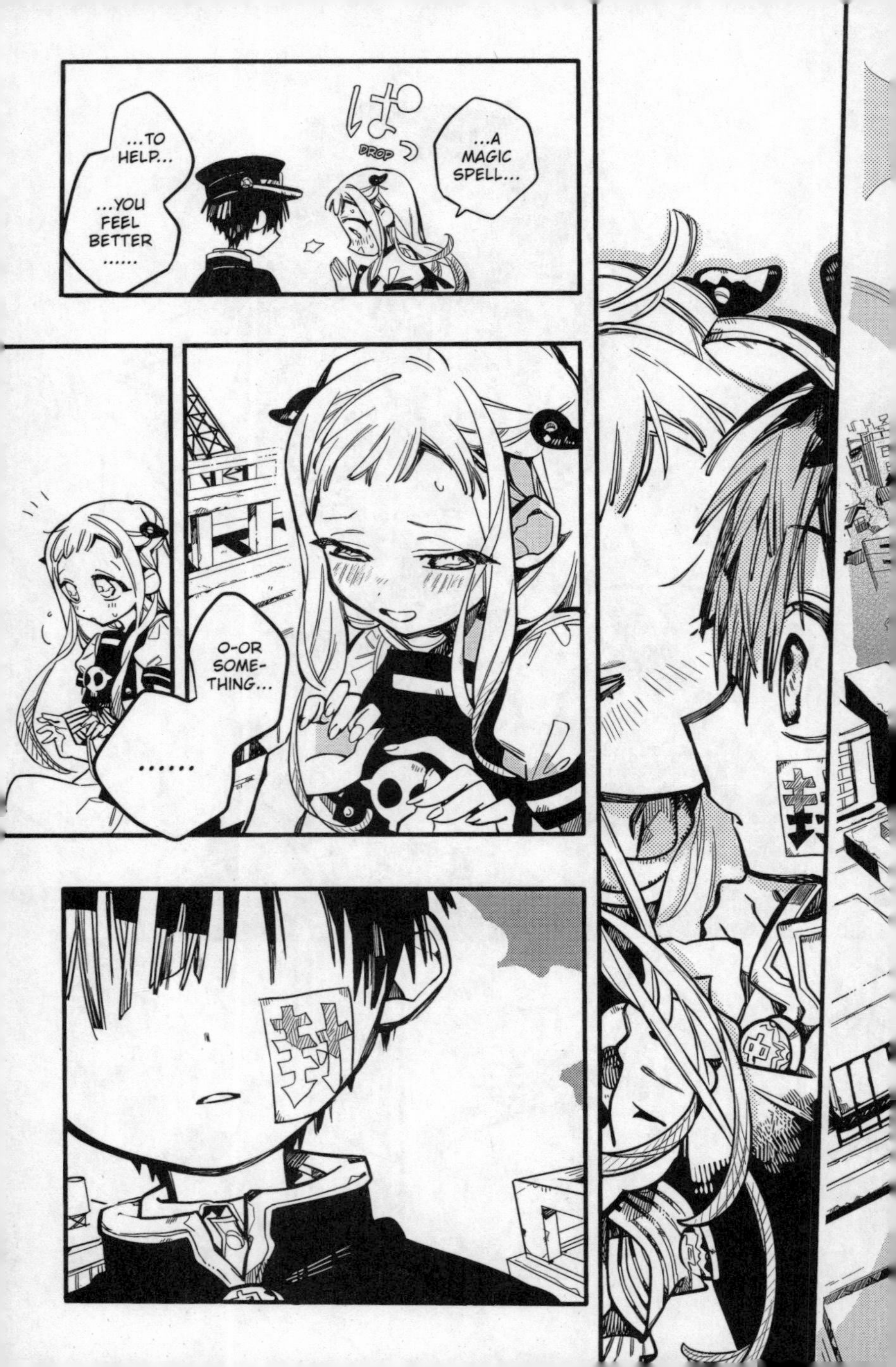
...A MAGIC SPELL...
ぱっ
DROP
...TO HELP...
...YOU FEEL BETTER ......
O-OR SOME-THING...
......

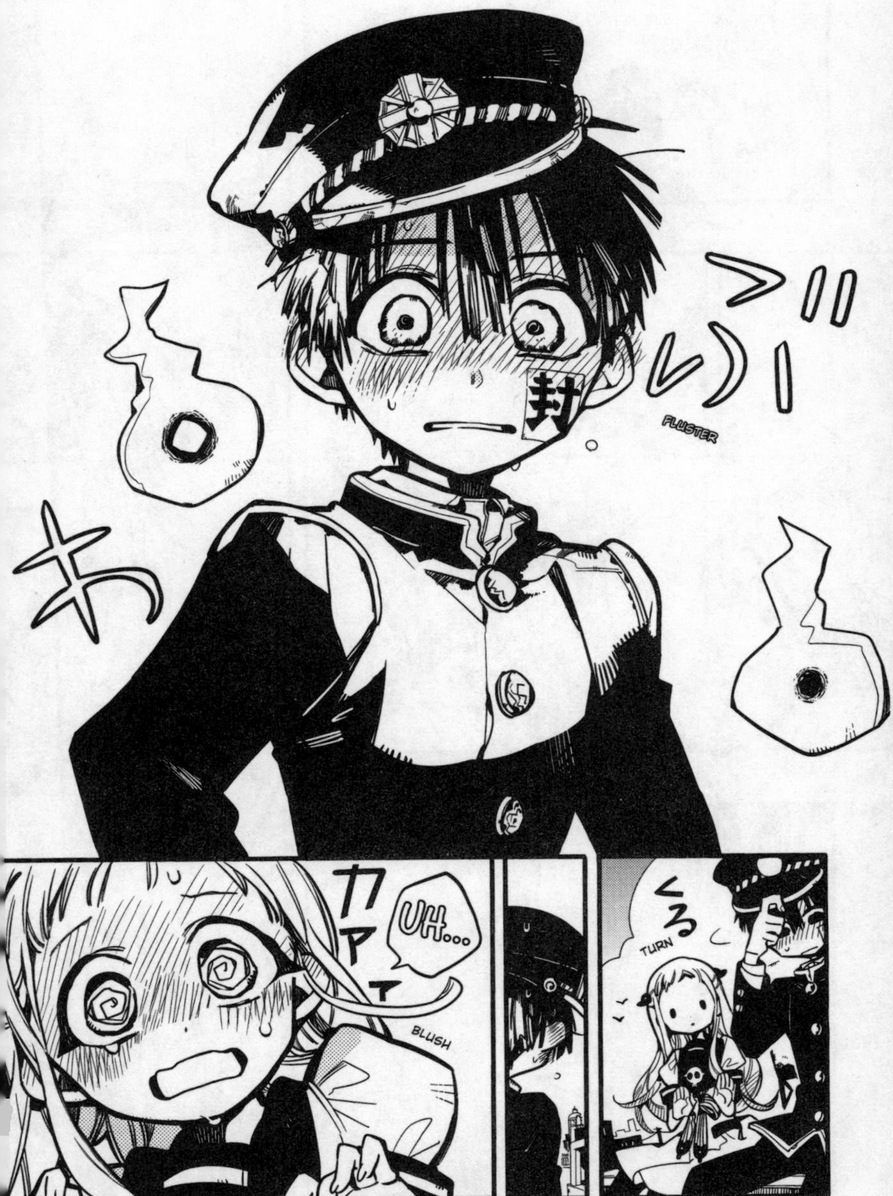
FLUSTER
くる
TURN
カアァ
UH...
BLUSH

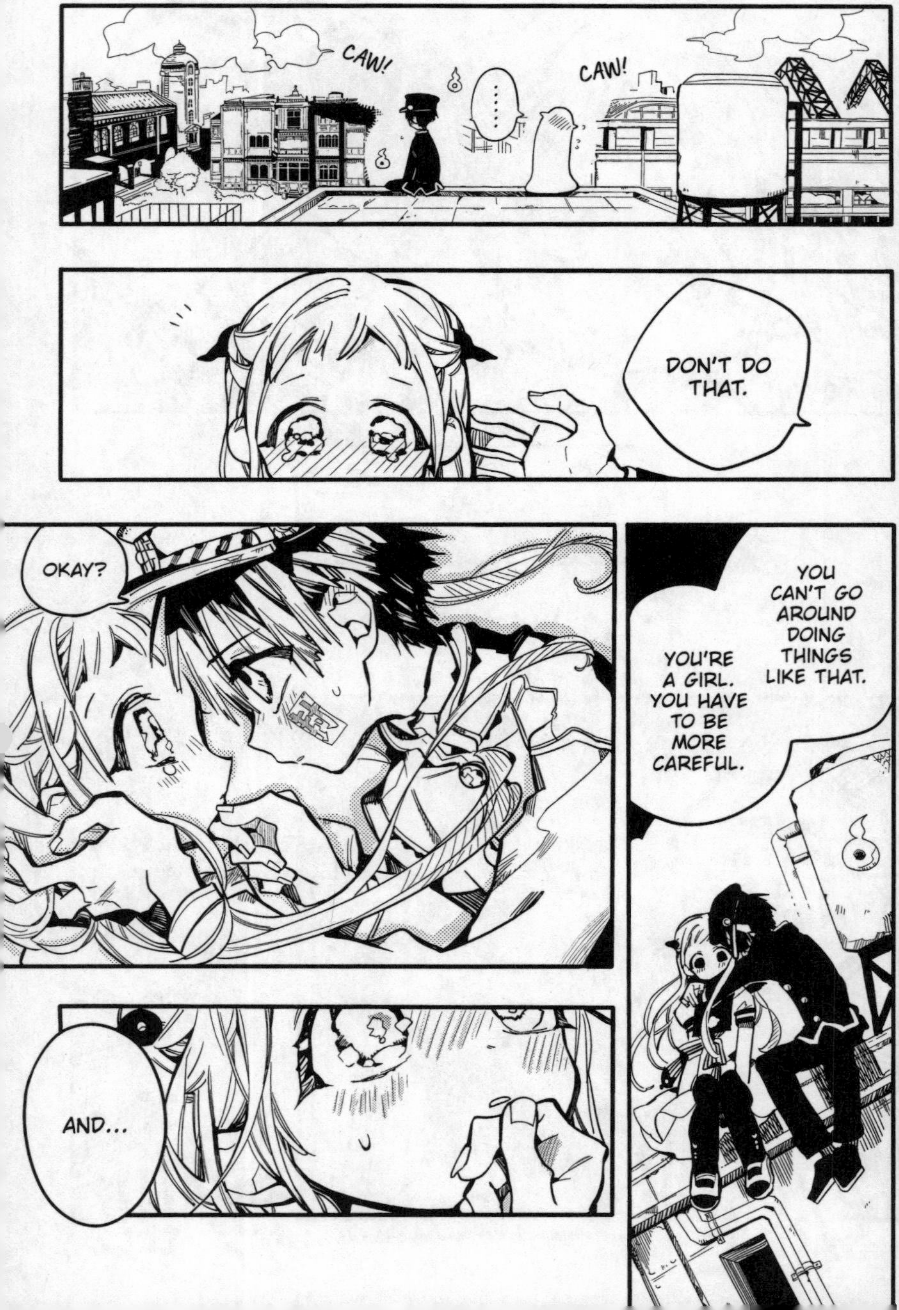
CAW!
......
CAW!
DON'T DO THAT.
YOU CAN'T GO AROUND DOING THINGS LIKE THAT.
YOU'RE A GIRL. YOU HAVE TO BE MORE CAREFUL.
OKAY?
AND...

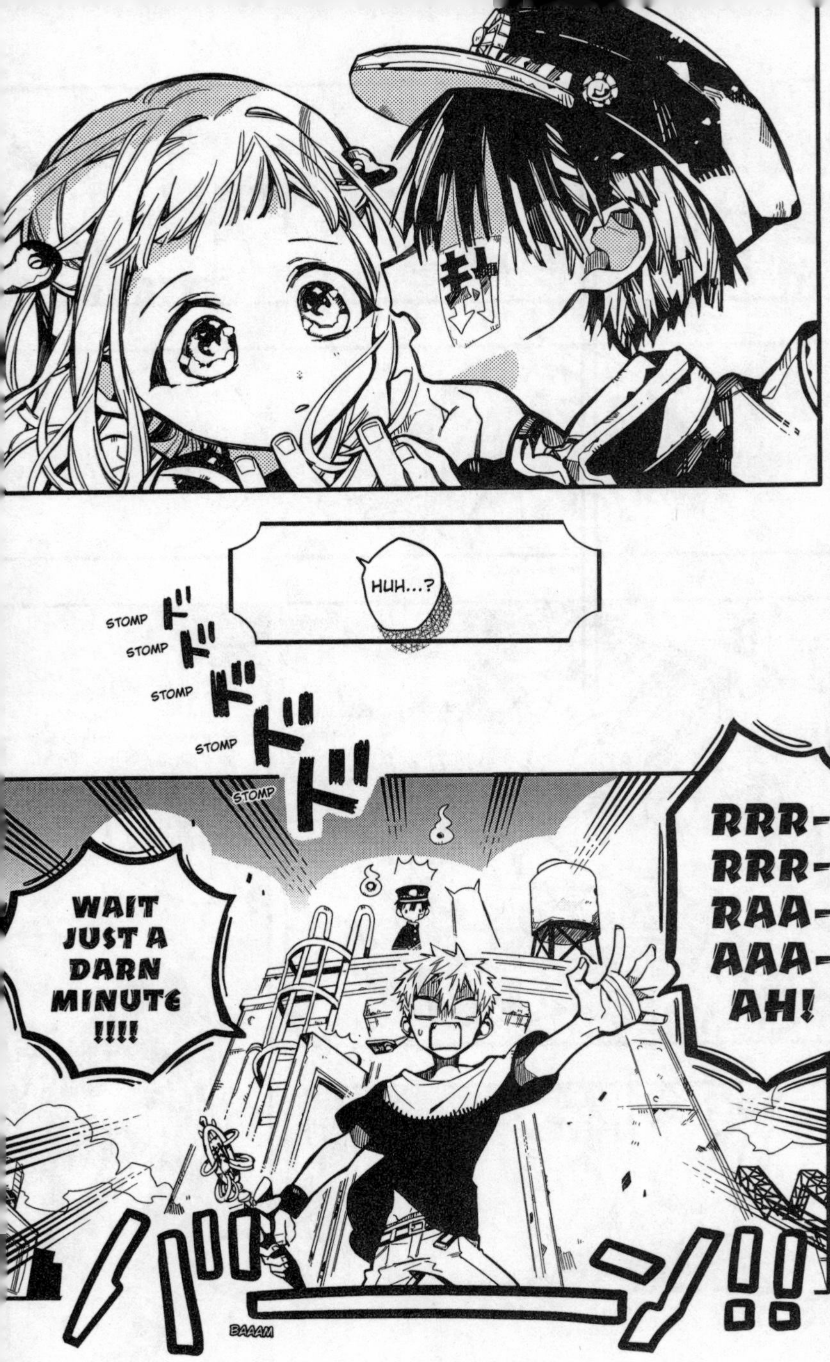
HUH...?
STOMP
STOMP
STOMP
STOMP
STOMP
RRR-RRR-RAA-AAA-AH!
WAIT JUST A DARN MINUTE!!!!
BAAAM

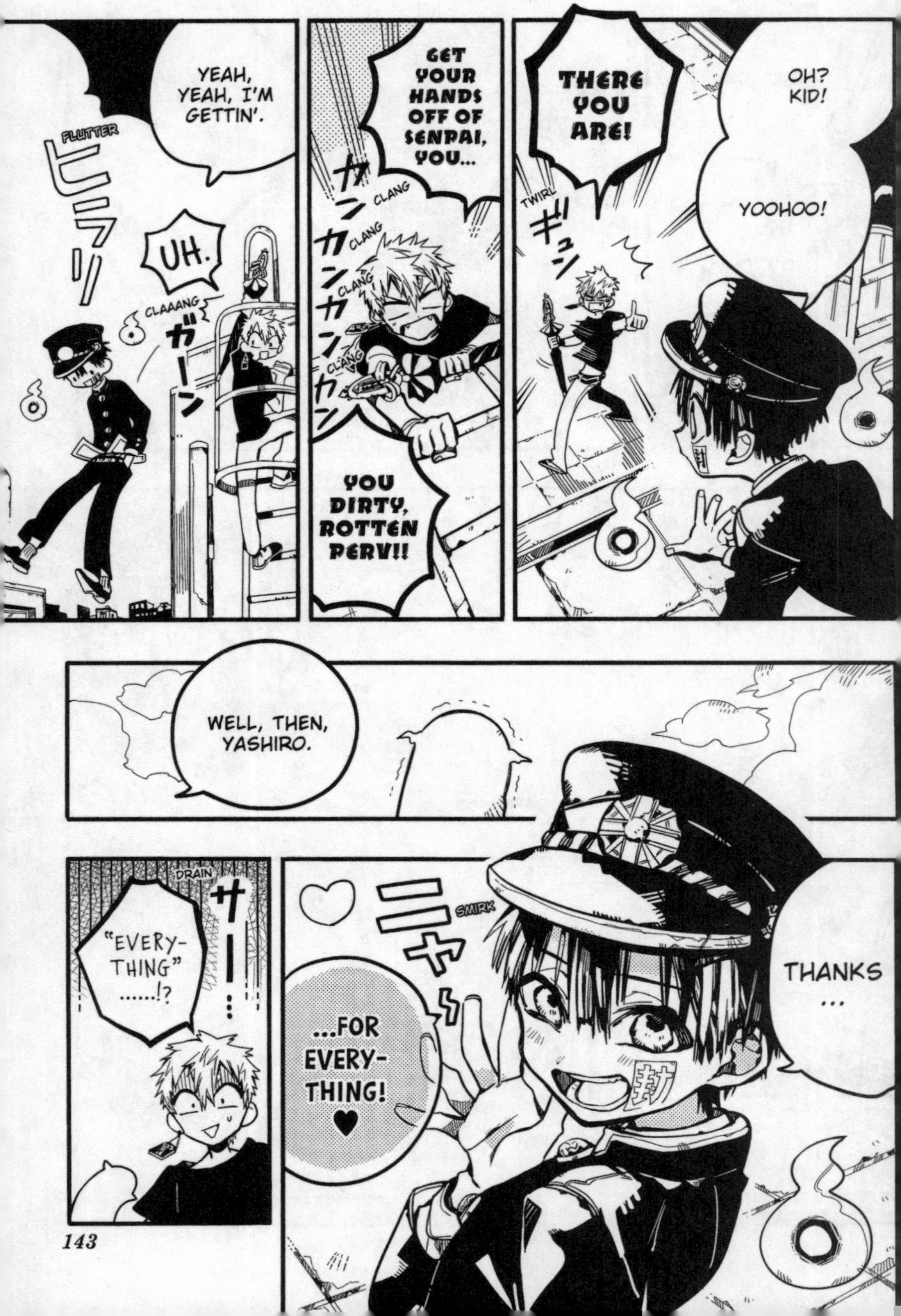
OH? KID!
YOOHOO!
THERE YOU ARE!
TWIRL
GET YOUR HANDS OFF OF SENPAI, YOU...
CLANG
CLANG
CLANG
CLANG
YOU DIRTY, ROTTEN PERV!!
YEAH, YEAH, I'M GETTIN'.
FLUTTER
UH.
CLAAANG
WELL, THEN, YASHIRO.
THANKS...
SMIRK
...FOR EVERYTHING! ♥
DRAIN
"EVERYTHING"......!?

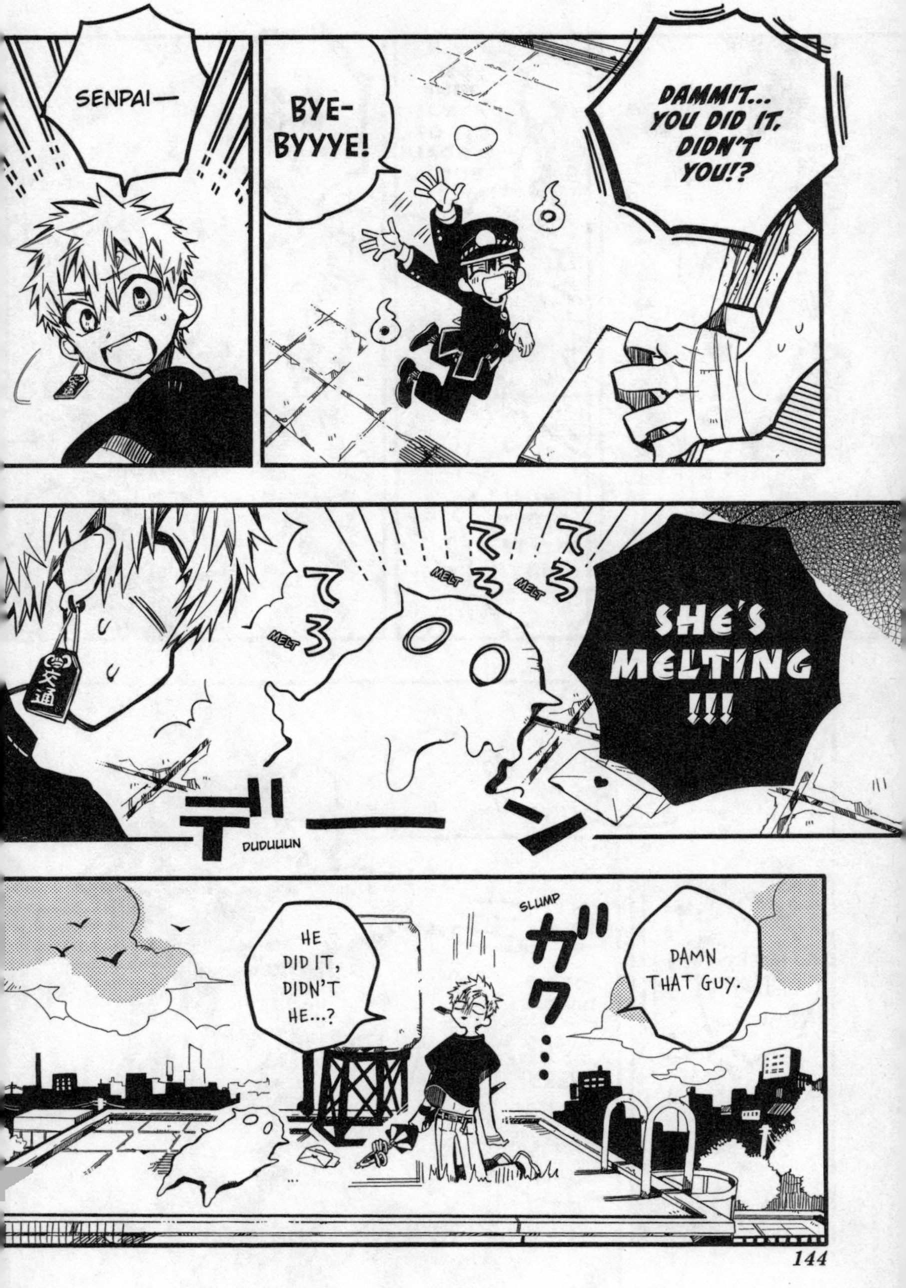
DAMMIT... YOU DID IT, DIDN'T YOU!?
BYE-BYYYE!
SENPAI—
てろ MELT
SHE'S MELTING !!!
てろ MELT
てろ MELT
デーン DUDUUUN
DAMN THAT GUY.
ガク… SLUMP
HE DID IT, DIDN'T HE...?
...

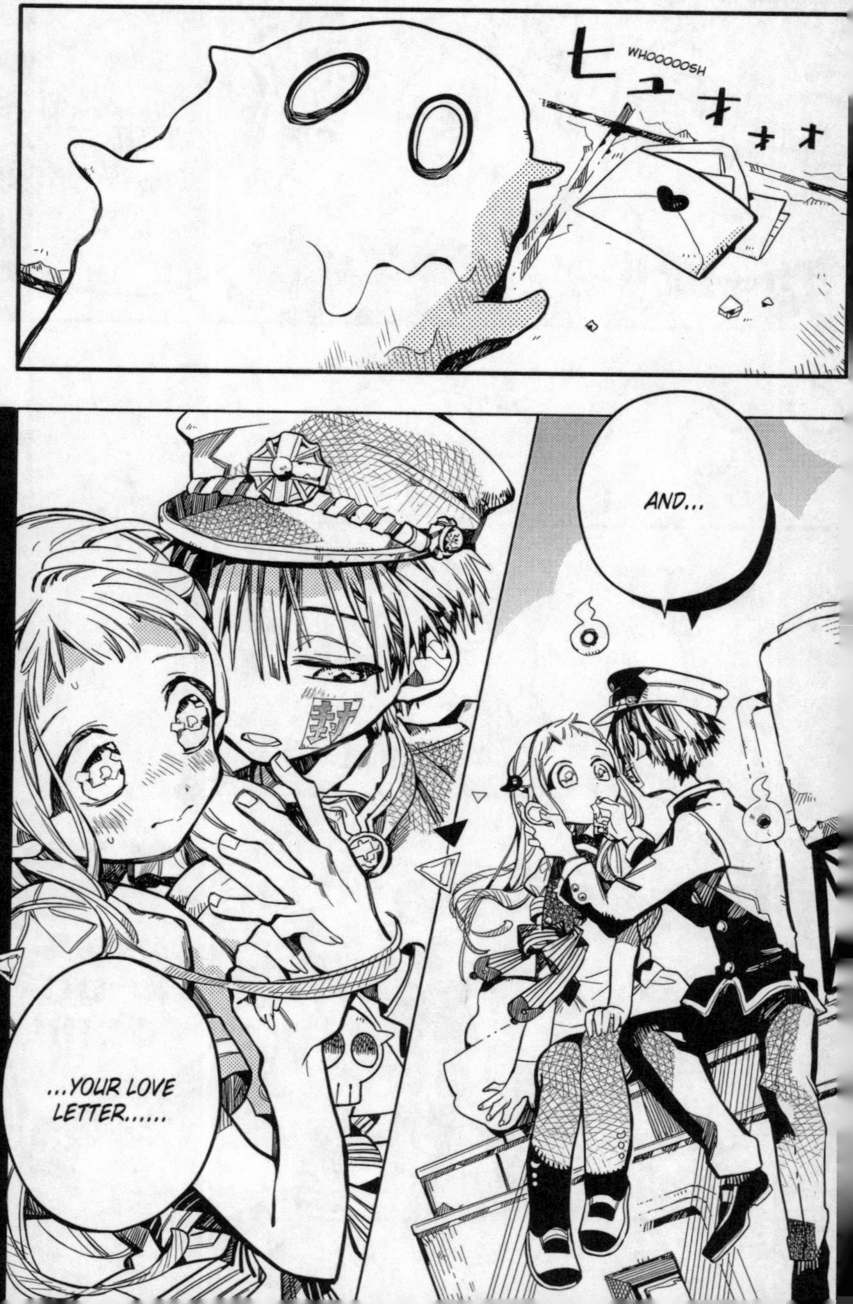
ヒュオォォ
WHOOOOOSH
AND...
...YOUR LOVE LETTER......

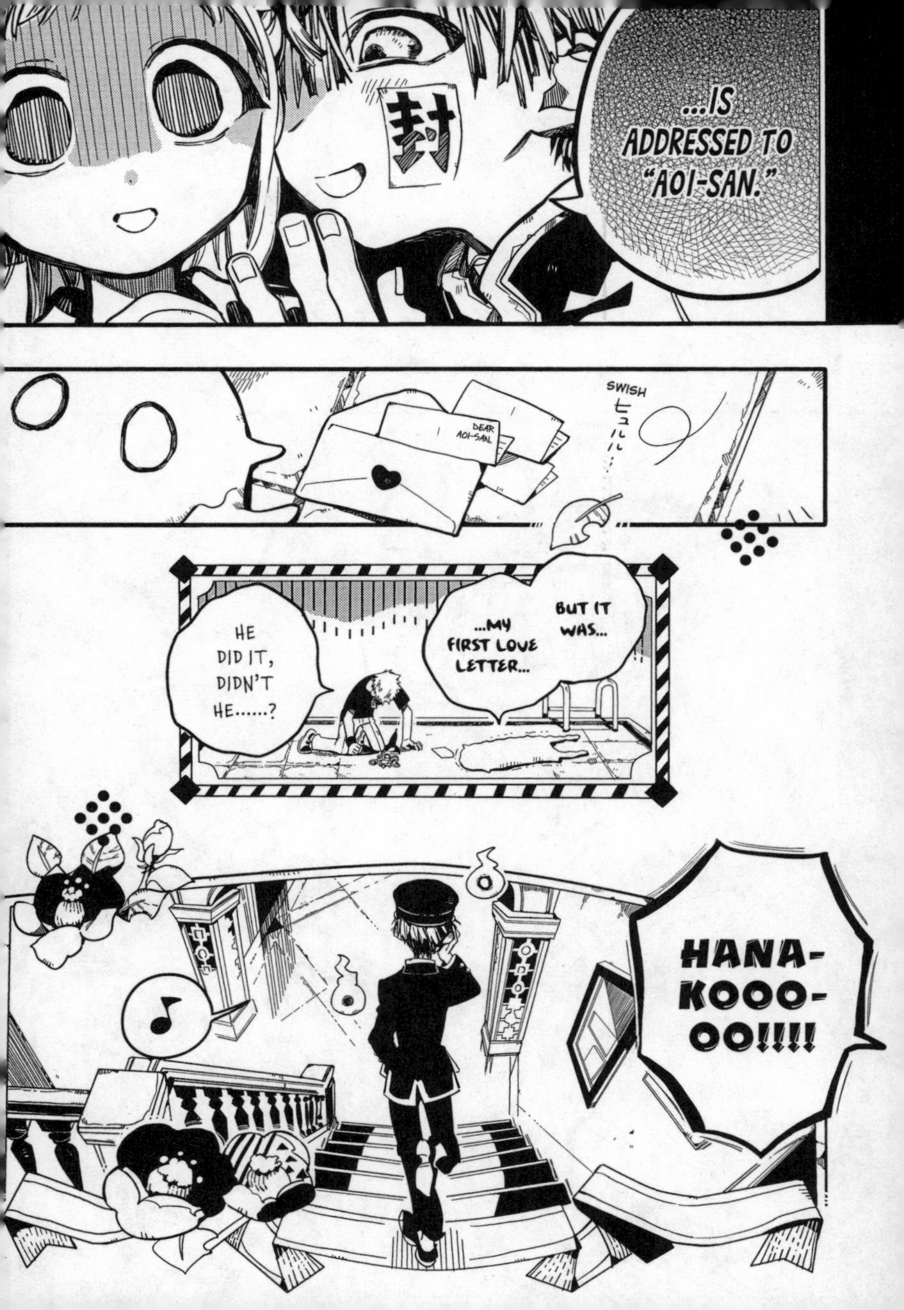
...IS ADDRESSED TO "AOI-SAN."
SWISH
ヒュルル…
DEAR AOI-SAN.
BUT IT WAS...
...MY FIRST LOVE LETTER...
HE DID IT, DIDN'T HE......?
HANA-KOOOO-OO!!!!!

ギョロ
SWIVEL
カサカサ
SKITTER
SKITTER
カサ
SKITTER
ベチャ
SPLAT
ズリズリ
DRAG
HMMM?
YEAH. PRETTY GOOD, DON'TCHA THINK?
MM-HMM. I LIKE IT.
I LIKE IT.
SPLRCH
SPLRCH

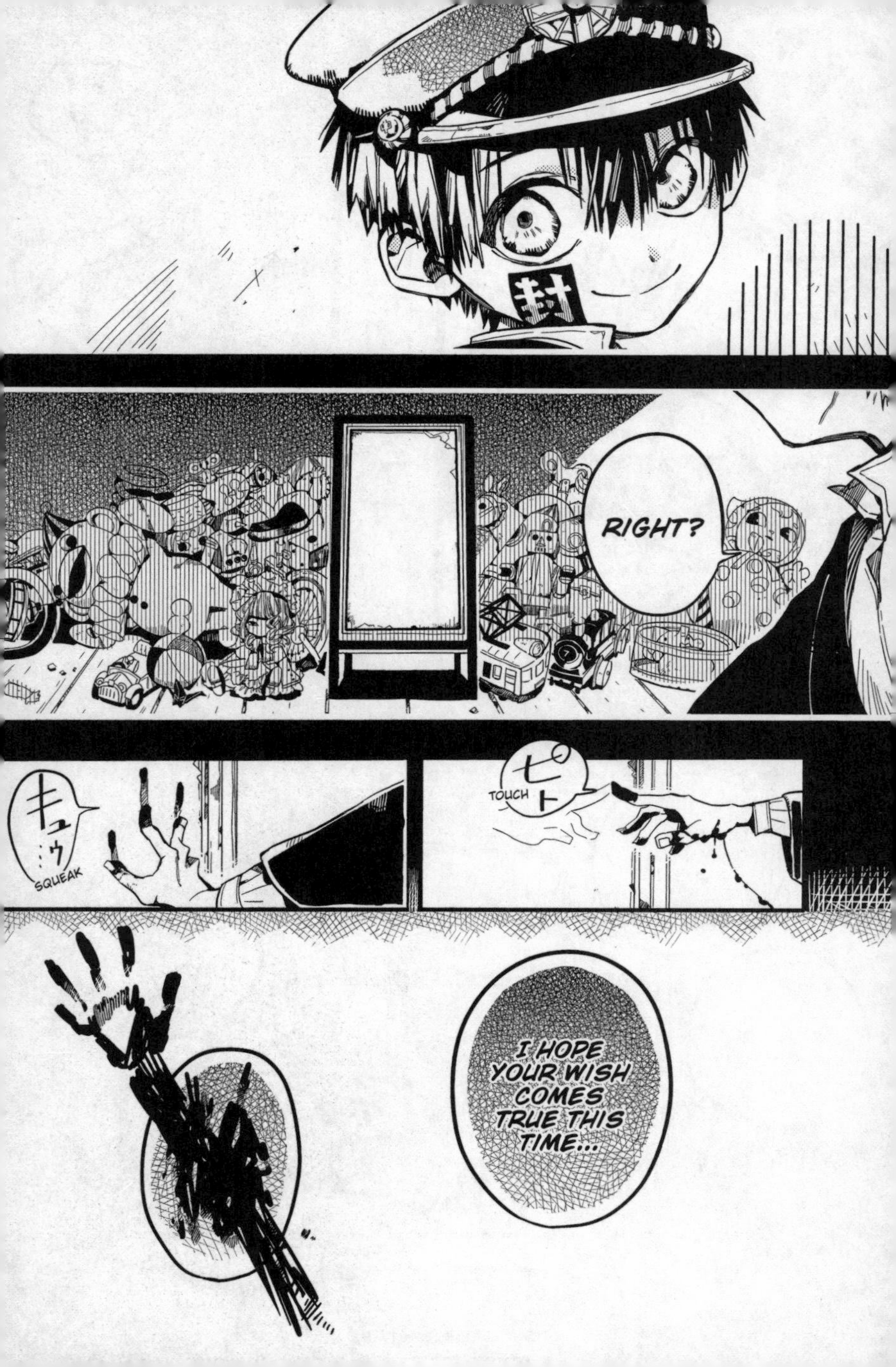
RIGHT?
ピト
TOUCH
キュウ
SQUEAK
I HOPE YOUR WISH COMES TRUE THIS TIME...

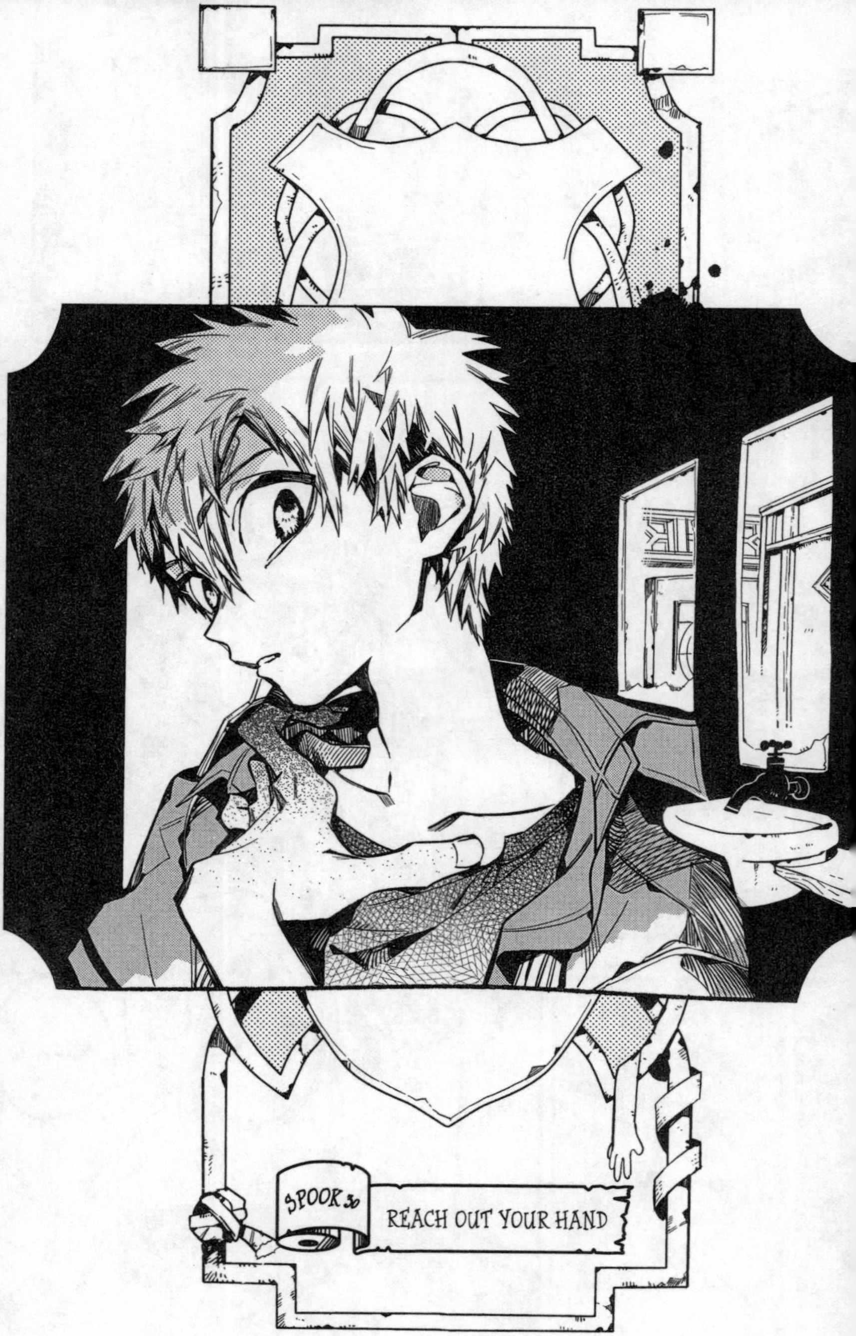
SPOOK 30
REACH OUT YOUR HAND

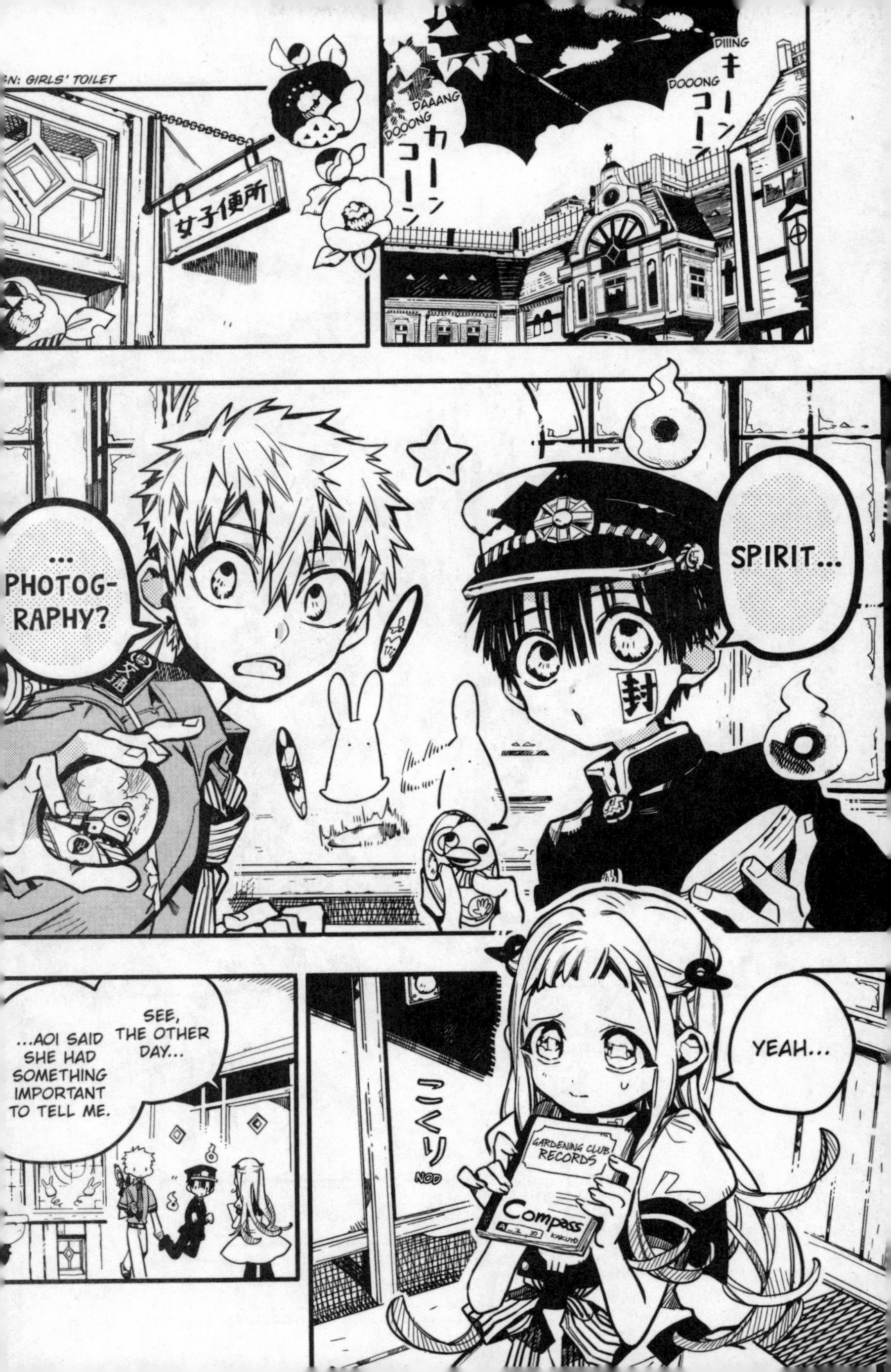
DIIING
キーンコーン
DOOONG
DAAANG
DOOONG
カーンコーン
GN: GIRLS' TOILET
女子便所
SPIRIT...
...PHOTOG-RAPHY?
YEAH...
こくり
NOD
GARDENING CLUB RECORDS
Compass
SEE, THE OTHER DAY...
...AOI SAID SHE HAD SOMETHING IMPORTANT TO TELL ME.

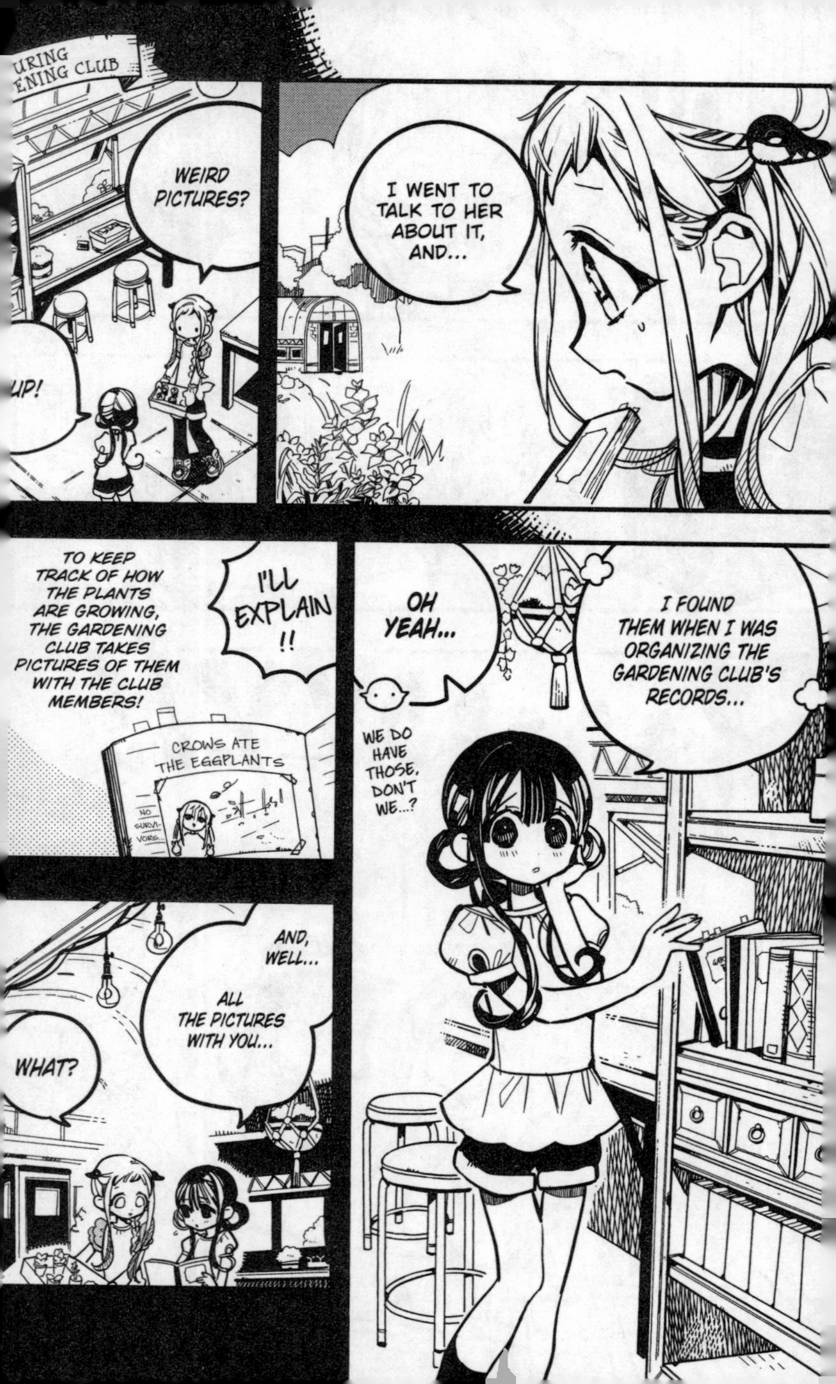
I WENT TO TALK TO HER ABOUT IT, AND...
WEIRD PICTURES?
URING
ENING CLUB
UP!
I FOUND THEM WHEN I WAS ORGANIZING THE GARDENING CLUB'S RECORDS...
OH YEAH...
WE DO HAVE THOSE, DON'T WE...?
I'LL EXPLAIN !!
TO KEEP TRACK OF HOW THE PLANTS ARE GROWING, THE GARDENING CLUB TAKES PICTURES OF THEM WITH THE CLUB MEMBERS!
CROWS ATE THE EGGPLANTS
NO SURVI-VORS.
AND, WELL...
ALL THE PICTURES WITH YOU...
WHAT?

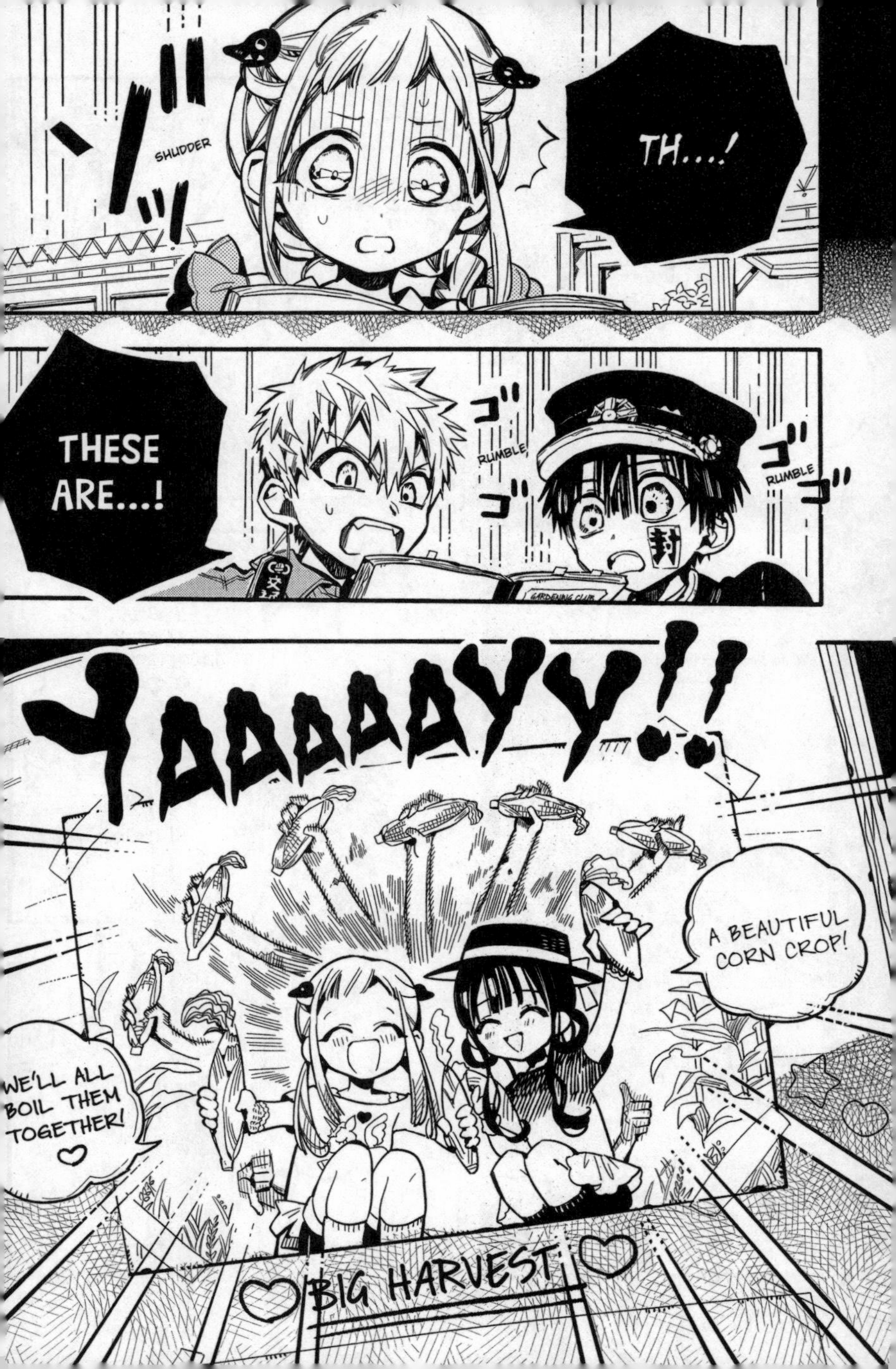

TH...!
SHUDDER
RUMBLE
RUMBLE,
THESE ARE...!
GARDENING CLUB
YAAAAAY!!
A BEAUTIFUL CORN CROP!
WE'LL ALL BOIL THEM TOGETHER! ♡
♡ BIG HARVEST ♡

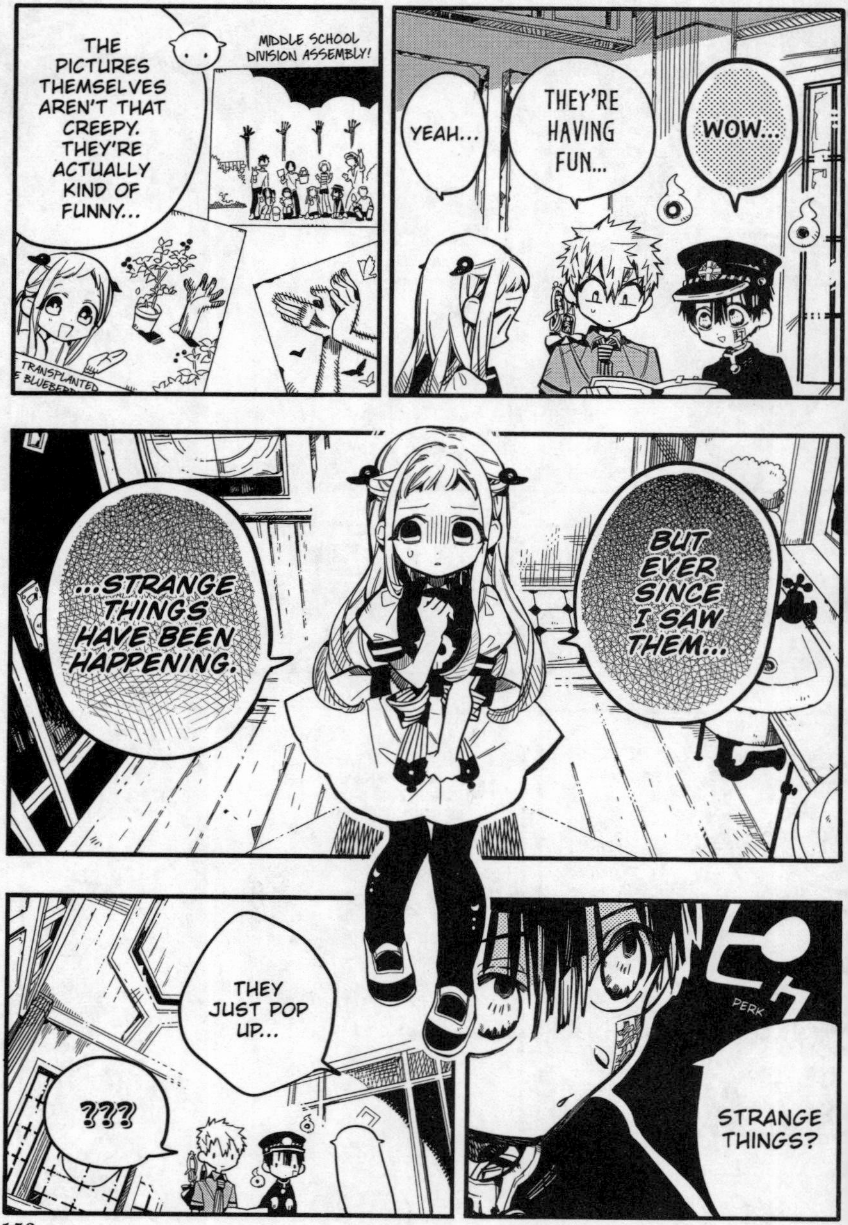

WOW...
THEY'RE HAVING FUN...
YEAH...
MIDDLE SCHOOL DIVISION ASSEMBLY!
THE PICTURES THEMSELVES AREN'T THAT CREEPY. THEY'RE ACTUALLY KIND OF FUNNY...
TRANSPLANTED
BUT EVER SINCE I SAW THEM...
...STRANGE THINGS HAVE BEEN HAPPENING.
ピク
PERK
STRANGE THINGS?
THEY JUST POP UP...
???

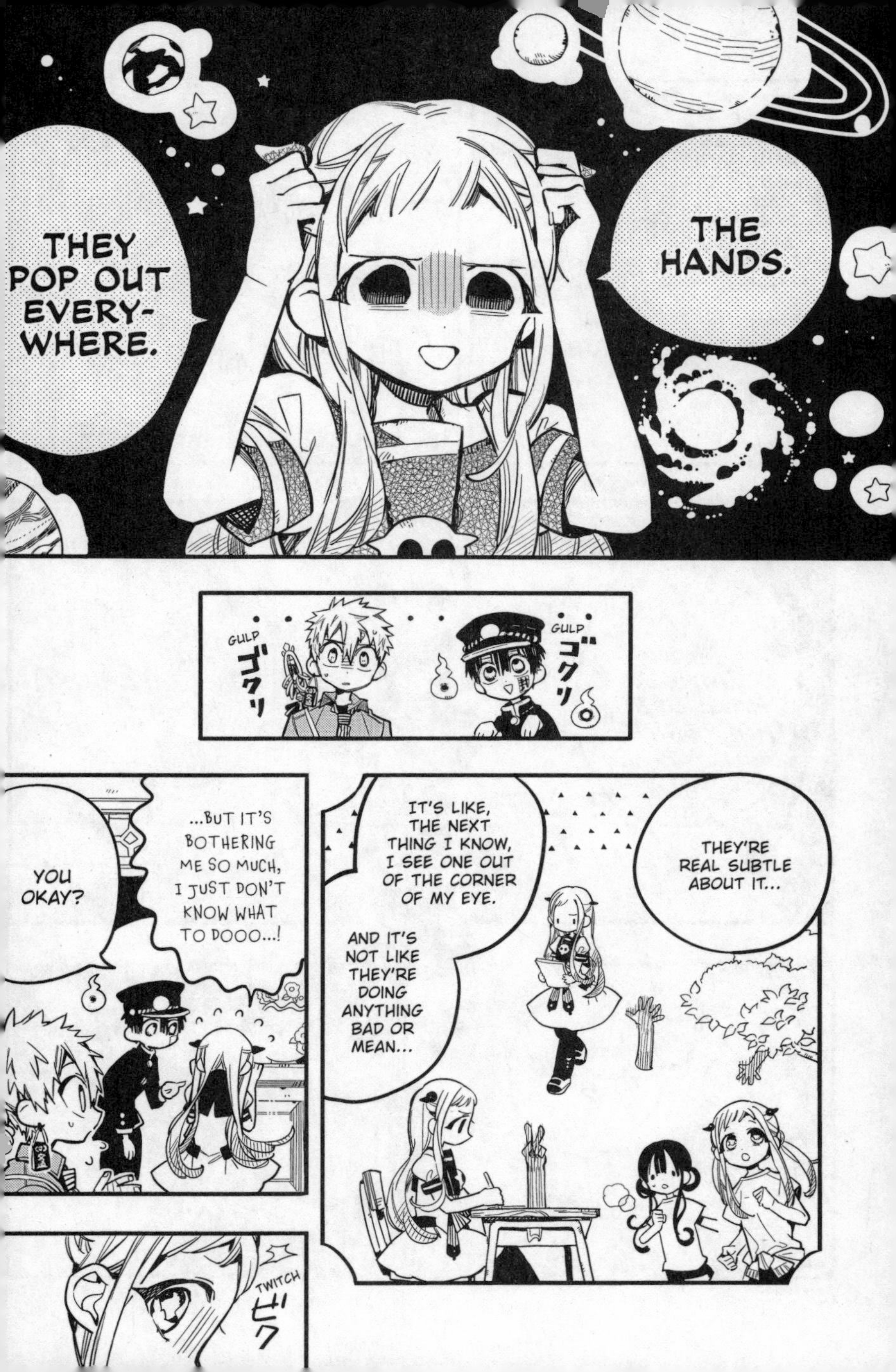
THE HANDS.
THEY POP OUT EVERY-WHERE.
GULP ゴクリ
GULP ゴクリ
THEY'RE REAL SUBTLE ABOUT IT...
IT'S LIKE, THE NEXT THING I KNOW, I SEE ONE OUT OF THE CORNER OF MY EYE.
AND IT'S NOT LIKE THEY'RE DOING ANYTHING BAD OR MEAN...
...BUT IT'S BOTHERING ME SO MUCH, I JUST DON'T KNOW WHAT TO DOOO...!
YOU OKAY?
TWITCH ビク

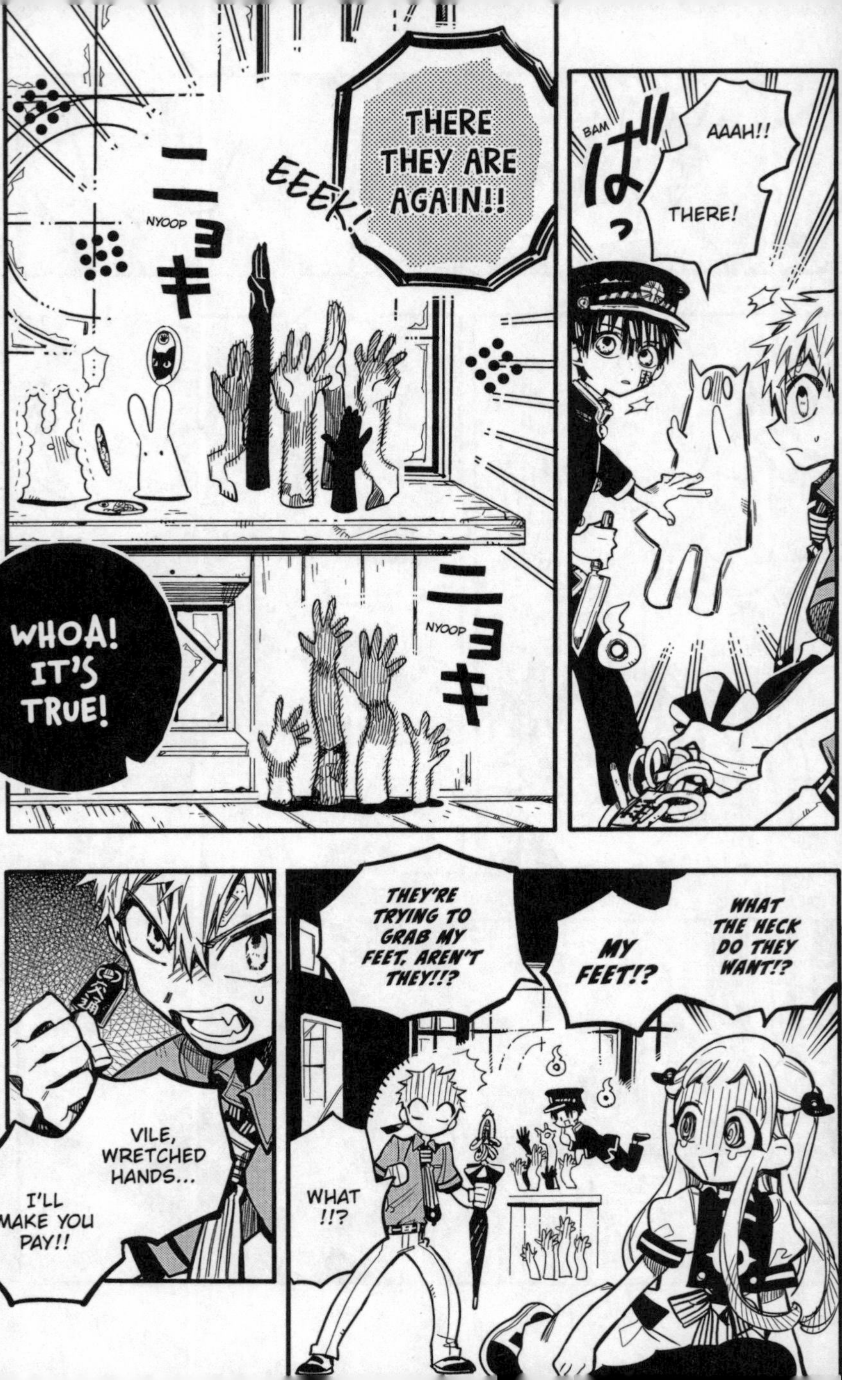
BAM
ばっ
AAAH!!
THERE!
THERE THEY ARE AGAIN!!
EEEK!
NYOOP
ニョキ
WHOA! IT'S TRUE!
NYOOP
ニョキ
WHAT THE HECK DO THEY WANT!?
MY FEET!?
THEY'RE TRYING TO GRAB MY FEET, AREN'T THEY!!?
WHAT !!?
VILE, WRETCHED HANDS...
I'LL MAKE YOU PAY!!

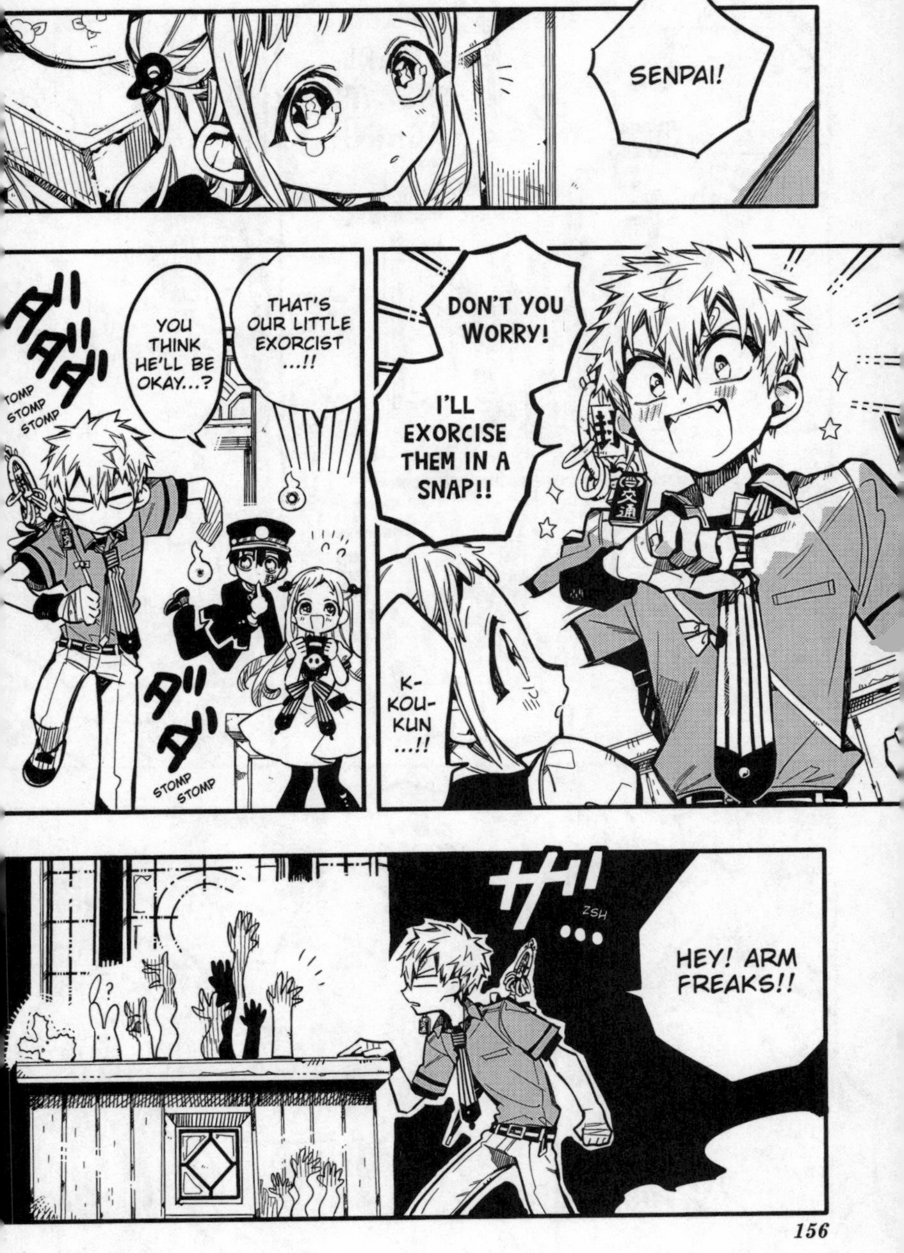
SENPAI!
DON'T YOU WORRY!
I'LL EXORCISE THEM IN A SNAP!!
K-KOU-KUN ...!!
THAT'S OUR LITTLE EXORCIST ...!!
YOU THINK HE'LL BE OKAY...?
TOMP STOMP STOMP
STOMP STOMP
ZSH
...
HEY! ARM FREAKS!!

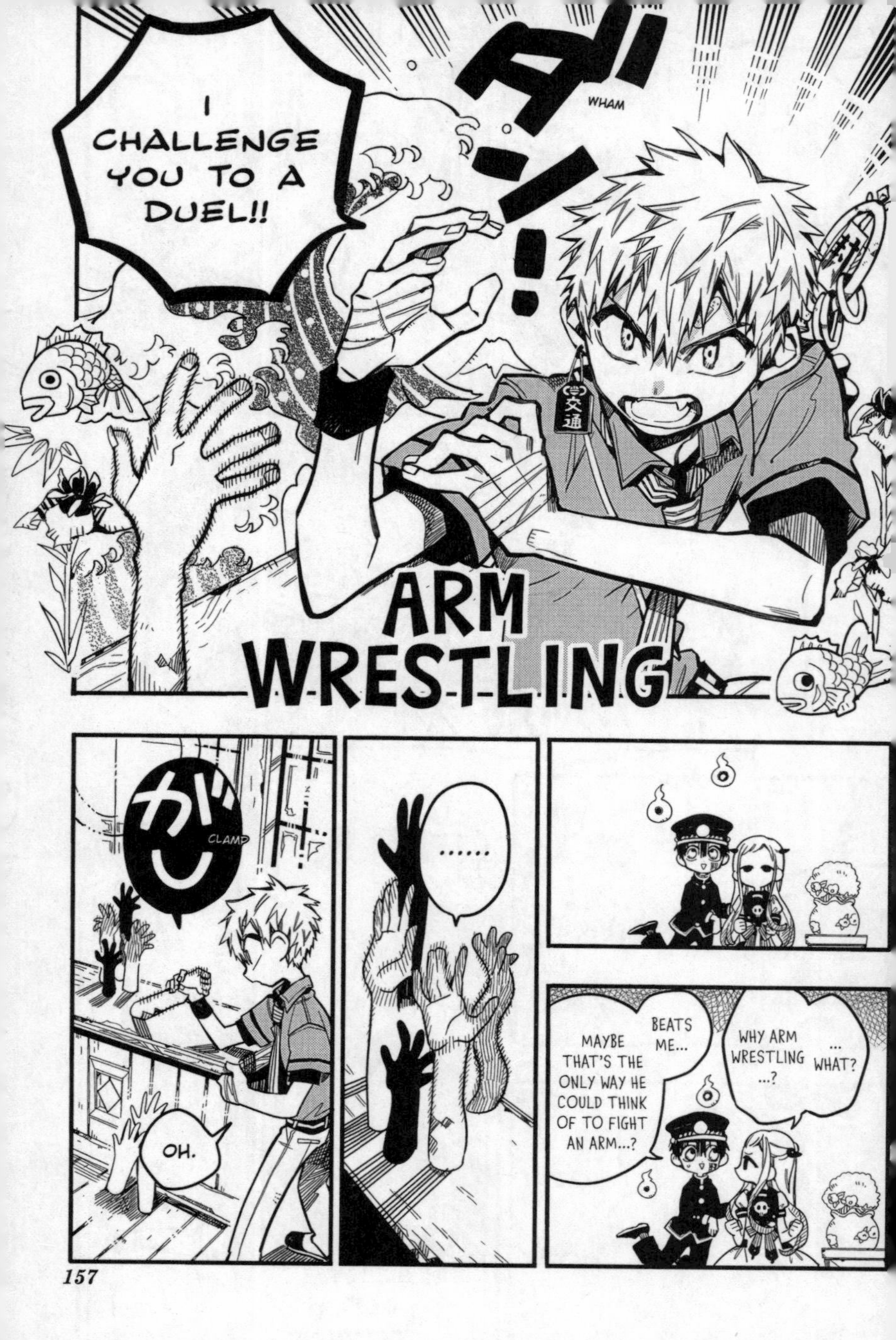
WHAM
I CHALLENGE YOU TO A DUEL!!
ARM WRESTLING
... WHAT?
WHY ARM WRESTLING ...?
BEATS ME...
MAYBE THAT'S THE ONLY WAY HE COULD THINK OF TO FIGHT AN ARM...?
......
CLAMP
OH.

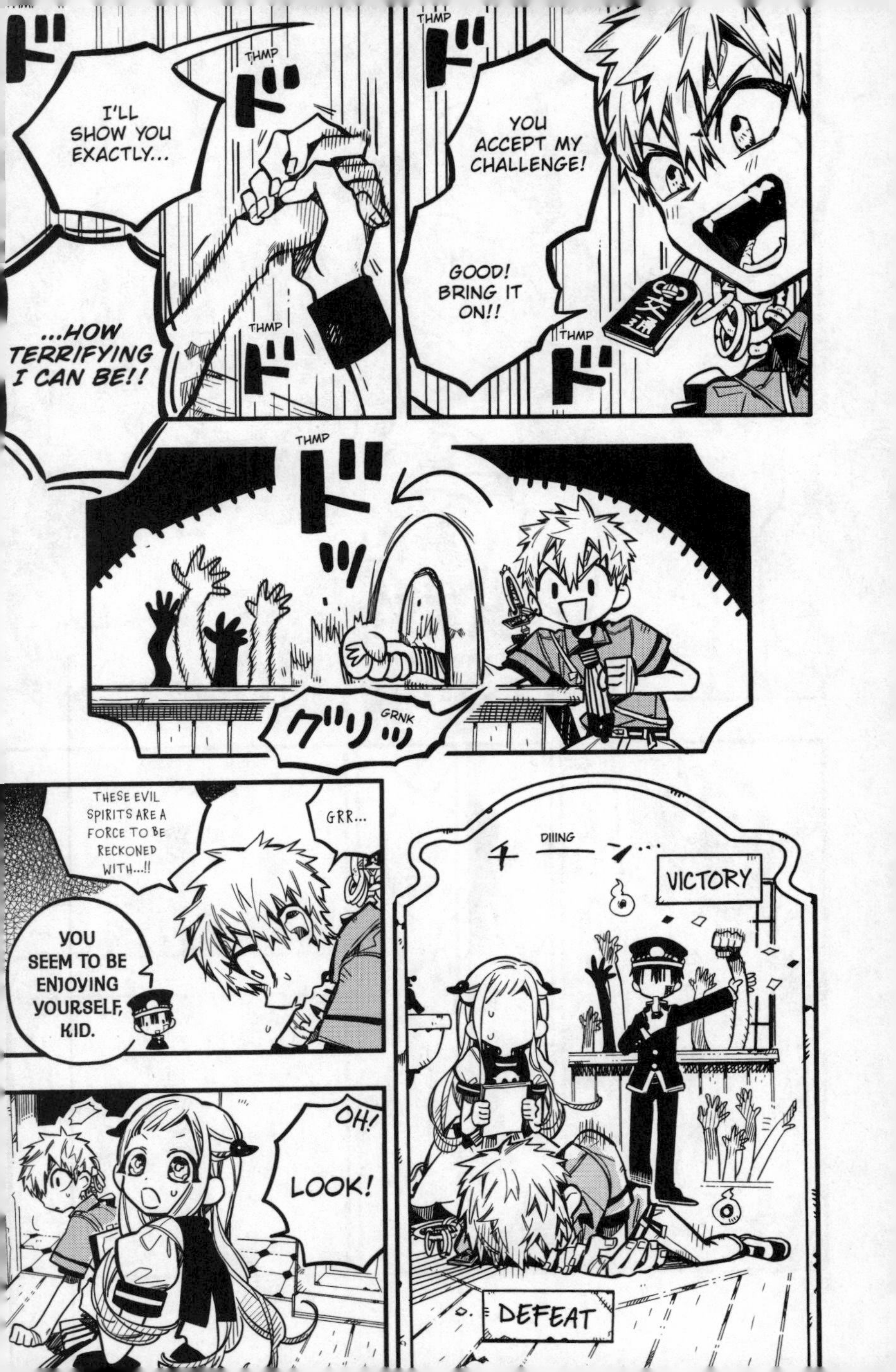

ド THMP
YOU ACCEPT MY CHALLENGE!
GOOD! BRING IT ON!!
ド THMP
ド THMP
I'LL SHOW YOU EXACTLY...
ド THMP
...HOW TERRIFYING I CAN BE!!
ド THMP
ド THMP
ッ
グリッ GRNK
チーン… DIIING
VICTORY
DEFEAT
GRR...
THESE EVIL SPIRITS ARE A FORCE TO BE RECKONED WITH...!!
YOU SEEM TO BE ENJOYING YOURSELF, KID.
OH!
LOOK!

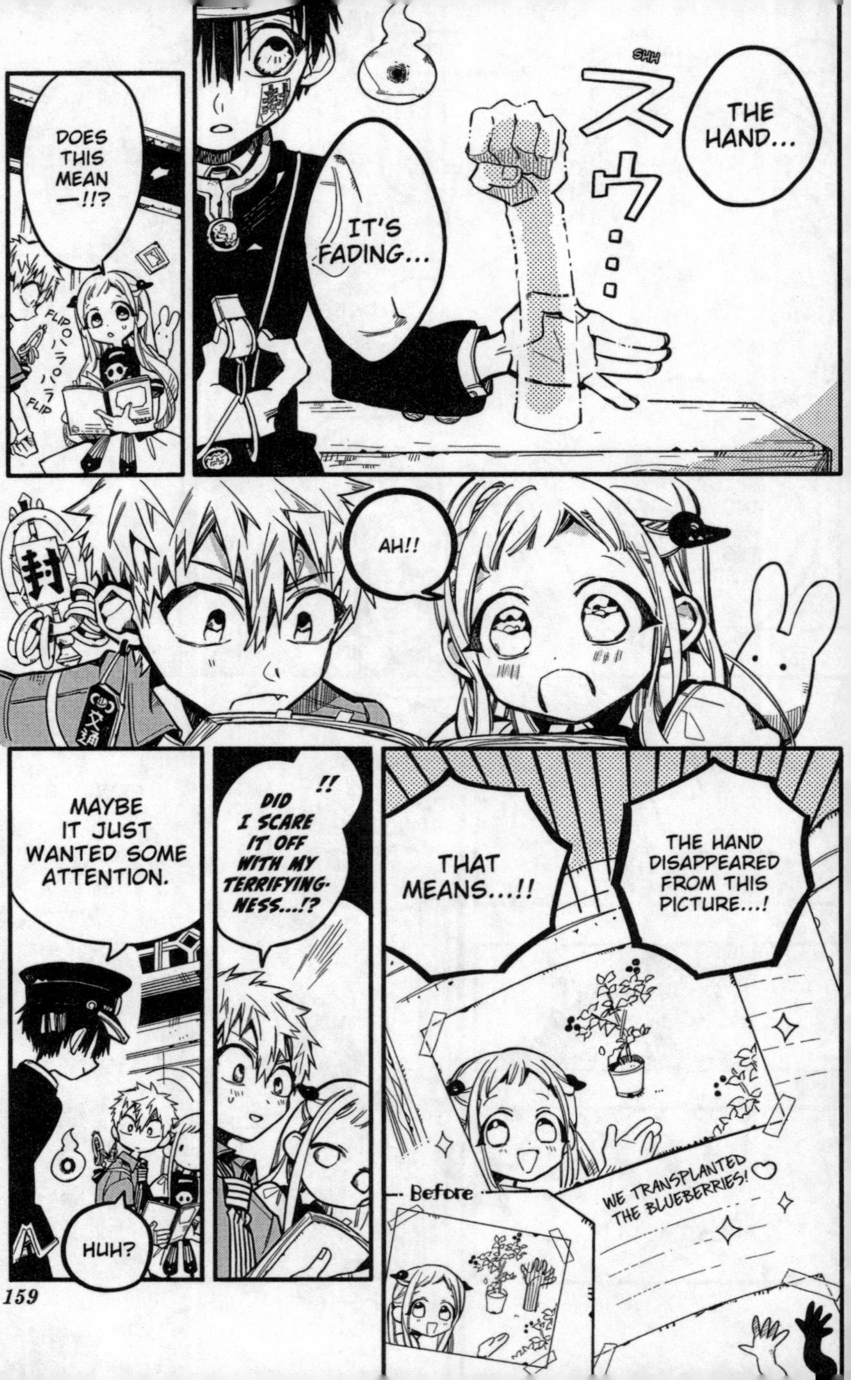
SHH
スゥ…
THE HAND...
IT'S FADING...
DOES THIS MEAN—!!?
FLIP
パラパラ
FLIP
AH!!
THE HAND DISAPPEARED FROM THIS PICTURE...!
THAT MEANS...!!
WE TRANSPLANTED THE BLUEBERRIES!
Before
!!
DID I SCARE IT OFF WITH MY TERRIFYINGNESS...!?
MAYBE IT JUST WANTED SOME ATTENTION.
HUH?

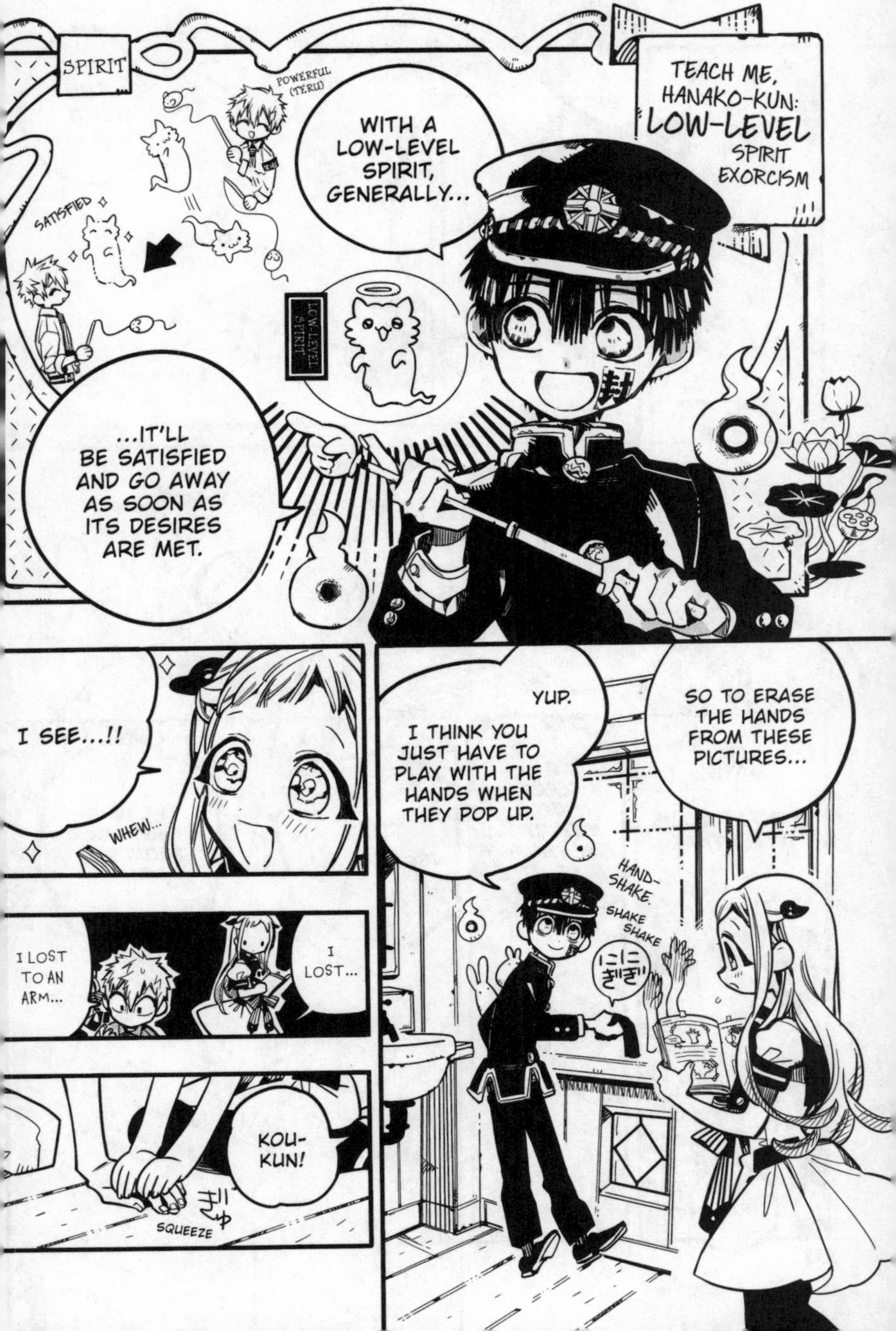
TEACH ME, HANAKO-KUN: LOW-LEVEL SPIRIT EXORCISM
WITH A LOW-LEVEL SPIRIT, GENERALLY...
LOW-LEVEL SPIRIT
SPIRIT
POWERFUL (TERU)
SATISFIED
...IT'LL BE SATISFIED AND GO AWAY AS SOON AS ITS DESIRES ARE MET.
SO TO ERASE THE HANDS FROM THESE PICTURES...
YUP.
I THINK YOU JUST HAVE TO PLAY WITH THE HANDS WHEN THEY POP UP.
HAND-SHAKE.
SHAKE SHAKE
にぎにぎ
I SEE...!!
WHEW...
I LOST...
I LOST TO AN ARM...
KOU-KUN!
ぎゅ
SQUEEZE

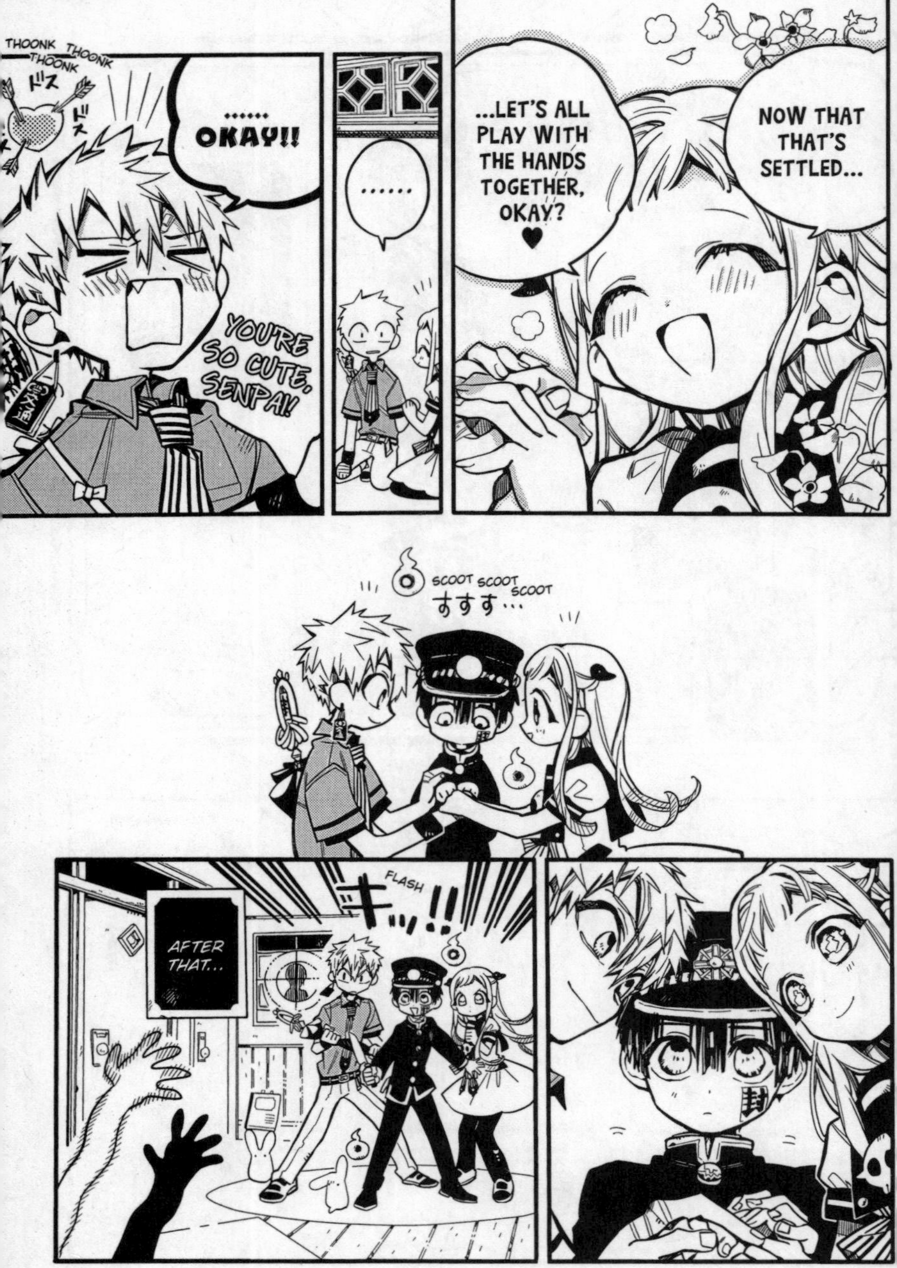
NOW THAT THAT'S SETTLED...
...LET'S ALL PLAY WITH THE HANDS TOGETHER, OKAY? ♥
....
THOONK THOONK THOONK
ドス ドス
...... OKAY!!
YOU'RE SO CUTE, SENPAI!!
SCOOT SCOOT SCOOT
すすす…
FLASH
ギッ!!
AFTER THAT...

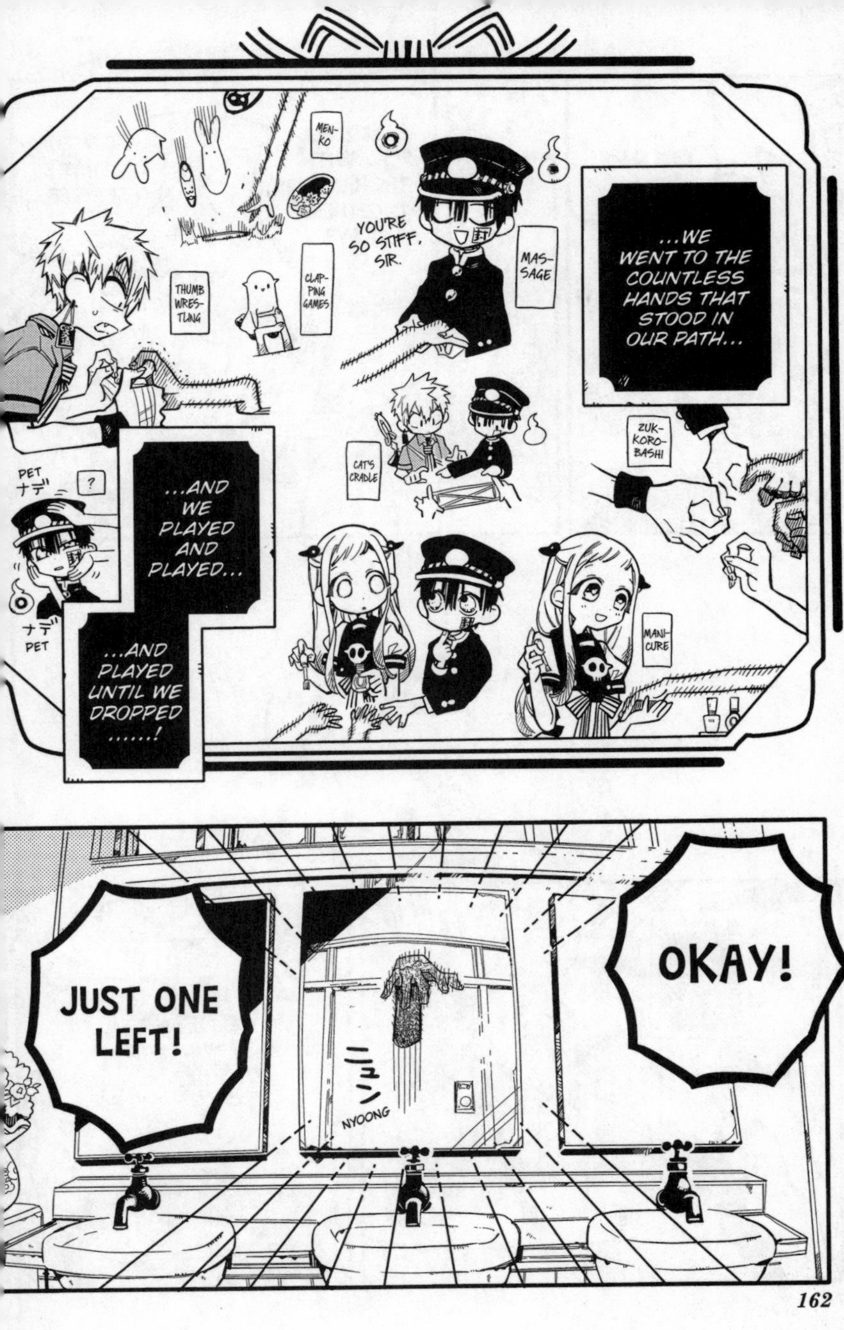
...WE WENT TO THE COUNTLESS HANDS THAT STOOD IN OUR PATH...
MEN-KO
MAS-SAGE
YOU'RE SO STIFF, SIR.
CLAP-PING GAMES
THUMB WRES-TLING
ZUK-KORO-BASHI
CAT'S CRADLE
MANI-CURE
PET ナデ
?
...AND WE PLAYED AND PLAYED...
ナデ PET
...AND PLAYED UNTIL WE DROPPED......!
OKAY!
ニュン
NYOONG
JUST ONE LEFT!

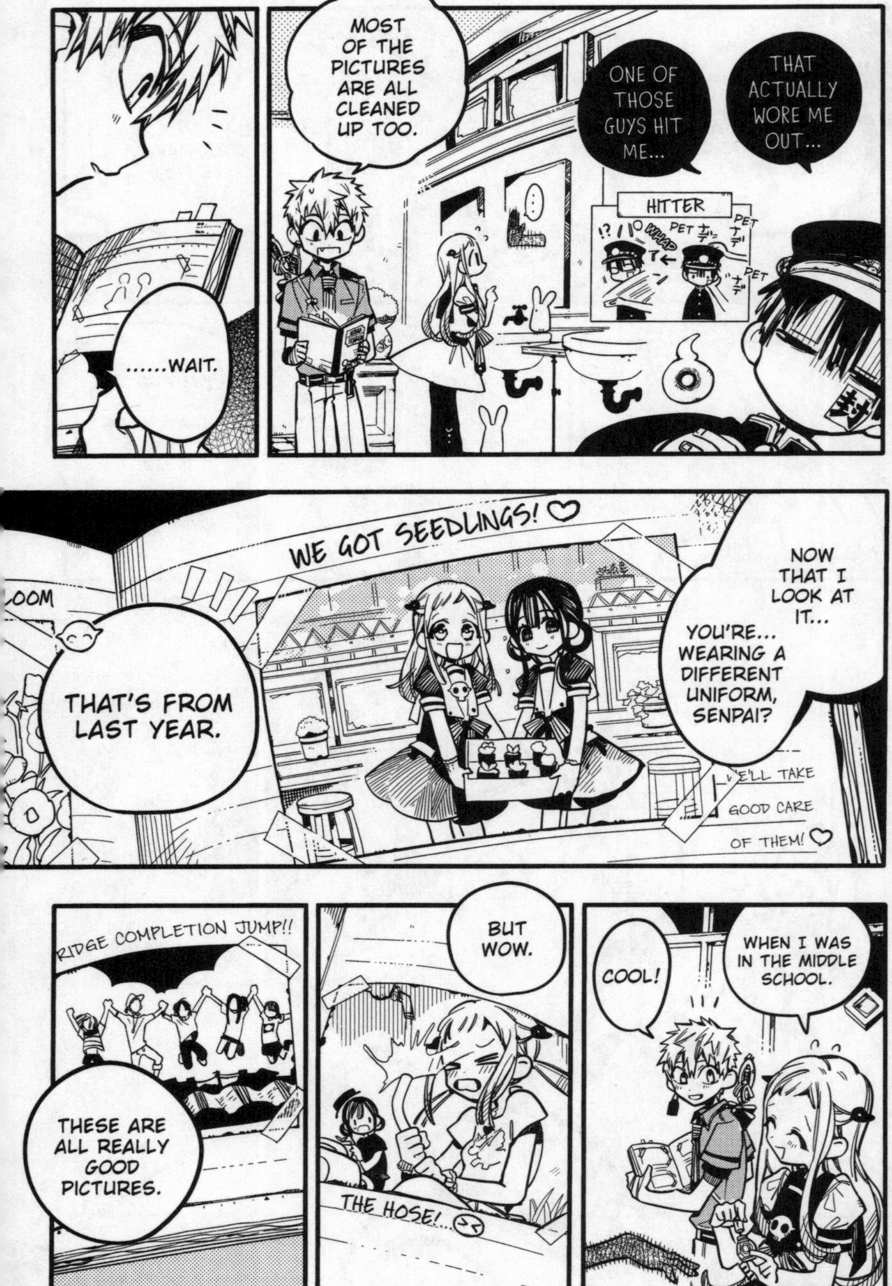
THAT ACTUALLY WORE ME OUT...
ONE OF THOSE GUYS HIT ME...
HITTER
PET PET PET
WHAP
!?
MOST OF THE PICTURES ARE ALL CLEANED UP TOO.
......WAIT.
NOW THAT I LOOK AT IT...
YOU'RE... WEARING A DIFFERENT UNIFORM, SENPAI?
WE GOT SEEDLINGS!
E'LL TAKE GOOD CARE OF THEM!
OOM
THAT'S FROM LAST YEAR.
WHEN I WAS IN THE MIDDLE SCHOOL.
COOL!
BUT WOW.
THE HOSE!
RIDGE COMPLETION JUMP!!
THESE ARE ALL REALLY GOOD PICTURES.

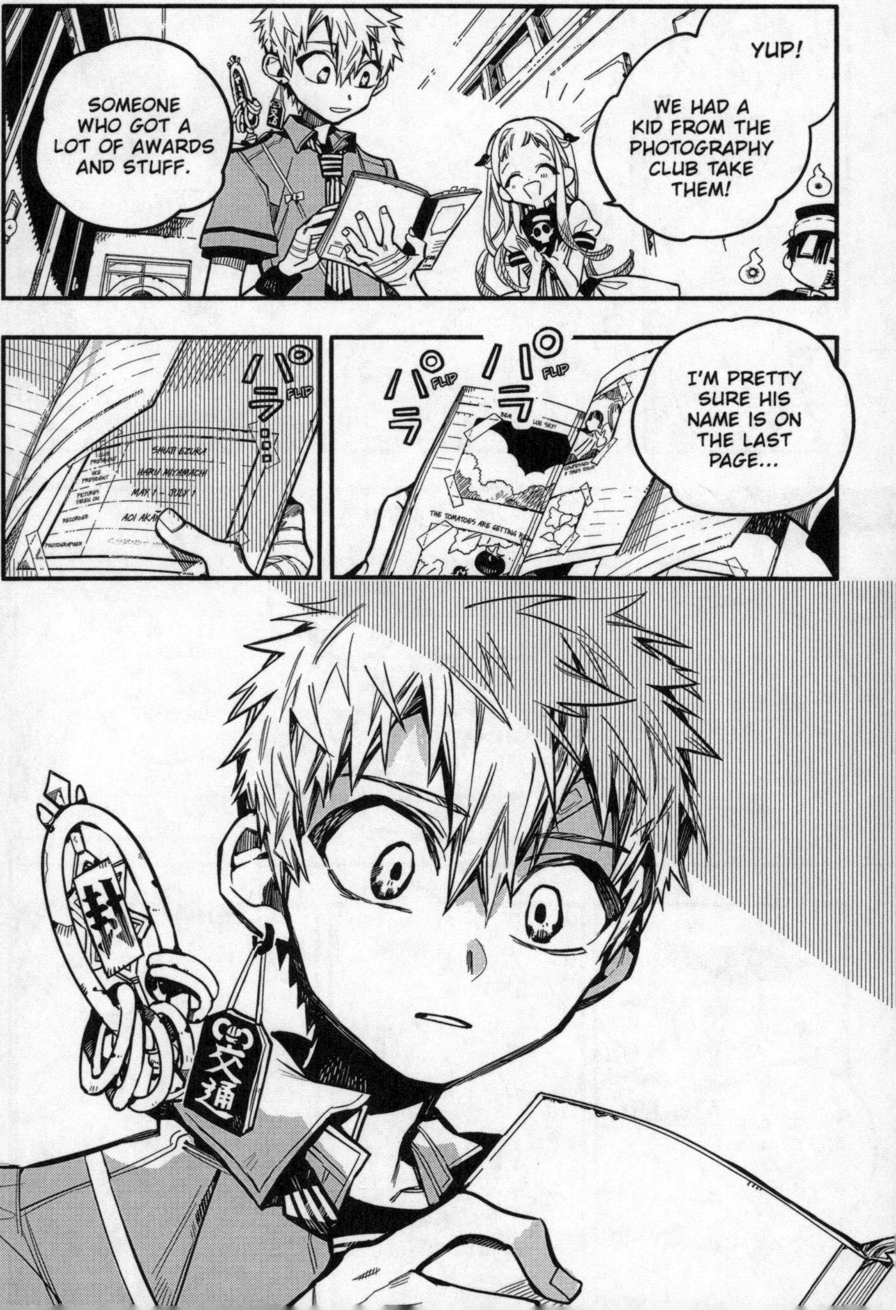
YUP!
WE HAD A KID FROM THE PHOTOGRAPHY CLUB TAKE THEM!
SOMEONE WHO GOT A LOT OF AWARDS AND STUFF.
パラ FLIP
パラ FLIP
I'M PRETTY SURE HIS NAME IS ON THE LAST PAGE...
THE TOMATOES ARE GETTING
パラ FLIP
SHUJI EZUKA
HARU MIYAMACHI
MAY 1 – JULY 1
RECORDER
PHOTOGRAPHER

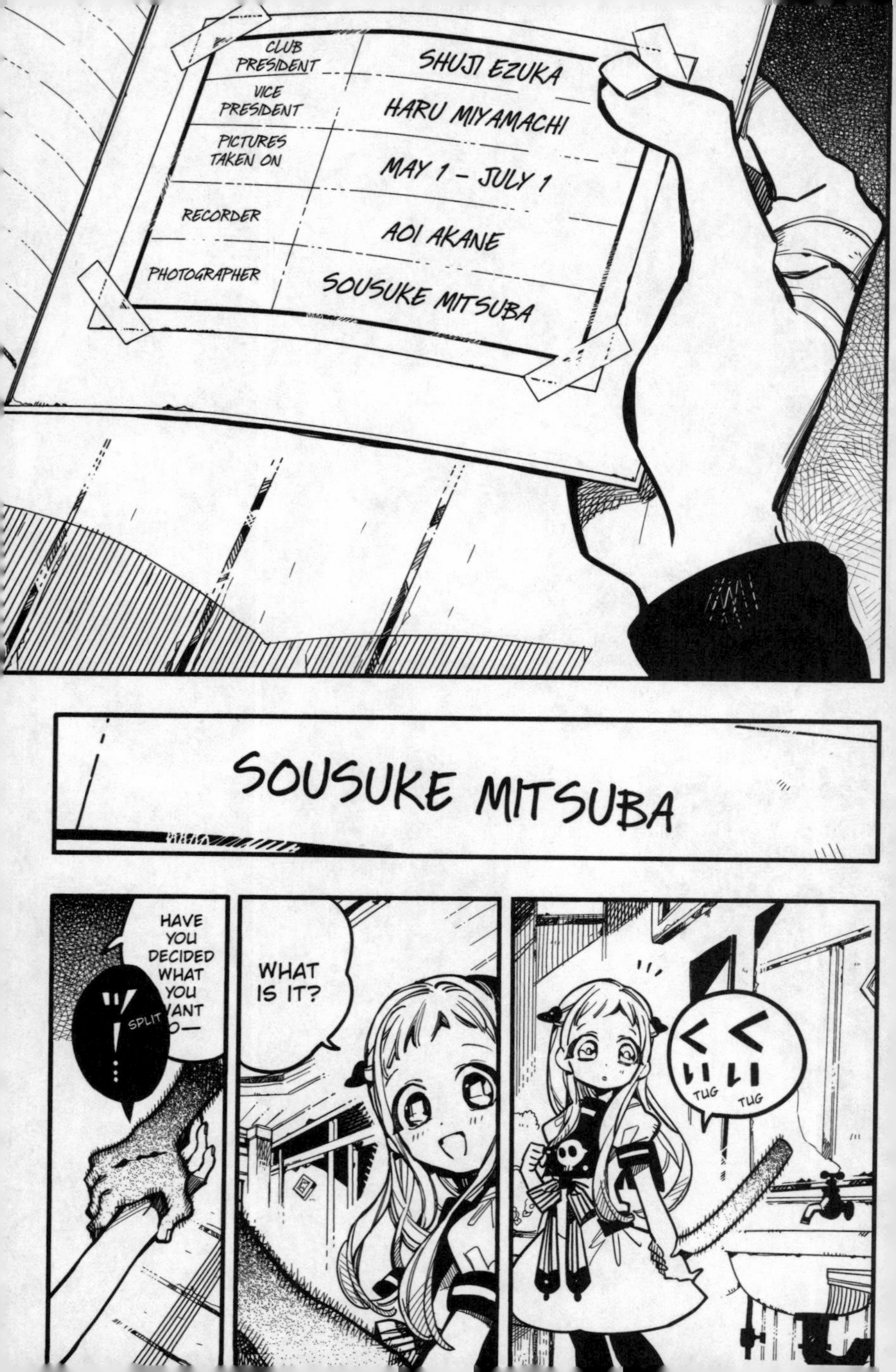
CLUB PRESIDENT
SHUJI EZUKA
VICE PRESIDENT
HARU MIYAMACHI
PICTURES TAKEN ON
MAY 1 – JULY 1
RECORDER
AOI AKANE
PHOTOGRAPHER
SOUSUKE MITSUBA
SOUSUKE MITSUBA
TUG
TUG
WHAT IS IT?
HAVE YOU DECIDED WHAT YOU WANT TO—
SPLIT
...!

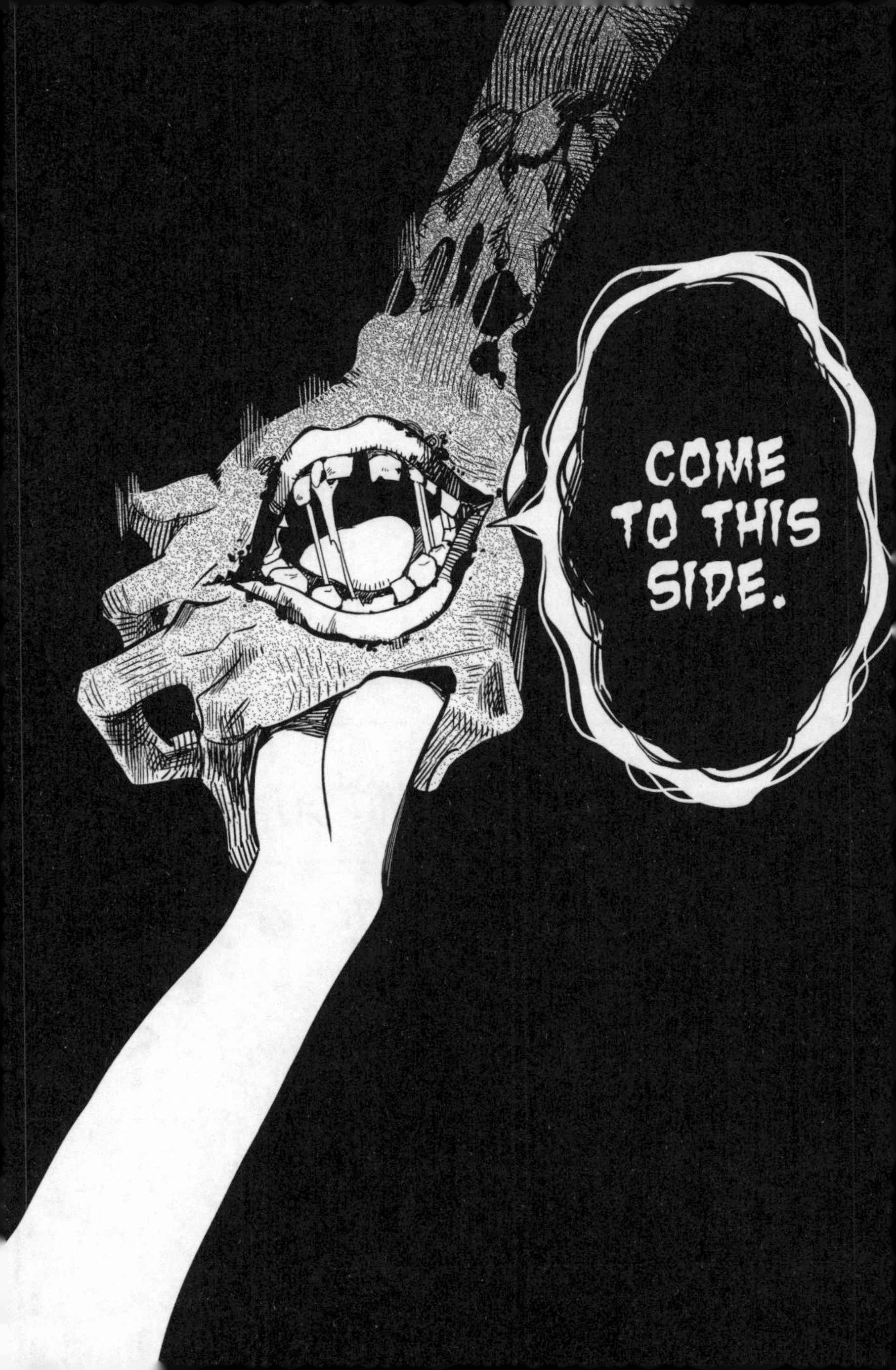
COME TO THIS SIDE.

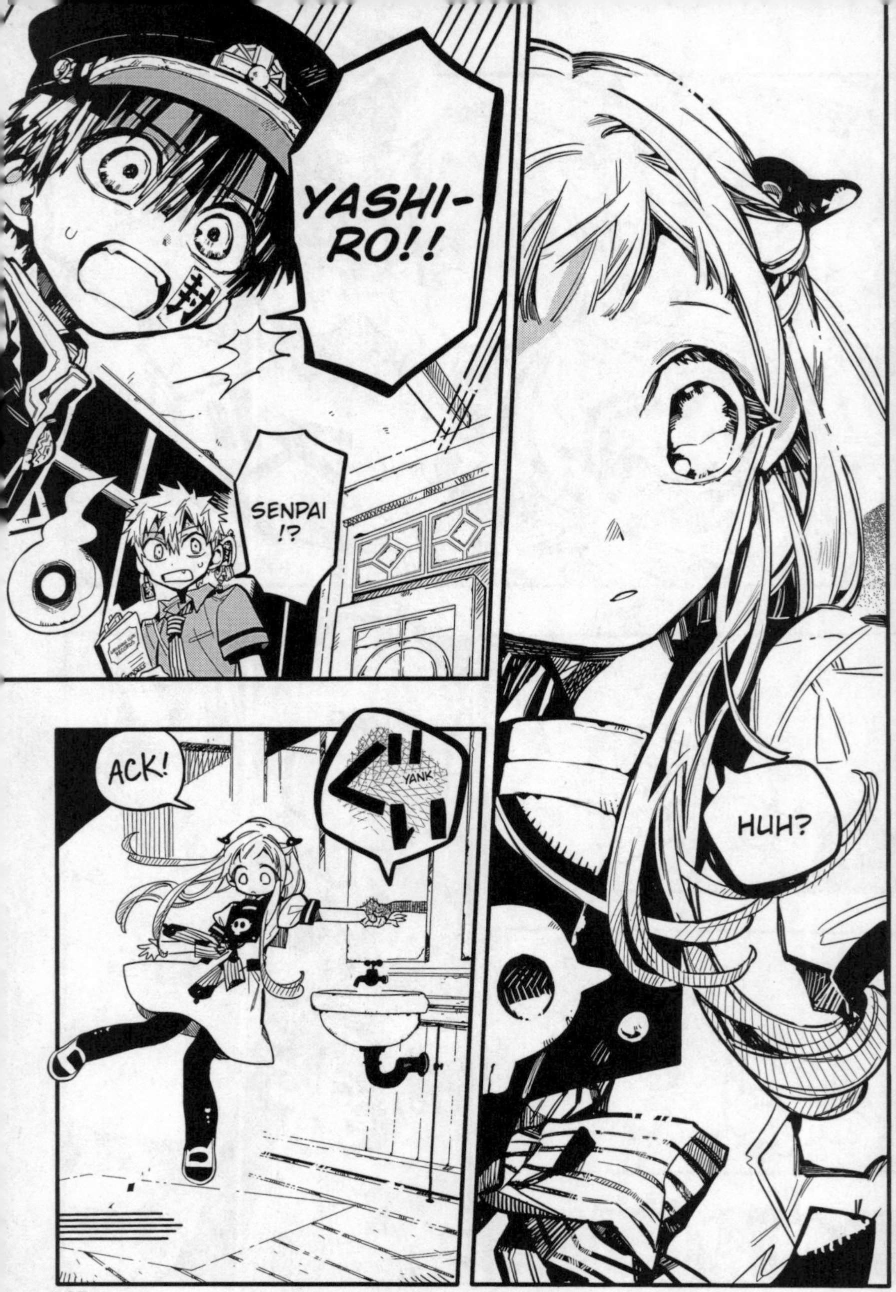
HUH?
YASHI-RO!!
SENPAI !?
ぐい
YANK
ACK!

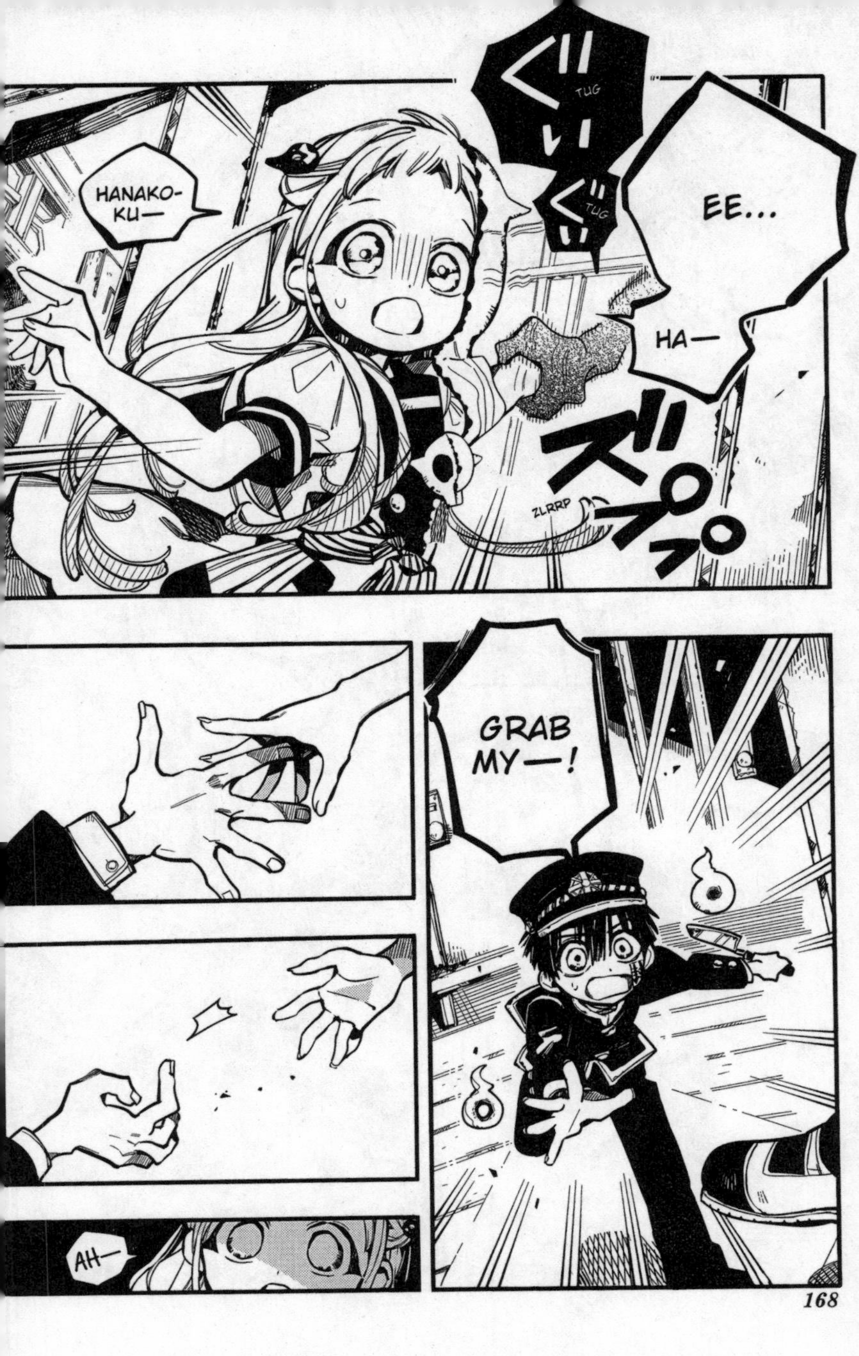
TUG
EE...
TUG
HA—
HANAKO-KU—
ZLRRP
GRAB MY—!
AH—

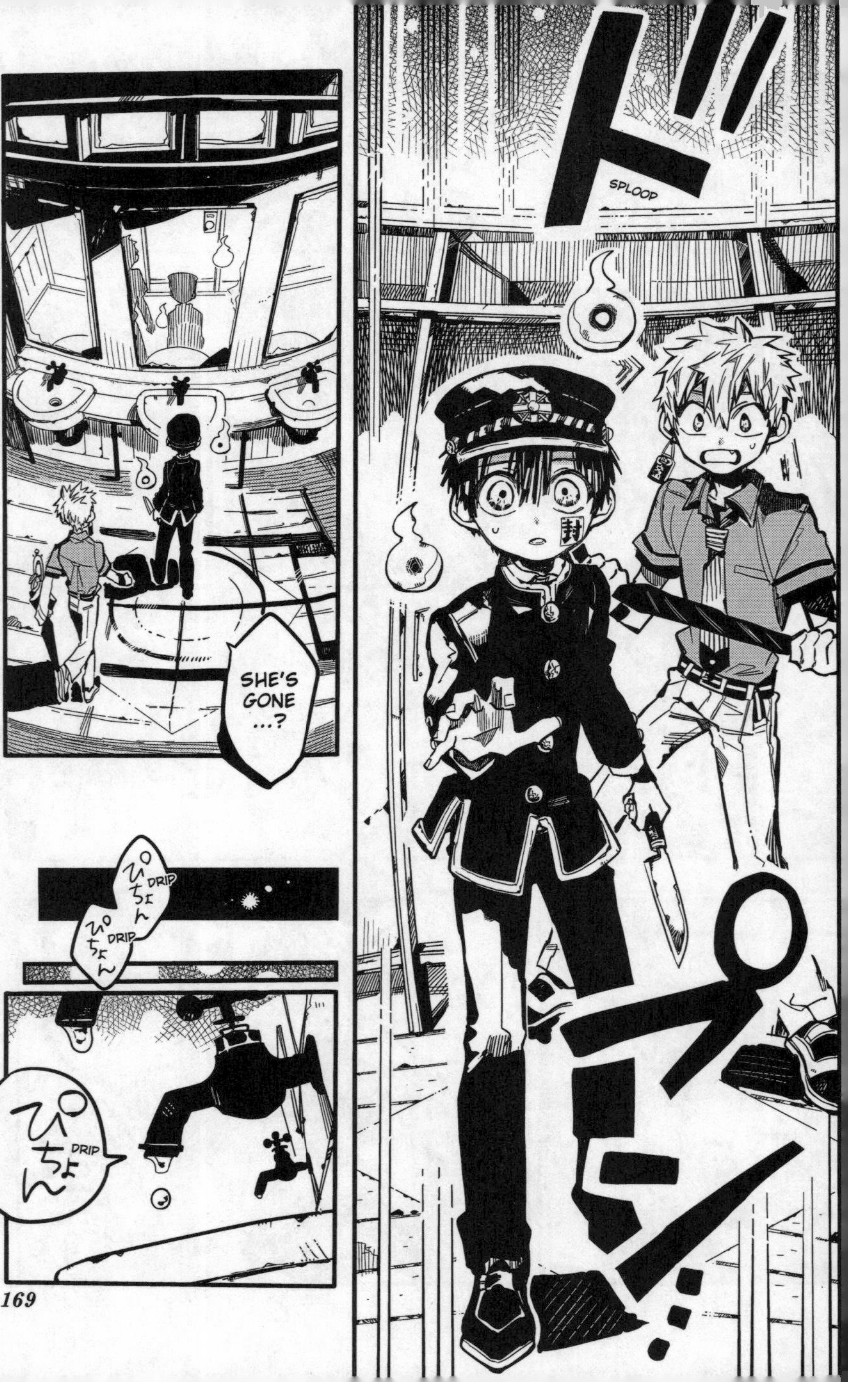

ドッ
SPLOOP
SHE'S GONE ...?
ぴちょん DRIP
ぴちょん DRIP
ぴちょん DRIP

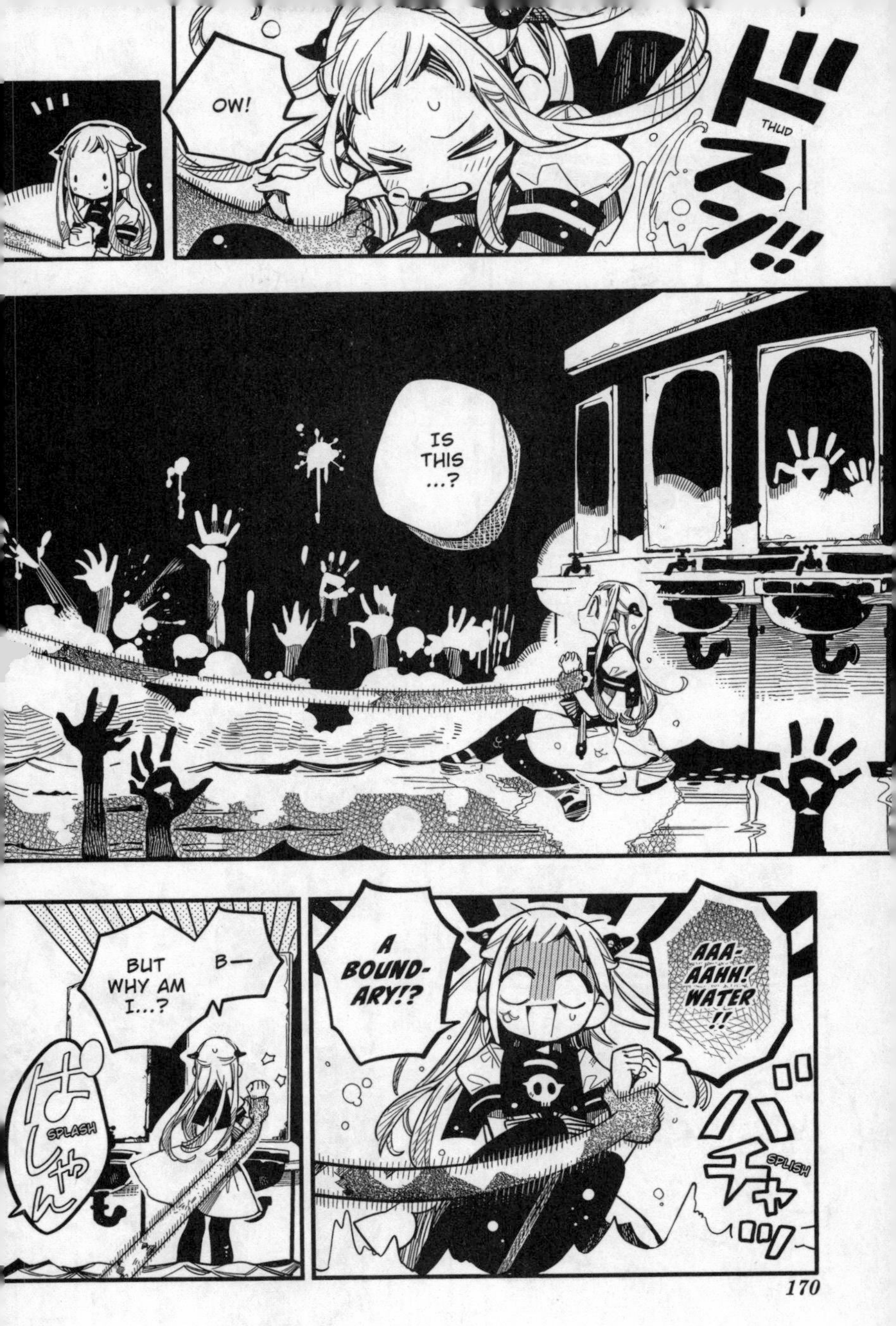
THUD
OW!
IS THIS ...?
AAA-AAHH! WATER!!
A BOUNDARY!?
SPLISH
B—
BUT WHY AM I...?
SPLASH

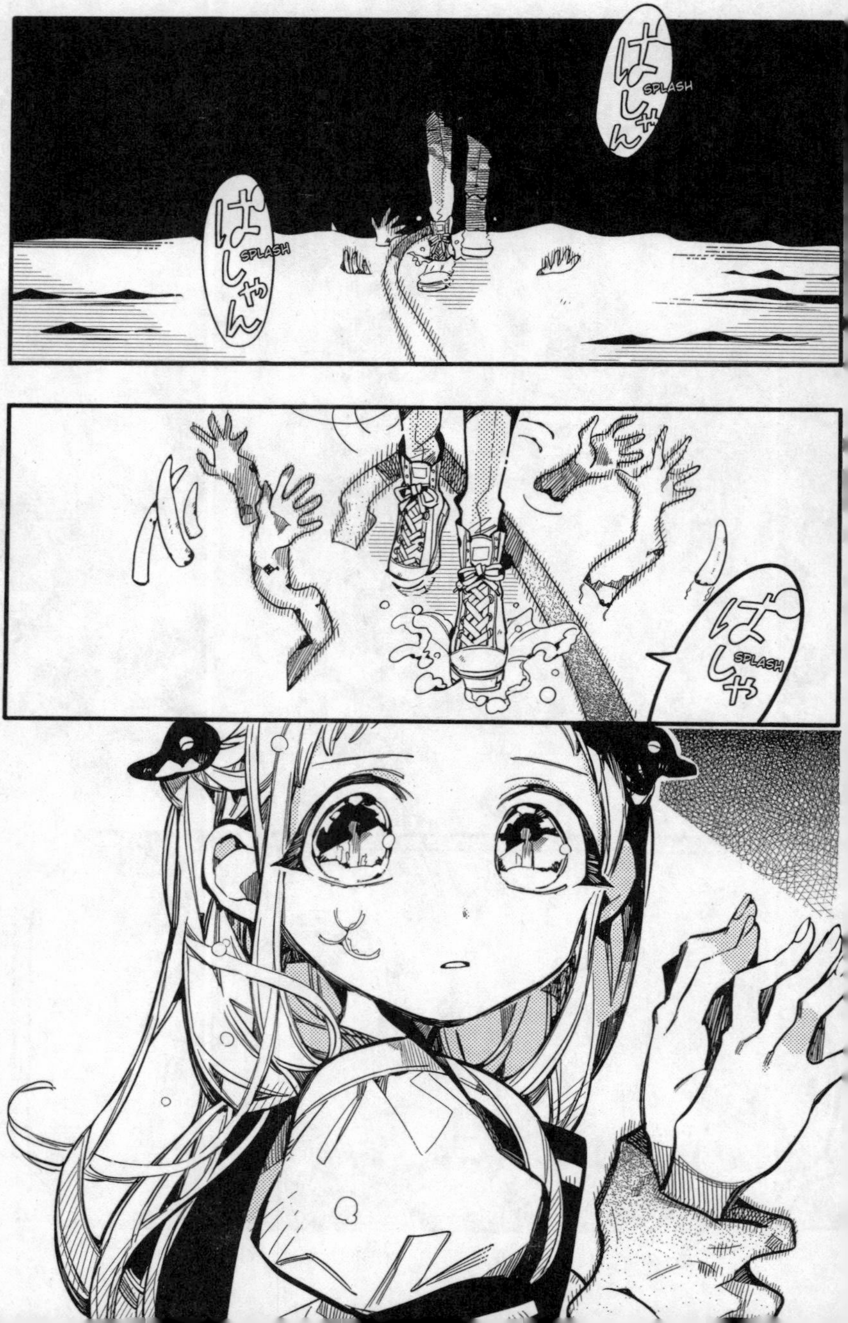
ぱしゃん
SPLASH
ぱしゃん
SPLASH
ぱしゃ
SPLASH

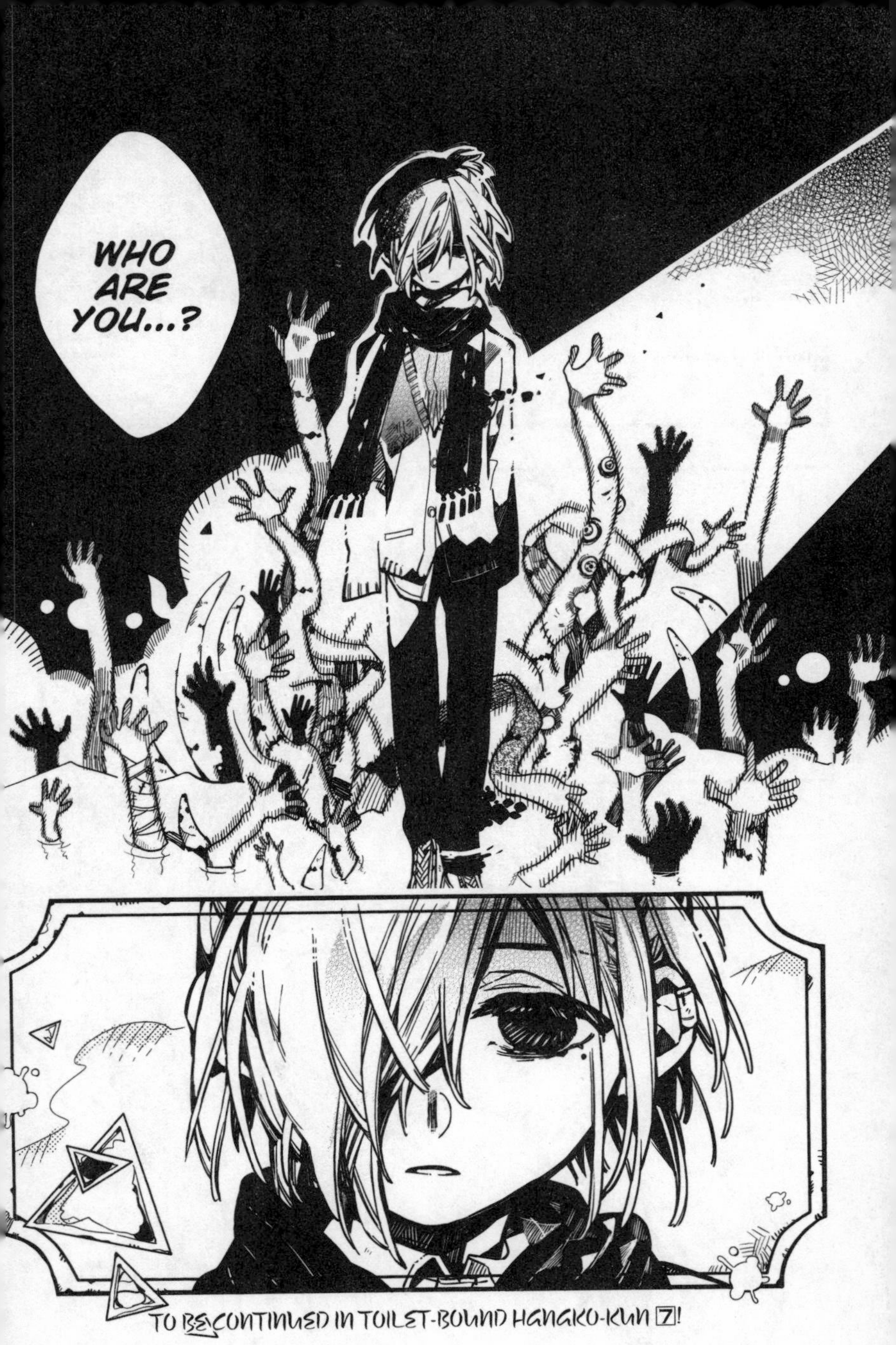
WHO ARE YOU...?

TO BE CONTINUED IN TOILET-BOUND HANAKO-KUN 7!

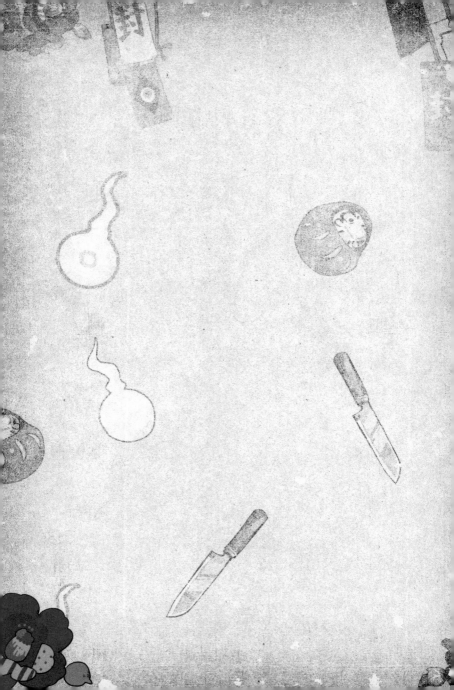

Sakura Nanamine

Q What's your favorite snack?

Hard candy.

Q What's your biggest concern lately?

Natsuhiko is annoying.

Tsukasa

Q What's your favorite snack?

Amane!

Q What's your biggest concern lately?

Amane!

Natsuhiko Hyuuga

Q *What's your favorite snack?*

Black-bean senbei.

Q *What's your biggest concern lately?*

The runt won't shut up.

Aoi Akane

Q *What's your favorite snack?*

Raspberry pie.

Q *What's your biggest concern lately?*

Nene-chan is so busy.

🥢 Akane Aoi

Q What's your favorite snack?

Raspberry pie!
(I love anything that Ao-chan makes!)
(Not that she's made anything for me yet.)

Q What's your biggest concern lately?
Ao-chan is so cute,
I'm happy every day.

🥢 Mirai

Q What's your favorite snack?

Agar jelly.

Q What's your biggest concern lately?

I can't make Honorable No. 7's
assistant all wrinkly.

TRANSLATION NOTES

Common Honorifics

no honorific: Indicates familiarity or closeness; if used without permission or reason, addressing someone in this manner would constitute an insult.

-san: The Japanese equivalent of Mr./Mrs./Miss. If a situation calls for politeness, this is the fail-safe honorific.

-sama: Conveys great respect; may also indicate that the social status of the speaker is lower than that of the addressee.

-kun: Used most often when referring to boys, this indicates affection or familiarity. Occasionally used by older men among their peers, but it may also be used by anyone referring to a person of lower standing.

-chan: An affectionate honorific indicating familiarity used mostly in reference to girls; also used in reference to cute persons or animals of either gender.

-senpai: A suffix used to address upperclassmen or more experienced coworkers.

-kouhai: The inverse of *senpai*, used to address those who are younger or less experienced.

-sensei: A respectful term for teachers, artists, or high-level professionals.

Page 4

Mirai's name means "future" in Japanese and—as Kou gets Akane to confirm on page 46—Kako's means "past."

Page 81

Sugoroku is a traditional Japanese board game with rules similar to Snakes & Ladders. Usually spelled with the kanji for "pair" and "six" (meaning "double sixes"), the former kanji has been replaced with two of the *hiragana* character pronounced *mi*, which is one way to say "three." Two threes add up to six, providing the "pair" of *sugoroku* in an unconventional way, which might be a hint to look out for something starting with "Mi" and the number three...

Page 109

A *kabe-don* is a famous anime and manga trope in which an aggressive character (usually male) will force the object of his devotion's attention onto him by trapping her between him and a wall (*kabe*). This is a sudden move that usually comes with a wham (*don*) sound effect.

Page 116

The Mokke are preparing to carry out an *ushi no toki mairi* ("ox-hour shrine visit") on the immobile Akane. So called because it is conducted during the hours of the ox (1:00 a.m. to 3:00 a.m.), this is a traditional method of cursing someone by nailing a straw effigy (visible on page 118) to a sacred tree on the grounds of a Shinto shrine while wearing three candles in a ring on one's head. The Mokke have glossed over a few of these exact details—including the fact that the curse is supposedly nullified if anyone witnesses the ritual—so let's hope for Akane's sake that they aren't expecting him to be in the same spot for the full duration, as the spell must be repeated every night for a week...

Page 162

Zukkorobashi refers to a nonsense song, "Zui Zui Zukkorobashi," that's mostly known for its onomatopoeia. The important thing here is that it's sung while playing a finger game, similar to "Eenie Meenie Miney Mo," where children will put their hands in a circle and point at each one in turn while singing the song. Whomever they're pointing to by the end of the song is the loser.

Page 162

Menko is a game where a bunch of cards are tossed onto the ground. Players slam other cards down on top of them, hoping to flip them over, and whoever flips the most cards wins. And since it's a traditional Japanese game, of course the Mokke get involved.

Page 174

"Hard candy" is *rakugan*, a traditional Japanese sweet made from sugar and rice that can be molded into various shapes before it hardens. Many modern versions are quite cutesy, clashing with Sakura's no-nonsense personality, but traditionally it had a more muted look.

Page 175

Senbei are savory rice crackers, a curiously unflashy and health-conscious pick for the ostentatious Natsuhiko.

Page 176

Known as *kanten* in Japan, agar was first discovered there and used to make jellies long before its more modern application, which is growing microbes.

AidaIro

Translation: Alethea Nibley and Athena Nibley
Lettering: Nicole Dochych

JIBAKU SHONEN HANAKO-KUN Volume 6 ©2017 AidaIro / SQUARE ENIX CO., LTD.
First published in Japan in 2017 by SQUARE ENIX CO., LTD. English translation rights arranged with SQUARE ENIX CO., LTD. and Yen Press, LLC through Tuttle-Mori Agency, Inc.

English translation © 2018 by SQUARE ENIX CO., LTD.

Yen Press
150 West 30th Street, 19th Floor
New York, NY 10001

Visit us at yenpress.com • facebook.com/yenpress • twitter.com/yenpress • yenpress.tumblr.com • instagram.com/yenpress

First Yen Press Print Edition: November 2020
Originally published as an ebook in June 2018 by Yen Press.

Yen Press is an imprint of Yen Press, LLC.
The Yen Press name and logo are trademarks of Yen Press, LLC.

Library of Congress Control Number: 2019953610

ISBN: 978-1-9753-1138-4 (paperback)

10 9 8 7 6 5 4 3 2

BVG

Printed in the United States of America